Judy Nunn AM is an Australian literary icon and master storyteller. In her thirty-year career, she has written over twenty books, which have sold more than a million copies in Australia alone. Readers everywhere are passionate about Judy's stories of her country and its people, told with her trademark authenticity and filled with unforgettable characters who live on long after the final page. From the stage to the screen and the page, Judy has always been a storyteller, and her significant service to the performing arts and to literature was recognised in 2015, when she was made a Member of the Order of Australia.

PILBARA

BY THE SAME AUTHOR

The Glitter Game
Centre Stage
Araluen
Kal
Beneath the Southern Cross
Territory
Pacific
Heritage
Floodtide
Maralinga
Tiger Men
Elianne
Spirits of the Ghan
Sanctuary
Khaki Town
Showtime!
Black Sheep

Short story collections
The Long Weekend
Stories from the Otto Bin Empire

Children's fiction
Eye in the Storm
Eye in the City

JUDY NUNN

PILBARA

HarperCollins*Publishers*

A NOTE FROM THE AUTHOR
Pilbara is set in the late 1800s, during the days of British colonialism. There may be terminology and references in the text that some readers could find offensive. I have made no attempt to change or soften the language and have chosen to write in the style of the times. To modernise the vernacular would not be true to the era, both historically and dramatically.

HarperCollins*Publishers*
Australia • Brazil • Canada • France • Germany • Holland • India
Italy • Japan • Mexico • New Zealand • Poland • Spain • Sweden
Switzerland • United Kingdom • United States of America

HarperCollins acknowledges the Traditional Custodians
of the lands upon which we live and work, and pays respect
to Elders past and present.

First published on Gadigal Country in Australia in 2025
by HarperCollins*Publishers* Australia Pty Limited
ABN 36 009 913 517
harpercollins.com.au

HarperCollins*Publishers*
Macken House, 39/40 Mayor Street Upper
Dublin 1, D01 C9W8, Ireland

A catalogue record for this book is available from the National Library of Australia

ISBN 978 1 4607 6847 1 (paperback)
ISBN 978 1 4607 1918 3 (ebook)
ISBN 978 1 0381 0133 4 (audiobook)

Cover design by Hazel Lam, HarperCollins Design Studio
Cover image by istockphoto.com
Map by John Frith
Author photograph by David Hahn
Typeset in Sabon LT Std by Kirby Jones
Printed and bound in Australia by McPherson's Printing Group

*To Donald Macdonald, with love and thanks for a
lifetime of friendship*

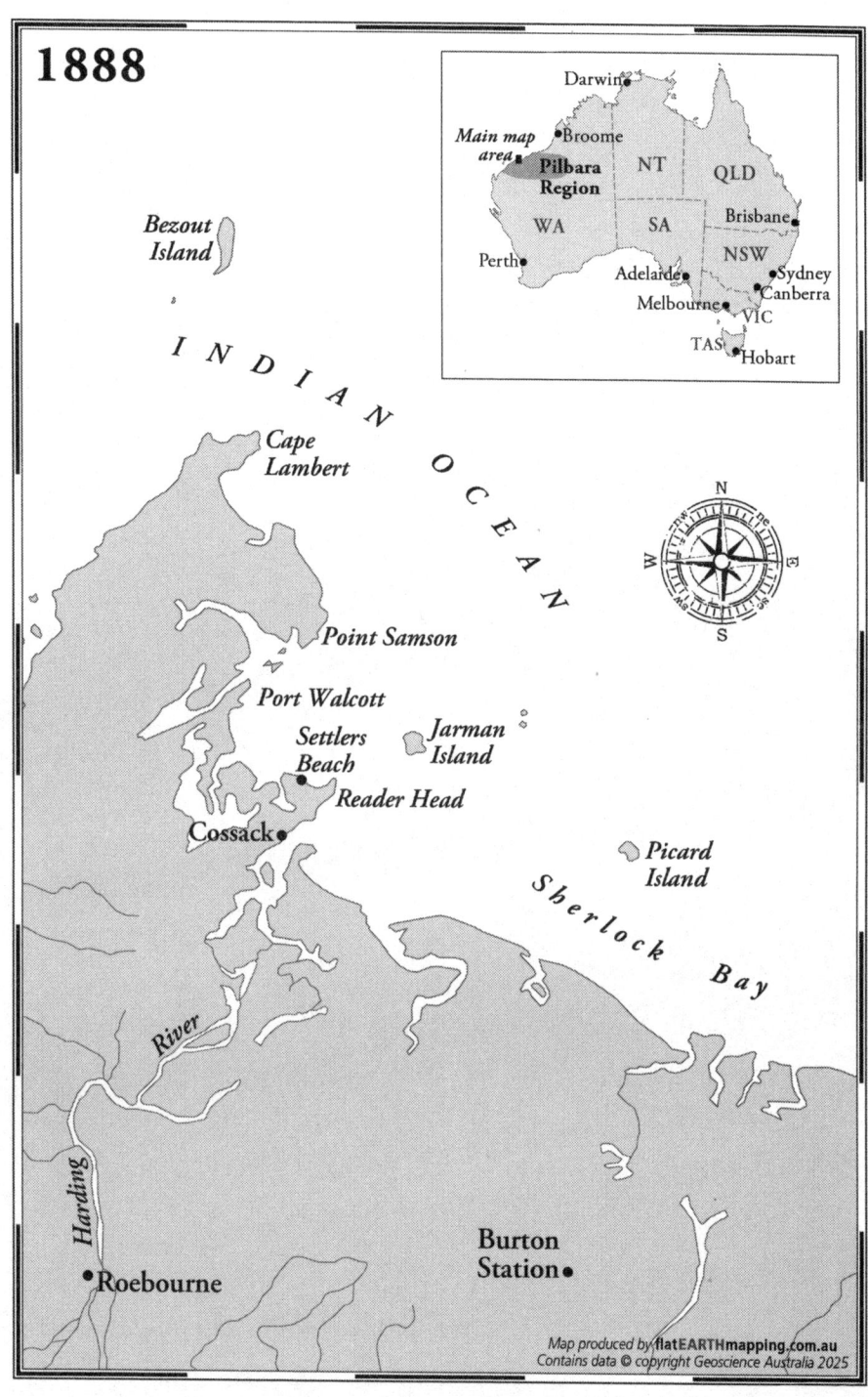

1888

Bezout
Island

INDIAN OCEAN

Cape
Lambert

Point Samson

Port Walcott

Settlers
Beach

Jarman
Island

Reader Head

Cossack

Picard
Island

Sherlock Bay

River

Harding

Roebourne

Burton
Station

N

W E

S

Darwin

Broome

Main map
area

Pilbara
Region

NT

QLD

WA

SA

Brisbane

Perth

NSW

Adelaide

Sydney

Canberra

Melbourne

VIC

TAS

Hobart

PROLOGUE

The majestic SS *Bengal*, pride of Britain's P&O Line, approached the rocky peninsula slow and steady as she goes on an azure-skyed, mid-summer morning.

'One of the finest land-locked harbours in the world,' the skipper boasted enthusiastically. 'That peninsula,' he pointed ahead, 'all but seals the entrance and serves as a breakwater.'

With his second officer at the helm, skipper Lars Bakker, a thick-set, bearded Dutchman who'd sailed the high seas in the employ of the British for thirty years or more, stood up at the bow. Beside him, Charles Burton and his three small children. 'Behind it, a magnificent accommodation for any number of vessels,' Lars continued, 'and the surrounding hills afford shelter from even the wildest of Southern Ocean storms ...'

The Dutchman went on extolling the virtues of Albany's harbour with all the zeal of a true seaman, and barely minutes later, the proud SS *Bengal*, at five thousand tons, one of the largest steamships of her day, rounded the peninsula and sailed into the Princess Royal Harbour of King George Sound.

'Oh, Father, how beautiful.' Eleven-year-old Victoria gazed in wide-eyed wonder at the pristine waters and flawless bay laid out before them like a masterly crafted work of art.

'It most certainly is, my dear,' Charles agreed, and even ten-year-old Edward, and Harold, soon to turn seven, both of rowdy disposition as a rule, stood jaws agape in silent awe.

Lars felt dutifully rewarded by their open admiration, having himself never tired of this perfect natural harbour at the bottom of the world.

'Yes, I must agree,' he said, 'quite, quite splendid.'

He remained with them a further five minutes or so before joining his helmsman. He enjoyed the company of Charles Burton. They had become well acquainted over the six-week journey from England, which many considered the most arduous test of endurance, but which young Burton had appeared to find nothing short of exhilarating. Indeed, young Burton had invested himself totally in the voyage from the moment they'd left Liverpool. He'd complained of no sea sickness at all on behalf of either himself or his children, and as they'd slowly steamed their way down the canal from Port Said to Suez, even the oppressive heat and humidity of the tropics had failed to dampen his enthusiasm.

'How fascinating,' he'd remarked, discarding his jacket and striding about the deck in his shirtsleeves as he admired the ingenuity of the Suez Canal. 'A remarkable feat of engineering, Lars, truly remarkable. A privilege to witness such a phenomenon, I must say. I am quite awestruck.'

Little wonder Lars had warmed to Charles Burton. Not

only was the fellow's enthusiasm for all that surrounded him refreshingly genuine, so too was the manner with which he instilled in his children the same sense of wonderment.

'Just look at that,' he would effuse to his young daughter and sons as he pointed out sights from the deck, be they an exotic foreign shoreline or a pod of dolphins in an endless ocean, 'have you ever seen anything like that before?'

'No, Father, never,' would come the answer.

'And I'll warrant you may never again,' he would advise them, 'so drink it in while you can, children, drink it all in while you can.'

Lars Bakker, ageing sea captain and a man who knew men, found Charles Burton a most impressive young fellow in both appearance and manner. A gentleman, he decided. But no wastrel. For all his English upper-class bearing, this was not one who spent his life lounging about in gentlemen's clubs. *You can tell by the way he moves*, Lars thought, *this is a man who has worked physically for a living. And it shows.*

Lars had been delighted to discover himself proved right. Charles Burton was a gentleman farmer no less, from a family property in Yorkshire.

'Been in the family for generations,' Charles had told him. 'My father's father and his before him worked that same land for years, and I shall no doubt return to carry on the tradition, as will my sons. But for now, adventure calls. I am bound for Western Australia, where I am to assist in the management of a sheep and cattle property my father owns there with his brother. My uncle, Geoffrey, is to meet me in Perth and we are to travel north together. It is my sincerest wish that by making a huge success of our joint venture, I may perhaps return to England with untold riches.'

Charles had smiled self-effacingly and with good humour. 'That is, if all goes according to plan. Impossible to predict, of course, for I have no first-hand knowledge of Australian stock farming, which will no doubt differ somewhat from its English counterpart.'

'Whereabouts would this property of your uncle's be, may I ask?'

'A place quite some distance to the north. A place called the Pilbara.'

'Ah. Never been there myself, but yes, I think you can safely assume it will be different.' The nod Lars had given had been solemn, and his tone dour. 'From what I've heard of the Pilbara, it is a hard, hard part of the world. The true "Wild West", I'm told.'

'Yes, so I have gathered from my Uncle Geoffrey's reports.'

Lars Bakker had felt privileged that young Charles Burton should choose to share with him such a wealth of personal information, and that he should do so in such a disarmingly unaffected fashion. *What an admirable young fellow*, Lars had thought. *Why, even the very look of him.*

With a square-boned, strong face and a fine head of dark hair, Charles was clean-shaven, which suited, highlighting the chiselled features as it did. His gaze, too, was direct, and his manner forthright. *An honest face*, Lars had decided. *Honest and highly principled, you can tell by the way he looks at you. A gentleman of the finest standing.*

Above all, Lars most admired Charles for his relationship with his children. But then it appeared everyone did. Charles had been met with praise, congratulated and complimented on a daily basis throughout the voyage.

'Oh, it's easy to be a good father,' he would reply, shrugging off any form of flattery with the natural grace that others found so admirable. 'The credit is hardly mine, but belongs to my children, for they are a constant source of delight.' And he would smile that easy smile of his. Little wonder everyone, and most particularly women, found him not only impressive, but highly attractive.

Charles Burton, at thirty years of age, was far too young to be a widower, particularly a widower burdened with three young children. At least, that was the opinion of most, who were quick to offer their sympathy, which, although graciously accepted, was not necessary.

'Yes, it is sad,' he would admit. 'I do miss Amy dreadfully, for we were childhood sweethearts, married at such a very young age, and there can be no other. But you see, I have the children.' Again, that smile. 'The children are my world.'

People soon stopped feeling sorry for Charles, who clearly did not consider himself in the least burdened.

'I shall miss you, Charles,' Lars said an hour or so later as they parted company, 'you and the children, you're a fine family.' He acknowledged the curtsey Victoria bobbed him and shook hands with both of the boys.

'And I you, Lars,' Charles said, offering his own hand. 'What a voyage of discovery it has been,' he added as the two shook warmly, 'I have enjoyed every day of our travels.'

'Yet more discovery awaits you at the Pilbara, I'm sure,' Lars replied. 'Good luck, my young friend.'

As Lars had suggested he should, Charles booked into the Horse and Groom Hotel on York Street, just a four hundred yard walk up from the wharf, the luggage following in a horse-drawn dray. The family was to remain in Albany for two days, awaiting the arrival of the Adelaide Steamship Company's three hundred ton SS *Franklin*, which was bound for Fremantle, the port that served the Western Australian colony's capital city of Perth.

'Terrible port, Fremantle,' Lars had explained, 'no port at all, in fact, no natural harbour. You have to come in alongside Long Jetty, and given the strong westerlies that prevail, that's damned troublesome, I can tell you. I wouldn't bring a ship this size in there, no respectable skipper would, bound to damage the vessel. Dangerous for all concerned.'

He'd given an airy wave of his hand, not wishing to frighten the children. 'Oh you'll have no trouble aboard the *Franklin*,' he'd assured them. 'She's small and she's manageable.' He'd chosen not to warn them, however, that travel aboard the *Franklin* would prove far rougher than that which they'd experienced aboard the solid and ever-reliable *Bengal*, particularly if heavy weather was encountered around the notorious Cape Leeuwin. They would find that out for themselves soon enough.

***

The family enjoyed their two days in Albany, an exceptionally pretty township nestled cosily into the south coast of Western Australia.

'The oldest settlement in the colony,' Charles informed the children the following morning as they took tea in the hotel's attractive front parlour, the windows of which looked out onto the street. 'Constructed a good two years before Perth – as a military outpost of New South Wales, I believe, in order to prevent the French from laying claim to territory on this western side of the continent. This particular site was chosen due to its natural harbour, which, as Lars pointed out to us, is quite extraordinary.'

Charles had had the most interesting conversation over a brandy with the publican, whose company he had sought after putting the children to bed the previous evening. Bowerbird-like, he did so enjoy gathering titbits of information wherever he could.

'I'm informed Albany remained the colony's principal harbour for decades,' he went on. 'It still is, really. Which is of course why we're here. Amazing, isn't it?' he added thoughtfully. 'Albany will probably remain the principal port until a proper harbour is built at Fremantle ...'

Young Victoria, as always, was paying avid attention to her father, being as eager to learn as Charles was to instruct. But Edward was squirming restlessly in his chair, impatient to set off on their promised climb up Mount Clarence. Seated beside him, Harold too was starting to squirm. Harold invariably took his lead from big brother Edward.

'We've finished our tea, Father,' Edward said meaningfully.

Charles laughed. The boy's tone was nothing short of accusatory, which was only fair, he decided, a promise was a promise after all. He often forgot he was talking to children, particularly when Victoria was hanging on his every word.

'You're quite right, Edward, we have finished our tea. We shall leave right away.' He stood. 'Does anyone need the lavatory?'

No-one did.

'Very well then. Off we go.' And they stepped out into the street.

They walked the one mile to Mount Clarence and scaled its slopes to the peak, which, at little more than five hundred feet, they all agreed did not really constitute a mountain at all, but from where the view across the whole of King George Sound was truly spectacular.

'Hardly surprising they chose this spot for the first settlement,' Charles remarked to Victoria, who stood beside him equally entranced, the boys having wandered off to a nearby tree that demanded climbing. 'I wonder if at any time the colony might have considered making Albany its capital rather than Perth,' he pondered before answering his own musing. 'Although I think perhaps not. I've heard the Swan River is quite lovely.'

'We shall soon find out, shan't we, Father?' Victoria gave him that 'special' smile they often exchanged, as if they shared a secret. Father and daughter were so extraordinarily like-minded.

'We shall, my darling girl, we most certainly shall.'

***

The warning Lars had chosen not to issue Charles and his family proved alarmingly correct, although not at the start of their three-day journey to Fremantle. The children having inherited their father's 'sea legs', the motion of the SS *Franklin* initially had no adverse effect upon them at all. To the contrary, the boys very much enjoyed the rougher conditions they were subjected to aboard the smaller vessel. Standing on deck, hands grasping spars, they whooped with excitement as the ship reared like a wild horse riding the crests of the waves.

The following day, however, it was a different matter altogether when, upon rounding Cape Leeuwin, they were hit by a storm.

Cape Leeuwin, although not the most southerly, was certainly the most south-westerly headland of Western Australia, and here being considered the meeting point of the Southern and Indian oceans, rough weather was always to be expected. Encountering a storm, however, and one of alarming ferocity, made for a daunting experience. The wind whipped the waves to a frenzy and the *Franklin* no longer reared horse-like, but rocked and rolled drunkenly, threatening at any moment to capsize. Or so it appeared, and so it felt to the horrified passengers, all of whose constitutions succumbed to the storm's violence. Confined to their cabins, they found themselves fearing the worst as they retched into buckets and chamber pots. Surely at any moment they would be plummeted to the very depths of the ocean.

Charles Burton and his children proved no exception on this occasion, despite the fact none of the four had displayed any sign of sea sickness on their entire voyage from England.

'Not even in the Bay of Biscay,' Charles said to the skipper the following day, when, having been among the few who had sufficiently recovered, the family was allowed back up on deck, 'and we encountered the most ferocious of storms there. The other passengers suffered terribly, but not we four, which I believe may have led us to think we were invincible. Not the case this time, though, I have to admit. Cape Leeuwin was quite an experience, Captain Briggs.'

'You're right, Mr Burton,' the skipper agreed, 'Leeuwin's known to kick up some exceptionally nasty weather. But you need have no fear aboard the *Franklin*, sir,' he added jovially, 'she's a fine girl.' A hardy Englishman who regularly did the run from New South Wales to the western port of Fremantle, Joseph Briggs was proud of both his seamanship and his vessel. He tapped the ship's railing like a fond father. 'She'll take whatever's dished up to her.'

Charles, in his customary engaging manner, had struck up an amiable acquaintanceship not only with the ship's captain, but several of the passengers, including one whom he'd been delighted to discover knew his Uncle Geoffrey. Mr J.D. Booker, manager of the National Bank of Australasia, had been conducting some business in Albany and was now returning to Perth.

'Jolly good to meet you, Mr Burton,' James Booker declared upon hearing Charles' story. 'I met your uncle some time ago. Haven't seen him for ages, didn't even know he had a nephew.' James gave a guffaw. He was a hearty sort of fellow, and this being the first day of their voyage, he was yet to experience the intolerable sea sickness that was destined to overwhelm him. 'Why, Mr Geoffrey Burton is a customer of our bank,' he went on. 'A fine chap indeed, and we continue to do business with him via his lawyer, Mr Goodiston, in Perth.'

'What a delightful coincidence,' Charles said. 'My uncle is to meet us when we arrive in Fremantle and we have an appointment arranged with Mr Goodiston at his office. Which is in Hay Street, I've been informed, not far from the Town Hall ...'

'That is correct.'

'After which, the children and I shall travel north together with Uncle Geoffrey.'

'Well, well, I shall look forward to renewing acquaintance with your uncle upon the ship's arrival,' James Booker replied, beaming happily.

He was not, however, destined to renew acquaintance with Geoffrey Burton, for the simple reason that, upon their arrival in Fremantle, Geoffrey Burton was nowhere to be seen.

Not that James Booker suffered any great disappointment at this fact, for he remained too ill to contemplate anything but booking into a hotel for the night before venturing on. He did however advise Charles upon the most efficient method of travel to Perth.

'Eastern Railway,' he said after they'd disembarked and were making their farewells. 'Runs from Fremantle to Guildford, via central Perth. Much quicker than going by road. Your uncle would have intended to take the train, I'm sure.'

'Most obliged, Mr Booker,' Charles said as they shook hands.

'Yes, yes, best of luck,' James replied, 'so sorry to have missed your uncle. Do give him my kindest regards.'

James Booker then made his departure as speedily as possible. The very ground beneath his feet still rocked with the motion of the ship and the mere sight of the ocean threatened the onslaught of another bilious attack, which was bound to prove a case of dry retching, he knew, for there was nothing left in his stomach to regurgitate.

After waiting a full hour in case his uncle was merely running late, Charles followed James Booker's advice and boarded the train.

The family very much enjoyed the Eastern Railway train ride from Fremantle, which was twelve miles south-west of Perth. Edward and Harold, leaning dangerously out of the open windows, oohed and aahed at the rugged coast of sweeping bays and broad white beaches; Victoria was mesmerised by the tangled forest that followed, the gangly eucalypts peppered here and there with flashes of bright yellow wattle; and Charles' principal enjoyment was gained from the children's reaction to every passing sight so foreign from the landscape of home.

Upon arrival at Perth's central railway station, he arranged for their luggage to be safely stowed while they sought out the office of Andrew Goodiston.

'Town Hall, you say?' Upon the enquiry made of him, the railway porter was most helpful. 'Easy, sir. Head that way.' He waved a hand in the general direction of the city centre. 'You can't miss it. Corner of Barrack and Hay, whopping great clock tower.'

They found the location of the lawyer's office with ease, an attractive two-storey stone building in Hay Street just a block along from the Town Hall. It bore several shingles beside its main entrance, one of which read *Andrew Goodiston Q.C.* His office was on the second floor.

They trudged up the stairs to the landing and Charles knocked on the door with the frosted glass window that again read *Andrew Goodiston Q.C.*

The door was opened by a clean-shaven, studious-looking young man with wire-rimmed spectacles, a stern air of authority and very straight hair.

'Mr Goodiston?' Charles enquired, surprised by the fellow's youth. *Why, he's barely twenty. How extraordinary.*

'No, no,' the young man said crisply, taking in the presence of the children with a disapproving glare, 'I'm Mr Goodiston's assistant. Do you have an appointment?'

'Yes, I do,' Charles replied, feeling distinctly ill at ease, but presenting a bold front. 'At least, I thought I did. I was to be here with my uncle, Mr Geoffrey Burton, who was to meet me at Fremantle. However, he did not arrive, so I have made my way here without him.'

'Oh, dear.' The young man's demeanour underwent an instant change. He now appeared flustered. 'You're Mr Charles Burton?'

'I am, yes,' Charles replied assertively, although in truth he felt far from assertive. *Something's wrong*, he thought. How he wished his uncle was with him.

'Oh, dear me, dear me. Do please come in, sir.'

Young Alastair Donegan, for that was his name, stepped aside, attempting a friendly smile at the children as they followed their father into the reception area.

'I shall let Mr Goodiston know you're here,' he said. He didn't suggest they sit, although there were several chairs in evidence, but left them standing beside the desk and filing cabinet as he walked to the rear of the room, tapped twice on the office door, then opened it and disappeared.

He was gone for only a moment or so before the door reopened and Andrew Goodiston Q.C. himself appeared, young Alastair hovering nervously behind him.

'Mr Burton,' the lawyer said effusively, stepping forward and offering his hand. The two shook. 'Do please come into my office. All of you,' he added with a welcoming smile.

As they filed through the open door, he turned back to his assistant and issued an order. 'Take out the Burton file for me, Alastair. I'll let you know when I need it.'

The young assistant headed directly for his filing cabinet, appearing only too relieved not to be included in the gathering as the door closed behind them.

Andrew Goodiston was a gentleman of around sixty, tending to the portly, with a neat goatee. He was smartly attired in a three-piece suit, a gold watch chain dangling from his waistcoat pocket. A successful man by all appearances. And clearly one of affable nature. But for some strange reason, he seemed a little unsettled.

'Do make yourselves comfortable, children,' he said, gesturing to the large sofa that sat against one wall. And to Charles: 'Perhaps you would care to join me, Mr Burton.' He indicated the carver that was positioned on the visitor side of his desk.

When all were seated, the lawyer circled the desk and, seating himself in his own carver, leaned forward, elbows on desktop, and lowered his voice, inviting an intimate exchange as if in the hope the children couldn't hear him, although they most certainly could.

'My assistant tells me you are unaware of the reason your uncle did not meet you upon your ship's arrival in Fremantle,' he said.

'That is so, Mr Goodiston,' Charles replied. 'I was quite mystified, to be honest. In our correspondence, Uncle Geoffrey's instructions were most specific, indeed, I was to follow them to the very letter.'

'I see …' The lawyer raised his hands and steepled his fingers, tapping the tips together and nodding thoughtfully in a way that suggested both he and his fingers were buying time. Which they were. 'Yes, yes, I see …'

'I was to meet my uncle at the docks in Fremantle. I was to accompany him to your office here in the city, where we were to complete some paperwork and arrange the transfer of bank finances. Then, several days later, the two of us were to board the SS *Otway*, bound for the port of Cossack in the Pilbara region where—'

'Yes, yes, I am aware of your uncle's plans.' The lawyer's fingertips stopped tapping, but the fingers themselves remained steepled as if pausing for thought. 'However,' he said slowly, 'there has been a change …' He stopped.

'A change?'

The eloquent fingers remained poised for a moment then gave up, the lawyer's hands returning to rest upon the desktop, defeated.

'We had no way of getting in touch with you, Mr Burton,' Goodiston said helplessly. 'You were at sea. We had no way at all of informing you ...'

'Informing me of what?' Charles asked.

'I regret being the bearer of such tragic news, sir,' Goodiston said with a mournful shake of his head, which was nonetheless sincere, 'but I fear I must inform you that your uncle died just one week ago.'

There was a collective gasp from the sofa, where the children had been astutely following every word.

Charles stared back at the lawyer disbelievingly. 'Uncle Geoffrey is dead?'

'I am afraid so.' A mournful nod this time, although once again sincere. 'His funeral was on Friday.' Andrew Goodiston did hope the young Englishman wouldn't enquire as to the reason for the hastiness of his uncle's burial. He had no wish to explain the brutal truth: that this was a common procedure; that bodies did not last long above ground in the height of a Western Australian summer.

Fortunately, no such query was forthcoming. Charles Burton remained dumbstruck. Andrew Goodiston felt sorry for the fellow.

'Were you and your uncle close, Mr Burton?' he asked gently.

'Yes, in a way,' Charles replied. 'If the truth be known, I barely remember what he looks like, for I was only a child when he left England and set sail for Australia, but I always felt I knew him through his letters to my father; the two were very close. And then during my adulthood, Uncle Geoffrey and I communicated personally. He wrote with such vitality, such enthusiasm, I so looked forward to our meeting again. I would like to have known him better,' he added wistfully. 'How very sad.'

'Yes,' the lawyer agreed, 'it is most sad. I knew Geoffrey well myself. He had been a client of mine for nigh on two decades. A fine man.'

'May I ask how he died?' Charles queried. 'He was suffering a long-term illness, this I knew, but his death is totally unexpected.'

'A tragic, senseless accident, I'm afraid. A fall. He had journeyed south from his property in the Pilbara to await your arrival and was staying, as he always did, at the house he'd purchased many years ago right here in Claremont. Apparently he'd decided that, in order to fill in the time, he would do repairs to the roof. That is what he told me when I was called to his bedside. Despite the dreadful pain he must have been in, I recall he even made a joke of it.

'"Never can bear to stand still," he said, "need always to be doing something. So I climb up on the roof and promptly fall off. What a damn fool thing." Those were his exact words.'

'Yes, that certainly sounds like Uncle Geoffrey,' Charles said with a glimmer of a smile as he remembered the tone of his uncle's letters.

'Did shocking damage to himself, I'm afraid. The house is a two-storey building leading down to the river, you see, and the fall was considerable. He broke his back. Internal injuries too, the doctor said.'

Andrew Goodiston decided that, much as he felt for young Charles Burton, now was the time to talk directly.

'Your uncle was aware his time was limited, Mr Burton,' he said briskly. 'I dare even to suggest he knew from the outset he was dying, for when the caretakers of his house sent their son to fetch the doctor, Geoffrey demanded they also send for me. He was determined to ensure all would be in order upon your arrival should he not be here to greet you himself. His action was most prescient, as this proved sadly to be the case.'

The lawyer rose, crossed to the door and, opening it, popped his head out into the reception area.

'I'll have that file now, thank you, Alastair.'

Returning to his chair, he continued, 'Your uncle left everything to you, Mr Burton: a comfortable enough sum in the National Bank of Australasia; the house in Claremont; and the Pilbara property to the north. I must warn you, there are certain debts you also inherit, for both properties are heavily mortgaged.

'Thank you, Alastair,' he added as his young assistant entered the room, deposited a file on his desk and silently disappeared, the door clicking closed behind him.

Charles, too, remained silent, simply because he could think of nothing to say. Things were moving too quickly. There was so much to take in.

'I have here,' the lawyer said, opening the file, 'your uncle's last will and testament.' He produced a pince-nez from the breast pocket of his jacket, clipped it to the bridge of his nose and started leafing through the document. 'Listed are the full bank details, the amount having been transferred to a new account set up in your name, Charles Edward Burton; the house in Claremont, which is not actually situated here in the city itself, but rather equidistant between Fremantle and Perth ...' He looked up, peering over his eyeglasses. 'A number of houses were built in that area during the fifties on allotments granted to semi-retired military officers charged with overseeing convict labour during the construction of the highway linking city and coast. It's become quite a pleasant location these days ...'

Returning to the file, he continued to read through its details. 'And we have the Pilbara property. This constitutes a well-established landholding of twenty-five thousand acres roughly ten miles east of Roebourne, with a farmhouse, several outlying buildings, sundry farm machinery and equipment, together with adequate livestock for transport – horses, oxen and the like.'

Once again he looked up. 'Mixed stock, some cattle, but mostly sheep are run on the property. I'm afraid I can't be specific with regard to the actual numbers, for I don't have the latest figures from the overseer, a fellow by the name of Lawson. Joe Lawson.'

He closed the folder and leaned back in his chair, unclipping the pince-nez and returning it to his breast pocket. 'I've not met Mr Lawson myself, but he's a long-time friend and employee of your uncle's. Geoffrey told me he'd hired Joe as a very young man and that he'd trusted him implicitly for the past decade or more. He furthermore assured me on his deathbed that Mr Lawson would have all the details to hand and that he would meet your ship's arrival at the port of Cossack. He said Mr Lawson would ably support your endeavours in the Pilbara, and was bound to prove your staunchest ally.'

It was only at that moment that the true magnitude of events dawned upon Charles. With a sudden sense of shock, he realised he was now to travel north unattended, that he and his children were to journey into the wilderness without the protection, guidance and expertise of Geoffrey Burton. The prospect was daunting.

'Your ship, the SS *Otway*, is due to sail in three days, Mr Burton,' Andrew Goodiston continued, 'and there is quite a deal to be done twixt now and your departure. Over the next day or so, I shall organise a meeting at the bank and we shall arrange the withdrawal of finances, the purchase of supplies and such. Firstly, however, we must sign and witness all the necessary paperwork here in my office, after which I shall convey you and the children to the house in Claremont, where you will be staying and where you can acquaint yourself with the caretakers there, a most agreeable couple, you'll find.'

He cast a benevolent smile at the children, who had remained seated on the sofa, having said not a word and moved barely a muscle, not even the normally restless Edward.

'My, my, you are such well-behaved youngsters,' he said, 'exemplary in fact.' He turned to Charles. 'You're to be congratulated, Mr Burton.' He stood. 'I shall call Alastair in to witness the documents.'

As the lawyer crossed to the door, Charles gave the children a nod of approval. They had passed the test and were indeed to be commended, but he wondered whether they had fully registered the enormity of what lay ahead.

Uncle Geoffrey had guarded their secret and paved the way well for them, it was true. And so far, the deception had proved successful. But a woman posing as a man and travelling unattended with her children to the wild north-west of the continent would present a challenge far greater than any they had so far encountered. And settling themselves as a family up there in that 'Godforsaken wilderness', as Uncle Geoffrey himself had referred to the Pilbara, would be the ultimate test of all.

The children stared back at their mother unflinchingly. They knew exactly what was expected of them, and their eyes signalled they were up to the task.

PART ONE

1874, Yorkshire, England

1.

The office of 'king's vavasor' was referred to by Chaucer in *The Canterbury Tales* to describe his character, the Franklin: *... an householder and great was he ... nowhere such a worthy vavasor.* Centuries later, the eminent philologist Walter William Skeat defined the term as a 'sub-vassal, next in dignity to a baron'. In the interim, it has been suggested that this country fellow (who referred to himself as a 'burel' man – one favouring rough, woollen clothes) functioned as a knight of his shire, at times a sheriff, and was quite likely the forerunner of that quintessentially English creation, the country squire.

Charlotte Elizabeth Burton was the daughter of just such a man.

William Edward Burton was the 34th Squire of Pendleton in West Yorkshire, a rambling estate of two thousand acres not far from Leeds. Dating back to 1348, during the reign of King Edward III, the estate of Pendleton had passed by marriage to the Burton line in 1714, following the ascension of King George I, and the Burton family had retained their squiredom ever since.

William Burton was intensely proud of his heritage. A responsible man, he was conscious of his position in life, but as one not prone to self-aggrandisement, he instilled in his daughter the virtue of humility.

'We are fortunate, Charlotte, to have been born into the landed gentry, but we are not of noble peerage and must always be aware we have a duty to others,' he would tell her. 'Our hard-working tenant farmers and their families, together with our own workers here on the estate, are reliant upon us, each and every one. We are therefore workers in our own right, my dear. We must never forget that fact.'

Charlotte loved her father dearly. She had no memory of her mother, who had died giving birth to a stillborn son when Charlotte was just two years old. Throughout the whole of her childhood, her father had been her world. Just as she had been his.

Despite mourning the death of his beloved wife, Elizabeth, and the son he had so longed for, William doted upon his strong, healthy daughter. He did not, however, spoil her by pandering to girlish whims, as some fathers might. Rather, he brought her up in the manner he might have reared his son. Which proved wise, as Charlotte needed no spoiling and had no girlish whims. Adhering to her father's advice, she embraced the role she was called upon to play and revelled in hard work, both physical and mental. From the age of ten, she loved nothing more than to labour alongside her father with the farm workers. By twelve she showed an avid interest in her father's collection of firearms and was a crack shot with a rifle. Study, too, presented no hardship, for she very much enjoyed her lessons.

William Burton, having attained degrees in law and engineering from Oxford as a young man, chose to school his daughter from home with the assistance of two live-in tutors, and Charlotte did him proud. She proved highly proficient in maths, sciences and literature, which formed yet another bond between the two. Father and daughter were everything to one another.

As the years passed, Charlotte continued to live a full and happy life, despite lacking the company of many youngsters her own age, which did not appear to bother her in the least. She had her father and the workers and the villagers she knew, all of whom were her friends.

But of late, things seemed to be changing. At least they did to Charlotte, and she was beginning to wonder if she might have cause for worry.

Sixteen-year-old Charlotte Burton stood on the crest of the hill gazing out over the Yorkshire Dales, long, dark hair whipped by the wind, horse's reins held loosely in hand. Beside her, Byron grazed peacefully enough, although his flanks continued to twitch, and every now and then he'd toss his head and give a brief snort. Byron, a six-year-old bay stallion, was not known for his placidity. Which was why Charlotte adored him, just as he adored her. There was a wild streak in both.

She looked down at Pendleton House nestled in the valley far below. Although always referred to as a house, it was more a castle, really, with its centuries-old stone walls and tower, surrounded by mediaeval gardens and intricate topiary of bushes that were hundreds of years old. The landscaped lake, too, contributed to the formal appearance, with its pretty little bridge and walkways. But the lake's ornamental design was far more modern. *It was probably just a boggy pond in its day*, she thought, *hardly mediaeval, but one must admit, most attractive.* She gave a slight shake of her head, bewildered by the memory. *How could Eleanor possibly have found all this unappealing?* But it seemed Eleanor had.

Charlotte had only recently learned it was Eleanor who was responsible for the change in her father's life, and therefore in hers too. Not that the elegant, stylish Eleanor's manner had been in any way untoward upon their introduction. To the contrary, Eleanor had been charming, albeit a little comically critical of Charlotte's choice of dress. Which had not been a dress at all, but hardy trousers and a rough, woollen shirt.

'When you visit us in London, I do hope you won't come in the guise of a boy,' Eleanor had said with a merry laugh to signal she was joking. At least, Charlotte had presumed the remark was intended as a joke. If it were not, it might well have been construed as an insult. She wisely chose not to interpret it that way.

'Yes, I promise,' she'd replied pleasantly, 'I shall be in a dress. These are my work clothes.'

'Of course they are,' her father had proudly announced with the broadest of grins. 'This is Charlotte in her "Charlie" role, isn't it my dear?'

'It is indeed, Father,' she'd replied, returning a broad grin of her own.

'I call her Charlie when we're working together,' William explained to Eleanor. 'The farmhands find it hilarious, particularly the older chaps. They refer to her as "Master Charles" half the time. Frightfully funny.'

They'd laughed then, all three of them, William delighting in the conviviality of this meeting between his daughter and mistress, which was progressing just as he'd hoped it would.

From the top of the hill, Charlotte's gaze now took in the estate's outbuildings: the stables and sheds, and the pretty little cottages, eight in all, allotted to the staff members and gardeners of Pendleton House. And there, barely half a mile away, the old stone church, which she considered particularly precious, the headstones of its burial grounds marking the graves of generations of local workers on the estate. The generations of Burton family were housed beneath the flagstone floors of the church itself, downstairs in the ancient crypt. *Such a wealth of history*, she thought. Yet Eleanor hadn't appeared overly impressed.

'How quaint,' Eleanor had said of the church.

Charlotte's eyes wandered further afield, to the tenant farms dotted here and there, and in the distance the picturesque village of Otley, everything so beautifully laid out among the lush, green hills and valleys of the Yorkshire Dales. *How could Eleanor possibly prefer smelly, smoggy London to all this?* she wondered.

'There's a distinct smell of mould, isn't there,' Eleanor had said when they'd given her a guided tour of Pendleton House, 'which I suppose is to be expected in a building of such age.'

Charlotte thought London smelled far more disagreeable. She'd been there many times throughout her childhood, staying at her father's apartment in the centre of the city, and on every occasion, she couldn't wait to get back to Pendleton. Her father couldn't either, in those days. He'd only ever visited

London when business demanded he should, and he'd often taken her with him for educational purposes. The two of them would visit museums and art galleries and places of historical interest. And as she'd grown older, she'd accompanied him to the odd fundraising occasion he attended for one of the several philanthropic causes with which he was involved. There he would instruct her in the etiquette required when mingling with the upper echelons of society. They both found such events and people a little tiresome and would breathe a joint sigh of relief upon their return to Pendleton.

But over the past six months or so, her father had been spending more time in London than he had on the estate, which at first Charlotte had found puzzling, even worrying. Until finally he'd been candid with her.

'I have met someone, Charlotte,' he'd said. 'She is a widow, and we have become friends. Very *close* friends, my dear,' he'd added meaningfully. An honest man, William refused to shy away from the truth, awkward though he now found the telling of it. 'This lady's name is Eleanor Witterson. We met at a charity ball, and we have become very fond of one another. *Very* fond, do you understand?' He was studying his daughter's reaction so intently he might even have been holding his breath.

'Yes, Father, I do.' Charlotte, always uninhibited and now only too relieved to know the reason for her father's long absences, had thrown her arms about him, embracing him wholeheartedly. 'And I'm happy for you,' she said, 'I am so happy for you.'

He returned the embrace. *Of course she understands*, he thought. *She'll be sixteen soon. She knows all about sex, she's seen animals mating ... She's helped with the delivery of lambs and foals. She's a highly intelligent girl ...*

William was relieved beyond measure. Since the death of Elizabeth, there had been no woman in his life and he had so feared his daughter might consider his current relationship a betrayal of her mother.

Charlotte's reaction was genuine; she was indeed happy for her father. He'd been a widower for fourteen long years, and now, at the age of fifty-six, it was only right he should seek female companionship, even marry again. She did not feel in the least jealous of another gaining a place in his affections. To the contrary, she looked forward very much to meeting Eleanor Witterson, the woman who shared an intimate relationship with her father.

And now she had finally met the Widow Witterson.

'No need to stand on ceremony, my dear,' her father had advised her in advance of their meeting, 'let Eleanor see us as we truly are. She's bound to love Pendleton and everything about the place. Including you, Charlie,' he'd added with a laugh that sounded positively boyish.

Charlotte had heeded her father's advice, although she now wondered whether she should have. Eleanor had laughed good-humouredly at her rough work clothes, it was true, but Charlotte had sensed no genuine amusement.

Not that it matters, she thought, tossing the reins over Byron's neck and preparing to mount. Whether or not she'd worn her customary work trousers and shirt that day two weeks ago was immaterial; she'd registered something else that was of far greater importance. For all Eleanor's wit and warmth, for all her engaging charm, this woman would never agree to live on the estate. It had been quite clear to Charlotte that Eleanor was not bred for the country. Eleanor Witterson was, without doubt, a creature of the city.

Charlotte mounted Byron, the animal whirling on the spot, eager to go, but she held him back as they made their way down the rocky slopes of the hill. Once on the grassy flat, though, she released her hold, giving the stallion his head, and they were off at a gallop across the green valley, a wild and windswept pair.

Charlotte revelled in the sense of freedom she shared with the animal, knowing that Byron felt the same exhilaration. She'd named the stallion herself after her favourite poet, Lord Byron. He'd been a newborn foal and she'd been ten years old at the time. They'd grown up together.

But even as she relished the ride, she could not rid herself of the lurking worry: Should her father decide to marry Eleanor Witterson, what would that mean for the future? Was their life about to change? And if so, how? And to what degree?

Arriving back at the stables, having jumped the fence – they did so love to jump, both of them – she dismounted Byron and handed the reins to Mac, who'd come out to meet them.

'Looks like you've had a good workout, the two of you,' Mac said drily. A weathered Scot who'd been stable master at Pendleton for twenty years, Mac knew them both well.

Charlotte answered the comment with a laugh.

She unsaddled Byron herself as she always did, watered him and brushed him down, then, after they'd shared a caress and a nuzzle, she left him in the care of the Scotsman.

'Thanks, Mac,' she said.

'My pleasure, Master Charles.' Mac returned a tap of his cloth cap by way of a mock salute.

She walked the several hundred yards to the house, entering by one of the side doors in the west wing that led directly to the family's living quarters. She seldom made her approach via the front carriageway and up the steps to the main doors that opened into the huge entrance hall with its Gothic ceiling and broad central stairway leading to the upper floor. The main entrance was principally for show and the welcoming of guests, who would then be accommodated in the east wing. She seldom used the doors at the rear of the building either, for these were the servants' entrances, reserved for the delivery of goods and leading to the quarters of the live-in house staff. The staff was modest in number for a house Pendleton's size: head butler, housekeeper, cook, under-butler, several maids, and a young footman called Teddy, who was the general dogsbody. All other Pendleton workers and their families – the estate manager and the gamekeeper, along with the groundsmen, the gardeners, the stable hands and more – were accommodated in the pretty little cottages dotted about the estate.

'Ah, you're back,' William called through the open door of his office as he saw his daughter cross the living room on her way to the stairs of the west wing; he'd been keeping an eye out for her. 'Teddy's just returned from Otley with the mail and there's a letter from Geoffrey. Jolly good stuff. Come on in and I'll read it to you.'

'Be with you shortly, Father,' Charlotte called over her shoulder as she jogged up the stairs. 'Give me ten minutes, I need to freshen up.'

In her room, she poured a basin of water from the fresh jug the maid had left on the washstand and, stripping off her work clothes, gave herself a flannel wash before slipping into a light cotton day dress. It was a warm summer morning, and a Saturday, which meant she would not be labouring in the fields. On a Saturday they addressed more bookish concerns, Charlotte her studies, William his business accounts, and Sunday was naturally a day of rest, following the morning church service.

After vigorously brushing her hair, Charlotte coiled it into a simple chignon, and a minute or so later was jogging back down the stairs. She couldn't wait to hear the news from Uncle Geoffrey.

William's brother, Geoffrey, his sole sibling and younger by four years, had set sail for Australia in 1868. With their mother long gone and their father recently deceased, William had borne the responsibility for their family's estate, and he'd been shocked by his brother's decision.

'But why, Geoffrey, why?' he'd demanded. 'I need you here. We have responsibilities, you and I.'

'No, we don't,' Geoffrey had glibly replied. 'Well, yes, you do, William,' he'd admitted. 'You're the Squire now and it's your duty to take over the reins. But you're well suited to the role. You embrace responsibility, and you're so very good at it. I'm not, I'm afraid. I crave adventure and I'd only get in your way if I remained here.

'But fear not,' he'd added, aware that William was about to interrupt, 'I shan't let the family down. It is my intention to make my fortune in Australia. There are limitless possibilities there, or so I have read and so I've been told. Believe me, William, I have given this a great deal of thought.'

Determined to convince his brother of his plan, Geoffrey continued in earnest, 'Mine is no empty dream, brother. I do not intend to join the herds infected by gold fever who are flocking to the colony of Victoria; I have set my sights on the west, where a man can acquire land for virtually nothing! Acres and acres of land. I shall create a farming property five times the size of Pendleton. Just think of that. I shall do the family proud, William. I shall expand our interests and acquire wealth in the process. The Burton name will be famed on the other side of the world.'

As always, Geoffrey's enthusiasm was contagious, but it was also persuasive, for he had done his homework, and the more detail he expounded upon, the more convinced William became that the plan was a good one. So good, in fact, that William found himself agreeing to invest in his brother's venture. They would become partners.

Within barely four years, Geoffrey's plan had started coming to fruition in a remote area of Western Australia known as the Pilbara. Having acquired a pastoral lease on a fifteen thousand acre property from the colonial government via the local warden, he had, during these four years, completed the purchase of the property.

It's ours, he'd written in a jubilant letter to his brother.

*Burton Station is all ours, William. They're known
as stations rather than farms in this part of the world,
so that's what I've called it, and I can now confirm
to you that, lock, stock and barrel, Burton Station
is ours! I have expanded the family's interests as
promised, and the acquisition of wealth will follow
in due course. As you well know, brother, I am a man
of my word!*

William had laughed out loud upon receiving the letter, Geoffrey's voice and incorrigible optimism so evident in every word. And over the following years, the same voice, the same optimism, the same humour rang loud and clear. William loved receiving his brother's letters.

So did his daughter.

'Here I am, Father,' Charlotte announced unnecessarily as she swanned into his office, heading straight for the sofa, where she plonked herself down. 'Edith's bringing us in some tea. I can't wait to hear Uncle Geoffrey's latest news. What does he have to say for himself? Do tell me.'

Letter and reading spectacles in hand, William rose from behind his desk and joined her, seating himself in an armchair opposite, the coffee table between them.

'This time around it's not so much about himself, I fear, but rather more about me,' he said.

'Oh, really?' Charlotte was surprised. 'How so?'

Her father's expression was a little shamefaced. 'Well, you see, I have to admit that in my last letter I wrote to him of having met Eleanor and of the relationship upon which we two had embarked. That was close to four months ago now, quite some time before I told you, I'm afraid. I do hope you don't mind.'

Charlotte smiled. 'Of course I don't mind, Father, why on earth should I? Uncle Geoffrey's your brother, the two of you share everything.' She leaned forward eagerly, an eyebrow raised in anticipation. 'So what was his reaction? Something a little risqué, perhaps?'

'Absolutely.' William returned his daughter's smile. How could he have felt even the slightest twinge of concern? Charlotte had welcomed Eleanor's place in his life, and the meeting between the two could not have gone more splendidly. 'In fact, true to form, my brother's reply is downright cheeky.'

Donning his spectacles, he settled back in his armchair and started to read, aware that only several weeks previously he would have baulked at reading such material out loud to his daughter. But he had registered of late that Charlotte had become quite a worldly young woman, no longer the little girl he'd assumed she'd remained these past years.

'Dearest Brother,' he read. 'Well, well, I delight in the news you share of the fair Eleanor. I must say I'm quite thrilled to hear of such goings on.' William glanced up from the letter. 'You see? He dives straight in and doesn't let up. You just listen to this.

'I must also say, "And about time!!"' Another glance at his daughter. 'Two exclamation marks, I might add,' he said, then returned to the letter. 'Truly, William, you've been living like a monk for the last God only knows how long. It's high time you found yourself a mistress, or at least availed yourself *of the feminine delights life has to offer. Good luck to you, old chap. I must admit to feeling a profound sense of envy. No such luck for me in this wilderness, I'm afraid. Women do not abound in the Pilbara, and the odd few who are here are strictly off limits. The married "salt of the earth" variety without whom, in my opinion anyway, their husbands would be unable to survive. Like Emma Withnell, the woman I wrote of earlier, known as the "Mother of the North-West", more saint than woman really. You recall I told you how she and her husband helped me through the cyclone of '72, even though their own farm had been completely destroyed? By heavens, if I could meet a woman like that, I'd marry, I swear I would. Emma Withnell is to be truly admired. She has all the resilience and strength of character one associates with a man, yet she's very much a woman. But I fear she's unique, besides which, she's taken—'*

There was a tap on the open door of the office.

'Ah, the tea,' William said. 'How lovely. Do come in, Edith.'

The maid, a young local girl of around seventeen, bustled into the room with a tray, which she placed on the coffee table.

'Ah, Cook's gingerbread biscuits,' William added, 'even lovelier. I'm both parched and starving.'

Edith looked a question at Charlotte.

'No, it's all right, thank you, Edith, I'll pour,' Charlotte said.

'Right you are, Miss Charlotte.' And the maid departed the room.

As Charlotte picked up the teapot, William selected a biscuit from the plate, took a bite and resumed reading.

'*Marriage therefore being out the window, I am forced to rely upon my annual business trip to Perth in order to satisfy any lustful cravings that might beset me ...*' He looked up from the letter. 'I should perhaps leave some parts out.'

'You most certainly should not,' Charlotte insisted, 'this is Uncle Geoffrey at his best. It's as if he's right here in this room.'

'Yes,' William agreed, 'it is rather, isn't it?' He went back to the letter.

'*I visit a very discreet establishment in the city not far from the hotel where I stay, which is quite convenient. No such discreet establishment exists in Roebourne, and I daren't risk availing myself of the occasional temptation on offer from the more squalid quarters of town. Word gets around in this tiny community and as my position in the local pecking order is currently becoming elevated, I daren't risk sullying my reputation.*

'*You must allow me a moment's indulgence now, William, while I boast of my newfound status. I'm sure you'll be impressed to hear that your younger brother will shortly be serving as Acting Government Resident in this vast area of North-West Australia.*

'I certainly *was* impressed when I read that,' William said to Charlotte as she passed him his tea. 'Thank you, my dear. I wondered how on earth such a position had become available to a simple farmer. But he goes on to explain.' William swallowed the rest of his biscuit, took a sip of his tea and returned to the letter.

'It all came about through the influence of Robert Sholl, the gentleman you'll recall my having mentioned now and then in previous letters. He's the senior government official and judicial officer in these parts.'

William and Charlotte shared a glance, nodding as they recalled the man's name. Geoffrey had revealed some time back that he'd developed a friendship with Robert Sholl, who was 'something of a character', he'd said.

A larger than life fellow, an explorer, a journalist, a harbourmaster, and more. He refers to himself as an 'entrepreneur', and there's hardly a sphere in which he hasn't dabbled. Well, he's now Administrator and Magistrate for the North-West region, which just goes to show how things work in this part of the world, where opportunities abound for the true adventurer.

Geoffrey's current letter now continued along similar lines.

'Impossible as it may appear, I am about to join Robert's posse of adventurers here in the wild west of the continent. He asked me some while ago to take on the part-time duties of Warden – he's appointed a number of Wardens in the area to assist in his jurisdictional duties; some farmers, others in the pearling trade at the port of Cossack. He doesn't seem at all fussy about specific qualifications. Anyway, he's decided that as I happen to be a Warden who actually does have a legal qualification, given my law degree from Oxford, I would make an ideal replacement for him while he attends to long overdue personal matters in Perth. Hence, for the *next three months, I shall be Acting Government Resident, a position of immense executive power, I might add.*

'Oh, and William, I simply must tell you, Robert's laissez-faire attitude was never more evident than when I told him I'd never once practised law. "All the Burton men go to Oxford," I said. "An Oxford degree is de rigueur, *but we never end up practising whatever profession it is that we study. We just go home to the family estate and become gentlemen farmers."*

'He roared with laughter when I said that. It mattered to him not one whit. "Who cares?" he replied. "You're well-read. Make it up as you go along. I always have."

'So there you are, dearest brother, I'm moving up in the world. And before you worry that I may be abandoning our farm, fear not! Burton Station prospers, thanks to our wonderful new foreman, Joe, whom I so wish you could meet. He's a perfectly splendid young chap. We had an excellent lambing season, our stock numbers measurably increasing, and we've acquired fifty head of cattle so we are now expanding our interests. Joe has even hired extra help. I assure you, we are well on the road to the vast success I promised.

'Enough of my rabbiting on. Let me close in wishing you everything you might wish for yourself in your relationship with the lovely Eleanor. An exciting mistress? A loyal wife? You gave me little inkling in your letter as to which option you favour. But should she prove to become a true partner in life, I do envy you so. As I said, no such luck for me here. The Pilbara is no place for a woman.

'*My fondest to you always, dear William,*

'*Your brother from far, far away, Geoffrey.*

'So there you have it,' William said, placing the letter on the coffee table and settling back with his cup of tea. 'He's in fine form, wouldn't you say?'

'Yes, I certainly would,' Charlotte agreed, although given the letter's closing words, her mind was now more on Eleanor than her uncle.

What exactly is your wish with regard to Eleanor, Father? she wondered. *Mistress or wife? And if it should be the latter, what is Eleanor's wish? She certainly has no interest in becoming the Mistress of Pendleton House. Of that I am certain.*

***

Charlotte was quite right. The city being Eleanor's natural realm, a move to the country did not attract her in the least. Which she realised was somewhat unfortunate, as William Burton was rich and she would willingly have married him. But she also realised marriage would demand she lead a rural life, the prospect of which was quite out of the question. She therefore had no choice but to make herself indispensable as a mistress. Given her experience, this would fortunately present no problem, for she had special talents in the art of love-making.

The 'widow' Eleanor Witterson, who had in fact never married, was forty years of age (although she professed to no more than thirty-three) and had recently lost her source of income. For ten years, she had been mistress to the Marquess of Farnsworth, an extremely wealthy man, married with three children, who had set her up in a London apartment where he could regularly visit during the trips he made to the city from his ancestral home in Buckinghamshire. During the season, the Marquess would bring his whole family to London, but they would stay at their townhouse in Mayfair, wife and children unaware of the true nature of his 'charity work', which was taking place only several blocks away.

Then, just one year ago, Eleanor's Marquess had had the temerity to die. A heart attack, quite unexpected. This had occurred at his country estate rather than his mistress's apartment, which might have proved awkward, but Eleanor was nonetheless distraught. She hadn't even known her lover was dead until she'd read a small column in the social section of *The Times*, lamenting the loss of the Marquess of Farnsworth. *A philanthropic 'nobleman' in the true sense of the word*, the column had said, *a man who nobly devoted his life and his vast fortune to those less privileged.*

Eleanor was now stranded. What on earth was she to do? The London apartment had been purchased in her name and recorded as a 'charity donation' in order to conceal any discovery of its ownership, so she was not destined to be left homeless, but how was she to live? And particularly in the manner to which she'd become accustomed. Much as she detested the Marquess, he had been extremely generous. Her only option was to find another wealthy lover, and with the prospect of turning forty, the clock was ominously ticking.

The arrival of Squire William Burton in her life had been a Godsend. By the time they'd met, she'd already sold half her substantial collection of jewellery and was desperate. She'd instantly set about charming the Squire, who was admittedly not as rich as the Marquess, but by then she could hardly afford to be choosy. And he'd been easily won. In reawakening his long dormant sex drive, he'd become hers to manipulate.

Eleanor realised William Burton would want more than sex in due course; he was that sort of man. He would eventually seek the companionship of a devoted wife, but she would face that hurdle when she came to it. In the meantime, she played her role to perfection: in social circles, the impeccably styled woman any man would wish to claim his own, and behind closed doors, the sexual experience any man could only dream of. The Squire was conveniently gullible too. He'd been more than keen to offer assistance when she'd mentioned *en passant* the hard times she'd been having since her husband's death the previous year.

'I've even had to sell my jewellery,' she'd said with a wan smile and a shrug, as if it didn't really matter.

Gifts, mainly of cash, had arrived regularly after that, presented tastefully in an envelope. 'I'm afraid you must choose your own jewellery pieces, my dear,' he'd said. 'I place no trust in my taste, which I'm sure would be quite abominable.'

Six months later, when he'd finally decided to introduce her to his country home and his daughter, she'd pretended interest and made the trip to the monstrous old mansion that many might have found impressive, surrounded by the endless formal gardens that many might envy. Eleanor certainly hadn't. She'd found everything about Pendleton irksome except the value of the place, which was evidence enough that William was rich. If only he'd sell his family estate and buy a mansion in the city, she might agree to marry him. *Yes, perhaps I could make that a condition*, she thought.

Loathsome as she'd found the three days of her visit, she'd nonetheless professed admiration for his home and laid on the charm, particularly when meeting his daughter. If he were to propose marriage, which she suspected he might, it would be wise to cultivate the daughter's affection.

She'd found the girl unfathomable, however, and also a little disconcerting. The more charming she herself had become, the more penetrating Charlotte's gaze. It was as if the girl were studying her, making judgements even.

And as for the girl's *looks*! Well, yes, that was another matter. The daughter had inherited her father's height and, like her father, carried herself well, but she was too tall to be considered pretty or fashionable. She could have been handsome though, no doubt about that, if only she'd taken some pride in her appearance. Oh my goodness, the garments she'd been wearing upon their first meeting! How could she allow herself to be seen in men's work clothes? And how could William have encouraged such a thing? He was actually *proud* of her appearance, he'd even found the fact funny and called her 'Charlie'.

Obscene, Eleanor had thought, *quite obscene*. She'd laughed, pretending to join in the joke, but even as she'd laughed, she'd been aware of the girl's scrutiny, which she'd found most uncomfortable. William's daughter seemed to be seeing right through her.

Charlotte had. To a certain extent, anyway. Nothing substantial, just a strange sensation, deep inside, but she'd had misgivings right from the start. This good-looking woman, whom upon close inspection she took to be around forty, appeared vaguely suspect to sixteen-year-old Charlotte.

As Eleanor had anticipated, William's proposal was not long coming; barely two months later. During which time, she'd been forced to endure three more interminable visits to Pendleton, each visit affirming her realisation it was highly unlikely William Burton would ever relinquish his family estate.

'Pendleton is who I am, Eleanor,' he'd proudly told her, and with irritating fervour. 'This place is in my blood, it's where I belong.'

And Eleanor, while smiling fondly as if she understood, had breathed an inner sigh of resignation.

The situation with the daughter had not improved either, although Eleanor was thankful the girl continued to play the game. They both recognised the truth: they did not like each other. But Charlotte wished her father to be happy, and Eleanor was the source of that happiness, so they both abided by the rules.

'Oh, William, my dear,' Eleanor now said, caressing his cheek as, having made his marriage proposal, he remained on one knee before her. *The true gallant*, she thought. *A ridiculous posture for one his age. How very silly he looks.* 'I do love you so.'

She was seated on the living room sofa in her apartment, and leaning forward, she gently kissed him.

'Is that a yes then?'

His boyish hopefulness was disarming, she had to admit. She was also forced to admit that she actually *was* rather fond of him.

'Stop being silly and come and sit here,' she said, patting the sofa.

He rose a little clumsily to his feet and sat beside her. Taking her hand in his, he gazed into her eyes with that same boyish hope, which she again found disarming. She decided at that moment that, strangely enough, honesty might be the best tack.

'There is one reason and one reason only why my answer must be no, William,' she said.

He waited, hope replaced by bewilderment.

'If I were to marry you,' she said, 'you would wish me to move to Pendleton, would you not?'

'Of course. We would live on the estate. Pendleton House would be our home.'

'And that is the reason I must say no, can you not see?'

He was puzzled. No, he couldn't.

'Pendleton is who you are, my dear. As you said yourself, it's in your blood, it's where you belong. But you must recognise the fact that it is not who *I* am. It is not in *my* blood.'

Bewilderment was now confusion.

'London is who I am, William. This city is in my blood.'

This city? William remained silent; he didn't understand. *How could this city be in anyone's blood?*

'You are an honest man, my darling, and you deserve honesty in return,' Eleanor said. 'London is my home. I was born and raised here to live in high society. I have been trained for the life I lead.'

It was absolutely true. Eleanor's mother had raised her two daughters, both beautiful and both well educated, to move in elite social circles, the aim being to qualify as the wives of wealthy men. And if not wives, then mistresses. Eleanor's younger sister, Alicia, had done particularly well, marrying a Polish count at the age of twenty. And Eleanor, although never marrying, had successfully allied herself to men of extreme wealth from the age of seventeen.

'You have come to know my circle of friends, William,' she went on, 'you must surely recognise this social aspect of my life. The opera, the theatre, the ballet ... And above all, the charitable work that I do ...'

Eleanor had indeed been involved in many a philanthropic cause through the Marquess. The social set with whom she'd mingled was aware she was his mistress, but no-one cared. Many wealthy men flaunted their mistresses. Such fraternisation was not frowned upon as long as mistress and wife were kept separate from one another. The only tasteless action would have been a meeting between the two. Any such clash was assiduously avoided.

'Why, society and the arts are the very air I breathe,' she announced, aware she sounded overly dramatic, but meaning every word. 'I would be suffocated in the country, can you not see that?' Professing to the truth, or at least to a part of it, was such a novel experience for Eleanor that she was actually enjoying herself.

'This, my darling,' she concluded, 'is why I cannot marry you.' She gave a regretful moue. 'Despite the fact that I love you.'

'Yes,' William said thoughtfully, 'yes, I understand.' He remained bewildered by her choice of lifestyle, having little in common with high society himself, but he very much respected her honesty. He admired her for it, aware that many a widowed woman in her position would have accepted his proposal in order to gain the security of marriage.

Eleanor broke the moment and laughed light-heartedly. 'Of course, if you were to sell Pendleton and move to the city, I would marry you in an instant,' she said, as if the mere suggestion were a huge joke. Which he took it to be, laughing along with her.

His laugh, although intensely annoying, was helpful, directing Eleanor as it did to her next course of action, which, this time, was not exactly honest. She would now embark upon an alternative plan.

Her burst of merriment over, she was suddenly serious.

'But I am prepared to be a wife to you, William, for I love you dearly.'

Cupping his face gently in her hands, she gazed into his eyes and kissed him with such tenderness William felt quite overwhelmed. But he was also puzzled. A wife? What did she mean?

Their lips parted and she spelled it out for him, still gazing into his eyes. 'Although not the Mistress of Pendleton, my darling,' she said, 'I would be a wife to you in all but the legal sense. I would be yours, here in London. Always yours, waiting for you right here, I promise. Your city wife.' Her smile was seductive now. 'That is, if you will have me.'

What could he say but yes? His body was already answering for him.

Barely two minutes later, they adjourned to the bedroom.

Eleanor's promise was no trivial matter. In offering herself as a full-time mistress, she was aware she would be exclusively his property as she had been the Marquess's, and she would happily honour the arrangement, for it suited her. She would always be available, she would continue to excite him, she would pander to his ego; everything a clever mistress did.

But it will cost you, William, she thought as she made love to him. *Oh, dear me, yes. Exclusivity takes money, my darling. A lot of money.*

2.

Charlotte had been waiting for her father to break the news she was dreading to hear. During Eleanor Witterson's last visit to Pendleton, it had been quite evident he was going to propose marriage – all the signs were there. His proud boasts of heritage and tradition, his family lineage and his duties as squire, the history of the estate ...

Poor Father, Charlotte had thought, *he's trying to impress her. Oh, dearest Papa, she will be marrying you only for your money. She hates the country, can't you see that?*

But her father clearly could *not* see that. He could see nothing but the woman he loved.

Charlotte and Eleanor had come to read each other well. Or so they both thought. To Charlotte, Eleanor was a woman bent on one purpose, which was to marry a wealthy man. Understandable of course for a widow, and particularly one of her age. But it didn't make Charlotte like her.

To Eleanor, Charlotte was the epitome of rebellious youth: unladylike, brash; at times, even hoydenish. She detested the way the girl looked her so boldly in the eye. It was downright rude.

But they both continued to play by the rules, for William's sake.

***

Upon her father's return from London, Charlotte cornered him in his office, steeling herself for the news. She'd expected the announcement to be immediately forthcoming, but it wasn't, which she found rather strange. He'd left for the city in such an ebullient mood she'd been quite sure he intended to propose.

'How was London?' she asked casually, watching as, seated behind his desk, he leafed through some papers.

'Pretty much the same as usual,' William replied without looking up. He was faintly amused, but not surprised. Charlotte was not known for her subtlety.

'And Eleanor? How was Eleanor?'

He stopped pretending to be busy and looked directly at his daughter. 'She turned me down,' he said.

'She *what*?' Charlotte was flabbergasted.

'She refused my proposal of marriage, my dear. An out and out "no", I'm afraid. Wouldn't even contemplate becoming the Mistress of Pendleton.'

'Oh.' Charlotte quelled a shriek of delight at this unexpected turn of events. 'Good heavens above, why?'

'She told me she couldn't live in the country.'

'I see.' Eleanor had actually said that! Charlotte couldn't believe it. How amazing. 'Well, that's very honest of her, I must say.'

'Yes, exactly what I thought.'

'So what happens now?'

'Eleanor and I will continue our relationship,' William said a little stiffly; there were, after all, boundaries to be observed when discussing such matters, even with one's daughter. Perhaps especially with one's daughter. 'You must understand, Charlotte, that we love each other very much.' And he went back to his papers. End of conversation.

'Yes of course, Father. I'm sorry, I didn't mean to intrude.'

Well, fancy that, Charlotte thought as she left his office. *Eleanor has denied herself the opportunity to become Mistress of Pendleton House. She has chosen instead to remain simply 'mistress'. With no legal status. Dear me, how bold.* Beneath her overwhelming sense of relief, Charlotte couldn't help but respect Eleanor for having made such a decision. *That would have taken courage*, she thought. *Good for her.*

Despite her renewed respect, she came to realise, however, that some sort of arrangement must have been agreed upon, for, over the following months, her father chose to spend more time than ever in London. He now seemed consumed by his love.

Charlotte missed the company of the father she adored, but her response was practical. She must wait for his affair to be over, it was as simple as that. Such a relationship would not stand the test of time, but was destined to wane. William Burton's love for Pendleton would eventually outweigh his passion for Eleanor Witterson.

***

Meanwhile, Charlotte determined to take over the duties her father was so sorely neglecting, one of which appeared to be the employment of a new head gamekeeper. She'd had a meeting with the estate manager in her father's office, where she'd set herself up to conduct business when required.

'Old Harry has to go, Miss Charlotte,' Leonard Asquith had told her. 'He's sixty now, nearing retirement age, and he's had another fall. He really can't handle the job anymore.'

'Oh, how sad,' Charlotte said. Old Harry had been with them for as long as she could remember and she was very fond of him.

'He's become a bit slack lately too, I'm afraid. We had another poaching incident last week. That's two deer in just over a month. Butchered on the spot and, same as last time, hind quarters only taken, so probably a one-man job.' He gave a solemn shake of his head. 'Won't do. Won't do at all. We'll have to let Harry go.'

'Oh, dear.' Charlotte felt a pang of concern. 'He'll be all right, won't he? I mean, we'll look after him.'

'Of course we will, miss, your father always looks after his workers. Old Harry will be handsomely rewarded for his years of service.' Leonard, an accountant by trade, middle-aged, middle-class and mild-mannered, gave a pleasant smile. 'His wife, Doris, is more than happy with the situation, turns out she's been wanting him to retire for some time. They're going to move back into the village to live with their son and his family.'

'I must say goodbye before they go.'

'Yes, I'm sure they'd like that,' Leonard replied. 'In the meantime, we need to hire a new gamekeeper. I've made some enquiries and there's a promising fellow from Leeds. He's experienced, comes highly recommended with good references, would you like to meet him?'

'I most certainly would.'

Leonard was not altogether surprised. She could have elected him to interview the fellow, which would have made things a lot easier, but that was not Miss Charlotte's way. She was the Squire's daughter and she was doing her father's job. Which, in her highly capable manner, she would no doubt do very well.

'Although I'm sure he won't relish being interviewed by me,' Charlotte added wryly.

'Possibly,' Leonard agreed, 'but if he wants the job, it's just something he'll have to put up with, isn't it?'

'Yes, Leonard, yes, it is.'

The candidate's name turned out to be Albert Midgely. A tough, nuggety man of around forty with a pug-like face, who, as Charlotte had predicted, did not enjoy being assessed by a female, and a very young female at that. From the outset, Albert Midgely made no attempt to disguise his hostility.

Leonard ushered him into the office, where Charlotte was seated behind the desk, and after making the introduction quietly took a seat in the far corner. He had no intention of playing a part in the interview process himself, but he could not leave the two alone together, it would be improper. Charlotte had assumed command as was her right, but she was still a young woman, indeed barely more than a girl.

'My father would normally be conducting this meeting, Mr Midgely,' Charlotte said pleasantly, 'but he has been called away to London on business, so I shall be taking his place.'

'Very good, miss.'

A sullen response, she thought, but she'd expected as much. 'Mr Asquith has supplied me with your references, which appear most impressive,' she went on, referring to the papers before her. 'You have a wealth of experience, it would seem—'

'Yes, miss, I do.'

A touch of aggression? '—and your previous employer writes glowingly of you.'

'I served him well, I did.'

Yes, definitely aggressive. 'Why did you leave your previous employ, Mr Midgely, may I ask?' Charlotte was genuinely interested. 'Why do you wish to make the move to Pendleton?'

Albert Midgely stared her down. This mere slip of a girl, admittedly handsome, but a girl nonetheless, dared throw a personal question like that at him? *Right then, missy*, he decided, *you'll get a personal answer right back in your face.*

'I was sharing single men's accommodation with two groundsmen at my previous place,' he said. 'I want more. I want a nice gamekeeper's cottage like you got here at Pendleton.'

The cheek! 'Oh, you do, do you?' Charlotte found his directness amusing more than anything.

'Yeah, I do. I'm looking to marry, see. I got a fiancée.'

'Congratulations.' Choosing to ignore the man's belligerence, Charlotte gave a light laugh instead. 'A conveniently happy situation for us both, then. Would your future wife possibly be seeking employment too? We like to engage couples here on the estate.'

'She might, yes.' Albert's defences were starting to weaken. What was it about this slip of a girl? She had a real air of authority. He might have been talking to a man.

The slip of a girl then went on to quote wages, conditions of employment and a possible starting date ...

'We must give old Harry time to vacate the cottage,' she said, as she rattled off all the details, 'but I think things are looking extremely promising, Albert. May I call you Albert?'

'You most certainly may, miss.' Albert's pug-like face broke into a smile. Although it had to be said, Albert's smile more resembled a grimace.

'Very well then, Albert.' Charlotte stood, signalling the interview was over, both men also rising to their feet. 'I shall leave any further arrangements to be sorted out with Mr Asquith here and bid you good morning.'

She offered her hand and Albert shook it, taken aback by the strength of her grip.

'I shall look forward to our working together,' she said. 'You'll be joining us at the right time, I must say. We've been having some poaching problems lately.'

'You won't have any while *I'm* in your employ, miss,' Albert replied, his expression grim. 'I'll catch this poacher, you have my word on that.'

'I'm very glad to hear it.'

Charlotte was relieved when her father returned to Pendleton in time to make his farewells to old Harry, and also to Doris, who'd worked in the laundry. They visited the gamekeeper's cottage together, trudging through the snow on a wintry day, the landscape so pretty, the trees laced in white.

'I don't want to go, sir.' Harry, grey-haired and bearded, shook his big shaggy head mournfully. 'I really, really don't want to go.'

'Yes, you do, Harry,' the ever-stalwart Doris firmly announced. 'Yes, he does, Squire. He does really, I promise you. He really, really does.'

William smiled. 'We shall miss you both,' he said, shaking Harry's hand. 'It's been a long time. Good God, *how* long? I can't even remember.'

'Twenty years, sir. Twenty years nearly to the day,' Harry replied proudly; he was good with dates. 'Mac and me come here the very same year. Mac's been with you twenty years too.'

'Yes, yes, of course. Jolly good, jolly good.' William turned to Doris, offering her his hand. 'My sincerest thanks to you both for your many years of service.'

'Been an honour, Squire,' Doris replied, and she gave a respectful bob.

'I shall miss you too,' Charlotte said, embracing first Doris, then Harry. 'It feels like the end of an era. I shall miss you so much.'

'As we will you, Miss Charlotte,' Doris said fondly.

'Indeed we will,' Harry agreed, before adding with a grin, 'You take care now, Master Charles.' The term was tantamount to a badge of honour shared among the oldest employees, who were the only ones to address Charlotte in such intimate fashion. They'd been calling her that since she was ten years old.

Charlotte was thankful for her father's personal farewell of Harry and Doris, who certainly deserved recognition from their Squire. But she'd been surprised by the lack of interest he'd shown in the poaching problem and the employment of a new gamekeeper. He'd seemed almost offhand when she'd told him. Yet poaching was an extremely serious crime, and the position of head gamekeeper was of paramount importance.

'You've done well, my dear,' he'd remarked distractedly, 'but you could have left it in Leonard's hands, he is our estate manager after all.'

'But *you* would not have left it in Leonard's hands, Father.' Her response to such an uncharacteristic remark had bordered on accusatory. 'You never leave the appointment of senior employees to Leonard, you always take a personal—'

'I would not have done so this time, Charlotte,' William brusquely retorted. 'I am far too tied up with business in London to involve myself in minor affairs that can be seen to by others.'

She was startled by his tone. *Why*, she wondered, *why is he so irritable?*

'I'm sorry, my dear.' William was instantly regretful. 'I didn't mean to snap, that was most unfair of me. It's just that I have a lot on my mind at the moment.'

She stood there, studying him, and he sensed she was seeking a little more information.

'I am involved in the acquisition of a new property in London, Charlotte,' he explained, 'which demands a great deal of my time. In fact, after attending to several matters here with Leonard, I shall be immediately returning to the city.'

He changed the topic then, successfully avoiding any further discussion.

'Believe me, my darling girl,' he said with a wealth of affection, 'I'm proud of the way you're handling things in my absence. I'm very proud and very grateful, I assure you.'

They hadn't talked any more on the subject and barely two weeks later William returned to London. To attend to his 'business', Charlotte presumed, which was the acquisition of a new property. She wondered if it had anything to do with Eleanor.

It did. William was in the throes of purchasing a townhouse for his 'city wife'. They'd been searching for some time now, and had recently found the ideal property in the ideal location. Mayfair, on which Eleanor had had her sights firmly set.

Eleanor was pleased to note that the property was only a stone's throw from the London home of the Marquess's family. She could see their townhouse a little further down the street, bigger and grander than the one that was to be hers, but no matter. She was soon to have a townhouse all of her own. And in Mayfair no less.

Her argument had been persuasive. At least, she had made it sound so. Indeed, it had appeared a debt of honour was owed to her.

'As your wife in all but name, my love,' she had said, 'I must have a proper house in which to live. Our respective apartments do not constitute a "home", William, and it is a home I wish to create for us. My greatest desire in life is to share a warm and loving home with you, my darling. This is surely the wish of any wife.'

He could hardly refute such an argument. And so it had been agreed he would arrange the sale of their respective apartments in order to purchase the new property. A townhouse in Mayfair being quite a deal more expensive than the combined worth of their apartments, however, he would need further funds. William had decided to put one of Pendleton's farm leases up for sale.

'It won't do us any harm to sell off a little land,' he said. 'Many of the larger estates are doing so these days.'

'Oh, my darling, how wonderful.' Eleanor had glowed with happiness. 'I shall create a true home for us, William, a nest all our own.'

He'd been a little taken aback by the next step she'd proposed: that the townhouse be purchased in her name. But, upon clarification, this too sounded perfectly reasonable.

'Do you not see, my darling,' she'd explained with infinite patience, 'that should something happen to you, the townhouse would be all I would have. With no legal claim to any property of yours, the home I share with you as your wife must be mine or I would risk being left destitute. Can you not see this?'

Yes, he supposed he could. In fact, it made complete sense. If she were to give herself to him totally, as she was prepared to do, then he must shoulder the responsibility for her wellbeing.

Eleanor fully believed in the authenticity of her claim to such rights as William's 'wife'. And she intended to earn them. She would be far more than a mistress to William Burton. With no legitimate wife in existence, she would assume the role in every sense of the word. Any wealthy man with a wife could keep a sexual plaything on the side, but few could boast a woman who served both purposes. She would be indispensable; vital to the man's very existence.

***

Albert Midgely took up his post as gamekeeper, moving into the cottage with his newly-wed wife, Milly, who in turn took up her position in the laundry. At least, Albert professed Milly to be his newly-wed wife, and Charlotte saw no reason to doubt him. In truth, she didn't actually care what their marital status was, so long as Albert proved good at his job.

Albert proved more than 'good'. Albert proved a man of his word. Two months later, just a week before Christmas, he caught the poacher. Or rather, one of the traps he'd set caught the poacher.

It was Charlotte who discovered young Tom Philby. She'd gone for a ride early on Saturday morning. There'd been no snowfall overnight and she'd taken the track through the woodlands that led to a large clearing where a number of logs served as excellent jumps. She and Byron loved this part of the woodlands, offering as it did such good sport.

They were approaching the clearing. She could see it up ahead, sparkling in the early morning frost. She could feel the stallion's anticipation, the extra spring in his step, he wanted to break into a canter, but she held him back.

Then she heard an unfamiliar noise. What was it? It wasn't the cry of an animal, but it was a cry. Something not quite human. A strangled, guttural sound. Something or someone in pain.

She drew Byron to a halt, dismounted cautiously and crept forward to investigate, keeping a hold on the reins, prepared to remount and flee should danger threaten.

Then, at the edge of the clearing, she saw him. Tom Philby. A youth from the village. Around eighteen years old, barely literate, Tom lived with his widowed mother and three younger siblings. The mother took in laundry and Tom was apprenticed to a smithy's shop. He also chopped firewood, which he sold to the locals, and always gave Charlotte a flirtatious smile when they passed each other in the streets of Otley. 'Morning, miss,' he'd say with a wink and a tap to his cloth cap. 'Good day for it, eh?'

'Morning, Tom,' she'd say, returning his smile before walking on. Tom was a cheeky lad all right.

But Tom wasn't cheeky this morning. Tom was on the ground, grunting with pain and exertion as he struggled desperately to free his leg from the vice-like jaws of a mantrap.

It was a grisly sight. The thick, hemp fibre of his trousers had protected his flesh, or so it appeared, for she could see no blood, but the leg was bent at an ominous angle and clearly broken.

'Tom!' Charlotte dropped the horse's reins and crouched beside him. She knew that Byron would not stray.

Tom ceased struggling and looked at her, seeing her for the first time. Consumed with pain, he hadn't noticed her arrival.

'Can't get the ruddy thing off,' he muttered through clenched teeth, 'been trying for God knows how long.'

Charlotte grasped the hideous mouth of the trap and tried to pry the jaws open, but she knew it was hopeless.

So did Tom. 'You'll never do it, miss,' he gasped. 'It's spring-loaded, you'll never do it. Oh, hell, oh, hell.' His whole body sagged with exhaustion and he appeared close to passing out.

'I'll fetch the gamekeeper. Albert will know how to free it.'

Charlotte jumped to her feet and mounted Byron. She had noted the cross-bow that lay on the ground beside Tom. *So you're our poacher,* she thought as she set off down the track, Byron breaking into a canter with no urging. *We needed to catch you, Tom, yes, but not like this! Not in a mantrap!* Charlotte was angry, but far more so with Albert Midgely than young Tom Philby. *We never use those ghastly things. They're banned, for God's sake! Father will be furious.*

Forty minutes later, she was back with the gamekeeper. She had not unleashed her anger upon Albert, not to the extent she would have wished. She would leave that to her father, who was returning from London the following day in order to spend Christmas at Pendleton. The estate's finest carriage was all lined up with driver and footman to meet the arrival of his train at Leeds, for he was to have Eleanor with him.

Although thankful to leave the matter in her father's hands, Charlotte had nonetheless made a caustic comment to the gamekeeper as they'd set off on horseback, Albert leading a spare mount for Tom.

'I doubt he'll be able to ride,' she'd said, 'his leg is broken. Badly too,' she'd added accusingly. 'That's why mantraps are banned, Albert. They're inhumane.'

'They work though, don't they?' Albert had smugly replied.

They arrived at the clearing to find Tom unconscious.

'Probably just as well,' Charlotte said, feeling for his pulse, thankful to discover he was still alive, 'he'd be in agony on the ride home otherwise.'

She proved accurate on both points. After Albert had released the trap's spring mechanism and freed Tom's leg, he roughly hoisted the youth's body up and over the saddle of the spare horse. At which point, Tom came to and gave a scream of agony. The excruciating pain continued as they set off down the track and after several minutes he once again lapsed into merciful unconsciousness.

While Albert ferried Tom back to the stables, where Mac had prepared a bed in the modest quarters out the back, Charlotte made a frantic dash into Otley to fetch the doctor.

When the two of them finally arrived at the stables, Tom had regained consciousness, but only barely. He was deathly pale and in a weakened state.

'You're right, Charlotte,' the doctor said after cutting away the trouser leg and making his examination, 'it's a bad break.' Reginald Langton could see instantly the cause of the break – the pattern of indentation and heavy bruising that indicated the teeth of the mantrap – but he made no mention. 'With a trauma injury like this, the whole body suffers,' he said. 'Luckily, young Tom's heavy trousers have kept the skin intact, which vastly reduces the threat of infection.'

Fifty-year-old Reginald, the village's most highly respected physician, knew the Widow Philby and her family. He was also on familiar terms with the Burtons, having had a long association with Pendleton workers and family members alike. He wondered how on earth a mantrap had come to be in use on the estate. Squire Burton would surely not have allowed such a thing. Now was not the time to query the matter though.

'Would you care to assist me, my dear,' he asked, 'or would you prefer Mac do so?'

Reginald received the response he both expected and hoped for. He knew Charlotte to be a highly capable young woman, not in the least squeamish and probably more deft than Mac would be.

'I'm happy to assist you, Dr Langton,' she said.

As Reginald unpacked his medical kit, Mac stood to one side in case he might be needed. Albert Midgely was not present. The gamekeeper had long since returned to his duties, not having enjoyed in the least Mac's scathing reaction to his use of the mantrap.

As instructed, Charlotte placed the drop mask over Tom's mouth and nose.

'Hold her there. Steady now,' Reginald said, and very slowly, he started to feed droplets of chloroform from a bottle onto the gauze cloth covering the mask. 'Breathe in, Tom,' he quietly intoned, 'breathe in nice and deep, there's a good lad, nice and deep now, that's the way.'

Tom did as he was told and within only minutes was once again unconscious.

'Right,' Reginald said, his tone now brisk and efficient. 'Keep the mask steady, Charlotte.'

The resetting of the bone was gruesome to watch as Reginald Langton dug his fingers deep into the flesh, realigning the fragments as best he could. Charlotte didn't flinch, focussing on the mask instead, but Mac turned away.

Then came the binding of the crepe bandage, firmly, but not too tightly.

'We don't want to restrict the blood circulation,' Reginald said. He turned to the stable master. 'We'll need two wooden splints to stabilise the limb. Do you think you could round those up for me, Mac? The length of the leg so that the knee is kept firmly in place.' He held up his hands. 'I'd say about so long.'

Mac nodded and left, thankful to escape.

Reginald and Charlotte worked on together in silence until, at last, the procedure over, they awaited the arrival of the splints.

'You'd make a fine nurse, Charlotte,' Reginald said, taking the mask from her and packing away his equipment.

'Thank you. Will he be all right?'

'Hard to say, really. Only time can answer that. If the bone knits well enough, he'll walk, but most certainly with a limp, and a pronounced one, I'd say. If not ...' A shrug implied the rest.

'Ah.' Reginald looked up as Mac entered, 'The splints.' He took the lengths of wood from the stable master. 'Excellent, just what we need. Come, Charlotte,' he instructed, 'hold these in place for me.'

Tom was regaining consciousness as the splints were being bound to his leg with yet more bandages, but Reginald continued unabated.

'The most important factor in the healing process is immobility,' he said. 'It's essential young Tom be kept immobilised while the bone knits. Is it possible he can remain housed here for the next ... oh, I'd say two months, at the least?'

Reginald directed his question to the stable master, but Mac immediately referred it to Charlotte.

'Not for me to say, doctor. It's up to Miss Charlotte here—' he would have said 'Master Charles', had he been on more familiar terms with the doctor, '—she's the boss while the Squire's away.'

'Of course it's possible,' Charlotte replied. 'These quarters are only used when an animal is ill or when a mare is foaling so that a stable hand can be in attendance at all times.' She smiled at Mac, who was always so devoted to his horses. 'Or more often than not, to house Mac, who deserts his cottage and his wife and family to camp out here.'

'Good. That's settled then.' Reginald handed her a small bottle. 'I'll leave you some laudanum, he'll be in quite a deal of pain. Just a modest dose now and then. No more than a sip or two.' He snapped his medical kit closed. 'I'll return in a few days to see how he's going. In the meantime if you need me, you know where I am.'

Charlotte accompanied Reginald to the door. 'Thank you, Dr Langton.'

'Always a pleasure, my dear.' He shook his head, acknowledging for the first time the cause of the injury. 'Terrible things, mantraps,' he said.

'I know. Father will be livid. We had no idea our gamekeeper had placed them. He is newly in our employ.'

'Of course.' Reginald nodded, satisfied his assumption had been proved correct, that Squire Burton would never condone the usage of such a monstrous device. 'I'll pop in to see Mrs Philby and let her know that her son has met with an accident,' he said meaningfully. 'I'll tell her Tom has broken his leg and will be recuperating here at Pendleton.'

'Thank you,' Charlotte said simply, but her eyes signalled the depth of her gratitude. It was imperative the use of the mantrap remain a secret.

***

'Good God, man, are you mad? Those blasted things have been illegal for nigh on fifty years! And with just cause! What the devil were you thinking?'

The following day, William Burton was more than livid, he was enraged beyond measure. Charlotte had never seen her father so irate. The normally composed Squire Burton was close to losing control.

'And how many more of the infernal contraptions have you placed around this property? Tell me, man, how many more?' William finally drew breath, awaiting an answer.

To give Albert Midgely his due, he did not appear to be quaking in his boots, but stood before his employer, sullen and defiant.

'Six,' the gamekeeper replied, looking William boldly in the eye. 'You had a problem with poachers. I was doing my job.'

'Doing your job!' The man's attitude only succeeded in enraging William further. 'Doing your blasted job ...!'

Charlotte exchanged a glance with Eleanor. The two of them were standing to one side, observing the confrontation, Eleanor equally taken aback by the fury she was witnessing. *Where has this come from?* she wondered, intrigued by the passionate show of rage from her usually mild-mannered lover. *And his anger was so instantly aroused,* she mused. *Why?* She personally thought the gamekeeper should have been congratulated for having caught a poacher.

The moment they'd alighted from the carriage at the main entrance to Pendleton House (William never escorted her through the side entrance), Eleanor had noted Charlotte waiting there, ready to pounce.

'The new gamekeeper set mantraps,' Charlotte had announced to her father without even acknowledging Eleanor's presence. 'We caught a poacher in one yesterday and his leg is broken. He's in the stable quarters. Dr Langton says he has to stay there for two months until the bone mends.'

'Mantraps?' William's face had been a picture of disbelief, quickly followed by outrage. 'He set *mantraps*?'

'Yes, Father.'

'Bring him to me.'

Charlotte had raced off to fetch the gamekeeper and Eleanor had found herself with no option but to follow William, as he'd charged ahead without her. She'd given a nod to the footman that her trunk be taken upstairs to her quarters and, gathering her skirts, had trailed in William's wake as he'd headed through the entrance hall and into the west wing. He seemed to have forgotten she was there, until all of a sudden they were in his office.

'I'm sorry, my dear,' he'd said, finally appearing to notice her, 'please forgive me, but this is something that must be addressed immediately.'

'Of course, my love,' she'd replied. She was not accustomed to being treated in so unceremonious a fashion, but remained intrigued by the cause of his distraction.

William had continued to be distracted for the next fifteen minutes; he hadn't even offered her a seat. But she'd felt his growing rage as she'd watched him pace the floor. *How very interesting*, she'd thought, divesting herself of her travel cape and neat little bonnet, carefully placing both on an armchair. *I've never seen him so agitated.*

Then Charlotte had arrived with the gamekeeper and William's tirade had been unleashed.

'You do realise, don't you, that in "doing your blasted job", you have broken the law!'

'I caught your poacher, didn't I?' Albert maintained his bravado. 'I'm not the only one around who still uses mantraps, I can tell you. That boy, *he's* the one who broke the law—'

'And furthermore,' William went on, ignoring the interruption, 'as gamekeeper in our employ, it means *we* have broken the law. You have threatened the reputation of Pendleton Estate.' He was getting himself even further worked up at the mere thought of the disgrace that loomed. 'Dear God, man, do you realise what you've done? You've risked the loss of our good name!' He glared at the fellow, whose indifference was infuriating. 'What do you have to say for yourself?' he demanded.

But Albert wasn't one to back down. 'I say poaching's a hanging offence, that's what I have to say. He should go to the gallows, that boy, he should.'

William controlled his urge to strike the man. 'Your services are terminated as of this minute, Mr Midgely,' he said tightly. 'You will collect whatever wages are owed you from our estate manager, but before you do so, you will gather up every one of your abominable mantraps and get them off this property. Mr Asquith will assign a groundsman to accompany you so we may ensure you carry out this order. Needless to say, you will receive no reference for your service here at Pendleton. Good day to you, sir.'

Albert made no reply, but glowered as he strode from the office.

After taking several deep breaths in an effort to calm himself, William turned to Charlotte. 'We shall go to the stables now and see to this poacher,' he said.

Then he crossed to Eleanor. 'There is no need for you to accompany us, my dear, you've witnessed quite enough unpleasantness as it is.'

'Oh, my poor darling,' she said, placing a hand to his brow, 'you have so upset yourself.'

Eleanor had no intention of accompanying them to the stables. She was wearing one of her best day dresses in silk taffeta and velvet and certainly wasn't going to risk the hem. She had packed other day dresses that were less valuable and more appropriate for traipsing about the countryside.

'Why, you're quite shaking with rage,' she continued, 'I can feel it. This can't be good for your constitution, William.' She was stroking his brow now, soothingly, a maternal action that seemed to be having some effect. 'There, there, my love, you must calm down. There, there, now.'

'Yes, yes, you're quite right,' William agreed, 'I must not let the man rile me so.' Aware that his daughter appeared to be closely studying them, he detached himself from Eleanor's ministrations and resumed command. 'I shan't be long, my dear,' he said, taking her hand from his brow and clasping it fondly in both of his. 'Edith will serve you tea in the front parlour and I shall join you shortly. Now, if you will excuse me ...'

He kissed her hand lightly, gave Charlotte a nod and the two of them walked out of the office, leaving Eleanor to find her own way to the parlour, where Edith was already waiting with the tea.

Charlotte had indeed been studying the intimacy between her father and his mistress. *She's mothering him*, she'd thought with a sense of surprise, *and what's more, he's loving it.*

As they walked out the side door of the west wing and set off for the stables, Charlotte wondered whether Eleanor had changed tactics. *What sort of game is she playing? And why has she resigned herself to a whole two weeks here at Pendleton? She never stays longer than three days.*

Charlotte had been pondering this ever since her father had told her he'd be home for Christmas and well into the New Year.

73

'Eleanor will be with me,' he'd said. 'She'll need to return to London for New Year's Eve and the start of the season; so many charity functions are held around that time. But we'll have a lovely family Christmas together,' he'd happily announced.

A lovely family Christmas? Charlotte had thought. *Eleanor will just hate that.*

Little could she have known that the 'lovely family Christmas' had actually been Eleanor's idea.

'I'm afraid I shall be away for well over a month, my dear,' William had told his mistress. 'I always spend the Christmas and New Year season with Charlotte. It's a family tradition and a precious time for us both. I simply could not bring myself to desert her.'

William, already suffering guilt over the amount of time he'd been spending away from Pendleton, was adamant in his decision, and quite prepared to leave his 'city wife' alone in London.

Eleanor had immediately sensed a *fait accompli* and had made no attempt to dissuade him from his course of action. She had an even better plan.

'Of course, my darling, what a splendid idea. I shall join you for Christmas at Pendleton. That is, if you'd like me to,' she'd added with a winsome smile.

William had naturally been delighted. 'I'd *love* you to join me, you know I would,' he'd said, gathering her in his arms. 'Oh, Eleanor, we'll have the most marvellous time. Christmas at Pendleton is such a cosy affair with house staff who are like family, and New Year's Eve we celebrate with the villagers in

Otley. A grand party is held at the Town Hall,' he continued excitedly. 'We provide a lucky dip for the children and—'

'Oh, I wouldn't be able to stay for New Year's Eve, dearest,' Eleanor quickly countered. *What a simply ghastly prospect*, she thought. 'There's always a gala charity ball on New Year's Eve, the first one of many to follow. But I shall so look forward to seeing Charlotte and spending a lovely family Christmas together at Pendleton.'

Eleanor had decided that, having now moved into her townhouse in Mayfair, she could afford to be generous. It was high time she and Charlotte developed a more harmonious relationship. After all, they both loved William Burton and they both wished to make him happy, did they not?

Her plan, furthermore, was eminently sensible. So long as she didn't have to stay too long in the country, she was quite prepared to be a substitute mother to Charlotte. *The girl needs a female influence in her life*, Eleanor decided, *and William will bask in joy at the knowledge his daughter finally has a mother.*

***

William Burton was surprised to discover the poacher was none other than young Tom Philby from the village. He'd presumed the culprit would be someone from further afield, Leeds perhaps. Tom and his family were locals.

'I'm sorry, Squire,' Tom said, shamefaced. 'I know I done wrong.' He felt really bad. The Squire had been good to his mum. It was because of the Squire they'd lived rent free for a whole year after his dad had died of a heart attack. 'I'm real sorry, honest I am.'

'But *why* did you turn to poaching, Tom?' William was genuinely concerned. 'Is your mum doing things hard? Not enough food on the table? *Why?*'

Tom shrugged. He was feeling strange, a bit groggy from that stuff Miss Charlotte had fed him with a teaspoon, and when he moved, the pain made his head spin.

'No, we're not doing too bad,' he said. 'I mean, we're not starving or anything. I sold the hind quarters of deer to a butcher in Leeds. Both times. Didn't eat none. Didn't want Mum to know I'd been poaching, she'd be so ashamed.' He gave another shrug. 'Just wanted to make some extra money for Christmas ... buy stuff for my little sisters ...' His voice trailed off and his eyes were starting to glaze a little. 'I dunno ... showing off, most like ...'

'I gave him some laudanum as Dr Langton instructed, Father,' Charlotte explained.

'I see. Well, Tom,' William said, 'I shall call upon your mother and—' He halted at the lad's instant expression of alarm. 'No, no, rest easy. I shall tell her that you've had an accident. That you broke your leg and that we're looking after you here until it mends.'

'Thank you.' Tom breathed an audible sigh of relief. 'I'm real grateful. Thank you, Squire, from the bottom of my heart.'

These were very much the sentiments Charlotte had felt.

'That's exactly what Dr Langton told me he'd say to Tom's mother,' she confided as they left the stables, 'virtually word for word.'

'Then we're lucky, all of us, aren't we,' William replied grimly. 'Young Tom, the Burton name, and the entire estate of Pendleton.'

They strode on towards the west wing entrance. 'I shall call upon Mrs Philby nonetheless,' he said. 'She'll no doubt need money to tide her over until Tom is fit to work once more, and she will be welcome to visit him here any time she wishes during his recuperation.' William cast a murderous glance in the general direction of the gamekeeper's cottage. 'That blasted man,' he cursed.

The following morning, Eleanor insisted upon accompanying William and Charlotte as they left for the stables to tend their patient. Attired now in a more practical day dress with a warm, woollen jacket, and having replaced her pretty suede shoes with a pair of sturdy buttoned boots, she was prepared to traipse about the grounds of the estate. 'I wish to be a part of all that is going on,' she declared.

Pendleton's young footman, Teddy, had been assigned the task of bedpan duties, which had been seen to first thing that morning, but father and daughter had undertaken the general care of the patient. A fact Eleanor found odd, to say the least. Surely this should be left in the hands of the servants. She said as much to William as she took his arm and delicately picked her way along the track.

'It is somewhat unusual for a gentleman farmer to take such care of one who has poached game from his property,' she mildly remarked.

'He's a lad from the village,' William replied. 'We're acquainted with his family.'

77

'Oh, how very kind of you, William,' she said. 'How very kind of you *both*,' she added, smiling warmly at Charlotte. 'I believe you have taken on a personal responsibility for this man's nursing, my dear.'

'In a way, yes,' Charlotte replied. 'I have been administering the laudanum dose needed in order to control the pain.'

'Kind. So very kind.' Eleanor didn't think the two of them kind at all. She considered their nurturing nothing short of outrageous. She agreed with the gamekeeper. Poaching was a hanging crime. This fellow should be sent to the gallows. Good heavens above, her Marquess would most certainly have insisted the man swing.

She was taken aback by the youth of the poacher, a sandy-haired lad who couldn't have been twenty, and further outraged by the manner in which William enquired of his comfort.

'Did you manage to sleep well enough, Tom?'

'On and off, yes, thank you, Squire.'

And she was outraged yet further as she watched Charlotte support the lad's head while feeding him two teaspoons of laudanum. The whole scenario was obscene, in Eleanor's opinion. But she said nothing, having determined to play her part as the caring mother.

***

For the whole of the ensuing two weeks, Eleanor continued to play her part, and with great success. Christmas turned out to be just as William had promised it would be, a cosy family affair. Even Charlotte had found it so. Eleanor had been warm and funny, endearing herself to the house staff. She had been affectionate and caring, not only to William but to Charlotte herself.

Is this a game you've been playing? Charlotte couldn't help but wonder as she and Eleanor made their farewells outside the main entrance of Pendleton House on the morning of New Year's Eve. Mac was there with the carriage, waiting to drive Eleanor to the railway station in Leeds, the footman was loading her trunk, and William was standing by to accompany her. *If it's all been a game*, Charlotte thought, *then I must say, you're frightfully good at it.*

'I'm sorry you're not staying on for the villagers' party in Otley, Eleanor,' she said, 'we always have such fun. I'm sure you would find it most enjoyable.'

'I'm sure I would too, my dear,' Eleanor kissed her fondly on both cheeks, 'particularly in your company.' As she drew away, her eyes remained affectionately upon Charlotte. 'I have loved our family Christmas.'

'Me too,' Charlotte heard herself say.

Surprisingly enough, they both meant it. Eleanor had perhaps played her part *too* well. She had found herself drawn into her motherly role and Charlotte had found herself responding to the show of female affection she'd never before known.

How strange, Eleanor thought as William assisted her into the carriage then climbed in to sit beside her. *I really do feel I've acquired a daughter.* She was relieved to be returning to London nonetheless. The countryside would never agree with her.

At the station, William drew Eleanor to him in a farewell embrace, the mere feel of her body so close to his setting him aquiver. Eleanor always had that effect upon him.

'I shall be with you in less than a month,' he murmured. And he kissed her. Openly, in public view. He didn't care what people thought. 'Until then ...'

'I shall be waiting for you,' she whispered in return, and they might have been making love right there on the station platform. Eleanor was fully aware of the power she had over him.

However, when he'd seen her safely settled aboard the train and had returned to the platform, she offered a word of advice through the open carriage window.

'That boy in the stables, William,' she said, 'it is unseemly Charlotte should be alone with him. You must ensure a servant is present at all times.'

'Yes, yes, of course, my love.' William's response was perfunctory. The train's whistle was sounding, the guard was calling 'All aboard', and William was drinking in his fill of her. Close to a whole month loomed without her nightly presence in his bed.

The train started slowly to chug from the station.

No, no, William, you don't understand, Eleanor thought as she watched him standing there on the platform, forlornly waving goodbye. *You can't see, can you? You really can't see at all. That boy is young. That boy is young and he's handsome. And Charlotte is shortly to turn seventeen.*

3.

'It was that boy in the stables, wasn't it?'

Eleanor remained elegantly poised in her hardback chair, bone china teacup halfway to her lips, little finger extended. The statement had come as something of a shock. Then, leaning forward, she replaced the cup and saucer on the coffee table and studied the girl seated on the sofa opposite her.

Charlotte nodded. She hadn't touched her own tea.

'Are you sure? Have you consulted a doctor?'

'Yes, I'm quite sure. But no, I haven't seen a doctor, I didn't want anyone to know.'

Charlotte's façade was crumbling. She'd managed a bold performance in the presence of her father, who'd been there when she'd arrived, fresh from the railway station, suitcase in hand. She hadn't expected him to be home during the afternoon, having presumed his days in London were spent on business.

'I thought it was time I paid a visit,' she'd said after they'd welcomed her inside, embracing her warmly. 'I've been dying to see the townhouse. And oh, my, my, isn't it glorious!' she'd exclaimed, gazing about admiringly.

'And oh, my, my, aren't *you* glorious, my dear!' Eleanor had exclaimed with equal admiration, holding her at arm's length. 'In a dress, I do declare, and a very attractive one at that. Oh, my darling Charlotte, you're as pretty as a picture.'

They'd all laughed, and Eleanor had immediately ordered her maid arrange tea to be served in the front sitting room. She had a full-time live-in maid and also a housekeeper-cook these days; the minimum number of staff required, she'd informed William.

Charlotte had been relieved beyond measure when her father had excused himself.

'No tea for me, I'm afraid,' he'd said, 'business calls. But I'll see you this evening, Charlotte. You'll be staying with us for a while, I take it?'

'Yes, Father, a few days, no more. That is, if I may.'

'You most certainly may. In fact, it's high time you did,' he'd said before setting off for his meetings, happily leaving the two of them to their own devices.

Charlotte had maintained her façade while the maid served tea. She'd commented upon the play of sunlight that was shining so attractively through the bay windows. The way it highlighted the decorative sitting room, she'd remarked. And also the stylish furnishings, which she very much admired. Her small talk had been masterful. Then, when the maid had finally departed, she'd steeled herself.

'It is you I came to see, Eleanor,' she said. 'Not Father.'

'Oh, yes?' Eleanor's response had been wary, although she'd remained composed as she'd picked up her cup of tea. The girl was looking her boldly in the eyes, the way she had in the days when they'd been testing each other's mettle, making judgements about one another. Was it a confrontation she was after? And if so, a confrontation about what? *Has she discovered the townhouse belongs to me?* Eleanor wondered. *What business is it of hers anyway?*

'I'm pregnant.'

The announcement had come as a shock, but Eleanor had known the full story in an instant. *You fool, William,* she thought, *I tried to warn you. But you didn't listen, did you? Oh, you foolish man.*

'It was that boy in the stables, wasn't it?' she'd said. And she put down her cup and saucer.

Charlotte had nodded. But this remote reaction from the one person she'd turned to as her only possible ally immediately undermined her defences. No, she said, she hadn't seen a doctor, she hadn't wanted anyone to know ...

Then all of a sudden, she found herself starting to sob. 'Oh, Eleanor, I didn't know where to turn, I didn't know what to do ...'

'There, there, my dear, there, there.' Eleanor rose from her chair and crossed to sit beside Charlotte on the sofa. She put her arms around the girl and drew her close. 'I'm here, darling, I'm here,' she said, rocking her gently back and forth. 'I shall look after everything, I promise you I shall. You're not alone, my dear, you're not alone.'

They were the words Charlotte needed to hear and she quickly fought to regain control, taking the napkin Eleanor passed her from the tea things on the coffee table and mopping up her tears.

'I'm sorry,' she said.

'Blow your nose, there's a good girl.'

Charlotte did so. 'Thank you,' she said. 'I'm all right now.'

'But you're not really, are you?' Eleanor commented drily. 'You're not in the least all right.'

'No, I suppose I'm not.'

They shared a wan smile.

'Your father must be told, of course,' Eleanor said crisply.

'I know. He'll be furious. He'll blame Tom …'

'Yes, he will.'

'But it wasn't Tom's fault. I was as much to blame …'

'Yes, yes, I'm sure you were.' Eleanor was determined to get down to business. 'How far gone do you think you are?'

'I've just missed my second monthly time.'

'I see. And which path might you wish to consider?'

Charlotte met her gaze blankly.

'Do you want to get rid of it?'

The question was brash, jarring, and Charlotte was shocked. Such an idea had not occurred to her.

'No,' she said, 'no, I couldn't possibly …'

Of course you couldn't, Eleanor thought, *and your father would never condone such a thing anyway, good Christian man that he is.* 'Very well,' she continued, 'we must plan where you will spend your confinement and safely give birth.'

'Yes,' Charlotte agreed, 'yes, we must.' Things were moving at such a pace she felt quite breathless, but she was grateful for the support on offer and would do anything Eleanor suggested.

'I know of a place,' Eleanor said, 'it's a nunnery. The Abbey of the Sisters of Adeneaux, roughly twelve miles out of London. The good nuns there will look after you, Charlotte.

As they have looked after many a young woman in your condition,' she added meaningfully. 'You will have no cause for concern, they will deliver your baby safely.' *They delivered mine, didn't they?* she thought.

'Oh, thank you, Eleanor,' Charlotte said, relieved beyond measure. 'Thank you so—'

'Now drink up your tea before it gets cold, there's a good girl. Then we'll take your suitcase upstairs and settle you in.'

***

Just as they had predicted, William lay the blame solely upon young Tom Philby.

'Why, that scoundrel,' he fiercely declared when Eleanor broke the news over pre-dinner drinks in the sitting room. 'This is the way the fellow repays a kindness, is it? By defiling my daughter!' He leapt to his feet, outraged. 'I'll have the wretch flayed alive. I'll see him hang for this. I'll—'

But Charlotte refused to suffer such histrionics.

'Tom did not rape me, Father,' she loudly declared. 'He didn't even seduce me. It was more a case of *me* seducing *him.*'

William halted his tirade to stare back at her.

'I wanted to know what it was like, you see.' She met her father's eyes brazenly before turning to Eleanor, who was sipping her sherry and watching in silence. 'I wanted to experience sex,' she said.

The glance Eleanor returned was eminently readable. *Of course you did, dear. You were just aching to experience sex. Seventeen is such a dangerous age.*

Eleanor looked up at William, who remained in an apparent state of shock. 'I did warn you, my darling. At the train station, remember? I told you she must not be left alone with him.'

'Yes, I remember,' he replied crossly. 'You said it was unseemly and that she should always be accompanied by a servant. I naturally assumed you were referring to a matter of etiquette. What else was I to assume?'

Oh, William, you are naïve, Eleanor thought. *Particularly for one whose passion is so easily aroused. Good God, man, do you not realise women, too, can be aroused?* She heaved an inward sigh. *But then men always seem blind to a woman's needs, don't they?*

'I think perhaps, my love, we should address the matter to hand,' she gently suggested, 'we must make plans, do you not agree?'

'Yes, yes, we must,' William said shakily, and like an obedient child, he returned to his seat. He was at a loss. What plans? What were they to do? He had no idea. He downed a hefty swig of his Scotch and water.

Eleanor took over. 'The boy,' she said, addressing Charlotte, 'I take it the boy has not been told of your condition?'

'No, he has not been told. And he will never be told,' Charlotte answered firmly. She felt strong now. 'I would not wish fatherhood upon him. You're right, he *is* only a boy. Just a country lad.'

The image of Tom's face flashed through her mind. The surprise in his eyes when she'd kissed him. She'd been sitting on the side of his bed, having brought him his meal, and he'd been thanking her for the care she'd taken of him over the past six weeks.

'From the bottom of my heart, Miss Charlotte,' he'd said, 'I don't know what I'd have done without you. You're an angel, that's what you are ...'

She'd leaned in and kissed him. And when she'd drawn away, she'd seen more than surprise in his eyes, she'd seen wonderment. She knew he was infatuated with her; she'd known from the very start. The way his gaze had followed her every movement; the way he'd started at the touch of her when she raised his head to plump his pillow or when she settled him into a more comfortable position. She'd found the effect she had on him intensely erotic.

So she'd leaned in and kissed him again, opening her mouth to him this time, inviting him to go further. And he had, his hand seeking her breast, their mutual arousal growing more urgent by the second as they clumsily fumbled with their clothes.

He'd felt mortified afterwards. Riddled with guilt, he'd begged her forgiveness.

'Oh, Miss Charlotte,' he'd said, 'I don't know how that happened. Do please forgive me. I'm sorry, I'm so very sorry ...'

'I'm not,' she'd said. She hadn't been, either. After the initial stabs of pain, she'd enjoyed their coupling. She now knew what sex was like and it was every bit as exciting as she'd hoped it might be. 'I'm not sorry in the least.'

'You've done the right thing in not telling the boy,' Eleanor said approvingly. 'Word of this must reach no-one. Your pregnancy must be kept an absolute secret, not only for your sake, Charlotte, but for your father's.' She cast a glance in William's direction. 'Such news would do irreparable damage to his reputation as Squire of Pendleton, you understand.'

'Yes, of course. I understand.'

'It really is most unfortunate you fell pregnant from the one experience.' Eleanor shook her head sympathetically. 'Downright bad luck, I must say.'

'It wasn't one experience, actually.'

'Oh?'

Charlotte was aware of them both staring fixedly at her, two pairs of eyes studying her intently: her father shocked, Eleanor taken aback.

'There were other times.'

'I see.' Eleanor swiftly gestured for William to be silent; he appeared about to explode. 'This does put a slightly different complexion upon things, Charlotte,' she said carefully. *The wretched girl hasn't fallen in love with the boy, surely,* she thought, appalled. *Young women these days can be so foolish!* 'So your relationship became an *affair?*'

'I wouldn't say an "affair", exactly. No, I wouldn't say that.'

Tom would have liked it to become an affair, Charlotte recalled. She'd had to be firm with him that day he'd left to return to the village.

'We won't be seeing each other again, Tom,' she'd said. 'Not like this, anyway. This was just an adventure we shared. You do understand that, don't you?'

'Yes, I do,' he'd said reluctantly. He'd have liked to

continue an illicit affair. He was aroused by the mere thought of secretly meeting her here in the stables. But, yes, he understood. They were worlds apart, the two of them, and always would be. 'A pity,' he'd added suggestively, 'we made such music, you and me.'

An hour or so later, there'd been a twinkle in his eye as he'd openly bade her farewell, Mac standing by the dray, waiting to take him home.

'I thank you for your care, Miss Charlotte,' he'd said with a respectful touch to the brim of his cloth cap. 'I shall no doubt bump into you in the streets of Otley.' And he'd given her a wink before lurching away on his crutch to climb awkwardly into the dray. Despite the fact his leg would heal a little further, he was destined to remain a cripple. But the cheeky young Tom Philby was back.

'You're not in love with the boy, then?' Eleanor challenged, her tone sharp.

'Good heavens, no,' Charlotte replied. 'As I told you, I wanted to know what sex was like. And I found out. As simple as that.'

Eleanor's smile was congratulatory. *Good girl*, it said. 'Right then, let's get on with our plans. We'll be called to dinner in ten minutes.'

Charlotte remained in London for only three days, the allotted period she'd allowed in the hope that Eleanor might have the answer to her predicament.

'I should be no more than three days, Leonard,' she'd told the estate manager, 'perhaps four at the outside,' and she'd left, praying desperately she might be proved right.

She had been, Eleanor having arranged her future so neatly Charlotte had even relaxed enough to enjoy the rest of her trip to London. Including her father's newly purchased property, which she found most impressive.

'This really is the most beautiful house,' she'd remarked that first night as they'd dined at the twelve-seater table, which, with its centrepiece added, could accommodate twenty. The dining room and main lounge, complete with grand piano, were the focal point of the townhouse. Eleanor very much liked to entertain.

'I'm surprised you should say that, Charlotte,' her father remarked tightly. 'I thought you hated the city.'

William was tense, his nerves jangled, his mind still reeling. How could Charlotte be so calm when she'd completely disrupted their lives? Eleanor too. They were chatting amicably as if nothing had happened. Yet the girl was pregnant!

He was guilt-ridden, furthermore, still smarting from Eleanor's comment. 'I told you she was not to be left alone with him.' *Is this all my fault?* he wondered. *Am I responsible for ruining my daughter's life?*

'You're right, I don't much like London,' Charlotte replied. 'I was merely commenting upon the house, which is quite lovely.'

'That's exactly why I'm surprised,' William said. 'You must be aware this house is typical of London architecture, particularly in this area.'

Charlotte knew why her father was being terse. *Poor, dear Papa,* she thought, *you're still in a state of shock. And who can blame you?*

'Yes, Father,' she agreed, 'very typical indeed of an inner-city townhouse.' Her smile was complimentary. 'Which makes it such an excellent investment,' she said.

It *was* a good investment, Charlotte thought, but hardly worth the sale of one of the farm leases. She'd been surprised when she'd recently discovered this, and via the farmer who'd bought the land, what's more. Neither her father nor Leonard Asquith had mentioned the fact, which she'd found most strange.

'Yes, a very good investment,' William replied. He did not look at Eleanor, addressing his rack of lamb instead.

Shortly before Charlotte's departure, Eleanor suggested William return to Pendleton with her, which was surprising, for, as a rule, she was extremely demanding of his company.

'It is Charlotte who now needs your companionship, my love,' she insisted, 'we must ensure she does not feel alone. When her condition is beginning to show, she will return to me here in London and I shall take her to the abbey, where she is to spend her confinement. We must face this dilemma as a family,' she announced, 'each one of us playing our part.'

Such selflessness was not typical of Eleanor, and both William and Charlotte were deeply appreciative. Charlotte was grateful for the show of female support, and William was proud of the maternal care displayed by his 'city wife'. The thought that they were a family pleased him immensely.

Over the ensuing months, Charlotte was indeed thankful for her father's company. Eleanor had been right; his presence was reassurance that she was not alone. There were even times when she felt they'd returned to the days of her childhood. Seated in his office, savouring the letters he read out loud to her, hearing Uncle Geoffrey's voice all the way from the Pilbara, she might have been twelve years old again.

I have acquired a property in Perth, Geoffrey proudly announced in a letter to his brother. *Well, it's not actually in Perth,* he corrected himself, *but rather it's halfway (and precisely so, I'm told) between Perth and the port of Fremantle. Most convenient, I must say. Not far from the railway line connecting the two, a place called Claremont.*

> *I hasten to add, dearest brother, that I have purchased this property in both our names as the necessary bank loan was raised on the value of Burton Station. You are now therefore co-owner of a frightfully pretty, two-storey house overlooking the Swan River. And, oh, William, I promise you, it is bound to prove the most wonderful investment ...*

They'd shared a laugh at that news. To Geoffrey, the perennial optimist, everything was 'the most wonderful investment'. 'Let's hope he's right,' William remarked drily.

Then in another letter, Geoffrey wrote of his position in the community, the township of Roebourne and the surrounding district ...

> *All once again due to the influence of Robert Sholl of course; dear God, the man is incorrigible. I serve as a virtual magistrate these days and yet, as you know, I have never once practised law. Until now, that is. Marvellous what an Oxford degree will do in a place*

*like this. I swear I seem a law unto myself. I rather
enjoy the power, I'll admit, but for the most part I
find it devilishly amusing. I mean, when all's said and
done, I'm only a farmer.*

*And speaking of farming, dearest brother, Burton
Station continues to thrive. Wool sales are well up
now, via a new Singapore route, and beef always
makes money. The farmhouse is not much to look at,
I must confess, but then no property in the Pilbara is.
There seems no point in building something of beauty
when the next cyclone (quaintly referred to by the
locals as a 'willy-willy' no less) is destined to flatten
the place. All one can do is ensure the animals are kept
safe ...*

On and on Geoffrey would go, his voice delighting both his
brother and his niece, while serving also to strengthen the
bond between them; the bond which, of late, had become
somewhat tenuous due to William's lengthy absences from
Pendleton.

But then came the time when Charlotte could no longer
disguise her swollen belly beneath the large shirts that she
wore loose over her work trousers instead of tucked in at
the waist. At least, she considered it unwise she should *try*
to disguise her belly. Men would perhaps not recognise her
condition, but women very well might. She must return to
London.

William accompanied his daughter on the train journey
south. But after they'd spent a pleasant week with Eleanor

at the townhouse, he was surprised to discover he was not to accompany Charlotte to the Abbey of the Sisters of Adeneaux.

Eleanor was most insistent over dinner, as the three of them discussed the following morning's departure plans.

'Having visited the abbey and having spoken with the nuns,' she said firmly, 'all is set in place, William. It is now only a matter of my delivering Charlotte to them, which I am happy to do on my own ...'

He was about to protest, but Eleanor continued.

'She has been lodged at the abbey under a false name, funds have been paid in advance, as *discussed*,' she added emphatically, her meaningful look telling him the funds had been as substantial as she had warned him, 'and you have been in no way associated with the process.'

In the brief pause that followed, William glanced at his daughter, but Charlotte's focus was solely upon Eleanor. It was quite clear she had placed herself entirely in Eleanor's hands.

'You must see, William,' Eleanor went on, her tone a little gentler yet still the voice of authority, 'that should you become involved, your reputation would be ruined. The Burton name would be forever tarnished.' She relaxed. 'Besides, my love,' she added, her smile patronising, humorous even, 'this is a women's issue. Men have nothing to contribute when it comes to such matters.' She turned her smile to Charlotte. 'Do you not agree, my dear?'

'Yes, most certainly,' Charlotte replied. She didn't altogether agree, and the notion that she should amused her. *Men surely have a great deal to contribute when it comes to women's pregnancies*, she thought. But she certainly agreed there must be no risk of tarnishing the Burton name. 'It is better you do not accompany us to the abbey, Father,' she said.

William nonetheless insisted upon seeing them both aboard the train to Erith, which left early the following morning from London Bridge Station.

'Take care, my darling girl,' he said, holding Charlotte close as they said their goodbyes on the railway platform. 'Oh, please, take care. Please be safe.' His plea was so heartfelt he might have been praying.

Returning her father's embrace and recognising the depth of his anxiety, Charlotte whispered words of comfort in his ear.

'Don't worry, Papa. Women have babies all the time.'

He stood watching as the train pulled away, and Eleanor, looking through the carriage window, thought once again what a forlorn figure he presented. 'I'll see you back at the townhouse in the late afternoon,' she'd assured him. 'I can't be sure of the time exactly, but I shall take a hansom cab from the station.'

William had no option but to simply go home and wait. Which he did, all day, anxiously, and when Eleanor returned shortly before dusk, the questions tumbled out.

'How is she? Is she being safely looked after? Were they there to meet her?'

'Yes, yes,' Eleanor replied, curbing her irritation, for she'd found the day intensely wearying. 'Everything went exactly as I told you it would. Two nuns were waiting for us at the station in Erith. Good heavens, there was even a driver standing by with the abbey's carriage and pair. They treated Charlotte like royalty.' *Hardly the way I was treated*, she thought, as the image of a nun and a dray flashed through her mind. 'As well they should,' she added, 'given the money they've been paid. And the ample funds Charlotte has with her will no doubt see her living there like a queen. She'll have a lovely room all to herself and the nuns will purchase for her whatever she wishes.' *Yes*, Eleanor thought, *they certainly won't stick her away with two other girls in that ghastly upstairs garret.*

'They drove Charlotte off in style the further mile or so to the abbey while I waited in the grubby little railway station for the next train back to London,' she concluded. 'Which took an age to arrive, I might add.'

'But the nuns, were they—'

'I have met them before, William,' Eleanor said, his interruption only serving to irritate her further, 'and I can assure you they are personable and efficient and will take excellent care of Charlotte. As will all the nuns at the abbey, my dear. As will the Mother Superior too. These are good women. You have nothing to fear.'

But still she could see he was worrying and fretting.

'It's a glorious place, the abbey,' she said by way of distraction. 'Right on the banks of the Thames, so pretty, lovely walks beside the river. Charlotte will be happy there ...'

But nothing could distract William from the dread of what might lie ahead. His daughter, his little girl, the person most dear to him above all others, was soon to give birth. *Women die in childbirth ... God forbid she should go the way of her dear mother.* He could not shake himself free of the hideous thought.

'Come, come, my dear,' Eleanor said, realising the only course of action that might prove successful was to take him to her bed; she could always distract him there. 'It is only three months before Charlotte will be back. You need have no fear, I promise. The nuns will send word when she has given birth, and I will fetch her home to us. Why, in just three months, she will be standing before you, right here at our front door.'

***

Eleanor's prediction proved correct. With one discrepancy, however. In just three months, Charlotte was indeed standing at their front door. But Eleanor had not fetched her home. And the girl held in her arms a newborn.

How has this happened? Eleanor's mind screamed. *There was to have been no baby; the baby was to have been taken from her. No girl leaves that place with her baby. How could the nuns have so disobeyed instruction?*

But her thoughts were interrupted as, beside her, William sprang into action.

'Good God, she's about to collapse,' he exclaimed, gathering Charlotte and the baby in his arms and ushering them inside. 'Oh, my darling girl, what has happened?'

He half-carried the two through to the front sitting room, where he seated his daughter on the sofa and sat beside her, Charlotte still fiercely clutching her newborn.

'You're not taking my baby,' she screamed, shrinking from him as he put his arm around her. 'You're not taking my baby!' Despite her state of near exhaustion, her voice was defiant and the strength of her grip on the child powerful. 'No-one's taking my baby! No-one, do you hear? She's mine! You can't have her!'

'Of course she's yours, Charlotte,' William said, stroking his daughter's hair, which was wild and ill-kempt, realising that, in her hysteria, she had not registered who he was. 'No-one's taking your baby, she's safe, my darling, she's quite safe. You're with me now.'

Charlotte's panic subsided at the sound of his voice and as her eyes met his, it was clear she recognised him.

'Father?'

'Yes, I'm here,' he said gently, still stroking her hair.

'I'm here too, Charlotte,' Eleanor said, seating herself on the arm of the sofa.

'Eleanor?' At the sight of the two of them seated either side of her, Charlotte finally felt safe. She was home. She was home at long last, and she felt herself relax, her body sagging with weariness.

The baby was crying now.

Eleanor leaned forward and, parting the blanket that swathed the newborn, she caressed the tiny cheek with her finger. 'Shush, little one, shush,' she whispered, 'all is well.'

She took the baby from Charlotte, who no longer resisted, and stood rocking the tiny body in her arms. 'There, there,' she crooned, 'there, there, all is well.' She swayed to and fro as she rocked the baby, whose cries were already turning to whimpers. 'You must sleep, little one, you must sleep.'

'You must sleep too, Charlotte,' William said, and he lifted his daughter to her feet.

She made as if to protest, reaching her hand out for the child.

'No, no, my dear,' William insisted, 'Eleanor will bring the baby, and we'll put her to bed right beside you. Come, come, now. You must rest. You're exhausted.'

The three of them climbed the stairs, William supporting his daughter, Eleanor carrying the baby, but when they reached the bedroom, the child was once again crying, more insistently this time.

'She's hungry,' Charlotte said, 'I must feed her.'

'Of course.' Eleanor passed the child to her.

As Charlotte seated herself on the bed, Eleanor turned to William. 'I shall stay with her, my love, and see them both settled for the night. You go on now, I shall join you downstairs.'

'Why has she no luggage with her?' William was mystified. 'She has nothing but that purse.' He indicated the drawstring reticule that dangled from Charlotte's wrist. 'What of her belongings? What of the trunk she took to the abbey? What of—'

'We shall find out in the morning when she will no doubt tell us all that has happened,' Eleanor said. 'Now go, William, I shall join you shortly.'

He left the women to their own devices and returned to the sitting room, where he poured himself a large Scotch.

His nerves were rattled by the events of the day certainly, but there was only one thing that truly mattered and for which he would be eternally grateful. His daughter was alive. The thought of her possible death in childbirth had been haunting him for months.

'A little girl,' Eleanor said, watching as Charlotte freed her breast from her bodice and started feeding the baby. 'How pretty she is.'

Charlotte gazed down at the perfectly formed fingers grasping her breast, the tiny mouth sucking away fiercely. 'Yes,' she said, 'they tried to take her away from me.'

'Really?' *Well, of course they did*, Eleanor thought, *that's their job*. She assumed an expression of shock, although it wasn't necessary, the girl's focus was solely upon her baby.

'But I fought them off,' Charlotte went on. 'Two of them,' she said proudly, 'I attacked them.' She'd chased after the nuns in her nightdress. They'd stolen the baby from her room in the early hours of that very morning, and she'd chased after them, screaming. 'They took her when they thought I was asleep,' she said. 'But I wasn't.'

She'd been like a tigress, she recalled, spitting and clawing and tearing at them.

'It's for your own good,' they'd insisted over and over, one of them clutching the baby, the other trying to ward off Charlotte's attack. 'Your child is to be adopted. It is for your own good, girl, do you not understand? It is for *your own good*.'

For my own good? She'd been aghast. *I'm expected to abandon my child for my own good!* Oh God, how she'd fought them. Right there in that deserted corridor of the abbey's west wing. How she'd fought them! 'You're not taking my baby!' she'd screamed. 'No-one's taking my baby! She's mine, you can't have her!'

She'd wrested the child from them but exhausted herself in the process; it had been only two days since she'd given birth. In her weakened state, she could then have been overcome, but she'd realised there was another avenue open to her.

'Money,' she'd declared, 'I have money!' She would buy her baby from them.

Her offer had gained the immediate attention of the nuns. They knew this girl had money. Everyone at the abbey knew she had money. They knew, furthermore, that it had come from her family, whoever her family might be. Which was unusual. Girls mostly arrived either destitute and abandoned by their family, or in need of keeping their condition a secret from their family. Or perhaps, in the case of a mistress, from their benefactor. They never had money of their own. The necessary funds to house them came from the considerable fees charged to the adoptive parents who wished to buy their babies.

Would they dare take a bribe? Charlotte had sensed the nuns were wondering whether they dare risk the wrath of their Mother Superior should they be caught. She could see the indecision in their eyes as they exchanged a furtive glance.

'No-one will know, I swear,' she'd promised. 'I'll just disappear. You'll never see me again. You can tell them I escaped with my baby early this morning. You had no idea I'd gone until you came into my room and discovered I wasn't there. Oh, please, please,' she'd urged, sensing them weaken, 'we have no time to waste.'

They'd returned to her room, where she'd given them half the money she carried in her purse. Then, as she'd hastily dressed, they'd made their departure. But not before letting her know where she might find the driver, who slept in the quarters near the stables.

'It was to their advantage I should escape safely,' Charlotte said, 'rather than be caught wandering about the abbey with my baby.'

'I see,' Eleanor replied, 'yes, of course.' Throughout Charlotte's story, she'd sat in the bedside chair, watching the girl feed her baby, listening to her every word. She was relieved Charlotte in no way suspected her of having any knowledge the child was to have been adopted. She was nonetheless a little surprised the girl had never contemplated this might have been the plan from the very beginning.

'I gave the rest of my money to the carriage driver,' Charlotte said, 'and he brought me all the way here. He'll no doubt lose his job when he gets back to the abbey, but I made it worth his while.'

'What a clever girl you are, my dear,' Eleanor said, 'clever and brave. Now let's get you to bed. Both of you,' she added. Having been fed, the baby was now fast asleep.

She helped Charlotte strip down to her undergarments.

'I shall give you a nightdress of mine tomorrow,' she said. 'For now, this will do, you're exhausted.'

After tucking mother and child into bed, Eleanor left both sleeping and went downstairs. This unexpected outcome had altered everything. There was a great deal to think about. She must change her plans.

'Poor, dear Charlotte,' she said as she joined William in the sitting room, 'she's been through such an ordeal.'

William listened, riveted, while she recounted to him every detail of his daughter's story.

'Oh, my goodness,' he said when she finally came to a halt. 'How terrifying that she should have had to do battle for her child. And that she should be forced to run away like that. All on her own.'

Eleanor had been studying him closely as she'd recounted the story, and she noted now that his horrified reaction appeared completely genuine. *Are you really that innocent, William?* she wondered. *What did you think was going to happen at the abbey? You surely didn't expect the girl to keep her baby.*

'Did it never occur to you, my darling,' she said with care, 'that the nuns' intention from the very start might have been to adopt the baby out following its birth?'

William stared back at her uncomprehendingly. 'No,' he admitted with a helpless shake of his head. 'I never thought about the matter, to be honest. I never once thought of the baby, only of Charlotte and the fact she might die giving birth. What would become of the child never entered my mind.'

Yes, Eleanor thought, *this is true, he's not lying.* William had spent the past three months so obsessing over his daughter's safety that she had been forced to offer him endless assurances. 'Women give birth all the time, my love,' she'd said again and again, 'you must not fret, it's a perfectly natural, everyday occurrence.' Never once had the child been mentioned. She had not brought up the subject herself, assuming he understood that adoption was the customary procedure in such circumstances. Good God, why else did a young unmarried girl disappear to give birth at a convent? Certainly not with the intention of bringing the child home.

He was looking at her a little strangely now. 'Did you know the nuns intended to take the baby from her and have it adopted?' he asked.

A tricky question. How should she answer?

Evasion was the best bet, she decided, evasion with a touch of honesty. William always admired honesty.

'No,' she said, 'not really. Although I admit I suspected such an option might have been offered her ...'

Option? Offered? The thought was laughable. *Dear God, the baby was always taken from the mother, or else the girl was simply told she'd given birth to a stillborn.*

'... An option that, had she chosen to take it, would have simplified matters a great deal,' she added, 'for Charlotte, and also for her future.' Eleanor's smile was tender, concerned. 'Life is not kind to a single mother.'

He nodded, appreciating her candour.

She was glad he understood, and thankful that her answer had proved the right one.

'But as Charlotte is determined to keep her baby,' she continued briskly, 'we need to make plans for her future, my love. Her reputation must be protected at all costs, as must yours, and above all, the Burton name.'

Eleanor rose from her seat and pulled the bell cord,

summoning the maid. 'I shall have a cold supper prepared,' she said, 'and we'll discuss the path we must take.'

Path? William wondered. *What path?* What was she talking about? He had no idea.

But he found out during the next hour or two. Eleanor's instructions were so clear and concise, no input of his was required. Just agreement. Wholehearted agreement.

***

The following morning over the breakfast table, all was revealed to Charlotte.

'Your father and I had a long talk last night, Charlotte dear,' Eleanor said, 'about your future. And the future of little Victoria,' she added with a smile to the baby who, having been fed, was wrapped up and sleeping peacefully in an armchair.

It had been Eleanor's idea the child be named Victoria barely an hour previously, when she'd brought a fresh change of clothes to Charlotte's bedroom.

'I fear the dress will be too short as you are so very tall,' she'd said, which sounded faintly critical. 'But it will do for the next day or so until we can buy you a new wardrobe.' Then, gazing down at the child, who was hungrily feeding at Charlotte's breast, she asked, 'What are you going to call her?'

'I don't know,' Charlotte admitted.

'What about Victoria?' Eleanor suggested. 'A name fit for a monarch when all's said and done.'

'Yes,' Charlotte had agreed. So, Victoria it was.

'And we have decided, your father and I,' Eleanor went on, 'that we must find you a husband as soon as possible.'

Charlotte cast a look at her father, who nodded. It hadn't been his decision at all, but Eleanor's argument had made such sense he could hardly refute it.

Eleanor, aware the girl was about to interrupt, seamlessly continued. 'You owe this to everyone, my dear, not least of all your daughter. You don't want little Victoria growing up a bastard, do you?'

'No, of course not ...'

'Exactly. And then there's your father's reputation as Squire of Pendleton and protector of the Burton name. You are now a mother, Charlotte, and all this would be at risk should your unmarried status be known.'

Charlotte had no answer to a statement so unequivocal.

'The plan your father and I have decided upon is this,' Eleanor said. She naturally meant the plan *she* had decided upon, but as there was no other course of action open to them, she was happy to share the credit with William. Both father and daughter were entirely in her hands. And surprisingly enough, she *did* feel responsible for them. *You are so naïve, the pair of you*, she thought, with a mix of wifely and motherly concern.

'You and little Victoria are to stay here with me, Charlotte,' she said. 'Your father will return to Pendleton, where he will let it be known you have recently married in London and that you and your husband are now on your honeymoon. In the meantime, I shall find a suitable choice for this husband of yours.'

Eleanor suspected such a chore would not be too difficult. That among her wealth of contacts there would be an eligible bachelor only too willing to marry the daughter of a prosperous squire with an estate like Pendleton. *It will cost though*, she thought, *the man will need money.*

She'd warned William of the cost, but he had unhesitatingly agreed, so long as it was stipulated this man could never inherit Pendleton Estate. Any male issue of the marriage would be heir apparent and, should there be no such issue, the squirearchy would revert to Geoffrey Burton. William would do anything and everything to protect his daughter.

'When you finally return to Pendleton, my dear,' she announced, 'you will be a respectable married woman with a child.'

Charlotte nodded obediently, as did her father, which Eleanor found rather touching.

You are such innocents, she thought. *I suppose living in the country does that to people.*

4.

His name was Harold Lindsay Bradford, and he was a lieutenant in the Royal Navy, which Eleanor thought rather convenient, under the circumstances. If poor, dear Charlotte didn't like the man – and this was quite possible, as Eleanor didn't much like him herself – then his long absences at sea would make the marriage so much easier to endure.

She found him within the first week of her enquiry, but then she'd known exactly where to head for direction: Phoebe Morris-Barrett. Phoebe knew everything about everyone and had brokered many a marriage, unofficially of course, and for a substantial introduction fee.

'He's twenty-nine years old and not frightfully bright, I suspect,' Phoebe had warned. 'Sufficiently educated to gain acceptance into the Royal Navy, but I doubt he'll ever rise above the rank of lieutenant. His family will be forever grateful to see him marry into a family with money.'

As fate would have it, Harold was currently on leave and in London, but the following month he would be returning to sea, so they would need to move swiftly, Phoebe said. All of which very much suited Eleanor's purpose.

She was introduced to him over afternoon tea in the front parlour of Phoebe's house in Hampstead and discovered him to be a rather uninspiring fellow, both physically and temperamentally. A strong young man, he could have been good-looking, but why wasn't he? *Solid in build and stolid in nature*, she thought. *Ah, well, beggars can't be choosers.*

Charlotte's reaction was much the same upon meeting her husband-to-be when he was invited around to the townhouse, once again for afternoon tea.

'He's not much of a conversationalist, is he?' she remarked after he'd departed.

'He's probably just shy, dear,' Eleanor replied.

'Perhaps.' Charlotte rather doubted this herself. She wasn't sure why, but suspected it was due to his reaction upon being introduced to baby Victoria.

'Ah, so this is my daughter, is it?' he'd said with just the faintest touch of a sneer.

Eleanor decided it best to speak her mind. 'Beggars can't be choosers, Charlotte,' she said.

'Yes, I suppose you're right.'

'I know I am.'

Charlotte and Harold were married a fortnight later. William, having been contacted by Eleanor and informed of the plans, arrived several days prior to the wedding and met with Harold at his gentlemen's club in The Strand. Harold was on his very best behaviour, which was hardly surprising. This, after all, was where the money was coming from.

'Seems like a nice enough chap,' William said upon his return to the townhouse.

'Yes,' Eleanor and Charlotte chorused in unison.

The wedding itself was an unceremonious affair, a civil service held in a register office, but William insisted upon booking the couple into the Langham Hotel, one of London's finest. Harold was returning to sea in barely a fortnight, and it was only right they should have a proper honeymoon. For two days anyway, during which time Eleanor could look after the baby.

Charlotte wasn't sure what to expect on her wedding night. She didn't love Harold, so her expectations were not unrealistically romantic, but she hadn't loved Tom Philby either and she'd very much enjoyed sex with him, hadn't she? As a sensual young woman, she was rather looking forward to reliving the experience.

She was destined for disappointment, however. Harold, with his thickset, clumsy body and what appeared to be an equally thickset, clumsy mind, was bent on nothing but his own gratification, pounding away until he was spent.

It was the same the following morning. And the next night too. And the morning after that. Charlotte couldn't wait to get back to the townhouse. If only their conversation had proved stimulating, she thought. If only, over the sumptuous breakfasts delivered to their stateroom in the mornings, or across the dining table of the Langham's fine restaurant at night, they'd communicated, she might not have minded. She could perhaps live without sexual fulfilment, but some form of mental connection was surely not too much to ask.

Back at the townhouse things were no better, although Charlotte was happy to be reunited with baby Victoria, whom she'd sorely missed. William had returned to Pendleton and the newly-weds were to stay with Eleanor until Harold's departure in just over a week, but even Eleanor, with all her social graces, was unable to coax any form of conversation from the man. His responses were for the most part monosyllabic and sometimes just a disinterested grunt.

'What a pity,' Eleanor admitted in private, 'he's turned out to be a rather drab choice, hasn't he? But he'll be away at sea a lot of the time, my dear, you can look forward to that.'

Harold himself very much looked forward to being away at sea. He liked being in the navy. He liked simply being 'one of the boys'. He didn't enjoy social intercourse. Never had. He didn't much enjoy the company of women, to be truthful – apart from in bed, that is. They talked too much.

Harold was beginning to find Eleanor and Charlotte irritating. He sensed they wanted more from him. But what were they after? What did they expect? He'd earned his money. He'd done his duty. He'd married the girl and given her baby legitimacy. What more did they want?

He was thankful when it came time to take his leave of them.

'I'll see you in six months,' he said as he kissed his wife goodbye.

Charlotte was relieved to see him go.

Over the months that followed, she felt cooped up in London, despite the fact Eleanor was pleasurable company and went out of her way to offer all forms of entertainment. It was upon Eleanor's insistence that they'd gone shopping together to buy her a new wardrobe, Eleanor herself thoroughly enjoying the experience, but Charlotte finding it stressful. There were too many people in the streets, the boutiques and the millineries were claustrophobic, even the clothes themselves were restrictive; everything seemed bent upon imprisoning her. She longed for the freedom of the countryside.

Of an evening, Eleanor would try to entice her out to the theatre or a concert or some sort of social event, but Charlotte preferred to stay at home with Victoria.

'The maid can look after the baby,' Eleanor would insist with a touch of impatience.

'Jane has quite enough to do without being at my beck and call for babysitting duties,' Charlotte would reply. She'd only recently discovered the maid had a name at all. To Eleanor, Jane was always 'the maid'. And indeed, the girl was worked quite mercilessly.

There were also those nights when Eleanor chose to entertain at home. When the house became a 'salon': a musician at the piano; a soprano or tenor, or sometimes both, singing arias and duets from favourite operas; a classical actor perhaps, performing Shakespearean speeches or sonnets; and always a gathering of society to admire and applaud and above all mingle while exchanging the latest gossip.

Eleanor loved her salon nights. Here, she was in her element. She would hire professional caterers and play the glittering hostess, entertaining all the right people in just the right way. And these days, she loved having Charlotte by her side. Her handsome young stepdaughter, elegant in the latest fashion, which she herself had personally selected. Eleanor was very much enjoying Charlotte's company. It was so nice to have another woman in the house.

Charlotte suffered the salon evenings, obligingly mingling with society as she knew Eleanor wished her to, but longing to be upstairs with her daughter, where the ever-dutiful Jane was keeping watch.

Her favourite pastime was in the mornings while Eleanor was still sleeping, when she would walk the perambulator along Upper Grosvenor Street to Hyde Park. Once there, she'd gather Victoria in her arms and stroll off across the grass, away from the main pathways and pedestrians. She'd point out all she could see to her baby, and she'd throw bread here and there to the pigeons, delighting in Victoria's gleeful gurgles. But Hyde Park was a very poor substitute for the hills and dales of Yorkshire.

Charlotte never voiced her dissatisfaction to Eleanor, thinking that to do so would appear ungrateful, churlish even. But she did admit her frustration to her father. William paid regular monthly visits to London when he would stay for a week, and she would plague him for all the news from Pendleton.

'I feel so useless in the city, Papa,' she said. 'What purpose do I serve here?'

'You're a mother, my dear,' William assured her. 'You're a mother now, that is your purpose. And motherhood is a purpose to be proud of, you must agree.'

'Rubbish,' she scoffed, 'giving birth doesn't mean a woman must give up the whole of her life. Motherhood and a purpose should go hand in hand. Victoria will not become the centre of my universe. She will not be mollycoddled but shall learn from me by example.'

Charlotte warmed to her theme. She was passionate about the plans she had for her daughter. 'I intend to bring her up the way you brought me up, Father,' she continued excitedly. 'By the time Victoria can walk, she'll be learning to ride. By the time she's ten, she'll be working alongside me in the fields, and at twelve, she'll be an expert with a rifle, and—'

'And let's not forget her studies,' William interrupted, 'her books and her lessons and her devotion to—'

'Intellectual pursuits. Exactly.' Charlotte laughed, relishing the bond they shared. 'She'll be reading by the time she's four. I shall teach her everything you taught me, Papa.'

William joined in her laughter. His visits to London brought him great joy, a fact to which he openly admitted as he basked in the company of his mistress and his daughter.

'How I love being with my two favourite women in the whole wide world, and now also my third,' he would say, dandling Victoria on his knee. Grandparenthood agreed with William, who simply adored his baby granddaughter.

***

Then at long last the six months were up, and the dour Harold Bradford was back.

All too soon, it would seem, Eleanor thought.

'Hello, wife,' Harold said as he and Charlotte shared a dutiful kiss.

'Hello, husband,' Charlotte replied, painting on a pleasant smile. She was unsure whether his comment was sarcasm or a clumsy attempt at humour, but trying to read whatever might be going on in Harold's mind was impossible. She'd discovered that on the very first day of their marriage.

Oh dear, they're not at all happy to see each other, Eleanor thought as she watched the couple's lacklustre reunion.

But strangely enough, Charlotte *was* happy to see Harold, for she had made up her mind. Harold's return would signal her own return to Pendleton.

'I'm going home,' she announced to Eleanor. 'It is time I introduced my husband and my daughter to Pendleton.'

Eleanor was aghast. 'But it's far too soon,' she protested. 'You married only seven months ago.'

'No matter,' Charlotte replied nonchalantly. 'The baby's birth may have been premature for all others know, and none will be bold enough to enquire anyway. Victoria's birthday falls in June of 1876, and I'll hear no more about it. Besides,' she added, 'I doubt they'll care. They are my friends at Pendleton, the staff and the workers and the villagers. And they're country folk, what's more. They do not judge others as city folk do.'

It was true that, upon her return to Pendleton, she sensed a mildly puzzled reaction here and there at the presence of little Victoria. And perhaps there might have been the shadow of conjecture behind closed doors about whether the baby was a premature birth or born out of wedlock. But no malice was attendant, because no-one cared either way. They were all pleased to see their Squire's daughter happily married and with a beautiful baby.

'You see, Papa, I was right,' Charlotte remarked. 'Unlike those in the city, country people are not bent on destroying each other's reputations, and therefore their lives.' Charlotte was pleased to have been proved correct, but she was not in the least surprised. 'City folk delight in vicious gossip simply as a form of entertainment,' she continued, 'regardless of the dire repercussions that may result. Here in the country, we do not.'

William's relief knew no bounds. The seeds of doubt Eleanor had sown about the wisdom of Charlotte's actions had taken such root he'd been living in a fog of dread.

'You must stop her, William,' Eleanor had declared, when he'd been summoned to London to collect his daughter, who threatened to return unannounced with her husband if her father did not agree to accompany her.

'She's behaving like a fool, and you must stop her,' Eleanor insisted. 'If she returns to Pendleton prematurely, she will bring us undone. All our plans will have been for naught. She will ruin her reputation, and she will ruin yours too. The Burton name will be ridiculed, shamed, you must stop her ...'

On and on, Eleanor had ranted. But there had been no stopping Charlotte, who had remained adamant.

And now it was Charlotte who had been proved right. William's fog had finally lifted.

'How and when did you become so wise?' he marvelled.

'I learned a lot in the city, Papa,' Charlotte replied with a smile. And she had, she realised. Her eight months in the city had taught her a great deal. *I've grown up*, she thought.

Despite Harold's apparent lack of interest in his newly acquired marital status, Charlotte was determined to make their marriage work. She so wanted her husband to embrace Pendleton as she did, to share with him her love of the estate and the life it offered. Besides, he had duties to fulfil. Victoria needed a father and William needed a grandson who would one day inherit the squiredom.

But the harder she tried to impress upon Harold the role she wished him to play, the more he withdrew, to the point where it was clear he resented her. He had no interest in the baby. He did not wish to be a father, and he did not wish to be a farmer. He was simply awaiting the time when his long-term leave would be over and he would be called back to sea.

The one duty he appeared quite happy to fulfil, however, was the provision of an heir as, on a nightly basis, he continued to pound away. Charlotte could only hope that conception might prove the turning point in her marriage, that the birth of his own child might awaken in Harold a natural sense of fatherhood. So, the following spring, when he finally returned to sea, she was delighted to find herself once again pregnant.

Edward William Bradford was born in early 1878. The baby was delivered at home in Pendleton House by the family's local physician, Dr Reginald Langton. A healthy eight pound six ounce boy. Squire William Burton could barely contain himself.

'Oh, my darling Charlotte,' he waxed rhapsodically as he sat by her bedside, cradling his grandson, 'you have delivered to us the future Squire of Pendleton. Oh, my dear, what cause for celebration!'

William was not alone in expressing such sentiments. The whole of the estate celebrated the birth of their future Squire.

Eleanor, too, was congratulatory. Upon hearing the news, she even went to the trouble of paying a visit to the estate.

'My, my, you clever girl,' she said, smiling down at the newborn in Charlotte's arms. Her personal aversion to squirming babies meant she rarely picked them up herself, although she had a talent for disguising her distaste when necessary. Indeed, no-one would have suspected, for she played the role of proud step-grandmother with great aplomb.

'What a beefy little boy he is,' she remarked fondly, tickling the tiny face with the perfectly varnished nail of her forefinger.

Harold Bradford arrived back at Pendleton to discover he had sired a son, but to Charlotte's profound consternation, this fact appeared to have little effect upon him. He didn't even want to hold the child. *Good God, man, where's your sense of kinship?* her mind begged. *This is your* son! *This is your flesh and blood!*

But Harold was as uninterested in his own son as he was in his acquired stepdaughter. Children, it seemed, were an irritating burden, and he wanted no part of them.

Once again, the more Charlotte sought her husband's engagement, the more he withdrew from her. Both on the home front and out working in the fields. Most *particularly* when they were out working in the fields.

Charlotte had resumed her farm-labouring duties when Edward was barely six months old, hiring a live-in nanny to look after her children. She chose worksites close to Pendleton

House so she could return home to feed the baby, but when Harold joined her in the fields, he offered minimal support.

'They're to be lined up this way, Harold,' she instructed. She was teaching him the correct method of fencing, demonstrating how the posts were aligned before being driven into the soil, but he averted his eyes. Deliberately. Infuriatingly. *He can't even bring himself to look at me*, she thought. She wanted to scream her frustration. But she didn't.

'Watch the way Benjamin does it,' she suggested instead. 'Benjamin's been with us for years. He's an expert fencer.'

Still Harold remained sullen, paying no attention to Benjamin, who was working with another farm labourer just up ahead.

'It is important we support our tenant farmers, and also our workers, Harold,' she reminded him tightly. 'Father has always maintained we are workers ourselves and must be seen as such.'

She'd irritated him with that remark.

'Yet your father is barely ever here, is he?' Harold retorted scathingly. 'The good Squire is more often than not with his mistress in London.'

It wasn't long before Harold opted to involve himself with farm labour further away from the house in an obvious bid to escape Charlotte's company. He wasn't afraid of hard work, if the truth be known. To the contrary, he was a strong young man who enjoyed exercising his muscles and exerting his considerable energy. He did not, however, wish to exercise his muscles and exert his energy working alongside the woman who was supposed to be his wife.

More and more these days, it appeared to Harold the only time Charlotte behaved as a wife should was when she lay thighs parted, obediently spreadeagled beneath him.

Finally, the time came when he decided he'd had enough. It was late afternoon on a Saturday, and he'd returned from the village, where he'd been drinking at the tavern with a bunch of the lads, as he so often did. And he was drunk, as he so often was. He left his horse at the stables to be looked after by Mac, or one of the stable hands, whoever was there. He never unsaddled and watered and brushed down his own horse. Why should he? That's what stable hands were for.

He walked a little unsteadily up to the west wing entrance. Once inside, he headed directly for the front sitting room, where he poured himself a large tumbler of neat whisky from the bottle that sat on the liquor cabinet and slumped into an armchair. He was fed up. There was another whole month to go before his return to sea, and everything about this place was driving him insane.

He swigged back half the whisky. How had he landed himself in such a predicament? He should never have agreed. The money, despite it being a substantial sum, hadn't been worth this. He was no farmer. Being stranded out here in the country with a wife who looked down on him, a wife who made it obvious at every turn that she considered him useless, was utterly intolerable.

He gulped down the remainder of the whisky in one hit. She was no wife, and this was no life! With all his might, he hurled the empty tumbler across the room, where it smashed into an ornate wall mirror, both glass and mirror shattering to the floor.

The noise brought Charlotte running down the stairs from the nursery, where she'd been with the children. She always spent Saturdays with the children.

'What's happened?' she called as she ran. 'Are you all right?' She'd seen him through the window as he'd walked up from the stables, and she could tell he was drunk. She presumed now he'd had some terrible accident.

Halting at the open door to the sitting room, she knew in an instant there'd been no accident. The scene spoke for itself: Harold drunkenly slouched in an armchair, the broken mirror on the wall, shattered glass all over the floor.

Behind her, two-year-old Victoria had also scurried down the stairs. Charlotte had told the child to stay where she was in the nursery with her baby brother, but Victoria was far too curious to obey.

The little girl now came to an abrupt halt beside her mother, staring in horror at the shattered mirror. She watched as her father rose to his feet and stood glowering angrily at them both. But what had she and Mummy done wrong? Why was he so angry?

Charlotte immediately took control. 'Go and find Nanny,' she said, bending down, a hand to the child's back, ushering her away. 'She'll be in her quarters. Tell her to look after you and Edward in the nursery while Daddy and I have a talk.'

'But why is Daddy angry?'

'That's what we're going to talk about, darling. Run along now, there's a good girl.'

As the child scampered off, Charlotte caught sight of the butler. Also alerted by the noise, Kenneth, looking more than a little concerned, was standing by awaiting orders.

'No cause for alarm, Kenneth,' she said. 'A bit of an accident, that's all. Just a breakage, no more.'

'I'll send Edith to clean it up,' he replied.

'No, no, don't bother. I'll ring when I need her.'

Kenneth gave a nod and left.

Charlotte closed the door and turned to face her husband.

'What's going on, Harold?' she demanded. 'What does this mean?'

'It means I've had enough. That's what it means.'

'Enough of what?'

'You,' he snarled, and he crossed to the liquor cabinet, where he picked up the whisky bottle, about to pour himself another glass.

'You've certainly had enough of *that*,' she said icily. 'I'd say you've had far more than enough.'

Something in Harold snapped. He slammed the whisky bottle down on the cabinet and whirled about.

'Don't you dare!' he screamed. 'Don't you dare use that tone to me, do you hear? I won't stand for it any longer!'

Charlotte was dumbfounded. The anger seemed to have sprung from nowhere. She could tell he was enraged. But why?

'What tone?'

'*That* tone!' he yelled. 'That superior tone. The way you talk down to me. The way you belittle me. I won't have it, you hear?'

'I have never talked down to you, Harold.' Charlotte was determined to remain composed, despite her confusion. 'You're in the drink and you're imagining things, my dear. It is the liquor doing the talking, not me ...'

'You see?' Her composure only served to incense him further. 'You see what I mean? That superior tone, the way you sneer at me. You both do, the two of you, you and your precious Eleanor, your father's fucking whore. Right from the very start you both looked down on me. Well, I won't have it, do you hear?'

He was closing in on her now, his rage ugly, threatening. But Charlotte stood her ground, refusing to back away.

'I have never looked down on you, Harold. You are my husband ...'

'Exactly,' he roared, 'I am your husband, and you are my wife! You will show me respect.'

He was barely a foot from her, his spittle flecking her face, but she didn't flinch, her eyes remaining locked with his.

'Know your place, wife,' he yelled, her fearlessness further maddening him. 'I'm a man, you're a woman. It's your duty to obey me!' And raising his right hand, he struck her with such force she staggered to one side before falling to the floor, where she lay among the shards of broken glass.

He gazed down at her, shocked to his senses by his own violence. He hadn't intended to do that. He looked away. *She deserved it*, he thought, *goading me the way she had. I was totally justified.*

He strode to the cabinet and picked up the whisky bottle. Then he stormed from the room and out of the house.

Charlotte remained where she was on the floor regaining her senses, waiting for the dizziness to pass. Her left ear was ringing. The left side of her face was smarting painfully and blood was already trickling down the right side from where a shard of glass had nicked her cheek.

She sat up, to discover that her right hand was also bleeding, and quite profusely, for it had taken the impact as she'd fallen. She staunched the flow with the hem of her summer dress, clutching the light blue cotton fabric tightly and holding it in place, willing the bleeding to stop. Upon brief examination, the wound did not appear too deep and would hopefully need no medical attention. Which was fortunate, she told herself, for this episode must be kept secret.

She hauled herself to her feet and sat in an armchair, the same one that Harold had been slumped in. She felt strangely sorry for him. Although it was probably pity rather than sorrow. *Poor Harold*, she thought, *how insecure you are. I never knew that.*

She remained in the armchair, dress bunched up around her hand, stemming the bleeding as she pondered the situation. Was it just her desire to labour alongside the farm hands that he found so threatening? Was it her donning of breeches and her lack of femininity that intimidated him so? But he'd also accused Eleanor of sneering and looking down on him, and one surely could not find a woman more feminine than Eleanor.

No, Charlotte decided, *his own insecurity is the cause of the problem. Eleanor and I are strong women, and Harold finds strong women confronting.*

She supposed in a way that they *had* looked down on him, or that their manner could have been interpreted that way. *When we tried to engage him in conversation, we certainly found his social skills lacking, but I don't recall either of us ever sneering at him.*

What was she to do? How was she to handle the situation? She must obviously temper her behaviour in his presence. She would not stop labouring alongside the farm workers, but she must show some pretence of 'obedience', whatever that might entail, when she was in his company. And she must feign respect, although she felt none. She clearly could not mould Harold to the husband she might have wished, but this must never happen again.

I will not be battered into subservience, she thought.

She checked her hand. The bleeding had stopped. She rose from her chair and rang the bell for Edith.

'Oh.' The maid gasped in horror at the sight of her mistress's dress saturated in blood. Her hand flew to her mouth. 'Oh my ...'

'Close the door,' Charlotte ordered.

Edith did so, her eyes never leaving the dress.

'It's not as bad as it looks,' Charlotte said, displaying her hand to the girl, 'it just bled a lot, that's all.'

Edith nodded, but gazed about the room, taking in the mess, wondering what had happened.

'Now, Edith, I want you to say nothing of this, do you understand? Nothing at all, to anyone. Not ever. This is to be our secret. Will you promise me that?'

'Yes, Miss Charlotte.' Edith wondered what exactly it was that was supposed to be a secret, but she made no enquiry. She would happily do anything her mistress asked of her. She adored Charlotte.

'Good.' Charlotte nodded briskly. 'Now, go up to the nursery and tell Nanny I'm on my way and that she can return to her quarters. Then let me know when the coast is clear, and I can get upstairs without being seen.'

Edith dived out the door and was back five minutes later.

'It's safe,' she said conspiratorially. 'I'll clean things up in here, then I'll come upstairs and see to your hand. You've cut your face, too, did you know that? And we'll need to get that dress washed as well,' she added.

Charlotte smiled gratefully. 'Thank you, Edith, what a true ally you are.'

***

Harold returned early the following morning. He'd saddled his horse and gone back to the village, where he'd stayed the night at the tavern. No mention was made of the previous day's incident. As the family breakfasted together, Harold did not comment upon his wife's bandaged hand, nor upon the angry welt on the left side of her face or the cut that was clearly visible over her right cheekbone. His very silence was comment enough, though. He was studying her intently. And he was waiting.

For what? Charlotte wondered. *Accusation? Condemnation? Damnation?* She offered him none. Perhaps this might be seen as her first act of 'obedience'. *Let him interpret my silence as he wishes.*

But she met his gaze boldly, just to let him know he had not cowed her into submission. She would keep his attack upon her a secret, yes, but it was not to happen again.

***

Exactly one week later, when William Burton returned for his monthly visit to Pendleton, arriving on a Saturday afternoon as was usual, the physical damage Charlotte had suffered was still plainly evident.

'What happened to you?' They were the first words he said when she greeted him at the front door, little Victoria jumping up and down beside her. 'Good heavens, Charlotte, what on earth has happened to you?'

'A fall from my horse last Sunday afternoon,' she glibly replied. 'Byron was frisky that day.'

'Grandpa, Grandpa,' Victoria squealed excitedly.

'Byron is always frisky.' William put down his bag and picked the child up. 'Hello, my little princess,' he said as she flung her arms around his neck and nuzzled her face into his shoulder.

'He was friskier than ever last Sunday,' Charlotte said. 'Come along now, Papa, Edith has afternoon tea ready and waiting.' She picked up his bag and William had no option but to follow, Victoria squirming happily in his arms and tugging at his beard.

But even as he followed his daughter, William questioned the glibness of her reply. Charlotte never fell from her horse. She and Byron were welded together, horse and rider seeming of one mind. That's what Mac always said, anyway: 'You can't separate those two, they ride as one.'

For the next half hour or so, as they sat chatting over the tea Edith poured and the scones with jam and cream she served, William continued to study his daughter's injuries. They did not seem to him consistent with a fall from a horse. The angry bruising and swelling were on the left side of the face, yet it was the right hand that was heavily bandaged, and there was a cut to the right cheek. Which way had she fallen? Wounds usually favoured one side or the other.

Afternoon tea was progressing so breezily he didn't dare voice any suspicion or make further enquiry. Nanny delivered baby Edward, who chortled away as he was bounced on his grandfather's knee, Victoria covered herself in jam as she gorged on scones and Charlotte chatted animatedly about the latest happenings at Pendleton. She and Edith both voiced their excitement about the birth of a brand-new foal.

'A coal-black colt, sir,' Edith boasted.

Throughout the entire conversation, not one mention was made of Charlotte's fall or the injuries that had resulted. The maid herself didn't even seem to notice her mistress was wounded. All of which William found most unusual.

He noted also Harold's absence. This too was unusual. His son-in-law was normally there to greet him, as a gesture of courtesy more than anything; they shared no great bond.

'Harold has friends in the village these days,' Charlotte had explained, 'he meets up with them at the tavern on Saturdays. He'll be home for dinner.'

'I see.' William had smiled and nodded, but he'd wondered, *Is all as it should be with this marriage?*

Dinner that night did not provide the answer, although it did rather tease his misgivings. William had not expected much by way of conversation from Harold, for the man had never been talkative, but he now seemed guarded. Wary. Why?

Aware that nothing would be forthcoming from Charlotte, he knew better than to ask, just as he knew he must not make enquiries of the staff or the workers. It was not his place to do so. Charlotte was the acting Squire of Pendleton these days, and he had no right to interfere. But as a father, he worried for his daughter's happiness, perhaps even for her safety. So, the following day, he did the most unethical thing. He enquired of his granddaughter.

'Are Mummy and Daddy happy?' he asked Victoria as she played in his office, baby Edward fast asleep in the cot nearby. The family had returned from church, and he'd volunteered his babysitting services while Charlotte went for her customary Sunday ride.

'Yes,' Victoria answered from the corner where he'd set up a cubby for her among a tumble of chairs and a blanket, as he always did, so adoring the child's company. 'Except for the time when Daddy broke the mirror,' she called over her shoulder as she pulled the blanket aside and crawled into her den.

'Oh? When was that?'

'I don't know.' Peering out from her hidey-hole, she shrugged. 'A while ago.' Victoria had little concept of time.

'What happened?'

'Daddy was angry with Mummy and me. I don't know why, and Mummy wouldn't tell me.' She emerged from her cubby, stood and crossed to him where he sat at his desk, the expression on her little face solemn and her voice deadly serious. 'But Daddy broke a mirror.' Victoria would never forget the sight of the broken mirror. 'And that's bad luck, Grandpa,' she said. 'Breaking a mirror is *very bad luck*.'

No more than that was needed to convince William.

The following day, he rode out to where his son-in-law was working in the far west paddock.

'A word with you, Harold,' he said, taking him aside, well away from the worker who was teamed with him. 'I need you to recognise something.'

'Oh, yes, Squire, and what would that be?' Harold's response was guarded. Once again, he appeared wary, which only served to confirm William's suspicions.

'I need you to recognise that, should you ever lay a hand on my daughter in anger, I would have you killed.'

'I would never do such a thing, sir. Never, I swear.'

Was that a flicker of fear? 'See that you don't, for even if I were not told of it, I would know, Harold. I would always know. And if I knew,' he added with deliberation, 'you would be a dead man.'

William did not await further answer but mounted his horse and rode off.

The remainder of his stay at Pendleton proved most enjoyable. He delighted in the company of his daughter and grandchildren, while barely noticing Harold, who seemed to drift about the periphery of their existence.

But Harold was present when William took his departure the following Saturday morning, and after shared hugs with Charlotte and little Victoria and Edward, William's farewell to his son-in-law was quite pointed.

'Goodbye, Harold,' he said pleasantly enough as his eyes issued a warning, which they both understood. 'I shall see you next month.'

He did not see Harold next month, however, for by then Harold had returned to sea, no doubt relieved to avoid not only his father-in-law, but his wife and the whole of Pendleton Estate, from which he so longed to escape.

***

For the following two years, Charlotte and Harold's marriage remained on tenuous grounds. There was no further outbreak of violence. Harold came and went, from land to sea and back again. He contained his anger although his frustration remained evident, and Charlotte, while still labouring in the fields, played the dutiful wife on the home front, particularly in bed, for she wanted more children. But the damage had been done. There was little to be salvaged from a union such as theirs.

The arrival of their second son, Harold, was a great salve to Charlotte, who named the baby after her husband in the hope this might please him. Sadly, it did not. The birth of another child proved only an irritation to Harold Bradford, serving as a further sign he was being buried ever deeper in the depths of Pendleton.

It was in early 1882, barely six months after the baby's birth, that Harold made his announcement.

'I have requested a posting to Hong Kong with Far East Command,' he told his wife. 'And from there they'll probably send me to India. I shall be gone for at least two years. Possibly longer.'

'Very well,' she replied. What else was she expected to say? 'When do you leave?'

'Next month.'

'That soon?' She was a little surprised. He'd only just returned from sea.

'Yes, that soon.'

The following month, their farewells were perfunctory. She didn't even accompany him to the railway station. But then she never had in the past, just as he'd never wanted her to, so there seemed little point in varying their ritual.

He didn't write while he was away, but again, he never had in the past, so why would he bother now?

Two years went by and still there was no word. It was as if Harold Bradford had ceased to exist in Charlotte's life. And in the lives of his children. Even little Victoria, who'd been five when he'd left, couldn't quite remember what he looked like.

Charlotte would occasionally show her children a photograph of Harold, just by way of a reminder. 'That's Daddy,' she would say.

The boys would nod dutifully, but with no recognition, while Victoria would say, 'Yes.' She vaguely recalled the face, but she remembered far more vividly the broken mirror.

Harold Bradford had never intended to return. Upon making his departure, he had suffered no remorse, no sense of disloyalty. He had not felt in any way that he was deserting his post as a husband and father, for he had served his purpose, even providing a future heir to his wife's estate. And a second son to be kept in reserve. What more could they want of him? He had finally decided it was time to be true to himself. He would lead the life he wished. And he would lead it with the person he wished by his side.

Lawrence Middleton had been Harold's best friend during their schooldays and throughout their naval training, the two having enrolled on the very same day. They'd been inseparable. They loved the navy and the life it allowed them to lead. What man wouldn't? Working hard and long, yes, but out there, free as a bird on the vast oceans of the world.

Harold had decided he would do just that. Like Spartan soldiers of old, he and Larry would spend the rest of their lives side by side, nobly serving their country.

And they possibly would have, had fate not dealt them the cruellest blow.

Much as Charlotte tried to keep the image of their father alive to her children, there came the day when Harold ceased to exist altogether. A letter of condolence arrived from the Royal Navy, informing her that her husband had succumbed to malaria in Bombay, while loyally serving his country.

Charlotte accepted with dignity the many condolences offered by those around her, but she did not make a public display of grief, knowing that to do so would have been hypocritical, for she could not bring herself to mourn the loss of her husband.

There was one who did mourn, however. Larry had been by Harold's side when he'd died, holding his hand and openly weeping. Theirs had been a friendship so close, perhaps something even akin to love.

Despite her lack of grief, Charlotte was deeply grateful to Harold Bradford. He had given her two fine, healthy sons and for that she would be forever thankful.

After observing a respectable period of widowhood, she reverted to her maiden name. She preferred to remain a Burton. Her children, too, were now Burtons. They were the Burtons of Pendleton.

5.

Dearest Lady Squire …

Geoffrey's letter to his niece opened with his customary greeting. Ever since William had informed him that Charlotte had become 'the Squire of Pendleton in all but name', Geoffrey, true to form, had playfully adopted the title.

Geoffrey Burton had been surprised to hear his older brother had relinquished the Pendleton reins with such apparent ease. He'd been quick to say so, what's more, albeit with mock humour.

Good grief, William, he'd written, *you, of all people! You, with your sacred devotion to duty! You, who preached constantly about the responsibilities of a squire, the preservation of Pendleton and the Burton name! I am horror-struck. How could you have so deserted your post?*

Despite his brother's good-natured joshing, William had responded in all seriousness, and with such brutal honesty, Geoffrey was left feeling guilty.

You're right, he'd replied,

> *I would never have thought myself capable of such desertion. I can only claim that love rendered me*

blind, for this was certainly the case in the beginning. When Eleanor refused to become Mistress of Pendleton and move to the country, I felt I simply could not live without her, so more and more of my time was spent in the city. I hasten to add, Geoffrey, under no circumstances do I offer this as a valid excuse, for I agree with you unreservedly. My dereliction of duty was, and for that matter still is, unforgivable.

However, as things have turned out, I am forced to admit, and to my shame, that Charlotte has proved the real Burton. As I told you in my last letter, dear brother, she is the true Squire of Pendleton in all but gender. Perhaps she should have been born a man …

Ever since then, Geoffrey had taken to writing directly to his niece rather than merely including mention of her in his letters to William. And his salutation was always the same: *Dearest Lady Squire …*

Charlotte sat cross-legged on the office floor as she read her uncle's latest letter out loud to her children, who were similarly seated around her: eight-year-old Victoria, Edward who was seven, and Harold, not quite yet four. It was Saturday afternoon, and the children had spent the entire morning in the classroom with their tutors, even little Harold, whose knowledge of the alphabet was so good he would soon be able to read a whole sentence all by himself.

Geoffrey well knew that Charlotte considered his letters educational, coming as they did from the other side of the world, and that the exercise of reading them out loud was part of the children's tuition. Bearing this in mind, he wrote accordingly, making his accounts of life in the Pilbara vivid, adventurous and above all informative.

'*I write this missive to you on the first of April,*' Charlotte read to the children, who were waiting in breathless anticipation, '*precisely one year after the near-death experience I had. An experience which, I can promise you, I will never forget.*'

She recalled he had written of this episode in a letter to her father. She and William had spoken of it. Geoffrey was now giving a full report intended purely for the children's edification and enjoyment.

It was on April Fools' Day last year in '84 and I had foolishly gone to sea aboard my friend's pearling vessel. We were in Lagrange Bay off the Kimberley Coast, some way north of the Pilbara, Geoffrey wrote. Charlotte was aware he was setting the scene, so she delivered her performance in suitably dramatic fashion

'*The bay is the site of the infamous La Grange Massacre, which took place back in 1865 wherein three white men were killed – by local natives it was presumed – and a party of vigilantes sought revenge, in turn killing twenty or thirty Aborigines. Oh, I tell you, my good Lady Squire, it is a dangerous and lawless place this West Coast of Australia.*'

Charlotte made a fearsome face for the children, each of whom was riveted to the story, as they always were.

'*To continue with my own adventure,*' she read on, '*it was up there in that very same area that a cyclone of great severity hit my friend's vessel, which foundered, leaving us all thrashing about in the sea. A wild, untamed sea determined upon drowning every single one of we unfortunates. It was only by the grace of God I survived the horrors by clinging to a broken piece of mast.'*

'A shipwreck,' Victoria interjected, 'just like *The Coral Island*.' She and Edward had recently finished reading R.M. Ballantyne's *The Coral Island*, which their tutor had set for them as a literary exercise.

'It is, it is too,' Edward agreed emphatically. 'It's *exactly* like *The Coral Island*.' He did so love an adventure story.

'What's the coral island?' Harold demanded, feeling left out.

'It's a book,' Edward said a trifle impatiently, 'you'll be able to read it soon. Go on, Mother.'

'I got to shore somehow,' Charlotte continued, *'where I managed to last a whole five days until a search party arrived, having come all the way up from Cossack, which is quite some distance south. They found me close to death, alone on the beach.*

'As it turned out, I was one of the lucky ones, for I was later to discover that, in a matter of only a few hours, one hundred and forty pearlers, including my friend and his crew, had been lost, along with nearly all their vessels.'

Charlotte looked up. 'Oh, my goodness, isn't that terrible?' The children nodded, too spellbound to make a comment. She returned to the letter.

'Being one of the few survivors, I can only thank our good Lord for delivering me from the watery grave that claimed so many.

'*I find it impossible to describe to you the ferocity of a cyclone, Charlotte. I can only impress upon you what a formidable place this Pilbara is. Indeed, it is a wonder our Burton Station manages to survive in this wild corner of the world where crime and violence, savagery and lawlessness are matched in severity by the very weather itself.*'

'I wish we could go to the Pilbara,' Edward said longingly.

'Me too,' Victoria agreed. Despite being a girl, she very much shared her brothers' adventurous spirit.

'Me too, me too.' Harold bounced up and down.

'*But survive we do,*' Charlotte ignored the children's interruption, '*despite the destructive force of many a cyclone. I cannot begin to tell you the number of times we have had our outbuildings and sheds flattened, on occasions even the homestead itself. But Joe and I, together with our loyal workers, rebuild every time. We not only survive, I am proud to announce. We thrive! I have purchased further lots, Burton Station is now 25,000 acres, and we are one of the most successful properties in the Pilbara. What do you say to that!*'

Having entertained the children with the recounting of his near-death experience, Geoffrey moved on to more mundane matters, including the increased financial value not only of the station but of the property he'd purchased in Claremont, which, he wrote, was rapidly becoming quite a popular area.

Geoffrey Burton had always enjoyed boasting of his successful enterprises to his older brother. He now chose also to boast to his niece.

So, as you can see, Lady Squire, he wrote in closing, *I continue to do the Burton name proud all the way down here in the wild west of Australia.*

And it is from here that I send my love to you always, dearest niece, your fondest, far away, Uncle Geoffrey.

Then he added in a postscript: *My love also to Victoria, Edward and Harold, from the great-uncle they have never met, but who wishes one day to make their acquaintance.*

'There you are, letter reading over,' Charlotte announced, and she stood. 'Come along now. Time to wash up before afternoon tea.'

The children rose.

'Uncle Geoffrey wants to meet us, Mummy,' Harold said. 'Why can't we go to Australia?'

'Because it's a very long way away, that's why.'

'It's on the other side of the world, silly,' Edward said scornfully.

'You can write to him instead,' Charlotte suggested, suddenly thinking what an excellent idea that was, and wondering why she hadn't thought of it before. 'You can write him a letter, all of you, after church tomorrow. Uncle Geoffrey would love that.'

'I can't write.' Harold looked glum.

'Yes, you can. You can sign your name.'

'Oh.' The little boy's face instantly brightened. 'Yes, I can sign my name.'

'Excellent. That's writing enough. Now off you go, all of you.'

She shooed them away. She would reply to Geoffrey herself later that night, when the children were in bed. She might even seek his advice, for some worrying events had recently come to her notice and she wasn't sure how to broach them with her father. Her uncle might perhaps prove a valuable ally.

She was unsure how she should voice her letter, though, as the subject was delicate and she did not wish to appear overly critical of her father's business management.

The fact was, Leonard Asquith, Pendleton's estate manager, had confided in her his concern about the additional farm leases that had been sold over the past several years.

'I'm aware many of the larger estates are selling off property,' he said, 'but it seems to me Squire Burton is reducing Pendleton land at an alarming rate. I did raise this matter with your father, Miss Charlotte, but he offered no further explanation than to say there had been many expenses of late, so ...'

Poor Leonard gave a helpless shrug. He'd hated raising the matter with William Burton's daughter, which could have been seen as something of a betrayal to his employer. But Leonard, too, had recognised Charlotte was more of a working squire than her father, and he simply had to inform someone of the danger they might face if the situation continued to get out of hand.

'Yes,' Charlotte agreed, 'it is true, Leonard, my father has been faced with many expenses over recent years.' *Some no doubt relating directly to me*, she thought, recalling her confinement at the Abbey of the Sisters of Adeneaux and the birth of Victoria, none of which would have come cheap, as Eleanor had told her. Then, also there was the payment to a husband in Harold Bradford. That too would have cost a pretty penny, as Eleanor had also informed her.

But surely the principal expense would have to have been Eleanor herself, Charlotte thought as she mentally listed the many extravagances: Eleanor's lavish lifestyle; Eleanor's demands for the finest clothes and jewellery; the expensive furnishings Eleanor insisted upon for the home in which she so loved to entertain, and in such luxurious fashion. Then there was the home itself, the townhouse her father had purchased for his mistress. Few properties were as expensive as a London townhouse, particularly in the choicest area of all – Mayfair.

'I shall discuss the matter with my father, Leonard, and get back to you in due course,' she said, and the estate manager nodded thankfully.

In the letter that she wrote to her Uncle Geoffrey that night, Charlotte worded the situation as delicately as she could. It took her a long time, for they were difficult issues. Not only did she wish to avoid criticism of her father, but she wished also to avoid painting too damning a picture of Eleanor, who had become something of a mother to her over recent years. The two had grown closer than Charlotte would ever have believed possible, particularly recalling, as she did, her initial dislike of the woman.

But she recalled also that her uncle knew quite a lot about Eleanor. Her father had openly written to him of his mistress many years ago. Charlotte clearly remembered Geoffrey's response – *Exciting mistress or loyal wife?* he'd queried in typically light-hearted fashion. Her father had no doubt kept his brother up to date with all further news of Eleanor, Charlotte thought; they wrote quite openly to one another. There'd even been a reaction to the purchase of the townhouse in one of the letters her father had read out to her.

A townhouse in Mayfair? Geoffrey had written. *My goodness, how extraordinarily extravagant. Surefire proof that you must be madly in love.*

Charlotte was glad Geoffrey knew of the townhouse, which made things a little easier as she penned her letter.

I am ashamed to admit that some of these added expenses Father has incurred over the years relate directly to me, she wrote, having explained the situation. She obviously could not say how the expenses that related to her had come about, but she wished very much to accept part of the blame. *He spent a great deal on my wedding and my marriage in general, but this alone cannot have necessitated the sale of so much Pendleton property.*

Finally, she was forced to get to the point.

*I fear a great deal of the expenditure pertains to
the lifestyle Father provides for Eleanor. But please
believe me, Uncle Geoffrey, when I say I have no
wish to speak harshly of Eleanor, who is a Godsend
to Papa. She loves him dearly, as he does her. In fact,
I have never seen him happier than when he is in her
company, and I can understand why. She is a strong
woman, while also good and kind and wise. I have
grown very fond of her myself. She has even become
something of a mother figure in my life.*

However, due to her wealthy former marriage, Eleanor has long been accustomed to a lavish lifestyle in London, and Father is obviously reluctant to deprive her of this. Hence the townhouse he bought and the style of living which he continues to fund, all of which I believe has led to this unfortunate situation.

Father has been disinclined to discuss in detail with Leonard Asquith the necessity for the sales of Pendleton leases, simply saying there have been 'added expenses of late'. Poor Leonard was reluctantly forced, therefore, to seek my advice, just as I am now seeking yours. I am at a loss, I must admit, for Father has also avoided any such discussion with me. What would you suggest I do, Uncle Geoffrey? Should I confront Father? Should I confront Eleanor? Should I confront them both? How do I go about curbing this ongoing expenditure and averting the sale of any further Pendleton lands?

I eagerly await your advice.

Your loving niece, Charlotte ('Lady Squire of Pendleton')

PS I am including herein letters from your grandniece and grandnephews, who await, with equal eagerness, news of your latest adventures.

The following day, after church, the children wrote their letters, Victoria and Edward both voicing their yearning to go to the Pilbara, and Harold proudly printing his name with a funny face drawn underneath. Then, on the Monday morning, Teddy, the young footman, took the envelope into Otley, where he posted it from the village post office.

***

Three months later, on a wet and wintry Friday afternoon, young Teddy returned from Otley. He proceeded directly from the stables to the laundry at the rear of the house, where he shook out his wet mackintosh, took off his sodden boots and left them to dry. Then, entering through the staff door, he slipped on his shoes, which he'd placed there before leaving, and proceeded to the hall stand in the west wing, where he deposited the mail he'd just collected from the Otley Post Office. The letter clearly marked from Western Australia he placed on the top of the pile, knowing how valued this correspondence was to both the Squire and his daughter.

Geoffrey's reply had arrived.

Charlotte took the letter directly to her bedroom. Her father was in residence at Pendleton and she could not risk him seeing the envelope addressed to her. They shared each of Geoffrey's letters these days, reading them out loud to one another, which could have proved a little awkward. For this reason, Charlotte had been keeping a close watch on the mail the past two weeks, although in truth her uncle's reply could not have arrived any sooner than it had, Geoffrey obviously having written immediately upon the receipt of her letter.

At that very moment, her father was in his office, studying the accounts and files, which had been delivered that morning by a worried Leonard Asquith.

In her room, Charlotte tore open the envelope and sat down to read, thankful that the weather had kept her indoors, and that the children were in the classroom with their tutor.

Geoffrey's reply was direct, harsh even. He did not write in his customary humorous vein. It was clear to Charlotte that her letter had shocked him. He did not even open with his *Lady Squire* salutation.

My dear Charlotte, he began,

I am appalled to hear William has landed himself in such dire financial straits that he has been forced to sell off Pendleton lands. He has said nothing of this to me. Nothing at all. We, who have always shared everything. For the whole of our lives, we have been as close as two brothers could be. Why? Why has he said nothing? I can only assume his silence in this matter is due to shame, that he is too proud to admit to his mismanagement, and this appals me further.
I would wish only to help him in any way I can. That he should choose not to confide in me is sure evidence he is tormented by guilt. You and I, dear niece, are the ones who must save him from this torment. So! On to our plans.

Despite the kind words you write of Eleanor, it is clear to us both that her penchant for extravagance has resulted in this catastrophic outcome. Your father even confessed that he'd been 'rendered blind by love' – his very words, I might add – when he admitted to spending more time in London than at Pendleton. That was when he boasted to me that you had become the 'true squire in all but gender'. I took this to be William's attempt at humour, which it obviously was not.

I must warn you, Charlotte, this newfound mother figure of yours, this Eleanor Witterson, is not good and kind and wise at all. Not in my opinion, anyway. I believe she is an opportunist bent on milking your father for every penny she can get. Why, he wrote to me many years ago that she had suggested he sell Pendleton and move to the city. He said she was joking, and I took him at his word. But was she? The more you tell me of her extravagances, the more I doubt it.

You asked for my advice, niece, and here it is. You must convince your father to sell the townhouse, there is no other way. It is a major asset that will realise substantial capital and prevent further sale of Pendleton leases. If his mistress truly loves him, as you say she does, although I must admit to doubting that fact, then she will agree to move to the country and live a more frugal life. If, however, she refuses, then she must simply be left in London to fend for herself. This would break William's heart, I know, but her refusal would surely be proof to him that her love was a pretence from the start.

I would happily offer this advice to your father myself, Charlotte, but I think it is wiser coming from you. William's guilt has obviously prevented him from confiding in me, and my intercedence would only add to his humiliation. You are there, in the centre of the whole sorry business, and you are, after all, the Lady Squire of Pendleton.

I await further news.

With love always from your faraway Uncle Geoffrey.

PS You will find enclosed a letter I have written to each of the children, whose missives I very much enjoyed. I do hope they will continue our correspondence.

Strengthened by her uncle's advice and support, Charlotte decided to confront her father the very next day.

'May I have a word with you, Papa?' she said, popping her head around the door of his office.

'Of course, my dear, of course. Do come in.'

She entered, closing the door behind her, and sat in one of the hardback chairs opposite his desk.

He half rose. 'Shall I ring Edith for a pot of tea?'

'No, no, Father,' she said, 'I wish to speak of business.'

'Ah. I see.'

William eased himself back into his chair, wearily, reluctantly, dreading what was to come. He was so very tired these days. Tired of the worry and stress that constantly dogged him, tired of life in general, but most of all, tired of himself. He'd been terse with Leonard Asquith yesterday when the poor man had delivered the previous month's paperwork.

'About the ongoing expenses, Squire—' Leonard had begun.

'Yes, yes, man, I know,' he'd snapped. 'I said I'd address the matter and I shall, I shall.'

'It's just that we simply cannot afford to part with any further—'

'I am fully aware of this, Leonard. Just as I'm sure you're fully aware that *I* am the Squire, and it is *I* who will make the decisions.'

'Yes, of course, sir, of course.' And the unfortunate fellow had backed nervously from the room.

How could I have done that? William wondered. *How could I have treated the man in such a manner? Poor loyal, hard-working Leonard, I treated him like a serf. And yet we're friends. Or we were.*

He looked at his grave-faced daughter now prepared to get down to the matter of business and his heart sank.

She is about to chastise me, he thought, *and she has every right, but what do I tell her? The truth?* He knew he wouldn't be able to, that the truth would expose his weakness, and yet in all honesty, he didn't know why. His arrangement with Eleanor had seemed at the time the right thing to do; the *only* thing to do; indeed the *honourable* thing to do. He had to admit it still seemed so. How was he to explain that to his daughter?

Charlotte thought how exhausted her father looked, exhausted and unhappy, and, yes, she decided, even depressed. She had never seen him like this, as if somehow he'd given up. *How unlike him*, she thought. But buoyed by her Uncle Geoffrey's advice and the need for immediate action, she decided to get straight to the point.

'I am aware, Father,' she said, 'of the sales of our leases due to the added expenses incurred over the past years.'

'Yes.' He nodded. 'As you would be and as you should be.' He presumed Leonard must have told her. Which, under the circumstances, he supposed was only right.

'And there is just one course of action we must take,' she continued firmly. 'In fact, there is just one course of action open to us, as far as I can see.'

He noted the peremptory tone and the use of *we* and *us* as if she were about to issue an order, which she probably was, and which, once again, he supposed was only right.

'And that is?' he asked, although he knew exactly what she was going to say.

'We must sell the townhouse,' she announced, and it certainly did sound like an order.

'*We* must, must *we*?' William couldn't help but feel a frisson of annoyance.

'Yes, we must.' Charlotte met his gaze directly. 'Or rather *you* must, Father.' Her voice softened a little as she added, 'But you know that, don't you?'

In his hesitation, he appeared cornered. *Why?* she wondered. 'It was an excellent investment when you purchased it,' she went on, 'and the property value will have no doubt increased a great deal since then, but the time has come to sell, surely you must—'

'There is a matter of honour at stake here, Charlotte.' Having mustered his courage, and more importantly his dignity, William's tone was sharp. Much as he loved and respected his daughter, he would not be talked down to. 'A matter about which you know nothing.'

'And what would that be?' Charlotte's tone was equally sharp, announcing she had every right to be told, as they both well knew.

'The townhouse was purchased in part with funds raised by the sale of two London apartments,' William said stiffly, 'one owned by Eleanor and one by me. The property is therefore as much hers as it is mine.'

There was a moment's pause as they eyed each other off like duellists.

He said purchased in part, Charlotte thought. *Two small London apartments would not buy a Mayfair townhouse.* She recalled it had been not long after the property's purchase that she'd discovered the first sale of a Pendleton lease. Her father's explanation was not at all satisfactory.

'This surely does not prevent the sale of the townhouse, Father,' she replied. 'A modest apartment could be bought for Eleanor in exchange for her initial investment—'

'That will do, Charlotte.' He cut her off abruptly and rose to his feet. 'As I told you, the townhouse is a matter of honour.'

She stood also and they faced each other across the desk. She was bewildered. It appeared he was dismissing her.

He was. 'We will speak no further on the matter,' William said and he sat, his attention once again focussed on his paperwork.

Recognising the futility of further argument, Charlotte strode from the office, but she was already planning the next action she would take.

The following day was Sunday and life proceeded as normal. The family attended church and lunched together, pleasantly enough, although things were just a little strained between father and daughter, as they were at the dinner table that evening.

Early Monday morning, however, saw Charlotte boarding the first train bound for London. She had made the necessary plans to avoid detection, for as long as possible anyway, Edith being her principal ally.

'When I'm not present at breakfast, tell Father I've gone for an early morning ride,' she'd instructed. She knew her father would make no enquiries throughout the day, presuming she was working with the field hands, besides which, he was far too preoccupied with his paperwork and his worries. The children would be well tended by their nanny and tutors, and Mac was to pick her up at the train station when she returned in the early evening. Her father would by then have become suspicious, certainly, but it would be too late, for the deed would have been done. She would have confronted Eleanor and convinced her the townhouse must be sold whether she liked it or not.

Things started out well enough.

'Oh, my dear, what a splendid surprise.' Eleanor was delighted to see her, greeting her effusively. 'Come in, come in.' She ushered Charlotte inside, then noted with surprise, 'But where's your luggage?'

'I shan't be staying.'

'Good gracious me, why ever not?'

'I just wish to talk to you, Eleanor. We have matters to discuss.'

'Oh, dear me, that *does* sound serious.' Eleanor gave a light laugh and led the way through to the front drawing room. 'In which case, we shall most definitely need tea.' She was about to ring for the maid.

'No tea, thank you.'

'Oh. *That* serious.' The two of them sat. 'Very well then.' Smiling encouragingly, she gave Charlotte her full attention. 'Fire away, my darling. What appears to be troubling you? I shall help in any way I can, you must know that.'

Charlotte returned the smile gratefully. She was sure Eleanor knew nothing of her father's situation and that the news would come as something of a shock, quite possibly a terrible shock. But she decided it would be best to get straight down to business.

'Pendleton is suffering financial trouble at the moment, Eleanor, and we need to sell the townhouse,' she said. 'But Father refuses to do so.'

Eleanor's expression was unreadable. She appeared neither shocked, nor even surprised, which in turn rather surprised Charlotte.

'Does he indeed,' she replied, 'and what reason does he give for his refusal?'

'You,' Charlotte said bluntly. 'He says the property was purchased in part by the sale of your apartment and that it is therefore as much yours as his. He says it is a matter of honour.'

'Is that so?'

Still Eleanor appeared enigmatic, unruffled, which, although puzzling to Charlotte, encouraged her to continue.

'We both know the sale of your apartment would have contributed a relatively modest amount, Eleanor,' she went on, 'and when the townhouse is sold, another apartment would be purchased for you, so—'

'But what if I do not *wish* to live in another poky little London apartment?'

Eleanor's tone remained gracious and her expression benign, but her words came as such a shock that Charlotte was struck speechless.

'You see, there's one detail you have overlooked, my dear,' Eleanor continued. 'Your father is not at liberty to sell the townhouse, for it is not his property to sell. The townhouse was purchased in my name. It belongs to me.'

Charlotte stared back at her, dumbfounded.

'This is the matter of honour to which your father refers,' Eleanor continued. 'The townhouse was a gift in return for my becoming a wife to him. Pendleton was to remain his "country wife" while I was to be his "city wife",' she added with a smile. 'Sweet, don't you think? Sweet and romantic. But your father is a very romantic man.'

'So the property was never purchased as an investment,' Charlotte said, a statement more than a question. She was horrified.

'No. Never. The townhouse was always to be my home. And surely no more than is due any wife, would you not agree? A safe and secure home of her own?'

Charlotte recalled the views Uncle Geoffrey had expressed in his letter. *Eleanor Witterson is not good and kind and wise at all ... She is an opportunist bent on milking your father for every penny she can get ... She had suggested he sell Pendleton and move to the city ...*

She recalled her own initial impression of Eleanor. *A shallow woman ... bent on one purpose ... to marry a wealthy man.* But when Eleanor had refused to wed her father, Charlotte had reassessed her opinion, hadn't she? And over the ensuing years, she'd been beguiled by the woman. *How could I have been so foolish,* she wondered, *so foolish and downright blind?*

'What a vile creature you are, Eleanor,' she said.

For the first time, Eleanor betrayed herself with a reaction. She was deeply offended.

'What right do you have to say such a thing?' she demanded. 'I have given your father the best years of my life.'

Charlotte jumped to her feet, infuriated. 'You have bled my father dry! He wouldn't sell Pendleton, so you've been taking it from him gradually, piece by piece. You've stolen his land, you've broken his spirit, you've cheated and deprived him of all he valued ...'

Eleanor rose, still with dignity, but equally infuriated, although determined not to display the extent of her rage.

'I have devoted my life to your father for the last ten years, Charlotte,' she said coldly. 'I have been more of a wife to William than any woman he might have chosen from your circle of *landed gentry,*' she spat the term out as something distasteful, which to her it was. 'I can assure you, without me, your father would never have known the true depth of love. It was I who awakened him to passion and all that gives life its meaning. I rescued him from the mundane convention of you and *your kind*, and I have remained constantly loyal throughout our relationship.'

Eleanor took a breath and regained her composure, which had momentarily threatened to desert her. 'A decade of loyalty deserves reward, my dear. I have accepted no more than my due.'

'You wouldn't know the meaning of love, Eleanor,' Charlotte replied. 'Your beauty and your wiles were more than a match for a defenceless man like my father, as you were very well aware. You've no doubt used this weaponry of yours for the whole of your life. You're no more than a parasite sucking off the blood of others.'

She strode to the door, where she turned back to deliver her farewell. 'I shan't see you again. Nor shall there be any contact between us. Father will probably never forgive me for having confronted you, in which case, you may well have caused a terrible rift in our family. I shall always hate you for that. I shall hate you for that more than anything.'

Eleanor felt powerless as she watched Charlotte leave. There was so much she would like to have said, so much she felt *needed* to be said. She'd been wrongly accused.

I was not born into a privileged family as you were, she would have told the girl. *What have I ever* had *but my beauty and wiles? I simply learned how to use this 'weaponry', as you call it, in order to create my own privileged world. What is so terribly wrong with that?*

But even as she thought of the conversation she would like to have had, Eleanor realised she had overplayed her hand, that she should have restrained her extravagances. She'd had no idea William had become so financially burdened. He'd said nothing to her, but then she'd shown no interest, so why would he? He'd just continued to indulge her. And now, due to this confrontation, he was bound to abandon her. What would she do? She still had her wiles, oh, yes, most certainly, but her beauty? She was now over fifty and her beauty had faded. Where would she find another benefactor at her age?

The townhouse was all she had. She would be forced to sell it before long, buy somewhere cheap and live off the profit, after which she would be destined to spend the end of her days in penury.

How unfair life is, she thought.

But there was something else that saddened Eleanor, and in the most unexpected sense. She had enjoyed being a family. She had enjoyed playing the role of wife to William and mother to Charlotte. She had loved William in her own way, and she had enjoyed Charlotte's company. She admired the girl's courage and independent spirit; she still did. In essence, they were really not all that dissimilar, were they? Strong women, capable of creating lives of their own in a man's world.

***

William Burton's reaction to his daughter's confrontation with his mistress was not what either woman expected. But neither was it in the least out of character.

'You should not have done that, Charlotte,' he said icily. 'As I told you, the townhouse was, and still is, a matter of honour. We shall not mention the subject again.' He would not allow this unpleasant incident to cause a rift in his family.

William was displeased by his daughter's actions, and the thought that Charlotte might well consider him weak was humiliating, but in essence, he agreed with Eleanor. Her loyalty and devotion had earned her the right to the townhouse. He did not regret his initial action of gifting it to her, and he would certainly not abandon her. Why would he? He loved her.

Charlotte wrote immediately to her uncle, recounting every detail of her confrontation with Eleanor.

Papa was angered that I had seen fit to take such a step, but I believe he understood why I did so, and that deep down he respects me for it.

However, we are powerless. The townhouse belongs to Eleanor. Father still maintains it's a debt of honour, and, unbelievable as this may seem, Uncle Geoffrey, he still loves her.

I have no doubt that Eleanor, now aware of his financial state, will curb her ridiculous extravagances, but what are we to do? I fear the only option may be to sell more land ...

The reply, when it eventually arrived, would have been astounding, had Geoffrey's money not already been received.

He opened in his customary light-hearted vein.

*Well, well, Lady Squire, proof positive indeed that love
is blind. Dastardly though the outcome has proved,
I am gratified at least to hear that my views on the
monstrous Eleanor proved correct. However, I have
made a decision which will save Pendleton from the
need for any further disastrous action. I have taken
mortgages out on Burton Station and also the house
in Claremont, or rather I have instructed my lawyer,
Mr Andrew Goodiston, to do so. The sums are to
be transferred to Pendleton's bank account in Leeds,
and will no doubt have arrived before you receive this
letter. I need go into no further detail here, Charlotte,
for I have just now written in depth on the matter
to your father. As I intend to post both letters from
Roebourne this afternoon, it is quite likely they will
arrive together ...*

They did. Both letters had been sitting on the hall table in
the west wing following young Teddy's trip into Otley, one
addressed to Squire W.E. Burton, the other to Squire C.E.
Burton.

William was in residence at Pendleton, as he mostly was
these days, spending little time in London, determined to
fulfil the duties of squire he had so long neglected. Geoffrey's
money having arrived a good six weeks before the letters, he
and Leonard Asquith were currently hard at work paying off
the accumulated debts and sorting out the estate's finances.

Father and daughter read their letters aloud to one another, Charlotte omitting Geoffrey's opening reference to 'the monstrous Eleanor', but it was William's letter that carried the fervour of his young brother's decision.

The monies, which you will have received by now, are rightfully yours, William, for you have always been partner to my enterprises here in the Pilbara and also my acquisition of the property in Perth. How trusting and generous you were, dear brother, in helping me on my way. Allow me now to return the favour in helping you rescue Pendleton from its current financial predicament.

He voiced no recriminations about how the family estate had become so financially threatened. No mention was made of Eleanor, nor of the townhouse. Instead, he offered sympathy.

Do not be angry with Charlotte for having shared with me the news of your troubles, brother. I am only saddened you felt you could not share them with me in person, and I presume this is because of the guilt you had taken upon yourself.

Oh, William, you are such a proud and honest man. I hate to think of you suffering in such a way. I beg of you, never close me out. Never again, please. You and I have always been so close. You are the one and only big brother I have and I value your love dearly, just as I know you value mine.

It is this love which I now send you from far, far away.

Your one and only youngest brother, Geoffrey.

There might have been the glint of a tear in William's eye as he placed the letter on his desk and leaned back in his chair. 'Well, well,' he remarked, 'not a joke to be had.'

Charlotte didn't reply, but they shared a smile.

'He says the monies I have received are rightfully mine due to our partnership,' William continued thoughtfully, 'but they are vastly in excess of such a sum, I am sure. I would say he has sent me the entire amount from the mortgaging of the properties, which I worry will leave him sorely in debt.'

'This is what Uncle Geoffrey wants to do, Father,' Charlotte replied. 'You must allow him that freedom.'

'Yes. Yes, I must, I know I must.'

***

True to her word, Charlotte cut all ties with Eleanor. She was aware of her father's disappointment, knowing how much he had enjoyed the semblance of family they'd shared, but even for his sake, she could not bring herself to offer any form of pretence. She detested the woman.

William soon gave up trying to heal the rift between the two, although at first he'd tried.

'Eleanor sends her warmest regards,' he would say after returning from a trip to London, but he would receive no more than a dismissive nod by way of reply.

He tried to persuade Eleanor to come to Pendleton for Christmas in the hope this might reignite the bond.

'I would not be welcome, my love,' she replied, 'as you very well know. Sadly, I'm afraid you must leave things be.'

So he had. Which was a shame, he thought, for he and Eleanor had become closer than ever over these past months. Insistent upon sharing his troubles, she had restricted her spending while displaying the most heartfelt contrition.

'You should have told me, my love,' she'd said. 'Oh, William, you should have told me.'

She'd even sold half her jewellery, and willingly parted with many of the more expensive items of furniture. 'Who needs them?' she'd gaily declared. The grand piano, however, had been retained, essential as it was for those evenings when she entertained. 'One cannot withdraw entirely from society, my darling,' she'd laughed.

William had tried to convey all this to his daughter, to convince her that Eleanor really did care, but Charlotte wasn't interested. She never even mentioned Eleanor's name.

So as the months rolled on to become years, William once again settled into the two lives he led: one a part-time existence with his mistress in London, the other the principal role he played in the country with his daughter and grandchildren, where he was the Squire of Pendleton.

It was in the summer of 1887 they received the news from Geoffrey, which arrived in a joint letter to them both. This was unusual, for Geoffrey had continued to correspond to them individually, knowing father and daughter shared his letters. He found the fact both amusing and complimentary, and took great pains to differ his anecdotes to each, his sole purpose being to entertain as much as to inform. Today's letter, shorter than most, was a different matter altogether.

'*Dearest Squire and Lady Squire,*' Charlotte read out to her father as they sat together in his office. '*I trust all goes well at Pendleton, and that life is treating you kindly. Regrettably, I cannot report the same from down here in the faraway land.*'

Geoffrey had decided to be blunt. *No point in shilly-shallying,* he wrote, *fact is, I've been told my days are numbered …*

Charlotte looked up from the page to meet the shock in her father's eyes before quickly reading on.

Now, now, before you both exclaim your horror at such news, let me assure you the term is not literal. I am not about to die in only days, nor even in months. Indeed I may quite possibly have years left yet. It's just that those were the doctor's exact words to me – 'Your days are numbered, Mr Burton,' he said, 'there is ultimately little or no escape from your condition.' How do you like that, eh? Doctors can be so brutal.

The fact of the matter is I have been diagnosed with tuberculosis, which I find somehow ludicrous. I mean how can anyone be consumptive in a place like this? Consumptives are always advised to go and live in a warm climate, aren't they? Well, you don't get any warmer than here, I can promise you.

I was convinced it must have been my trip
to Perth during last winter that brought on this
condition. The place seemed downright freezing,
although of course it would bear no comparison to
the Yorkshire winters I so vividly remember. But
the doctor dismissed the notion out of hand. His
practice is in Perth, I might add – I recently travelled
south to visit a specialist after I found myself
coughing up blood. In fact, he pooh-poohed the idea
altogether. 'Good God, man,' he said, 'you don't
catch tuberculosis as you would a chill. This is not a
case of a head cold or catarrh, it's a highly dangerous
bacterial infection that will eventually kill once it's
taken hold. And believe me, yours has taken hold, so
all I'm saying is be warned. Be warned, Mr Burton,
your days are numbered.'

I'm making him sound like a bit of a monster, this
doctor, aren't I? But he's not really. He's a nice enough
fellow who simply doesn't pull punches but prefers to
deliver the truth, and I respect him for that. Good to
know where one stands, what?

His advice I find somewhat amusing, I must say.
'Get plenty of fresh air,' he tells me. Hah! Easily done.
When am I not getting fresh air? 'And make sure also
you get plenty of rest,' he says. Hah! Not so easily
done. The good doctor has never been called upon to
manage a sheep and cattle station.

At the moment I'm handling things quite well,
although Joe's being more hard-worked than ever as I

find myself short of breath. Good, steady labourers are hard to come by too. Our blackfella workers tend to walk off the job when they've made enough to get by for a while. Only return when they need more tucker or tobacco or money to see them through until the next walkabout urge hits them. They're a good people for the most part, good-hearted and kind, with a distinctly spiritual connection to the land. But, oh my goodness, they're a different breed altogether.

So there you have it. I'm sorry to have been the bearer of sad tidings, but thought it best to let you know sooner rather than later.

Sending love always to you both from your ailing brother and uncle in the far, faraway wild west of Australia, Geoffrey.

Silence reigned as Charlotte put down the letter, father and daughter both shocked to the core and both thinking the same thing. Geoffrey needed help. Especially as he would now be under extra pressure due to the debt he had incurred on their behalf.

'We must do something.' William was the first to voice their mutual thoughts, but Charlotte was one step ahead.

'I shall go to the Pilbara,' she announced. 'I shall go to the Pilbara and work alongside Uncle Geoffrey's friend, Joe. Together we will take over the management of the station, at least until the mortgages have been repaid.'

'What about the children?'

'They shall come with me.'

Her father's expression was one of sheer disbelief.

'They have been longing to go to the Pilbara for years, Papa,' Charlotte continued, 'and just think of the educational value. Edward is one day to become Squire of Pendleton. Imagine how much he will learn from such an experience. Which,' she added wryly, 'would be of far greater practical use than an Oxford law degree, I should imagine.'

'No, no, my dear, I won't hear of it,' William protested, 'and I'm sure Geoffrey wouldn't either. Quite out of the question ...'

'Why?' Charlotte demanded. 'You cannot go yourself, Father. Hearty and healthy you may be, but next year you will turn seventy, hardly an age to be gallivanting off to the other side of the world. Besides which, you're the Squire of Pendleton, you're needed here.'

He was about to interrupt, but she charged on. 'And as you very well know, I am not only capable of performing the work of any man on a daily basis, I am more than qualified to take command of a sheep property, including one that also runs cattle.'

William could not refute any of this.

They talked at length on the subject, and finally wrote a joint letter to Geoffrey stating their plans. Charlotte and her family would travel to the Pilbara, where she would tend to her uncle and take over the management of Burton Station. William would fund his daughter's enterprise, and she would be prepared to leave within the year.

Geoffrey's reply, which arrived three months later, once again addressed to them both, was succinct. And, as usual, humorous.

Dearest Squires Burton of Pendleton,

I do applaud you on a wonderfully fanciful idea,
which I would most certainly have accepted were you
not, these days, Charlotte, without a spouse. What
a pity Harold died all those years ago. Do you think
you might perhaps acquire another husband in the
immediate future? If this were remotely possible, I
swear I would be there to greet you in person upon
your arrival in Perth. You see, dear brother and
niece, as I have written on many a previous occasion,
the Pilbara is no place for a woman, particularly a
woman travelling alone with three children. Sheer
madness.

Again, father and daughter talked at length, William
suggesting they might perhaps hire a male travelling
companion. But again, Charlotte was one step ahead, and
had an idea that was revolutionary.

'An unnecessary expense,' she said dismissively. 'I shall
travel alone with the children, and I shall travel as a man.

'No, no, hear me out,' she demanded as her father openly
scoffed at the suggestion. 'I shall have the protection of
Uncle Geoffrey during the journey from Perth to the Pilbara,
and once there, with his help, I shall keep up the deception.
Workers respond far more readily to the command of a male
boss than that of a female. I have experienced this right here
in the heart of Pendleton, where I am known and held in high
regard. I dread to think of the reception a female boss might
receive in the Pilbara.'

As Charlotte warmed more and more to the common sense of her argument, the very thought of what might lie ahead started to excite her. She had recently read a book on the subject.

'Other women have done this before me, Papa,' she continued. 'I have read a number of stories about women who have lived as men. Some have even fought in wars as men. There was an Englishwoman by the name of Hannah Snell who assumed the identity of her brother-in-law. She served in the British Royal Marines and fought in India over a century ago. Eventually, she sold her story to a London publisher and opened a pub called The Female Warrior.'

William was about to interject, but on she went.

'Then there was an American woman, Deborah Sampson. She enlisted in the Continental Army and fought against us during the Battle of Yorktown in the seventeen-eighties. And, far more recently, Sarah Edmonds, an American, joined the Union Army and fought in the First Battle of Bull Run. Don't you see? By comparison my job will be far easier than theirs ...'

Charlotte continued to harangue her father until he finally accepted defeat. And once again, they wrote a joint letter to Geoffrey.

Charlotte has the same spirit of adventure you have, little brother, William wrote in a postscript. *I must admit there is virtually nothing I can do to stop her, so you might as well start preparing for her arrival as a man.*

Geoffrey's own sense of adventure aroused, he embraced the idea with an excitement that matched Charlotte's.

Stranger things have happened here in this wild place, he replied, *where farmers are magistrates and so much is not as it appears. I shall start paving the way immediately for the arrival of my nephew.* Then followed his list of instructions.

Charlotte Elizabeth Burton was to become Charles Edward Burton, bound for Australia to be met by his uncle in Perth's port of Fremantle.

Throughout your voyage, make people aware of your connection to me as my nephew, he suggested to Charlotte, *particularly in the journey from Albany to Perth, where I shall be waiting. There will quite likely be some on board the SS* Franklin *who know me, if not personally, then at least by name.*

A further suggestion he made directly to his brother:

Given your interest in weaponry, and your handsome collection, William, I would advise you include in Charlotte's luggage one or two firearms of your choice. I leave the selection to you, being the expert you are, but perhaps even one of those new-fangled pump-action things, which would be handy for her as added protection in this crime-ridden corner of the world.

Then after a further exhaustive list of instructions, he finally signed off. Very briefly this time:

I eagerly await your company, Charles,
With warmest regards, Uncle Geoffrey.

PART TWO

1890, The Pilbara, Western Australia

6.

Charles was accustomed to this country now. He'd experienced its heat and its cold, its rain and its violent winds; even its cyclones, the fierce and destructive likes of which his Uncle Geoffrey had written. Why, just the previous year, on March 1st of 1889, there had been one of such proportion it had all but destroyed Burton Station. The fencing, the outbuildings, the very homestead itself all but flattened. They'd only now finished rebuilding.

He remembered with vivid clarity the experience he and the children had shared. Nothing to that point in their lives could have prepared them for the storm that nature had provided. He'd read of tropical revolving storms, also known as cyclones, typhoons and hurricanes, and while Uncle Geoffrey's letters had mentioned them, Charles had never imagined he would experience one personally, and any description had faded from his memory. Now they would be etched in his mind forever.

Charles recalled how, when he'd first laid eyes on the homestead at Burton Station, he'd been astounded to see large ship anchor chains extending over the roof and bolted to sturdy boulders sunk in the ground around the foundations.

His first reaction had been to laugh at the absurdity of it, but he'd soon discovered anchor chains were in place on the main buildings in the local townships of both Cossack and Roebourne. Cyclones, or the ridiculously named 'willy-willies' or 'big blows' as the locals referred to them, were seasonal in the Pilbara and justly feared by all. The wind gauge at Roebourne Post Office, one local told him, had registered up to one hundred and fifty miles an hour, at which point it had broken.

So, when a 'big blow' had threatened the previous March, Charles had heeded the advice of his station manager, Joe Lawson, and together they'd prepared as best they could.

'Time to batten down the hatches,' Joe had jovially declared. They'd rounded up the stock too, gathering the animals protectively in the more sheltered areas of the property. 'Although there's bound to be losses,' Joe had declared, also in jovial fashion. Nothing much seemed to adversely affect Joe Lawson, who had obviously weathered many a storm.

It had come from the north-west as cyclones invariably did, striking the coast and thundering across the countryside, until finally blowing itself out inland. Charles and his children would never forget the experience. For the first eight hours or so the wind had increased steadily to an unbelievable level, in excess of one hundred miles an hour. Then, all of a sudden, it had ceased altogether for thirty minutes or more as the eye passed over them. The wind then came from the south-east with the same terrifying speed until, once again and all of a sudden, it ceased. The nightmare was finally over. The storm had disappeared on its way inland, leaving them physically and mentally shattered.

The family had huddled throughout the ordeal, a whole day and night, among the piles of boulders set up specifically for cyclone protection. Terrified, they'd witnessed the devastation being wreaked all about them. Trees and the roofs of outbuildings flew through the air like giant kites, the playthings of gods gone crazy. The noise was deafening. Thunder and lightning screamed overhead and a constant heavy downpour all but drowned them as they crouched there together. The boys openly screamed out their fear, but Charles couldn't help noting that Victoria, although equally terrified, watched and observed every occurrence. He knew his daughter was analysing each moment, creating precise memories for her own future use. This was always Victoria's way.

They had survived, but Burton Station had not. All of the outbuildings had been destroyed, their roofs torn off and the flimsy wooden constructions scattered over several miles. The station homestead, despite the anchor chains, had also lost its roof, but its foundations remained. The well-established town of Roebourne, they found out later, had suffered much the same fate. Apart from a number of the larger stone edifices, the place had been virtually flattened.

The rebuilding and repairs had started immediately, Charles and Joe eventually acquiring a cartload of corrugated iron sheets for the station homestead and three other buildings.

It had taken them many months to restore Burton Station's modest stone homestead with its surrounding verandahs. But as so often happens, good comes from adversity. The whole family felt somehow privileged now they had experienced the devastation of a cyclone. Edward and Harold had written to their grandfather declaring they were now fully-fledged Pilbarans, while Victoria, from notes made following the event, created a small hand-written volume, which she titled, 'Cyclone Survival Instructions', to be strictly observed by all at Burton Station.

Yes, we survived, Charles thought, *but by the grace of God. It was certainly a day and a night we'll never forget.*

After nearly two years, Charles Burton was accustomed to the Pilbara's every mood and he nodded to himself as he opened the flywire screen door, stepped onto the front verandah and looked out at the dullness of the mid-morning sky. Rain clouds had formed over the rocky rise barely a quarter of a mile off and it was beginning to spit. Nothing much would get done today.

His partner, Joe Lawson, had left for Roebourne several hours ago with the last of the station hands. By now, they would have met up with foreman, Billy 'Bud' Norton, and the other stockmen, who had been gone for two days, having taken delivery of the new sheep stock that had arrived at the port of Cossack. After joining forces at Roebourne, seven miles to the south, the boys were then to drive the flock back home to the station.

It was silent without the men.

The Aboriginal women were not present either. They'd left to attend a local tribe meeting about a marriage or betrothal and they'd taken their children with them. Only forty-year-old Nina, the Jaburara woman who had been in Geoffrey Burton's service as the station's housekeeper and cook for the past twenty years, had remained, but she was nowhere to be seen.

Apart from thirteen-year-old Victoria, who was studying quietly on the back verandah, accompanied by her ever-present cup of tea, Charles was alone. Edward and Harold were both at school in Roebourne, travelling there in the rickety two-team horse and buggy that rounded up a number of children from various stations along the way. A two-hour journey there, and a two-hour journey back for the Burton boys, neither of whom minded.

Charles was relishing the peace and quiet. The house and its surrounds were usually a noisy free-for-all: women chattering as they worked; kids squealing as they played; and always the general racket of everyday activity. Now there was only the sound of the animals, the bark of a dog from the kennels, the crow of a wandering rooster, the neigh from a horse in the home paddock. No vestige of noise that was human.

The silence was palpable and Charles smiled, content.

Until he saw them. The three men on the rise, all looking his way. All white men, he noted, and all armed. He'd been aware of their presence on the property the previous day but had thought little of it. People crossed the station's land periodically, travelling to who knew where, and often they'd call into the homestead, usually to enquire of directions or to request water before moving on. But these three had made no request, and they had not moved on. These three were observing the homestead with obvious intent, and had no doubt been doing so for some time. They would have seen Lawson and the last of the station hands depart, they would know the place was virtually deserted. The signs were ominous. *This is not right*, Charles thought. *This is not right at all.*

Feigning a lack of concern, he re-entered the house, the screen door slapping shut behind him, and once out of sight, dived for the gun box that sat in the corner of the front sitting room. As he did so, he called urgently for his daughter.

'Victoria! Get yourself in here.'

His voice rang through the open door to the breakfast room and the further open door that led to the back verandah. During the hot months, all the station's doors were left open to channel whatever breeze there might be, the outer doors each having flywire screens.

As Victoria entered, he handed her the heavy Enfield .476 calibre revolver that he'd taken from the gun box.

'There are three men on the rise out front and they're armed. Get yourself out the back, make your way across the yard and take cover in the trees.'

'But why—'

'Do as I say, Victoria! Should anything untoward happen, shoot first from behind cover, then ask questions later.'

'Yes, Father.' The girl spun on her heel and disappeared through the breakfast room to the back verandah.

Charles took the Spencer pump-action shotgun from the gun box and loaded five 12-gauge cartridges into the magazine. He cocked it and crossed to the front door, peering through the flywire screen. The men were gone from the rise. He held the shotgun, finger on the trigger, and let it dangle by his leg.

It was some minutes before he heard the footsteps coming from the harness and tackle shed that stood forty feet distant from the verandah. Then they halted, and a man called out.

'Hello?' The voice was gruff, demanding. 'Anyone home?'

Charles pushed the screen door open and stood leaning against the frame, ensuring the shotgun was not visible. A big, bearded man was planted, legs astride, not thirty feet away, both hands suspiciously behind his back.

'Good day to you, sir,' Charles called to the man. 'Can I be of assistance? What is your business?'

'On my way to Roebourne. I'd appreciate a drop of water.'

'Travelling alone, are you?'

'Yes, that's right, all on my own.' The man attempted a smile, which failed.

'So, the men I saw you with on the rise not fifteen minutes ago are strangers to you, are they?'

The man's attempted smile twisted into a grimace, and he produced a handgun from behind his back, the barrel pointed unwaveringly at Charles. Then he began his slow advance towards the door, assertive, threatening.

'I was hoping things wouldn't have to go like this,' he said with an ugly leer. 'You're right, there are three of us. We wish you no harm, sir, but it would be wise not to cross us. We require any valuables you may have, and any ready money to hand.'

'So, it's robbery under arms then, is it?'

'I'm afraid so.'

The man was no more than six feet away, about to mount the steps to the verandah, when Charles raised the shotgun and discharged it into his face. He fell back dead, all features erased, nothing remaining but a bearded pulp. But even as the man fell, a bullet missed Charles' head by only inches.

Another man had appeared from the shed and, handgun raised, was now running straight at him.

Charles pumped the Spencer, this time shooting the man in the stomach. Then, as two more bullets hit the wall beside him, he bounded down from the verandah and raced to the shed, zig-zagging his way across the short distance that separated the two.

After making his ground, he flattened himself against the wall of the shed and pumped another cartridge into the breach.

'I know there's someone in there,' he called loudly through the door, which was slightly ajar. 'If you come out unarmed with your hands above your head, I promise I won't harm you.'

'Oh, you won't harm me all right, matey,' the voice from the shed sneered. 'I've got a friend of yours in here with me, see?'

There was a shuffling of feet, the door was pushed open and the sturdy figure of Nina appeared. But this wasn't the normally tough, confident Nina. The man was shielding himself behind her body, one arm locked around her neck, free hand pressing a pistol to her temple, and she was clearly petrified, the whites of her eyes rolling in terror.

'Any wrong move from you and your darkie here gets it, see?' The comment was delivered with bravado, despite the fact Charles could clearly see the man was shaken by the deaths of his companions.

'Let Nina go!' The voice was lightly pitched and youthful, but the delivery firm and steadfast in its purpose. 'Let her go or I'll shoot you.'

Charles turned to see Victoria not forty feet away, on the front verandah. She was leaning on the railing, arms extended, the big Enfield .476 in her hands pointing directly at Nina and the man.

'Ha! Hello, darlin',' the man scoffed. The kid with the big handgun didn't scare him half as much as this bloke with the pump-action shotgun. 'Who's a brave little girl then?' he jeered.

Charles turned back to the man, concerned that his daughter had not remained hidden as instructed, having chosen instead to circle the verandah. He was further disturbed that she had witnessed the carnage that had unfolded, but he issued a threat nonetheless.

'I'd do as she says,' he warned. 'She's the best shot in the family.'

'Hey, little one, you don't want your dear old abo nanny here to die, do you? Nah,' the man teased, 'a course you don't. That'd be—'

The .476 exploded. The bullet travelled the forty feet required, missed Nina's ear by an inch and hit the man in the right eye, killing him instantly.

As he dropped to the ground, Charles turned once again to look back at his daughter, who was motionless, gun still focussed upon her target, or rather where her target had stood, and where a terrified Nina now remained frozen to the spot.

Then, slowly, Victoria lowered the weapon.

'That took some nerve, young lady.'

Charles crossed to her, expecting any moment that her courage would desert her, that she might even collapse at the enormity of what she'd done and the horror she'd witnessed.

'Don't look,' he said as, passing the man's bearded but faceless body, he stepped up onto the verandah by her side.

But Victoria *had* looked. She'd looked at the man with no face, but more importantly, she'd looked at the man sprawled on the ground over there by the harness and tackle shed. *An excellent shot*, she thought. She'd been aiming for the right eye.

'Are you all right?' Charles asked.

'Yes, Father.' Victoria shrugged off the comforting arm he put around her, handing him the gun instead. 'The kettle's still hot. I'll brew us a fresh pot of tea, shall I?' she suggested, and walked off without awaiting an answer.

Charles watched her go, aware she didn't wish him to follow, but wondering what her reaction might be when the shock set in. He was in a considerable state of shock himself.

Over by the shed, Nina had recovered herself and was grinding her bare heel into the crotch of the dead man who'd used her as a shield. 'Dirty pig,' she swore. 'Dirty, filthy pig.'

This bloke had put his hand up her frock in that shed, and he'd grabbed her breasts, and he'd whispered filth while they'd waited in there for his mates to carry out the job at the house, robbing and killing, whatever was necessary. He'd have raped her if he'd had half a chance. And his mates probably would have too. But his mates had copped it from the Boss, hadn't they? And now he'd copped it from the missy, hadn't he? *Good onya, missy*, she thought.

Through the light cotton of the man's trousers she could feel his testicles rolling around like jelly and she ground away with her heel even more fiercely. 'Dirty, rotten, filthy, fuckin' pig,' she swore. Then she heard the Boss.

'Help me cover the bodies, Nina,' Charles called. 'Lawson and the boys can look after them when they get back from Roebourne.'

'Righto, Boss.' And she dived into the shed for some empty chaff bags and potato sacks.

They worked as a team, covering the men's bodies, particularly the bloodied parts that were already proving a magnet to flies, despite the fact the spit of rain was threatening to become a downpour. And all the while Charles wondered how Victoria was faring.

'Tea's up,' a voice called from the front door, and there was Victoria, waving them over.

Charles gathered the two weapons he'd left on the verandah and he and Nina joined her. *Cool as a cucumber*, he thought as they followed his daughter through the sitting room and into the breakfast room, where Victoria had laid out a plate of biscuits beside the pot in its tea cosy, three mugs lined up in a row beside it.

Charles and Nina sat together on one of the two benches set either side of the big central table, watching as Victoria stood opposite them, pouring the tea. They exchanged a glance, but neither said a word.

Then, when all three mugs were filled, sugar and milk added, Victoria picked two biscuits up from the plate. 'I'll be out on the verandah,' she said. 'I'm going back to my studies.'

Charles stood. 'Victoria,' he said, his voice stern, but also disbelieving, perhaps even a little accusatory, 'are you not aware of what happened here today? We just killed three men.'

'Yes,' she replied evenly, 'three men who would have killed us had they been given the chance.'

'And you're not ...' he paused, unsure what to say next, '... you're not ... *troubled* by the action you were forced to take?' *What an inadequate way of putting it*, he thought.

'No.' She shook her head and gave the faintest suggestion of a shrug. 'We did what we had to do.' A pause, then she smiled. 'Don't worry, *Papa*,' she said, with a slight emphasis on the casual form of address she occasionally adopted, as if she was sharing a joke with him. 'I shan't break down given the knowledge that I have now killed a man, and certainly not a man like that, who deserved to be killed.'

Then she left, taking her mug and her two biscuits out onto the back verandah.

Charles was left speechless. But Nina wasn't. Nina was lost in admiration.

'She right, Boss,' she said. 'Missy Victoria saved my life today. She a brave girl, that one.' Grabbing a biscuit from the plate, Nina took up her mug and stood. 'I'll have me tea in the kitchen,' she said. 'Gotta get on with the boys' tucker. What with the Aunties away, I got no help and they'll be needin' a feed when they get home.'

And disappearing through the open door, the flywire screen slapping shut behind her, she crossed the verandah and went out into the kitchen that sat at the back of the house, a necessary precaution given its wood-fired stove.

Charles watched her go. It seemed Nina didn't find the killing of three men particularly difficult to deal with either, which, given the violence of her background, was probably not surprising. But Victoria? The girl was only thirteen years old.

He peered through the flywire screen to the verandah, where he could see his daughter quite clearly, hunched over her papers and books, pencil in one hand, mug of tea in the other, just as she'd been before the arrival of the men.

The sight was unnerving. More and more these days, he found Victoria's behaviour strange. Distant. Rebellious, even. She'd refused to attend school the previous year, maintaining she would learn far more from the books she could order via the catalogue she'd acquired. He'd been proud when she'd been proved right, but it hadn't altered the disturbing reality that her nature seemed to have changed, and radically. He'd put this down to the fact that she had now matured, having started menstruating shortly after her twelfth birthday. Which was a little earlier than most girls, he'd supposed.

Yes, that must be it, he now told himself, *she's grown up. But even so, surely killing a man should mean something.* He watched as she sipped her tea and made a further note with her pencil. *Apparently not*, he thought.

He turned away, lost in thought and wondering how she could be so unaffected by the events of this hideous day. He felt quite sickened himself. Certainly, he'd seen many a bloodied body since he'd come to the Pilbara, where violence abounded. But he'd never been the cause. He'd never killed a man. Now he'd killed two. And his own daughter had killed another. The knowledge was shocking.

Gazing through to the sitting room, his eyes fell upon the pump-action shotgun leaning up against the wall where he'd propped it. *Thank God for that weapon, we'd probably be dead without it*, he thought, remembering Uncle Geoffrey's advice: *Given your interest in weaponry, and your handsome collection, William,* Uncle Geoffrey had written, *I would advise you include in Charlotte's luggage one or two firearms of your choice ... perhaps even one of those new-fangled pump-action things ... handy for her as added protection in this crime-ridden corner of the world.*

Charles could remember the advice, practically word for word, in that letter all those years ago when he'd been Charlotte. *All those years ago.* Good God, it was only two, and yet it felt like a decade. He could remember, as Charlotte, his father teaching him about that weapon, the very one he could now see leaning up against the sitting room wall.

'This is a Spencer shotgun, Charlotte,' William had said, 'a twelve-gauge, five-shot, pump-action weapon. Just the sort of "new-fangled thing" Geoffrey recommends.'

And Charles could remember, as Charlotte, his father instructing him how to use the shotgun, setting up target practice out there in the rich countryside of the Yorkshire dales, so very different from the primitive landscape of the Pilbara. Eleven-year-old Victoria had been with them at the time. Every Burton child was taught to shoot at the age of ten, and Victoria's fine marksmanship with a rifle, and even a hand gun, had by then been evident.

Charles had all but forgotten what it was like to be Charlotte. The children appeared to have forgotten too, although every now and then there was a tiny reminder from Victoria. Just now, for instance, when she had added that slight emphasis to her fond usage of 'Papa', Charles had recognised the inference. A joke perhaps, but given the circumstances, he'd decided it was more of a 'dare', as if she'd really been saying 'Mama'. Another example of the girl's rebellious nature.

The boys, however, seemed to have happily embraced their mother's change of gender, even appearing at times to have forgotten she'd ever been their mother. But then she'd always been both parents to them, hadn't she? In some ways, perhaps more father than mother; the stern disciplinarian who dressed like a man and worked alongside the farm labourers. For Edward and Harold, neither of whom had ever known their real father, the stretch may not have been as extreme as one might have imagined. And she'd drummed it into them.

'I am "Father" to you now,' she had instructed all three. 'I am no longer "Mother" but "Father" to each one of you. Do you understand? *Father*,' she'd emphasised, 'always *Father*! Do I have your word?'

'Yes, Father,' they'd chorused obediently. The whole thing had seemed such fun to them.

'And now and then,' she'd added with a smile, 'when you're feeling fond, you may call me *Papa*.'

It had been far more than fun back in those days. Every step along the way had been the greatest adventure imaginable.

Including even the chopping off of her long, dark hair. The children had gathered for the ceremony, the boys whooping with excitement as each lock fell to the floor. Edith had proved a talented hairdresser, instructing her mistress in the art, ensuring Charlotte would be able to maintain her masculine appearance

Edith had assisted, too, in a further process. One to which the children had not been witness – the construction and fitting of the broad, elasticised crepe band, which she was to wriggle herself into in order to disguise the swell of her breasts. It had been most uncomfortable at first, but she'd quickly adapted, thankful that she'd never been large-breasted anyway.

She and Edith had constructed two of these elasticised bands in order that they could be secretly rotated in the laundering of clothes. The material had reminded Charlotte of the heavy crepe bandages she had bound around Tom Philby's shattered leg. Amazingly enough, she thought of Tom now and then, during those odd moments when she was reminded of Charlotte.

So many memories, Charlotte thought, still mesmerised by the shotgun propped against the wall, still blessing Providence and Uncle Geoffrey for its being here with them in this 'crime-ridden corner of the world'. *I suppose killing a man makes a person's mind run rampant*, she told herself.

She had no idea how long she'd been sitting there staring at that shotgun, revisited by the past, no doubt in order to escape the horrors of the morning – which she realised had now become afternoon – but suddenly she was aware of a ruckus outside. Horses. Men. Livestock. Joe Lawson and the boys were back.

Charles rose from the breakfast table and strode out onto the front verandah, where the rain, which had been pelting down for some time now, was starting to ease. He'd been so distracted he hadn't even heard it turn into a downpour.

He could see the Aboriginal stockmen herding the newly acquired flock towards the paddock up near the rise, while, barely five yards away, Joe and the station's foreman, Bud Norton, had pulled their horses to an abrupt halt and were gazing about in disbelief at the carnage. Three dead men lay covered in rain-drenched hessian sacks, puddles of blood eddying around their bodies like miniature whirlpools.

The men dismounted, Joe handing his reins to Bud. 'Look after the horses,' he said.

While Bud, a middle-aged, nuggety man, led the horses off to the stables, Joe joined Charles on the verandah, taking off his hat, rivulets of water running from the brim.

'It appears you've had a spot of bother,' he said in the typically understated way that Charles at times found so annoying.

He found it particularly annoying right now. 'Yes, you could say that.'

'Want to tell me what happened?' Joe enquired after a pause.

'They were armed and tried to rob us,' Charles said abruptly. 'I killed two. Victoria killed the third.'

'Is she all right?' A touch of concern.

'Yes. In fact, she's remarkably calm about the whole affair.'

'Strange.'

'It certainly is,' Charles agreed. 'I must admit to being a bit shaken myself. I've never killed a man before.'

'Of course you haven't. Hardly *de rigueur* for a member of the Yorkshire landed gentry.'

Charles glared at the man. Was he trying to be funny? Did he mean to be rude? Or was this just another laconic comment intended to show nothing bothered him? Charles could never work Joe out.

'Sorry, old chap,' Joe said, aware he had offended, which had not been his intention. 'Just trying to put you at your ease. I can tell you're rattled. First time *does* come as a shock, I realise that.'

Charles nodded his acceptance of the apology.

'You'll get used to it, though,' Joe added. 'I'm surprised it hasn't happened sooner, actually.'

Another flash of irritation. *Why does he do this?* Charles cursed.

Charles had given up trying to work out the mystery that was Joe Lawson. The man was a contradiction in every possible way. Around forty years of age, he spoke like an Englishman, and a well-bred one at that, but he looked like a Chinaman. Or mixed race at least. Furthermore, the way his English practicality and common sense mingled with an inscrutability that could only be Chinese made him an unsettling mix.

Charles vividly remembered the shock of their first meeting when, as promised, Joe had been there to greet them upon their arrival at the port of Cossack.

'How do you do,' he'd said, hand extended, 'I'm Joe Lawson, Burton Station's manager.'

'Good God,' Charles had blurted out as they shook, he'd been unable to help himself, 'you're Chinese.' He'd never met a Chinese person before. He'd never even seen one.

'Yes, that is correct, or rather, half correct. My mother was Chinese, my father English. How do you do, children.' And one by one, he'd shaken hands with the children, knowing each of their names. 'Welcome to the Pilbara,' he'd said.

They'd stayed the night at Cossack, Joe having arranged accommodation, and the following day they'd travelled along the broad government-constructed road linking the port town of Cossack to the bustling centre of Roebourne. Then along the smaller dirt road to Burton Station, passing the occasional modest farmhouse and property along the way. And, as they'd travelled, luggage and children all piled in the back of the dray, Joe had at least cleared up the mystery that was his name.

'It's rather amusing actually,' he'd said, 'no-one around here knows how I came to be Joe Lawson. No-one apart from your Uncle Geoffrey, that is. My real name is Loh Kai Wah, and in Hong Kong, I was known as Loh san, which is simply "Mr Loh" in English. However, when I arrived in the Pilbara, everyone took "Loh san" to be Lawson. Then they very quickly started calling me Joe, because in those days I'd greet everyone with "good morning" in Cantonese, which is "joh san".'

In response to Charles' obvious confusion, he added apologetically, 'Cantonese is a tonal language, you see. A different inflection on "san" makes for a different word altogether, difficult for the English to comprehend really.

'So, there you have it, Mr Burton,' he'd concluded with a laugh. 'As the result of a perfectly ghastly bilingual disaster, I became Joe Lawson to one and all. Your uncle found it frightfully funny. Geoffrey Burton himself adopted the Anglicised version, and he never explained to others the origins of my name. Not even to your good self, sir. Not even in communication with his very own nephew.'

'I'm flattered you should think to tell me of this, Mr Lawson.'

'From the shock on your face upon meeting me, sir, I felt somewhat obliged to do so. However, you'll discover there are many of Asian origin in these parts. Japanese, Malays, Chinese. We abound, having gravitated here for the pearling or the gold.' His smile was disarming. 'Orientals are invariably opportunists. You'll find many like me in the Pilbara.'

By the time they'd arrived at Burton Station, Charles had thoroughly warmed to the man.

'Please do call me Charles,' he insisted.

'Of course. And I'm Joe.'

Now, two years later, even though they had become partners and despite the fact he had met many 'Orientals', Charles had yet to find any like Joe Lawson.

'I'll have a couple of the boys load the bodies into the dray,' Joe said, 'and I'll take them into town. I presume you'll come with me to report the matter to the police?'

'Of course.'

As Joe left to organise the dray and the workers, Charles fetched his mackintosh and broad-brimmed bush hat to ward off the rain, although by now the deluge had all but come to a halt.

He popped out onto the back verandah.

'Joe and I are taking the bodies into town,' he instructed his daughter, 'and I'll report the incident to the police. We might be gone for some time.'

Victoria barely looked up. 'Very well, Father,' she replied.

Good grief, Charles thought, *I might just as well have told her we're going shopping.*

He returned to the front verandah and watched the bodies being loaded into the back of the dray. The last of the corpses to be tossed unceremoniously alongside the others was the bearded man with no face.

'You did a good job,' Joe remarked.

'Thank you,' Charles replied stiffly.

'The pump-action shotgun, I take it?'

Charles nodded. 'I'm deeply grateful Uncle Geoffrey advised my father to acquire one.'

'Yes, I should imagine you are.' They climbed in, seating themselves side by side up the front. Joe gave the reins a flick and the hardy pair of greys set off at a trot.

It was late afternoon when they arrived in Roebourne. Situated on the banks of the Harding River and established in 1866, Roebourne was the oldest and largest township in the vast north-west region, boasting any number of impressive stone buildings lining its broad and normally dusty streets, which today, however, were not dusty. Despite the rain having long ceased, the streets of Roebourne remained a sodden, muddy mess.

The Police Quarters were located in front of Roebourne Gaol, a forbidding sight known for the atrocities that took place behind its massive brick and stone walls.

Charles and Joe stepped down from the dray just as the main door of the quarters opened and James Arthur Fry, Sergeant of Police, appeared. Fry was a legend in the Pilbara, a tough man in a land full of hard men and not one to be challenged. To those who knew him well though, beneath the hardy exterior there rested a good heart. The big, bearded policeman gave them a hearty welcome and beckoned them in with an eager wave of his arm.

Once they were seated, he allowed them no time to state the reason for their visit, nor did he even make enquiry, but chose instead to launch into his own dilemma.

'My word, Mr Burton, sir, your arrival is most timely, most timely indeed.'

'How so, Sergeant?' Charles enquired.

'I have some matters that need to be adjudged, sir, and I was intending to send young Constable Royden out to Burton Station to inform you your magisterial skills were required, post-haste ...'

'Ah, yes ...' Charles muttered, 'speaking of magisterial matters ...'

He was about to bring up the particular matter of the three bodies outside in the dray, but once again was allowed no time to continue.

'I wouldn't trouble you with this if it were not that Mr Owen, our warden, is currently absent, being unwell. As he appointed you a Justice of the Peace for this area in his absence, you are needed to conduct these magisterial duties.'

Charles heaved a reluctant sigh at this untoward turn of events. Upon his arrival in the Pilbara, he had been overwhelmed to discover that his Uncle Geoffrey, in paving the way, had boasted that his nephew, Charles, had all the requisite skills and knowledge of the law as he himself had and was bound to prove a blessing to the region.

Taking on the duties entrusted to him as a result of this boast had been daunting but, given his father's tuition from childhood, Charles had risen to the task, and had come to find the occasional challenge fulfilling, enjoyable even. Now, however, with those three bodies lying out there in that dray, this really was not the right time.

'Yes, of course, Sergeant.' He glanced at Joe, who shook his head as if to say, *Can't help you here, old chap.* 'You have the offenders in custody, I take it?'

'I do indeed, sir. They're all under supervision in Roebourne Gaol, but several are quite youthful and need to appear in court as soon as possible so that they can then get on with their lives.' He coughed uncomfortably, hoping he hadn't sounded presumptuous. 'That is, if they aren't sentenced back to gaol.'

'And what are the charges?'

'Thievery and assault, sir, apart from one, that is. A fifteen-year-old lad.'

'What's his charge?'

'Murder.'

'Good God,' Charles exclaimed, taken aback. 'Fifteen years old? Who did he murder?'

'His father.'

Charles and Joe sat in silence as the Sergeant went on to explain.

'Clifton Stroud, the deceased person, is, or more correctly *was*,' Fry said, 'a damnable drunk. In fact, I'd say he was the second-worst drunk in the whole of the Pilbara ...'

'The *second*-worst?' It was Joe who asked the obvious question. 'Who's the worst?'

'Alwyn Stroud, the boy in custody.'

'Good God!' Charles exclaimed once again.

'Old Cliffy was a wild Welshman and he began feeding the boy alcohol from when he was a little tyke,' Fry continued, 'around two years old, and nowadays the boy's constantly drunk. The two of them would drink together day and night and inevitably they'd argue and it'd always end with Old Cliffy begging young Alwyn to shoot him because he didn't want to live on anymore. "Shoot me, boyo! Shoot me!" he'd yell. I've locked them both up time and again for disturbing the peace and always over this very same argument. On and on they'd go. Their behaviour's been the talk of the town for I don't know how long. "When is Alwyn going to shoot Old Cliffy?" people have been asking.'

'What prompted him to do it finally?' Charles was mystified. *This could only happen in the Pilbara. This whole place is a world unto itself.*

Sergeant Fry shrugged. 'I've asked the boy that question any number of times, but he can't answer. He's got no memory of the incident, you see. He's a mess and he cries constantly over his father's death. Alwyn's had no mother and no siblings for the whole of his life. His mum was Aboriginal and she died giving birth. He's never known family in any form. Hasn't even resided in a proper house, living with his father mostly in the wild. I've no doubt the boy loved his dad, but something in his head finally snapped and he did as his father told him to do. Shot him in the head at point-blank range.'

Conversation now over, the three men sat in reflective silence for a moment or so until Joe drew Charles' attention to their own matter at hand.

'Right. Now what about our little problems in the dray?'

'What's that?' Sergeant Fry asked. 'You got problems with your dray?'

'No.' Charles shook his head. 'Not *with* the dray. *In* the dray.'

***

At ten o'clock the following morning, Charles took his seat in the magistrate's chair on the bench in the Roebourne Court House. Seated at the table below the bench was the Police Sergeant, and in the first row was Joe Lawson and a man with a mop and bucket who'd been cleaning the place until told by Fry to sit down. At the back of the court sat a number of wardens from Roebourne Gaol with their prisoners, each prisoner individually shackled.

Police Sergeant Fry stood. 'All rise,' he bellowed.

The motley row of wardens and offenders rose to their feet, chains clinking.

'I declare this court is now in session, the Honourable Charles Burton, JP, presiding,' Fry intoned, then looked to Charles. 'Are we ready to proceed, Your Worship?'

'We are, Sergeant Fry.'

Further clinking as the motley crew sat.

'Proceed with your first case, Sergeant.'

'Yes, Your Worship. The court calls Francis Morley.' Fry turned towards a scrawny young man of Aboriginal appearance, not yet an adult, more a youth really, indicating he should stand in front of Charles' bench.

'Your Worship, this young man is charged with stealing three cats from the Jubilee Hotel. Cats which the publican owned as pets. The animals have not been located.'

'How do you plead?'

'Guilty,' the young man replied.

'What did you do with the cats?' Charles asked.

'I ate them.'

'Why did you do that?'

'I was hungry.'

Charles closed his eyes briefly. *Is this really happening?* he wondered. *Oh dear, not again.* English law in the Pilbara was nothing short of bewildering. Then, pointing a judicial finger at Francis Morley, he announced, 'It is the decision of this court that you proceed immediately to the Jubilee Hotel and apologise to the publican for stealing his cats. You are to remain at the hotel for three hours and assist the yardman with any work he requests you do. Then you can go home.'

Several similar cases followed, Charles realising that
the Sergeant was genuinely concerned for the welfare of
these young men, or boys more accurately, and mostly of
mixed race, whom he'd been forced to place in custody in
the ghastly confines of Roebourne Gaol. It was here, in this
terrible place, infamous throughout the entire region, that
hundreds of men lived in appalling conditions and brutality
was rife.

Charles accepted pleas of guilty from the boys and, on the
advice Sergeant Fry had offered the previous day, fined them
each one pound sterling to be paid over two years.

'You are now free to leave the court,' he announced.

After the boys had been unshackled and ushered away,
three men were presented, charged with creating an affray.
Charles ordered each of them returned to the gaol, where
they would be incarcerated for one month, warning them
that 'brawling, drunkenness and disturbing the public peace
will not be tolerated'.

He felt just a little hypocritical saying that. The streets of
Roebourne were a constant scene of brawling, drunkenness
and the disturbance of public peace.

Then came the moment when Sergeant Fry presented two
sworn statements to the court, both of which Charles knew
had been written by the Sergeant himself.

The statements contended a robbery under arms had been
attempted at Burton Station the previous morning and that
the three perpetrators had been shot and killed by station
employees. The Sergeant then informed the court that the
two witnesses who had made the statements, Andrew Smith

and James Jones, both itinerant gold miners, had since moved on from the Pilbara and had left no forwarding address.

'The three deceased felons are being buried as we speak, Your Worship,' said the Sergeant. 'And if it please the court, this file will be forwarded to the Office of the Colonial Coroner in Perth, where it shall remain *in situ* as a public record.'

'*In situ?*' Charles queried.

'If it please the court,' the Sergeant replied with a respectful bow of his head, which Charles thought may have been gilding the lily.

'*In situ.*' Charles nodded stern-faced. 'Quite right, Sergeant. Just as it should be.'

'And now, if it please the court.' Fry gestured to the rear, and the remaining warder pushed forward a frail, mixed-race Aboriginal boy of fifteen. Little more than a child, he stood before the bench, gazing up at Charles, trembling and red-eyed, a forlorn mess.

'Alwyn Stroud,' Fry intoned. 'You are charged that, on the Saturday the fifteenth of this month, at the rear of the Victoria Hotel in the town of Roebourne, you did unlawfully kill and murder one Clifton Stroud by shooting him in the head. How do you plead?'

The boy slowly turned, wide-eyed and confused, to the Sergeant, who mouthed the word, 'Guilty'.

Alwyn then looked back up at Charles and said, 'Guilty ... sir.'

'Sergeant Fry,' Charles announced, 'I am fully aware of the facts in this case and the circumstances surrounding them.'

'Yes, Your Worship.'

'I am bound by law to sentence Alwyn Stroud to death or imprisonment for this capital crime. I have decided upon this and believe a term of imprisonment will be appropriate. Therefore, Alwyn Stroud, I hereby sentence you to a term of imprisonment not exceeding the rising of this court.'

He stood.

'And now, as there is no further business outstanding, I declare this court closed.'

'All rise,' Fry bellowed.

***

It wasn't until the afternoon, when they were in the dray making their way back to Burton Station, that Charles finally commented on the day's proceedings.

'I simply cannot comprehend what occurred in Roebourne Courthouse this morning,' he said. 'It never ceases to astound me. Are we not in a colony of Queen Victoria's British Empire? Are we not subject to the rules of its law?' He gave a sigh of resignation. 'How could that charade possibly have happened?'

'I thought it went rather well.' Joe Lawson smiled contentedly.

'It was a Molière farce!' Charles exclaimed. 'An English court of law was appallingly disrespected. It simply won't do.'

'Oh, come along now, Charles, stop being so stuffy, everything worked out perfectly. In fact, as you landed gentry might say, *spiffingly.*'

'Oh, do stop that,' Charles snapped.

'Stop what?'

'Making fun of me.'

'I'm not, old man,' Joe protested, 'I'm deadly serious.' And he was. 'Today, justice was served to the highest degree,' he went on. 'Everyone received precisely what they deserved, Fry can close the cases he's had in abeyance, and you have done your duty to the Crown. The whole "charade", as you call it, was a display of sheer genius. In Hong Kong we might even say, "Mo dak ding." In other words "indescribable"!'

Joe Lawson often ended a lecture of his with some Chinese saying, no doubt his intention being to annoy. But this time Charles knew he was right.

Both men fell silent as the horses, sensing their home nearing, quickened their pace.

In the back of the dray, legs dangling over the rear, scrawny bottom seated upon a heavily scrubbed-back stain of dried blood, Alwyn Stroud gazed about at the quiet surrounds and wondered what was to become of him.

7.

Alwyn Stroud had been at Burton Station for three months now. It had been hard at first. Very hard. Much harder than he could ever have imagined. He'd got over the worst of the shakes during the week he'd spent in Roebourne Gaol and he'd thought that would be the toughest part, because he'd never suffered from the shakes before. Not *really*. He'd never been sober long enough.

'Only one way to rid yourself of the tatas, boyo,' his dad used to say on the odd occasion he'd wake a little shaky from the grog, before handing him a bottle of the hard stuff.

But as Alwyn had now discovered, even worse than the tatas he'd experienced in gaol was what came after. The longing, the craving, the desperate desire for grog. Any sort of grog. Or anything that offered a similar kick to grog. Alwyn would have knocked back meths or kero if he could get his hands on them. But they hadn't let him, had they? Nina had made sure of that. She'd shackled his wrist to the bedpost of his bunk in her hut each night for a whole month so he couldn't sneak off to the native workers' camp, where they were bound to have grog. And then during the day, if she couldn't keep her eyes on him while he was doing whatever chores he'd been allotted, she'd lock him in the harness shed. Nina was tough all right.

Putting the boy in Nina's care had been Joe's idea.

'We'll let Nina look after him,' he'd told Charles, 'she'll know what to do. She's an alcoholic herself.'

'She's what?' Charles had been astounded. 'But she never touches the stuff.'

'That's because she's an alcoholic,' Joe had spelt out very slowly, with infinite patience.

'I never knew that.'

'There's a lot you don't know about Nina. She used to be a prostitute too.'

'*Nina?*' Charles couldn't believe what he was hearing. Nina was the virtual backbone of Burton Station, the homestead's housekeeper and cook with her very own hut right next door to the house.

'You've never told me any of this,' he said accusingly. *You're deliberately being irritating, Joe*, he thought.

'Didn't feel there was a need, old chap,' Joe replied. 'But with the arrival of the boy, I think it right you should know of her background, because I believe the two will be good for each other. Nina has no family of her own, you see, she lost everyone in the Flying Foam Massacre of 1868. In fact, I'd say she's probably one of the very few Jaburara mob still around.'

'Oh.' Charles felt instantly chastened, recognising there was a purpose to Joe's story. 'I didn't know that.' He'd heard of the infamous Flying Foam Massacre, which had taken place on Dampier Peninsula. Everyone had. The episode had been shameful, even in this part of the world notorious for its brutality. Roughneck men known to relish the slaughtering of natives had been officially sworn in as 'Special Constables' by the Government Administrator, Robert Sholl. These 'Special Constables' had been hired to avenge the Indigenous killing of several men who the Jaburara claimed had kidnapped and raped one of their women. As a result, the entire Jaburara mob had been all but wiped out.

And Nina belonged to that mob, Charles thought. *Of course*. He'd known she was Jaburara, but he'd never known she'd been part of the massacre.

'How sad,' he said. 'How terribly sad.'

'Yes,' Joe agreed. 'She was only eighteen at the time and with her whole extended family gone, she was utterly lost. When your Uncle Geoffrey came upon her, she was on her last legs, a hopeless alcoholic selling herself to the pearling lugger crews for grog and a roof over her head. He took her in and cared for her, got her off the grog and gave her a home. She'd be dead by now if it hadn't been for Geoffrey. Eventually, when she was healthy and sober, he employed her as his housekeeper and cook.'

Joe smiled, lightening the mood. 'So I think it would be a nice idea to put young Alwyn into her care. Who knows? The two might even become family to one another. What do you say, old chap?'

Charles returned the smile. 'I say it's a jolly fine idea, old chap.'

The plan had worked. Although now, three months down the track, Nina continued to keep an eagle eye on the boy.

She, of all people, knew that the temptation would always be there. She spread the word around the native workers' camp too, letting the men know to keep any grog well away from young Alwyn.

The men were happy to oblige. There was no unruly drunkenness among the local Ngarluma employed at Burton Station anyway, for intoxicating liquor was not allowed at the work camp. It was a known fact that they brewed their own 'sugar beer', which had quite a kick, but they were aware they'd be sacked if they hit the grog hard. Their work ethic was different, certainly, as most Aboriginal men's work ethic was. When they had the urge to go walkabout, they'd disappear at a moment's notice, but they'd come back to Burton Station when it suited them because they liked the Boss. They liked working for Charles Burton. They liked Joe Lawson too, but Charles Burton had become a bit of a hero since word had got around about how he'd saved the poor little half-breed from Roebourne Gaol. The boy would have spent the rest of his days in shackles and been worked to death on a blackfella chain gang. No place for a kid, not even a half-breed.

The men didn't have much time for those of mixed race as a rule, but they all agreed this kid who'd shot his white father was a sad case. What's more, they'd come to discover that, when you got to know him, young Alwyn was a nice boy. And he had a way with horses. The kid sure could ride.

It was true, Alwyn loved horses. So had his dad. Despite being a Welshman, old Cliffy could ride like a blackfella. But then, he'd spent more time with the blackfellas than the whites. Father and son had worked as itinerant stockmen, always drunk, but when they were in the saddle, you'd never know it. Even when they could barely walk, they could ride like the wind, and the horses obeyed their every touch. That's what old Cliffy called it – 'Having the touch, boyo, it's all about having the touch.' They'd invariably been given the sack, though, simply for not turning up.

Things were different now. Alwyn's life had undergone a radical change, and as his cravings had become manageable, he'd come to recognise the amazing fact that he now had someone akin to a mother in his life. Albeit a tough one.

'You a hard woman, Nina,' he told her on many an occasion.

'Yes,' she'd reply sternly, 'and I intend to stay that way. You need a hard woman, boy.'

There was no denying the closeness of the relationship they shared, however. They could very well have been mother and son, just the way Joe had hoped they might.

But Alwyn had gained far more than a mother at Burton Station, he'd gained a whole family. The boy worshipped the very ground Charles walked on, knowing only too well the hideous future from which Charles Burton had saved him. He'd seen those coffles of black men, chained together like animals. Charles Burton was both his father and his hero.

He had little brothers too. Little brothers who looked up to him, what's more. He had taught Edward and Harold a lot about this land. For instance, where to find witchetty grubs and how to eat them. They'd turned their noses up at first, refusing to eat them raw, blackfella style, but when Nina had agreed to cook their catch, frying the bugs to a crisp, they'd accepted the challenge, even enjoying the taste.

'Like chicken,' they'd said.

And just lately, in a tribute to the trust they now placed in Alwyn, they'd become bold enough to try the grubs raw. Edward had gone first, the way Edward always did. He'd held the bug by the head as instructed and bravely bitten off the body.

'Totally different,' he'd remarked, feigning nonchalance, 'more like nuts, almonds perhaps.'

Screwing his eyes up tightly so he didn't have to see the squirming bug, Harold had then followed suit, the way Harold always did.

'I like them cooked better,' he'd said, resisting the urge to vomit.

Alwyn had taught his little brothers about the eagles too.

'See,' he'd said, pointing skyward to two wedge-tailed eagles circling overhead. 'That mummy eagle and baby eagle. Baby eagle learn how to hunt. Mummy and baby circle like this, make sure animals down here can see 'em. Animals run away and hide to escape these two, but they don't see daddy eagle far away up high. He watch where animals go. Then he swoop down and catch 'em. This family work as team, you know? Mummy and daddy eagle, they mate for life. They teach baby before baby leaves nest. Eagles very smart.'

Harold squinted up at the sky, frantically searching. 'I can't see daddy eagle,' he said.

Alwyn's laugh was buoyant, confident, he was becoming quite a cocky lad, particularly in the presence of his little brothers. 'No, daddy eagle way, way up high. He can see from far, far away. All eagle can. You wait. He come.'

And suddenly there it was, a giant wedge-tailed eagle, swooping out of the vast blue, then plummeting at breakneck speed to earth, legs extended, to rise only seconds later, a baby rock wallaby grasped in its powerful talons.

'See?' Alwyn declared triumphantly. 'See? I tell you.'

The boys watched in awe as the three eagles united, circling higher and higher, finally to disappear from sight.

'They go home now,' Alwyn said. 'Time for their dinner.'

Edward and Harold did indeed look up to Alwyn Stroud. Which was a novelty for Alwyn. He'd never been looked up to before.

But there was one among his newly acquired family who, in sheer value alone, reigned supreme over all, and this was his little brothers' big sister, Victoria.

Victoria had made Alwyn Stroud her mission in life.

'The boy's fifteen years old, Father,' she'd insisted. 'He's fifteen years old and he's never once set foot inside a classroom. He can neither read nor write. It's outrageous. I intend to teach him the basic skills.'

Her attitude had come as quite a surprise to Charles, for she was currently consumed by her study of law.

'Very well, my dear,' he'd replied, 'if you're willing to give up some of your valuable study time, I see no reason why—'

'Two hours each morning, week days only,' she'd replied, her pretty girl's face, framed in its deep brown pretty girl's curls, stern and forbidding. 'I can spare that much of my time. Everyone deserves an education. It is a human right no-one should be denied.'

'I agree entirely,' Charles said with a smile. Victoria was becoming something of a martinet, he thought.

He'd proved right. Victoria had taken up her role with fierce intent and was now the sternest of taskmasters. *She's more than a martinet*, Charles thought as he watched young Alwyn being relentlessly hounded, *she's a downright bully*.

But Alwyn didn't mind being bullied. Victoria was forcing him to concentrate as he'd never concentrated before. He'd never concentrated upon anything other than the grog, where and how to get it. Now, when he was working with Victoria out on the back verandah, studying the letters on the page, trying to reproduce them with the pencil she'd taught him how to hold, he didn't even think of the grog. He was too busy learning to read and write.

Charles delighted in Alwyn's rehabilitation. With each passing month, the boy was growing stronger, his little brown body filling out, his confidence, too, gaining strength. Alwyn was still small in stature and probably always would be, but he was no longer scrawny, and no longer insecure.

Joe was right, Charles thought, *justice was served to the highest degree that day*. He was pleased he'd taken the action he had in that farce of a court case, which had so flouted British law. He was proud, too, of the part his children were playing in the boy's rehabilitation. It meant that, in several years' time, when they returned to England, Alwyn Stroud would be a healthy young man capable of standing on his own and earning a decent living. Joe would see to it that he was permanently employed here at Burton Station, if he wished to be.

'When we return to England' was a constant refrain in Charles' mind, for he had a plan. He'd always had a plan, although he'd never discussed it with his children. The most important factor in the deception of their lives was the ongoing and immutable belief that he was their father. Should his children be aware of a time limit to the deception, it could prove a distraction, which might make it difficult for them to play out their roles.

Charles' plan was quite simple. His intention was to pay off the debt he and his father owed Geoffrey Burton within five years. The fact that Uncle Geoffrey had died had in no way altered his plan. The debt remained a matter of honour, and when it had been repaid, he would return to England. Once there, the deception would be over. Charles would cease to exist. Charlotte and her children would have returned to Pendleton. Fifteen-year-old Edward would complete his education at Eton and be enrolled at Oxford in preparation for the role he was one day destined to play as the Squire of Pendleton.

Charles kept his father well informed of his progress, but even in their correspondence he remained 'Charles', and William responded in kind to his 'son', both aware of the threat should their letters be intercepted. The children were encouraged to include notes to their grandfather, but they too observed the rules, always referring to 'Father' in their correspondence. This had by now become simply a matter of course to Edward and Harold, who unreservedly accepted Charles as their father, appearing never to question the fact. Victoria was a little more difficult to read, but then Victoria always had been. And now, since she'd matured, more so than ever.

Dearest Charles, William had written in his most recent letter,

I am delighted to hear that your business dealings with the colourful Benny McCartney continue to prove fruitful. What a find, eh? How very like Geoffrey to have come up with such a bold idea, and how very fortuitous that your good friend, Joe Lawson, saw fit to advise you of the proposed venture despite being against it himself. Most importantly though, how very adventurous of you to follow through with the scheme. You are, as I have always said, dear boy, so very like your uncle. Daring, impetuous and as bold as brass, the two of you. Ready to take on the world, regardless of any risk or danger that might present itself. I do so miss my brother, Geoffrey, as you well know, but he lives on in you, son, I swear he does. I am so very proud of you, Charles ...

There was always a hidden message to Charlotte in her father's letters. And these hidden messages were very precious to her, reminding her as they did of just who she was.

Despite Geoffrey Burton's untimely death, which had prevented him from carrying out his audacious plan to join forces with 'the colourful Benny McCartney', and despite Joe Lawson's initial warnings, the idea had indeed proved fruitful.

'I doubt it could possibly come to anything,' Joe had advised Charles when, shortly after their first meeting, he'd told him of Geoffrey's plan. 'Benny's a hopeless old drunk, as I warned your uncle on many an occasion. Hardly the sort of chap with whom to go into business.'

'You say the man has talent though.'

'Oh, yes, he certainly has talent. That is, if you can keep him sober long enough for him to make any particular use of it. He normally works for just enough money to keep himself in the drink.'

'No harm checking things out though, eh?' Charles had questioned. 'I'm here to make money, after all. The Burton Station mortgage isn't going to pay itself off, and I intend to investigate any possible venture that might hasten the process.'

Burton Station's business in stock was continuing to make a profit. Sheep and beef products were selling well, and a recent sideline of horse trading via Singapore was proving a bonus. Charles, however, was eager to ensure he meet his five-year deadline in paying off his uncle's debt, and possibly with a little time to spare.

'Right you are then, old chap,' Joe had replied affably. 'We'll call in on Benny tomorrow. Better leave good and early so we get there before he hits the bottle.'

They'd ridden to the bustling township of Cossack first thing the following morning, where they'd visited Benny in his dilapidated one-room shack that stood not far from the water's edge and barely fifty yards from the old stone wharf. Which was convenient for Benny as he dealt in pearls, and had done so for the past thirty years or more.

Benny McCartney had turned out to be as colourful a character as Joe had painted him. An Englishman somewhere in his late sixties, he had a rural accent that was impossible to pinpoint, as he'd spent the whole of his adult life travelling the world.

'Don't know where I comes from anymore,' he said with a jagged smile displaying the lack, here and there, of several teeth, 'but I s'pose I'd own to bein' from around these parts, Cossack havin' been home for a good long time now.'

He'd welcomed them warmly into his shack and was particularly delighted to meet Charles.

'Oh, my lad,' he said with a fervent handshake, 'I was so saddened to hear of your uncle's death. What a *good* man. What a *fine* man.' Each emphasis was given an added squeeze of the hand. 'We was real good friends, Geoffrey and me. I shall miss him sorely, I swear I shall.'

Being not yet mid-morning, Benny was stone-cold sober, but eager to socialise. He always enjoyed a good chat. 'Care to join me?' he asked, raising a bottle of cheap whisky, and when they declined the offer, he said, 'You won't mind if I do,' which was not a question at all. 'I can get you a cuppa if you'd like,' he said as he poured himself a drink, 'but it'll take a while, I haven't stoked 'er up yet.' He gestured at the wood stove.

They said they were quite happy without, thank you, so he poured them each a glass of water from the jug that sat on the bench in the corner and they walked outside to the small front verandah, where they settled down to talk, Benny placing the whisky bottle on the floor beside his chair.

Charles opened the conversation. 'Joe here tells me you're a man with a rare gift, Benny. He says you're a great judge of pearl.'

Joe had actually been directly quoting Geoffrey Burton at the time. 'He's a great judge of pearl, Joe,' Geoffrey had enthused. 'It's a rare gift. You should just see him at work. Why, he can peel pearl like no-one I've ever seen! And he can clear them of all blemishes in a way that enhances their value enormously ...'

'Doesn't mean you should go into business with a hopeless drunk,' Joe had patiently argued, and not for the first time.

But Joe now left the talking to Charles Burton, aware that, just like his uncle, young Charles was determined to explore this avenue.

'Oh, yes, I know pearl all right,' Benny said, 'and pearl *shell* too. In some parts of the world, mother-of-pearl shell, or nacre as it's known, has more value than the pearl itself. Learned all that in French Polynesia way back in the forties when I set out on me travels, little more than a lad I was. Course they have black pearls there.'

'Black?' Charles queried. He'd never heard of black pearls.

'Aye. Black, or dark grey, some of 'em even a silvery colour. Pretty, but nowhere near the value of the ones we get hereabouts. I used to peel them black pearls for me bed 'n' tucker. Sell 'em to the vendors at the markets who'd make bracelets and necklaces and such.' He took a healthy swig of his whisky. 'I liked it way out there on those islands.'

Charles was intrigued. 'I don't know much about that part of the world.'

'Oh, it's a wondrous place, my young friend, a truly wondrous place. Some islands are mountain peaks that rise straight up out of the sea and into the clouds. Especially the northern islands, the ones called the Marquesas. Way, way, way out there in the middle of the ocean they are, a million miles from anywhere, these great volcanic peaks that reach up to the heavens. A wondrous sight.' He shook his head in admiration and took a further swig of whisky.

'But I was restless to move on, with such a lot of world left to see, you know, the way young men are. So I travelled. I travelled and I travelled, until finally I ended up here. That'd be close to thirty years ago now, I'd say, and I tell you what ...' another shake of his head, a final swig to empty his glass '... those days in French Polynesia, all that learnin' about pearls, it stood me in right good stead here at Cossack. I hadn't forgotten a thing, and I've learned a great deal more over all this time, I can tell you that much. And I've taught many other pearl workers their trade too. There's quite a number around these parts owe their talents to me.'

He laughed as he picked up the bottle, refilled his glass and sat back, prepared to reminisce. 'There were many in need of teachin' too, for it was still early days when I got here, and the business of pearling was only just startin' up. The local Ngarluma mob had been gatherin' oysters in the shallows since the beginnin' of time, and the European settlers were quick to notice the mother-of-pearl necklets they were wearin', for decoration and such. The natives used the shells to make fish hooks and the like too, very inventive, these locals. Well, it didn't take long for the Europeans to realise there was money to be had out of this shell business and before you knew it there was any number of small luggers working the shallow banks, hiring teams of natives to do their diving for 'em. The skippers were after the shell at first, nacre sold very well in London, mother-of-pearl buttons bein' so popular and all. But after that ...' A shake of his head and a hefty swig of his whisky.

'Oh, my goodness, you wouldn't believe it, Cossack became the pearling capital of the west. Nah, nah, more than that, far more, this 'ere place became the pearling capital of the whole darn country. A sleepy little port we were back in them days, and then we turned into a thrivin' town.' He waved a hand around expansively. 'I mean just look at us now. Thrivin' we are, thrivin'.'

Joe had been expecting Charles to interrupt the old man's reminiscences; the young Englishman must surely wish to speed things along. But he hadn't, so Joe continued to sit patiently waiting, offering not a word. Joe was the most patient of men.

'Course it hadn't been long before the shallow banks was fished out,' Benny continued, 'and after that, the boats got bigger. They needed luggers and schooners that were built for deep water. And that's when the divers changed too. Well, most of them did. Most of the locals didn't want to dive deep, you see, they didn't like the equipment needed for deep diving. So teams was brought in from Asia, Malays for the most part, some Chinese and Japanese too.'

He gave a proud chortle. 'We got quite a mix of folk around here at Cossack,' he said, raising his glass as if in a toast before taking a swig. 'And though a good deal of the pearling industry's movin' north to Broome these days, we're still goin' strong after all these years. As we will be, I swear, for many a year yet.'

He raised his glass again in another toast to Cossack, which Charles took as a direct invitation to get down to business.

'And you intend to remain an active part of this industry, do you?' The query was sharp, authoritative.

'Eh?' Benny was bewildered by the brusqueness of his tone.

'You're prepared to practise your craft on a business level along the lines my uncle discussed with you?'

'Oh.' Benny was more than bewildered, he was taken completely by surprise. He'd thought these two had just popped in for a natter, that Joe had wanted to introduce him to Geoffrey's young nephew, newly arrived in the area.

'Well, yes, we did have a bit of a chat some time ago, Geoffrey and me,' he admitted. 'About him gettin' together with a couple of pearlin' skippers I know, and me workin' alongside some of the lads I'd trained. Just a bit of a chat, that's all it was, over a glass or two while he watched me work. He liked watchin' me work, Geoffrey did ...'

'I'm here for more than a bit of a chat, Benny,' Charles said, interrupting briskly, 'I'm here to discuss the business venture my uncle had in mind. So let's get on with it, shall we?'

And they had.

'Firstly, where's the real value in pearling?' Charles demanded. 'Is it the shell or the pearl?'

Benny put his glass down. He recognised the question was from one with little, or no, knowledge of the business. However, this young man was smart and genuinely wanted his curiosity satisfied.

'Well, now.' Benny looked Charles directly in the eye. 'The shell has the least work to it. Its inside is lined with mother-of-pearl, and that's what people want. They make buttons and bracelets and such. All we have to do is clean it, pack it safe and send it away.'

'Right.' Charles nodded. 'Purchase, pack and export. I see.'

'Yeah, but the pearl itself is a different game altogether. You see, pearls ain't a natural part of an oyster. All there is inside the shell is the oyster itself, what you eat. With pearls, what happens is a bit of muck or a grain of sand or whatever gets inside the shell and the oyster doesn't like that. So, it puts a thin layer of nacre – that's what mother-of-pearl is called – around the foreign thing to protect itself from harm. And it keeps putting more and more thin layers around it until it gets quite big. That's how a pearl is formed. When you get hold of the pearl it's usually dull and not much to look at, but when you "peel" it' – Benny wiggled his fingers in front of his face – 'you see the bright nacre show up beautiful and then people will pay a lot of money for it.'

'So, peeling is the difficult part, is that what you're saying?'

'Oh, my word. You use a microscope and a knife. A very, very *fine* knife,' Benny said, 'and you delicately peel off the thin layer of skin. Like peeling an onion, it is, but not peeling the layers as such, more like the very fine film in *between* the layers, you know what I mean?' He looked at Joe Lawson and winked. 'And I'm one of the only people around here who can do it right.'

'So, you're saying, there's not a pearl in every oyster?'

'Oh no!' The old man shook his head. 'Whenever one of the lads 'ere is shucking the oyster and finds a pearl, or the start of a pearl, they bring it to me and if there's enough of a pearl there, I do the peeling.'

'Can any of your lads do the peeling?'

'Oh yeah, most of them can. A lot of the time they bugger it up though. It's a fine art, you know. Mostly I have 'em just shucking the oysters and polishing the inside of the shell to bring up the nacre shine. They get to eat a lot of oysters, and whatever they don't eat, we sell to the pubs. Then they pack up the shells for shipping to London.'

'I see.' Charles smiled. 'So that's how it's done. Righto, Benny. I think we're in business.'

Things had moved quickly after that. Barely a week later, Charles had met the pearling skippers, and in the months that followed, he'd had long-overdue repairs made to Benny's shack, adding a workshop extension to the side, which would allow additional space for several more pearl workers. These were men Benny had already lined up, each of whom had been personally trained by him in the art of polishing nacre and peeling pearl.

Also, during this time, Charles had made direct contact via his father's many connections with Streeters of London, arranging deals for the supply of expertly treated nacre and prime pearls.

'We're off and running,' he'd proudly announced to Joe, and his words had proved prophetic. By late 1889, after just one year of production, they'd made three thousand pounds from their dealings in the pearl industry. Benny, although the same drunk he'd always been, now appeared happy to work for more than just his alcohol supply. These days, he approached his labours with fresh application, enjoying the close company of fellow workers, the camaraderie it offered and the productivity that resulted.

Geoffrey Burton's plan to form a partnership with the 'hopeless old drunk' Benny McCartney was proving a winner, thanks to his young nephew, Charles.

***

But it was now late 1890, well into their second year of production, and they'd hit a snag. A snag, as it turned out, of considerable proportion.

The problem may well have arisen from the very source of Joe's initial concern – Benny's drunkenness – but Joe was not one to say 'I told you so'. Rather, it was his style to address and remedy the situation.

'You did warn me about him after all,' Charles said, prepared to accept sole responsibility. 'I should have known something like this would happen, shouldn't I? And it'll go on happening while Benny remains a drunk.'

'No, no, old chap,' Joe protested. 'It's not altogether Benny's fault. It's the criminal scum that abounds in these parts. When word gets around that someone's successful, these scum creep out from wherever it is they've been skulking.'

'But Benny could've protected the place, couldn't he? I mean, good God, there's a perfectly good lock on the door, the whole place is secure, I'd made sure of that from the start.' Charles' voice rose in frustration. 'But the door was wide open and he was passed out on the floor, an invitation to one and all.'

They were back at Burton Station, discussing the robbery of the previous night, having reported it that morning to Raymond Hatley, the resident constable at Cossack Police Station. Much purpose that he served, they both agreed, for it was next to nothing apart from filing reports when necessary. Ray was a nice enough bloke, but he'd lost any bite he might once have had and should have been put out to pasture long ago.

'Must've been professionals,' Ray had said as he'd focussed on his paperwork. 'Didn't hear a thing myself. Mind you, there's always a bit of racket around here, particularly on a Thursday, which is payday for some,' he went on, scrawling away laboriously. 'My new young copper was over at the pub sorting out a ruckus or he'd have come upon them on his night patrol. But the thieves probably knew that. Yep, professionals, I'd say.'

They'd not been robbed of much money. Benny kept little cash in his old shack, and they wouldn't have entrusted him with money anyway, but there had been a wealth of product. Perfectly treated nacre and pearls all neatly packaged, awaiting collection and shipment the following day.

'The thieves would have known that too,' Ray had said when they'd told him.

'Just as well Benny was passed out,' Joe remarked. 'If they were professionals like Ray said they were, they'd have slit his throat to keep things quiet. I must say,' he added thoughtfully, 'I'm rather surprised this hasn't happened earlier.'

To Charles, in a state of anger as much with himself as poor Benny, who was back there in Cossack, riddled with remorse and no doubt again drinking himself into oblivion, Joe's complaisance was intensely irritating.

'So, what do you propose we do,' Charles demanded, 'just sit and wait for it to happen all over again?'

'No.' As usual, Joe refused to be riled. 'We organise some form of protection for Benny, that's what we do. We pay someone to look after him.'

'And exactly who would you suggest?'

'No idea.' Joe ignored the disdain in Charles' voice. 'But I know of whom I would enquire if I were you, old chap.'

'Oh, really?' The tone was positively icy now. 'And who might that be?'

'Your good friend Sergeant Fry, that's who. Fry is Sergeant of Police for this entire area of the Pilbara, including Cossack, he thinks the world of you and would do anything you ask of him. Within reason, of course,' Joe added. 'And I believe your seeking his advice would be entirely within reason.'

'Oh.' Charles' irritation abated as he realised this was an excellent suggestion. 'Yes,' he said a little tightly, aware he'd been unnecessarily acerbic. 'I'll ride into Roebourne tomorrow morning and pay him a visit.'

'What a jolly good idea.'

Joe's smile was so amiable it ignited a further surge of annoyance in Charles. That damned Eastern inscrutability was infuriating.

The following morning, as he was saddling his horse at the hitching rail out the front of the house, young Alwyn appeared by his side.

'You goin' for a ride, Boss? Can I come with you?' the boy asked eagerly. He often accompanied the Boss on a ride, usually counting the stock numbers, or checking on fences that might be in need of repair.

Charles hesitated. This was a business trip into town after all.

'It's Saturday, so no lessons with Victoria,' Alwyn added, 'and I chopped wood for the stove, done my work, I have.'

'Shouldn't you check with Nina?' Charles asked.

At that very moment, Nina appeared on the front verandah carrying a rattan carpet beater and a rug, which she placed over the railing. She was keeping her eye on the boy as she always did. She met Charles' eyes and gave him a nod.

'Would you like to pay a visit to an old friend of ours in Roebourne?' Charles asked, and when Alwyn looked up at him, confused, he said, 'I'm off to visit Sergeant Fry at the Police Quarters. You're welcome to come along for the ride if you'd like.'

Alwyn paused. Such a decision warranted serious thought, the image of Roebourne Gaol seared into his brain as it was. And the Police Quarters was right in front of the gaol. Then he remembered the big policeman who'd looked so fearsome, but had turned out to be not such a bad bloke at all. That copper had helped the Boss get him off free.

The decision made itself in only a moment. Anything was worth a ride with the Boss. Even the sight of Roebourne Gaol.

'Yeah, Boss,' he said, 'I'm comin' into Roebourne with you,' and he scampered off to the home paddock to whistle up his horse. The mare always came to his whistle within seconds. She adored him. They adored each other.

It was late morning when they tethered their horses to the hitching rail outside the Police Quarters, and the big Sergeant greeted them heartily at the front door.

'Mr Burton, sir, what a welcome surprise,' he said, shaking Charles' hand effusively. 'And young Alwyn Stroud, I do declare.' He shook Alwyn's hand too. 'My, my, but you've filled out, boy. They must be looking after you well.'

He ushered them both inside, Alwyn thankful to lose sight of the gaol that loomed so ominously in the background.

'May I offer you a cup of tea?' Fry asked. 'Constable Royden here would be happy to oblige.' He indicated the young policeman who stood behind the front counter.

'No, thank you, Sergeant,' Charles replied, 'my visit will be brief. I don't wish to take up too much of your time, and work awaits me back at Burton Station.'

'Of course, of course, come in, come in.' Fry led the way through to his office. 'So,' he asked once they were seated, 'to what do I owe the honour, Mr Burton?'

'I seek your advice,' Charles said, and he went on to explain the sequence of events over the past twenty-four hours, the burglary at Cossack on the Thursday night, the discovery and reporting of the incident on the Friday.

'I see, I see,' Fry said, stroking his beard thoughtfully. 'And Ray suggested it may be the work of professionals who'd been observing your work premises, you say?'

'Yes, and Joe and I tend to agree. The thieves would have known we had product awaiting shipment and they would have known Benny as the hopeless drunk he is. They no doubt witnessed him pass out, leaving the place wide open.' Charles added caustically, 'He certainly made things easy for them.'

'Yes, yes, I see. And the new young constable I placed there recently was up at the pub sorting out a ruckus, you say?'

'Yes, that's what Ray told us. So, as you can see, Sergeant, we have something of a problem, and that problem is Benny. He can't be trusted when he's in the drink, which is virtually all the time. Joe thinks we should employ someone to look after him, and he suggested I ask your advice. We must provide personal protection for Benny or this will become an ongoing predicament.'

'And you're after my suggestion as to who this protector should be?'

'Yes, Sergeant, that's exactly what I'm after. Who he might be and where I might find him.'

The big policeman grinned broadly. 'The answer is staring us right in the face, sir. I have the very man for you, and he's there on the very spot where you need him.'

Charles looked a query.

'The new fellow I employed just a month or so back. I placed him in Cossack because Ray's getting a little past his prime and we need a fresh pair of fists on permanent call in a port town like Cossack. I'm sure young Constable Jeff will be only too happy to receive some added coin, given the meagre wages he's on. And I shall be happy to turn a blind eye to his extra-curricular duties.'

'Why, that sounds ideal, Sergeant.' Charles was delighted by the simplicity of the plan. 'I'm most deeply obliged to you.'

Fry gave a conspiratorial wink. 'It's a wee bit irregular, so we'll keep the arrangement between ourselves, but I'm sure it'll work out just fine.

'I shall be doing the rounds of the district next week,' he went on. 'I'll make Cossack my first port of call on Monday and stay overnight, as I always do. What say we meet at the police station there mid-morning and I'll introduce you to Jeff. You might then wish to pay a call on Benny and discuss the matter between the three of you. How does that sound?'

'It sounds like a marvellous idea,' Charles replied and stood, young Alwyn jumping to his feet beside him.

Fry rose also and the two men shook hands.

'You'll like Jeff,' he said, 'nice lad. Only around twenty, but he can certainly handle himself. Been at sea since he was ten years old, and my, oh my, can he fight!'

He accompanied them to the front door.

'I shall look forward very much to meeting young Jeff,' Charles said as they parted company.

Fry stood watching Charles Burton and the boy mount their horses and set off down the street. *Jeff's name isn't really Jeff at all, is it?* he thought. But he couldn't for the life of him remember what the hell it was, something French sounding and far too complicated. 'Jeff' had been a far easier choice.

As Sergeant Fry closed the front door and returned to his office, he remembered that time, over a month ago now, when he'd first met young Jeff.

He'd been doing his monthly district rounds, staying the night in Cossack, before moving on to the next town the following morning, and he'd been hanging about in the shadows observing the Weld, one of the town's two pubs. The Weld was a shanty-like mess full of drunken pearlers and sundry villains and there was bound to be a bit of a barney before long. He wouldn't intervene, though, until it appeared things might be getting out of hand.

Then from nearby he'd heard voices, ugly and demanding.

'Hand over your purse, boy,' one voice said.

'Come on now, whatever you're carrying, give it over,' said another.

A brief scuffle followed as the victim protested, and the tussle between the three drew them out into the shaft of light that spilled from the Weld.

From where he stood in the shadows, Fry could see them quite clearly, two thugs and a young man. He was about to intervene, but it became quickly apparent there was no need.

In defending himself, the young man hit out swiftly, his punches potentially lethal, powerful, first one thug, then the other, each blow finding its mark.

Fry watched on in admiration. The attackers had become the victims, they didn't stand a chance, and within less than a minute, both lay unconscious on the ground.

After which, the young man straightened up, breathing deeply. But Fry could tell that he wasn't gasping for breath, he was deliberately and methodically filling his lungs as if preparing himself for a further attack.

Fry couldn't resist. From the shadows where he stood, he started a slow round of applause. He watched as the young man's hands once again balled into fists, and the lad turned, fully prepared to meet whatever fresh aggressor this might be.

That's when Fry stepped out to confront him, still clapping.

To the young man, the big policeman obviously appeared a threatening figure of authority.

'Are you a fighter, son?' Fry asked.

'No, sir, Sergeant. It was an accident.'

'I know all about accidents, boy,' Fry said, 'and that was no accident. Where did you learn to use your fists like that?'

'Ran away from home and I've been at sea since I was ten years old, Sergeant. You learn to look after yourself or you don't last long.'

Fry eyed him up and down. 'I'm guessing you're new to the Pilbara, am I right?'

'Yes, sir.'

'And I'm guessing you're looking for gold, am I right there too? All you fresh-faced, young new arrivals are heading for the goldfields around Mallina way.'

'Er, that's correct, sir, yes.'

'You won't find it, son. Not on the surface, anyway. Not anymore. These days you've got to dig for it.'

'I don't have near enough money for prospecting yet.'

'Right then.' Fry nodded. He'd thought as much. 'I've got just the job for you. Until you're wealthy enough to go seek your fortune in the soil, that is.' He smiled. 'I can offer you free accommodation and ... barely enough money to get by.'

'What would I have to do?' The young man tried not to sound eager, but the offer of free accommodation already had him interested.

'You'd serve as my assistant here in Cossack.'

The lad was clearly astounded. 'Are you asking me to be a copper?'

'Police officer!' Fry growled, then checked himself. The boy had meant no disrespect. 'Yes,' he admitted, 'I am. You'd be a junior constable. I'd swear you in and you'd learn as you go, that's the way we tend to do things around here.' Aware the explanation sounded a little lame, he shook his head, admitting to his frustration. 'Son, I need someone who can use his fists and you're it!'

'Ah, well, um ...'

'Don't even think of saying no. By the way, what's your name?'

'Jean-François Fabron.'

'Christ alive, boy,' he exclaimed, 'that's far too long, 'I'll never remember it, let alone spell it. "Jon Frans" something, you said?'

'Yes sir. Jean-François ...'

'Right. Let's make it J.F.' That sounded a lot easier, he decided. But then he had another thought. J.F? No, we can do much better than that. 'Better still,' he said, 'we'll call you Jeff.'

They were interrupted by a series of groans. The men on the ground were regaining consciousness. Fry cuffed the wrists of the two together.

'C'mon,' he said, 'help me get this scum down to the station and I'll swear you in.'

Yep, that's how it happened all right, Fry now thought, glancing through the reports that sat on his desk, but not really seeing them as his mind retraced the happenings of that night.

The following day, Constable Jeff had been ensconced in a wooden shed at the rear of Cossack Police Station that held a bed, a chair and a small table. An outhouse stood twenty feet away with a bore-water showerhead next to it. Young Jeff had been quite happy with his accommodation. And he still was.

But what the heck was his real name? Fry wondered. *That fancy double-barrelled French moniker, what was it? Funny too, because he doesn't sound at all French. What the heck was it?* He couldn't for the life of him remember. From that day on, the boy had become simply Jeff.

Sergeant James Arthur Fry liked Jeff, and was genuinely glad he was able to steer the boy in the direction of Charles Burton, who was known as a just man, one who would pay well for the services of the 'protector' he needed. Fry was glad also that he was able to be of service to Charles Burton, a man he deeply admired.

He hoped the meeting between the two on Monday would go well and that the deal would prove beneficial to both.

But he also hoped, perhaps even prayed, that this new arrangement wouldn't mean he'd lose Jeff to the goldfields in the near future. Young Constable Jeff was a damn fine cop.

8.

Jean-François Fabron was born John Francis Boyle in the very heart of the City of London. His mother died when he was eight years old, and, shortly after, he ran away to escape the tyrant of a father whom he despised. For two years he lived on the streets of Whitechapel and Limehouse, a member of one of the many urchin gangs referred to as 'guttersnipes', who managed somehow to survive and even thrive in old London Town.

At the age of ten, he stowed away on a French cargo ship bound for Marseille but was quickly discovered and put to work as a cabin boy. Life aboard the SS *Mistral* was hard, but John Boyle, already toughened by the back streets of London, met every demand made of him, relished his freedom and developed a great love of the sea.

The boy's devotion to duty did not go unnoticed by the skipper of the *Mistral*, Captain Pierre Fabron, who took John under his wing with the intention of protecting him from the other youthful members of the crew, of whom there were a number, French lads for the most part. The pecking order being prominent aboard ship, young John, still only a boy, was destined to be bullied.

But Fabron soon realised young John had no need of protection, that he was already quicker with his fists than lads five years his senior. Yet there was no vestige of violence about the boy, who was fair-haired and good-looking. If anything, the first impression he made was one of innocence. But when confronted, he was fearless, and could certainly fight back. All of which Fabron found quite remarkable.

When they arrived in Marseille, Pierre Fabron invited John to remain aboard as a member of the crew, an offer John eagerly accepted, and over the following years the young English boy learned much from this man he so admired. He learned not only seamanship, but how to read and to write and also how to master both languages. It wasn't long before he was bilingual, even at times thinking of himself as French.

Pierre Fabron had by now become far more to John than his skipper and mentor. Pierre Fabron had become the man John looked up to as the father he wished he'd had.

Then in 1884, disaster struck. The *Mistral* was wrecked in a typhoon off the coast of Tahiti. The vessel was destroyed and the crew lost at sea, or so it was presumed. Fourteen-year-old John Boyle, however, made it close to the shore of Moorea, where he was rescued by a local fisherman.

He found himself in Papeete on the French Polynesian island of Tahiti, but search as he might there was no sign of any other survivors, including the ship's skipper, Pierre Fabron.

That was when John Francis Boyle became Jean-François Fabron, a tribute to the man he saw as his father.

For the following three years, Jean-François worked aboard a supply schooner that serviced the French Polynesian

Islands from Tahiti as far north as the Marquesas Islands, almost a thousand miles north-east of Papeete. He grew to love the Tahitian and Marquesan islanders, gentle people that they were, and would have stayed living happily among them.

Until another disaster struck, claiming the lives of so many he loved, leaving Jean-François devastated. He could no longer stay in this land that carried nothing for him but heartbreak.

Then came the day he met the two Australians who offered escape, who boasted of their country as 'the place to be'. Young men in their early twenties, they had embarked upon their great adventure. 'We're off to see the world,' they said, 'but there's really only one place to be.' The gold strikes of Australia were 'the order of the day', they told him. After they'd satisfied their itch to travel, they were going back to make their fortune on the goldfields that were 'popping up all over the country'.

'Australia's the future for any young man who wants to get rich,' they declared.

So, Jean-François embarked upon the next leg of his own adventure, arriving in Sydney, New South Wales, on January 26th, 1888, a day which, upon discovering it to be the centenary date of Australia's first European settlement, he took to be most auspicious.

In need of funds to undertake his search for gold, he secured a job on board an Australian cargo ship and, in the winter of July 1889, found himself in Perth, Western Australia, or rather Fremantle. It was in one of Fremantle's many rough pubs that he heard the story of young Jimmy Withnell of Mallina Station, 'which is way up north between Roebourne and Port Hedland', the man at the bar told him.

'Two years ago, it was,' the man said. 'Young Jimmy was out in the scrub, and he picked up a stone to chuck at a crow that had knocked over his tuckerbag. Then he noticed there were flecks of gold in the stone. So, he took a good look around and blow me down, he found there were nuggets just the same all over the place. Strewn about like manna from heaven they were, all these stones, flickering away.

'I tell you, mate,' the man declared, 'it was that boy who personally discovered the Pilbara gold, and folks have been flocking up there ever since. True as I'm standing here, every word true.'

But there was a fellow drinker seated nearby in the pub's crowded bar eager for a bit of one-upmanship.

'Yep,' he agreed, raising his voice so everyone could be in on the joke, 'but you wanna know the real funny part to that story? The Withnell kid took the stone into Roebourne to be assayed, and when the Government Resident found out it was the real thing, he telegrammed the Colonial Secretary in Perth. His telegram read: *Jimmy Withnell picked up a stone to shy at a crow*, but the bloke was so excited he forgot to add anything else. The reply he got back said: *Did he really? What happened to the crow?*'

Everyone in the bar burst out laughing. The story was famous. Some had heard it, some hadn't, but those who had all knew it to be true.

The story was enough for Jean-François Fabron. Inspired to investigate, he set off for the Pilbara like many a young man before him.

Arriving in Cossack in the late spring of 1890, it was there he'd met Sergeant James Arthur Fry, and it was there Jean-François Fabron had become simply 'Jeff'. He'd been a little confounded at the time and in many ways still was. Jeff. It had happened so quickly and it took some getting used to. He still wasn't quite sure exactly *how* it had happened. But Jeff he was. Constable Jeff. And he was stationed at the port town of Cossack.

***

'This is Constable Jeff,' Sergeant Fry bluntly announced. Then followed a more formal introduction. 'Jeff, this is Mr Burton of Burton Station, whom I wish to inform you happens also to be appointed Justice of the Peace for this area.'

Fry thought it necessary to add this piece of information, which Jeff, being new to the Pilbara, was probably unaware of, simply because he didn't want to appear to be doing a favour merely for a 'friend'. He would rather it be apparent he was prepared to stretch the rules just a little in order to oblige a man of great significance to the community.

Charles offered his hand. 'Good to meet you, Jeff.'

'How do you do, sir.'

The two shook.

Although they'd not met previously, Jeff had certainly heard of Charles Burton. Burton Station itself was well known to all, and he was aware also that this was the man who was in partnership with old Benny McCartney.

'I must apologise, Mr Burton,' he said, 'for my failure

to prevent the robbery that took place at your workshop premises last Thursday. Unfortunately, at the time I was—'

'Yes, I know,' Charles interrupted, 'you were sorting out a ruckus at the Weld. Constable Hatley told me.'

Constable Raymond Hatley was currently nowhere to be seen. Upon arrival, Sergeant Fry had sent him off to do the morning rounds, aware it was essential the three of them have a private meeting at the police station.

'Nevertheless, sir,' Jeff went on, 'I feel guilty such a thing should happen on my watch.'

'No need for apology, Constable,' Charles assured him. 'You can hardly be in all places at once. The thieves were professionals, we've decided, and Benny had left the place wide open, literally inviting them in. So ...' He gave a helpless shrug that conveyed all.

Charles found the young Constable Jeff impressive. He'd expected to meet a thug. 'Been at sea since he was ten years old, and my, oh my, can he fight,' Fry had said, which had certainly sounded descriptive of a thug. But this young man carried himself well and was good-looking to the point of being handsome. He was well-spoken too, his voice virtually accentless. *Intriguing*, Charles thought, *I wonder where he comes from.*

'Which brings us to the matter at hand,' Fry said. 'Mr Burton has a proposition to put to you, Jeff, regarding the vulnerability of his premises here at Cossack.'

He gave a nod to Charles, which said, *Over to you.*

In his customary manner, Charles got straight to the point. 'As you've no doubt gathered, Constable, old Benny

McCartney is a liability to my business. The man's an expert with pearls and the most talented worker there is, but not when he's drunk, which is most of the time. I'm willing, therefore, to pay you one pound a week to keep an eye on him.'

Sergeant Fry couldn't quite believe what he'd just heard. *A whole pound a week!* he thought. *Crikey, five bob'd be enough, surely. Ten at the very outside.*

His surprise and the pause that followed may have been readable, for he realised that Jeff had turned to see his reaction. But perhaps the young man was just seeking permission.

'I'm happy for you to accept Mr Burton's extremely generous offer, Jeff,' he said magnanimously, 'so long as you make sure this in no way interferes with your policing duties.'

'Yes, sir.'

'In any event, given the thieving incident last week, it would be within your duties to ensure Mr McCartney's premises were locked up at the end of each workday, would it not?'

'Yes, sir, it would.'

'We need say nothing of the added remuneration Mr Burton has kindly offered for a little further attention, however,' Fry added. 'It's somewhat unorthodox and could lead to misinterpretation.'

'Yes, sir, I understand.'

'Well, then …' As far as Fry was concerned, the meeting was over. 'I suggest, Mr Burton, that the two of you now pay a visit to Mr McCartney and inform him of your arrangement.'

His look to Charles said, *About which I know nothing.*

'Yes, Sergeant,' Charles agreed, 'that is exactly what we shall do.' He shook Fry's hand with fervour. 'I am deeply grateful to you, believe me, I am.'

As they walked out the open front door, Fry heard Charles Burton's friendly query of the young policeman.

'What's your first name, Constable?'

Fry allowed no time for the young man to answer. 'Jeff,' he called after them. 'He's just Jeff.'

Once they were outside, Charles looked a query.

'Yes,' Jean-François replied, 'Jeff. I'm just Jeff.' Things were easier that way.

They chatted about the additional duties Charles would require of Jeff as they walked the several hundred yards or so along the waterfront to Benny's shack and the workshop, and once there, the meeting lasted barely ten minutes.

'Yes, I understand, Boss, course I do. I really, really do, and I can't begin to tell you how sorry—'

'Yes, yes, I know you're sorry, Benny, you've told me any number of times,' Charles replied brusquely. They'd stepped out onto the shoaly shore where they couldn't be overheard by the other workers, and Charles had briefly explained the new arrangement to Benny, Constable Jeff nodding agreement.

'So, this is the way it will be from now on,' Charles concluded. 'A bit of added protection, that's all. Constable Jeff, here, will pop in on you from time to time to check work is going well, and above all, that the premises are kept secure.'

Benny nodded vigorously at Constable Jeff. The two knew each other, not well, but in amiable enough passing fashion.

'Yes, yes, Boss, got all that.' More nods.

Benny, at this stage of the day quite sober, presented a somewhat pathetic figure. Still squirming with a mix of guilt and remorse, he was genuinely ashamed of himself, and it showed in his manner. His use of the term 'Boss' was usually delivered in jovial fashion, he and Charles Burton were after all 'partners'. Well, *sort of* partners, he'd supposed. But now the use of 'Boss' was subservient to the extreme. Benny was only too grateful Charles Burton was prepared to remain in business with him.

'Leave you with it then, Benny,' Charles said, 'I'll let you get back to work.' He turned abruptly, heading back to the police station, where his horse was tethered.

'Yes, Boss, right you are, Boss.'

Jeff, who'd been silent throughout the meeting, apart from an initial 'hello' to Benny, gave the old man a nod. 'See you tomorrow, Benny,' he said, and joined Charles. Not a word had been uttered about the money that was to change hands for this 'added protection', which was just as it should be. No-one needed to know.

It was close to midday the following morning when Jeff called around to check on Benny. He was disappointed to note from a distance that the old man was sprawled out on the mothy sofa that sat on his front verandah, glass in hand, whisky bottle on the floor beside him.

Damn it, this won't do, Jeff thought, *I'll have to drill a bit of sense into him right from the start.* But he decided to opt for the amicable approach rather than play the bully. It would be simpler all round if they remained friends.

'Morning, Benny,' he called, 'taking an early lunch break, are we?' He could see the other pearl workers at their benches in the open-sided workshop area. 'Not yet midday ... a bit premature wouldn't you say?'

'Well, well,' Benny called back, 'if it isn't my new bodyguard. Or should I say, as of yesterday, my new gaoler.'

'Bodyguard will do,' Jeff replied, stepping up onto the verandah. 'Friend would be even better.'

"*Ia ora*, Constable,' Benny offered, 'as they say in the Society Islands.' Benny was proud to show off now and then with the bits and pieces of Tahitian he remembered.

'*Maita'i*,' Jeff replied, and stood smiling down at the old man. '*E aha tō 'oe huru?*'

'You speak Tahitian?' Benny sat bolt upright, nearly spilling the contents of his glass as he stared up in amazement at the young policeman.

Jeff grinned. '*E parau Tahiti au.*'

'Me too! Well, once upon a time, I did.' Benny shook his head. 'I haven't heard that lingo since I left Tahiti and that'd be thirty years ago now. I used to speak it real good, but I've forgot most all I know these days. Where on earth did you learn it?'

'Where on earth?' Jeff laughed. 'Why, in French Polynesia. Where else?'

'How'd you come to be in Tahiti?'

'Shipwrecked. The SS *Mistral* out of Marseille.'

'The *Mistral*. Yeah, I've heard of her.' Benny nodded and swigged from his glass. 'Around six years ago, it was. I heard of her from a pearler who worked on the luggers here some time back. Terrible business. All hands lost, they say.'

'All but one,' Jeff corrected him. 'I was rescued by a local fisherman near Moorea Island and taken in by his family in Papeete. I lived there for a few years. Worked on local schooners as far north as the Marquesas Islands.'

'Aah, the Marquesas.' Benny's face took on a faraway look. 'Now there's a place I'll never forget. Truly beautiful. Can't think of a word to do 'em justice.'

'"Unforgettable" might be the one you're after,' Jeff said in hearty agreement. 'The way they appear out of nowhere, rising from the ocean like the spires of great cathedrals. Once seen, never forgotten, Benny, that's for sure.'

'Aye, they're locked in my memory, that they are.' Benny drained the remnants from his glass, an action that did not go unnoticed by young Constable Jeff. 'But most of my time was spent on Rangiroa.'

'Yes, I know it well.' Jeff waited for the old man to pick up the bottle. 'Stopped there regularly, dropping off supplies and transporting the odd passenger or cargo to Papeete.'

'I lived in the little village of Avatoru. That's where I learned about pearls and the art of drunkenness.' Benny threw back his head and cackled, a sound more like a cough or a wheeze than a laugh. 'An old Frenchman used to grow vines. He made his own wine and shared much of it with me. Truth be known, I drank nearly the whole lot.'

Benny was thoroughly enjoying himself now. He picked up the whisky bottle to pour himself another. But in a flash, Jeff snatched it away.

'Sorry, Benny, *'o vau tō 'oe ti'a pāruru.*'

'What's that mean?'

'It means "I'm your bodyguard" and don't you forget it.' He waved the bottle in Benny's face; time to read him the rules. 'You can have this back at three o'clock,' he said, 'and after that you can drink yourself senseless. You see, Mr Burton not only wants you safe and sound, he wants a good day's work from you. And that means each and every day with the exception of Sunday.'

Benny made a lunge for the bottle, but Jeff held it aloft.

'I'm here to keep you safe, and only a little bit drunk, my friend,' he said. "*O vau tō 'oe ti'a pāruru.* That's my job and you'd better get used to it!'

Benny lunged once again for the whisky bottle, and once again it was held out of his reach.

As the old man rose to his feet, Jeff knew that he'd won. This round of the battle anyway. There would no doubt be many more.

'*E pīrau pa'i tō 'oe ure, 'a marua roa ai!*' Benny growled. His Tahitian was coming back to him now, and with a vengeance.

Jeff laughed. 'That's wishful thinking, Benny. Unlike you, I'm young and I'm healthy. My penis will not rot and drop off!'

He was still laughing as he walked away. The old man was bound to have more grog stashed in his shack, but he wouldn't get stuck into it now; he'd go back to work. The first lesson had been learned, and others would follow. But Jeff was happy enough. Already they'd developed a friendship – of sorts.

***

Over the months that ensued, Charles himself was more than happy with the arrangement they'd set in place at Cossack, and he said as much to Joe Lawson.

'We're back in business, Joe. All thanks to Constable Jeff.'

It was true Benny would always remain a hopeless alcoholic, but these days he was never drunk until after three in the afternoon. Or if he was, one would never know it. And the Cossack premises remained safe under the watchful eye of Constable Jeff.

'He's a fine young man, our Jeff,' Charles declared when, by mid-1891, the profits from their pearling enterprise were once again soaring.

Charles was also keenly aware that he was, by now, halfway through his five-year plan to pay off Burton Station's mortgage. He was well on track, and had recently had a further idea to raise yet more money.

'I've decided to sell the Perth property,' he announced to Joe one afternoon. It was a Friday, and they were out in the mulga scrubland checking the fencing, a packhorse alongside carrying supplies should there be the need for repairs here and there. Alwyn Stroud was with them, and the boys too, who were on their school holidays. Edward and Harold enjoyed working hard physically and young Alwyn Stroud simply loved being anywhere with the Boss. All three were good hard workers and experienced in fence repair.

It was a blisteringly hot afternoon and the two men were taking a break, swigging from their water bottles as they sat beneath a scrawny mulga tree, watching the youngsters at work.

'The Perth property?' Joe queried, taken aback. 'You mean the house in Claremont?'

'Yes, that's right. It's not necessary. I rarely visit Perth, and you *never* do. Why should we keep it? There's no need. Any business can be conducted by telegraph, and the money from its sale could go straight into paying off the station mortgage.'

Joe remained silent, staring contemplatively at the boys, who were completing a minor repair, Alwyn driving a mallet with full force onto a fence post while the two younger ones trustingly kept it in place, although there was little risk, as Alwyn was known to have a fine eye.

'I doubt your uncle would like to see the house sold, old chap,' Joe said finally, after appearing to have given the matter due thought. 'Geoffrey very much enjoyed his regular visits to Perth.'

Something in the languid manner with which he'd made the comment irritated Charles.

'Yes, and I know why,' he replied, 'Uncle Geoffrey enjoyed his regular visits to the brothels available in Perth.' Aware he'd been unnecessarily sharp, Charles softened his tone. 'My uncle was very open about that in his letters to father. And those to me, I might add. Fortunately, Joe, I feel driven by no such need.'

Joe smiled good-naturedly. 'No, of course you wouldn't, old man. After all, you are not your Uncle Geoffrey.'

Is that meant as an insult? Charles wondered. *Is this yet another hint that you consider me 'stuffy'?*

'You know, Charles, you really should find yourself a woman,' Joe said in the same languid manner. 'And I don't mean in a brothel, I mean a proper physical relationship with a member of the fairer sex. Good grief, you're a young man with a young man's appetites, don't you feel the occasional yearning?'

Was the question rhetorical or was this further goading? Charles wondered, but he made no reply, which didn't bother Joe in the least, as he went on.

'Why not give it a go, old chap? I'm sure there are several young women around here who'd be more than interested.'

Yes, Charles thought, *there are indeed several, one of whom must be avoided at all costs*. Felicity Coburn had become a thorn in his side.

'Time to head home,' he said, rising to his feet. 'I shall most certainly sell the Perth house,' he added as he crossed to his horse. 'I shall telegraph Mr Goodiston tomorrow.' This would hopefully put paid to Joe's flippant insults, he thought.

***

Charles was accustomed to women finding him attractive and had learned how to cope with it from the outset, warding off attention aboard ship on the journey to Australia. He portrayed himself always as a devoted father to his children, a man who had little time for anything else in his life. This made him even more attractive to women, but they respected him for it and kept their distance.

Felicity Coburn's approach, however, had been particularly

difficult to avoid, for she was the boys' schoolteacher and her interest in their welfare gave her every right to intrude upon Charles' life. Or so she appeared to believe. Twenty-five-year-old Felicity was fiercely determined to work her way into Charles Burton's affections, and she had chosen to do so via the very children whom he'd used as a barrier.

Her determination was never more apparent than when Charles bumped into her at the post and telegraph office in Roebourne the following afternoon. He'd driven the buggy into town as he had his daughter with him, Victoria having decided to take a break from her studies.

They left the horse and buggy in the care of the boy at the nearby stables and wandered down Sholl Street to the post office. Charles was intent upon sending his telegraph to Andrew Goodiston and Victoria was most keen to pick up the new books she'd ordered from the latest catalogue, even though her father could have collected them for her. Charles visited the post office every second Friday.

Felicity Coburn was all too aware of Charles Burton's regular visits to the post office, and aware also that these were always made late in the day after the deliveries had arrived. Which meant they hadn't really 'bumped into' each other at all.

'Ah, Mr Burton, what a pleasant surprise,' she said as they almost collided in the outside foyer of the Roebourne Post and Telegraph Office, where she'd been waiting for a good twenty minutes. 'And Victoria, my dear, I haven't seen you for such a long time. My, you get prettier by the day. And what a lovely bonnet.'

Victoria accepted the compliment with a brief nod and a tight smile. She didn't like Miss Coburn and knew the feeling to be mutual. Miss Coburn had never approved of her refusal to attend school and had openly said as much to her father upon their arrival in the area.

'Do you think it wise, Mr Burton,' Miss Coburn had remarked when he'd visited the school with his children to enrol the boys, 'allowing your daughter to remain at home?' She'd smiled to soften any appearance of criticism, for he was a very attractive man. 'You see, sir, I am a modern woman, and strongly believe girls deserve an education.'

'Oh, she will most certainly continue to receive an education, Miss Coburn, you can be sure of it. Victoria is already at tertiary level, and she firmly believes school would hold her back.'

Miss Coburn hadn't liked that one bit.

'Are the boys enjoying their holidays?' Felicity Coburn dived in, before Charles could move off into the post office proper.

'Yes, I believe so. I've put them to work, certainly, but boys being boys, they rather like being out in the scrub, labouring alongside the men.'

'Of course.'

They shared a smile, and Charles was once again about to move off, but once again Felicity dived in. She had planned this meeting and was not going to let him get away.

'I'm so glad we bumped into each other, Mr Burton,' she said. 'There is a matter I have intended to bring up with you for some time. A small problem regarding your boys, which you might wish to discuss. Would you perhaps care to join me for a cup of tea at Renshaw's General Store? Mrs Renshaw serves a delightful Devonshire tea on Friday afternoons. That is, if you have the time?'

Charles didn't dare look at Victoria, knowing full well she was glaring.

'Certainly,' he replied. 'I'll just post these letters,' he patted his top pocket, 'and collect the mail. I know there is a delivery awaiting us, for Victoria is expecting some books.'

'Lovely.' Felicity didn't even glance at the girl. 'I shall wait here for you in the foyer.'

As they left, Charles muttered under his breath to his daughter, 'Well, I could hardly say no, could I?'

Ten minutes later, the three of them walked down Sholl Street, Victoria clutching her valuable books to her chest, Charles with a letter from his father tucked in his pocket, Felicity chatting away happily about the weather, then turned right into Padbury heading towards the river and left into busy Roe Street, where Renshaw's General Store did a bustling trade.

Once settled at their table at the rear of the store, Felicity continued to chatter on to Charles about absolutely nothing of any importance, which Victoria found extraordinarily grating. Had he partaken of Mrs Renshaw's excellent scones before? He hadn't? Oh, my goodness, he was in for a treat then, they were truly amazing, the very best scones imaginable. And dear me, here they were in Roebourne, of all places!

Victoria gazed at the woman, who had not once glanced in her direction. *I might as well not be here*, she thought.

'Being an Englishman, Mr Burton,' Felicity continued, 'you are no doubt highly accustomed to the finest of scones, but I doubt you'll find any better than Mrs Renshaw's.' And there followed a girlish laugh.

The woman's a simpering fool, Victoria thought, *and what's more, she's flirting. She's flirting just as hard as she can!*

Charles was equally aware of Felicity's flirtatiousness; he was well accustomed to it by now. He studied her machinations with interest and a touch of bemusement, recognising every ploy as he did.

Yes, men would probably find you attractive, he thought, even as he wondered why. *You're a pretty woman, certainly, but you're also an intelligent woman. Why the need for this silliness?* He supposed such frivolous behaviour appealed to men's vanity, but there were women who could do it so much better.

The image of Eleanor sprang to mind. Eleanor's beauty. Eleanor's intelligence. *Now there's a woman to whom flirtation is an art form*, he thought, the memory of her automatically arousing anger.

He was thankful to be distracted from his thoughts by the arrival of the tea and the highly acclaimed scones, complete with bowls of strawberry jam and cream in full Devonshire style.

'Ah, here we are.' Felicity sighed ecstatically. 'And now for the test.' She took off her gloves in preparation. 'You must try one, Mr Burton, while I play mother.' And picking up the teapot, she started to pour. 'I defy you to prove me wrong.'

After slathering their scones with jam and cream, they

all dutifully performed the taste test, Felicity breathlessly awaiting Charles' verdict.

'Very nice indeed,' he said, although he'd tasted better, particularly the cream, which was most certainly not up to the standard of that produced from the milk of the dairy cows that fed on the lush pastures of Yorkshire.

'Yes, yes, they are, aren't they,' Felicity trilled, nibbling away delicately at her own scone. 'A treat, such a treat.'

'What was the matter you wished to talk about with my father, Miss Coburn?' Victoria asked bluntly, by now thoroughly fed up with the woman's coquetry, which she found grotesque.

'Oh.' Felicity was a little startled. She'd all but forgotten the girl was there. 'Yes, of course, Victoria, you're quite right, high time I got down to business.'

She took a sip of her tea, returned the cup to its saucer and dropped the flirtatious manner, becoming once again the serious, responsible teacher she considered herself to be and as she wished to be perceived.

'You may or may not be aware, Mr Burton, that we have recently moved into our brand-new, stone schoolhouse in Hampton Street, a building of which we are most proud.' When referring to the school, Felicity always used the royal 'we'.

'Yes, I did know of the new schoolhouse, Miss Coburn,' Charles replied, 'the boys have told me all about it. And I'm so sorry I haven't paid a visit to the building, which I believe is quite splendid.' He'd deliberately avoided paying a visit to the building, wishing to avoid Felicity herself.

'It is indeed most splendid,' Felicity agreed, 'we are proud to have such a schoolhouse in Roebourne. We've even had a private residence built on to the rear in which to house our headmaster. You really must allow me to give you a personally guided tour—'

'What was the problem about the boys?' Victoria interrupted once again, this time in a tone that clearly said, *Get on with it.*

Felicity gave her a schoolmarmish look that said with equal clarity, *You are a very rude girl,* before redirecting her focus to Charles.

'It is the fact that your sons, Mr Burton,' she said, 'are surprisingly mature. Edward in particular, whose education is so far in advance of his peers.'

'Yes, this is not altogether surprising,' he replied. 'They were schooled from a very early age in England, not only by me, but also private tutors, as was I in my boyhood. Such is the family custom.'

'I see,' she said, nodding thoughtfully, as if herein lay the problem.

'But upon our arrival in a place so foreign as the Pilbara,' Charles went on, 'I considered their socialising with children their own age to be more advantageous than further home schooling, indeed that they would quite likely learn from the local youngsters.'

'Yes, you may have been right to a certain degree,' she said doubtfully, 'but ...' She paused, leaving whatever the degree might have been dangling.

'What exactly appears to be the problem, Miss Coburn?' Like Victoria, Charles was wishing she'd get to the point.

'It is Edward about whom I am most particularly concerned,' Felicity replied. 'I do so hate the thought of him being held back.'

'Held back? In what way?'

'He is thirteen years old, Mr Burton, and about to embark upon the secondary stage of his education. However, he is already so advanced that unless he receives specialised tuition, he will be held back by the limitations on offer at the school where he can learn only what is being taught to others his age.'

Charles felt a stab of concern. He was also a little confused. Was this a ploy or was the woman sincere? Could there be a real problem?

Registering his worry, Felicity's expression became one of deepest sympathy.

'Oh, you poor man,' she said, 'I understand how difficult it must be for you, having journeyed to this treacherous part of the world with three young children in your care and no woman to share the burden.'

She reached out and placed her hand gently over his, the touch of her bare skin delivering a brief shock. In the past when they'd shaken hands, she'd always been gloved.

'Charles,' she said, then added, after the briefest hesitation, 'I may call you Charles, mayn't I? We have after all known each other for well over two years. I would be willing not only to offer extra tuition to Edward after school hours, but also to tutor him at Burton Station during the weekends. I would happily make the journey out there to assist you and your son.'

Charles did not withdraw his hand, but like his horrified daughter watching on, was quite aware of the proposal being put before him. The woman was not offering her services. She was offering herself.

He smiled gratefully. 'That is very kind of you, Miss Coburn—'

'Felicity,' she interrupted, returning his smile, her fingers curling warmly around his, 'Felicity, please.'

'Yes. Felicity,' he replied, not flinching, appearing even to return the gesture of affection with a slight pressure from his own fingers. 'Thank you for your concern, Felicity, it is most kind of you.' Another grateful smile and only then did he withdraw his hand, giving the impression he needed to do so in order to drink his tea. 'I shall certainly give the matter my full consideration, I assure you.'

'Do, Charles.' Her eyes never left his as he sipped his tea. 'Please do.'

They reverted to small talk, Felicity leading the way, and the following half-hour evolved around the charity ball to be held next month at the Victoria Hotel, she did so hope he would be there; the Roebourne Races, 'Oh my goodness, such excitement'; and the annual Boat Regatta and Sports Day, when the fleet was in port at Cossack, 'quite the highlight of the year'. Felicity always kept herself well informed of social events.

Charles responded with polite interest, while Victoria remained ominously silent until finally they were able to make good their escape.

Outside in the street as they exchanged farewells, Felicity offered her hand, now gloved, to Charles, but as they shook, she managed once again to make the gesture intimate, clasping his hand fervently in both of hers.

'Do consider my offer, Charles,' she said, 'please do. I would so like to assist Edward in his studies.'

'I shall, Felicity,' he replied, 'I shall give the matter a great deal of thought.'

Father and daughter said not a word as they retraced their steps to the stables on Sholl Street, although Charles was awaiting Victoria's outburst all the while. He knew she was simmering with rage, and wondered when he was going to cop the full blast.

He didn't cop it until they were in the buggy on their way home and then his daughter let loose with a vengeance.

'She wants to *assist Edward in his studies*?' Victoria all but screamed. 'What absolute rubbish! She wants you! She wants you to bed her, that's what she wants!'

'I know, I know,' he patiently replied. 'She's been wanting exactly that for two years now.'

'It was sickening to watch,' Victoria went on, glaring at him accusingly. 'And you pretended to believe all that nonsense about the need for *specialised tuition*! You said you'd give the matter *a great deal of thought*. For heaven's sake, are you *enjoying* this game? You even made it look as if the prospect of her weekend visits might be *attractive*!'

'What alternative did I have, Victoria?' He turned to her in all seriousness, not expecting an answer, only confronting her with the dilemma that constantly presented itself. 'You tell me. Exactly what alternative did I have?'

Victoria did not rise to the challenge, but nor did she appear subservient. She continued to glare back at him, then directed her gaze to the passing countryside and remained silent until they arrived at Burton Station, by which time it was dusk.

Edward and Harold had just returned home from their labours and were cleaning themselves up in preparation for dinner. They were starving, as always after a hard day's work, and seven o'clock saw the family seated around the breakfast room table, Nina bringing the evening meal in from the kitchen: a huge chicken casserole and a large bowl of potatoes. Joe Lawson occasionally joined them for dinner, but was not present tonight as it was shearing time and he was eating with the men out at the cookhouse.

Having served the Burton family, Nina retired to her hut where she and Alwyn dined together, a family unto themselves. It was a routine that suited all, but as far as Victoria was concerned, particularly tonight. Tonight she wanted the family all to herself, for she had an announcement to make, which was for their ears only. She would wait until after dinner, she decided, as she watched her brothers dive into the casserole dish and the bowl of potatoes; she'd get scant attention from them now.

'I have a letter from your grandfather,' Charles announced, taking the unopened envelope from his pocket and placing it on the table. William's letters invariably included comments to the children, who wrote notes to him regularly, so his correspondence was always read out loud to the family. 'I shall read it to you after dinner,' he said.

'Why not now, Father?' Victoria suggested, and as he looked a query, she rose from the table, leaned over and picked up his plate. 'I shall serve your meal for you,' she said with the warmest smile, 'and you can read Grandpapa's letter out to us while we eat.'

He recognised something meaningful in her suggestion. He could not imagine what it might be, but was thankful to see that at least she was no longer angry.

'Very well, my dear,' he agreed and he opened the envelope.

'*Dearest Charles,*' he read, '*I embark upon this letter with some rather sad news, although news which will hardly come as a surprise, for he'd reached a good age and we must all go some time. It is with a heavy heart, son, I must inform you that Byron is dead ...*

'Oh.' As Charles looked up from the letter, he noted his children were now paying avid attention, even the boys, who'd been so preoccupied with their meal. They'd all known the bay stallion who'd been so precious to him. 'Oh, dear me, yes,' he said. 'That is sad.' He returned to the letter and read on.

'*With the cold weather now upon us, he'd been brought in from pasture and settled warm and cosy in the stables, but just yesterday morning I found him in some distress. He was lying on his side, breathing heavily, and couldn't get to his feet, although he tried. I don't know what it was, a heart attack perhaps, who can tell, but I sat there comforting him while Mac fetched the rifle. There was nothing else one could do. He seemed at peace with the feel of my hand stroking his neck and he closed his eyes. I like to think he felt no pain at the end, Charles, but knowing what the animal meant to you, I'm sure you will be saddened by this news.*'

Charles paused in order to embark upon the meal Victoria had served up and set before him, but also to give himself a moment's reflection. He remembered how, as a ten-year-old, he'd been there in the stables at the foal's birth, how he'd named the foal himself, after his favourite poet. But he'd been Charlotte then, and it was Charlotte to whom his father was now writing. He took his time, eating several mouthfuls of the casserole, barely tasting the chicken, then read on.

'But you must admit, son, your Byron had a good life. Twenty-three years is not too bad an age for a horse. I must say at seventy-three, I am probably his equivalent in human years. Who knows what lies ahead, eh?

'On now to news from your side of the world. What a Godsend your Constable Jeff has proved to be, I must say. Indeed quite the saviour. And as for your thoughts about selling Geoffrey's house in Perth. Yes, I can see it would hardly serve the same purpose to you as it did to him. A jolly fine idea all round.'

William continued to write in similar light vein to his son, the odd signal here and there directed to his daughter, which as always was of great comfort.

He ended with messages to his grandchildren, each of them humorous. Had Victoria completed her law course yet? If not, she'd better get a move on, she'd be sixteen next year. How very impressive that Edward could now ride bareback, and what a pity Harold couldn't master a boomerang, whatever exactly that was.

And then he signed off in typical fashion.

'My love to you all, dearest son. Continue to live safely in that wild place you have chosen to inhabit. I do admire you so.

'*Your loving father and grandfather.*'

Charles folded up the letter, returned it to its envelope and finished his meal, while the children, the boys in particular, dug into the pudding Nina had left them. 'Not for me, thank you, dear,' he said when Victoria offered him a serve.

She didn't have any herself and, watching her brothers scrape the last from their bowls, she decided dinner was over. Time to make her announcement.

'I have the perfect answer, Father,' she said.

Charles was bewildered. 'The perfect answer to what?'

'The way we can rid ourselves of any further contact with Felicity Coburn.'

Edward, whose principal focus had been upon his meal, was instantly attentive.

'Why would we want to rid ourselves of contact with Miss Coburn?' he asked. 'She's an excellent teacher.'

'Yes,' Harold piped up. 'I like her a lot.'

'Because she wishes to tutor you, Edward,' Victoria replied. 'Out here at Burton Station. On the weekends,' she added meaningfully. '"Special tuition", she calls it.'

'Why?' Edward was puzzled. 'Why would I need special tuition? I'm head and shoulders above everyone else in my class.'

'That's exactly why she wishes to give you "special tuition",' Victoria said scathingly. 'She doesn't want you to be held back by the limitations of your classmates.'

'Why? I don't mind being taught alongside them, even if I'm more advanced in some subjects. My classmates are my friends.'

What an innocent you are, Victoria thought, and she decided to spell things out in no uncertain terms. 'It's not you she's interested in at all, Edward,' she bluntly announced. 'It's Father.'

'Oh.' Edward was an innocent, certainly, but he was also a very bright boy, and in that moment everything fell into place. He had for so long now played son to a father who was really his mother that he'd all but lost sight of the truth. 'Oh,' he said again, before turning to his father, who remained stern and silent. Recognition flooded his young face, and he nodded. 'Yes,' he said. 'Yes, I understand. That would be difficult.'

Ten-year-old Harold was in a state of utter bewilderment. 'What would be difficult? What do you understand? What's going on?'

Charles looked at his elder son, at that astute, intelligent boy he so loved, but not for one moment did he drop the façade, which must be maintained at all costs. Victoria had broken the rules in speaking so plainly.

'What exactly is it you propose, Victoria?' he demanded, his voice carrying a distinct reprimand.

'I shall take over the secondary stage of Edward's education, Father,' she coolly replied. 'I shall become his personal tutor. That way, Felicity Coburn need make no unnecessary trips out here to Burton Station.' Victoria's expression was brazen and her smile challenging. 'Home-schooling has proved very successful for us in the past. After all, you were home-schooled yourself, weren't you, Papa?'

The cheeky, suggestive use of 'Papa', as if they were sharing a joke, was not as it had been in the early days, and Charles found it unsettling in the sure knowledge she was deliberately goading him.

Does she despise me? he wondered, recalling the force of her anger on the buggy ride home, the outright accusation she'd hurled at him. 'Good God, are you enjoying this game?' she'd said. *Does she despise me for what I'm doing? Does she despise me for the role I'm playing?*

Far from despising her mother, Victoria was lost in admiration. It was true she had never liked her mother becoming her father. It had never been the joke to her that it had been to her brothers and she had never enjoyed 'playing the game' as they had. But she very much respected her mother's strength in so boldly carrying out the deception.

Having of late become acutely aware of her own sexuality, Victoria could imagine no woman apart from her mother who would so dare deny herself all vestige of femininity. She did not in the least despise her mother. She *did*, however, despise Felicity Coburn.

'I am quite happy to inform Miss Coburn that her services are not required, Papa,' she offered, again with a brazen smile.

'Thank you, Victoria,' he replied, 'but I shall do so myself.'

Oh dear, Charles thought, *I fear I may have a rebellion on my hands.* Victoria's attitude was a worry.

9.

Felicity Coburn was deeply disappointed to discover Charles Burton would not be accepting her generous offer to tutor his son at Burton Station. And the casual way in which he informed her of his decision came as a crushing blow, for she'd been so excited when he'd called in to see her at the school, instantly convinced as she was that his personal visit signalled a definite 'yes'.

It had been barely a week since their cosy *tête-à-tête* over Devonshire tea at Renshaw's General Store and only several days until the new school term, the final of the year, was to resume. She and the other teachers, together with the headmaster, were in the common room discussing the various syllabuses and schedules. They always did so during the last week of the holidays, taking notes, making plans.

'Why, Mr Burton,' she exclaimed, jumping to her feet as he tapped at the open door, offering his greeting to the assembled company.

'Forgive the intrusion,' Charles said to the headmaster, 'but I wondered whether I might borrow a few moments with Miss Coburn.'

'Of course, Mr Burton.' The headmaster nodded benignly, always pleased to see the parents of his pupils taking an interest in the school and its teachers.

'Shan't keep her long, I promise,' he said as Felicity virtually skipped out the door with him.

'How lovely to see you, Charles,' she said when they were well clear of the common room. 'Have you come for the tour of the school that I promised you?' Her eyes were sparkling in the knowledge that he hadn't.

'I'm afraid not,' he replied, 'I could hardly drag you away from your teachers' meeting.'

'So then I am at a complete loss,' she said, still pretending innocence. 'To what do I owe the honour?'

How very readable you are, Charles thought.

'I just wanted to let you know,' he said, 'that I shan't be availing myself of your very kind offer to give Edward special tuition.'

'Oh.' She stared back at him in such stunned, open-mouthed amazement that Charles couldn't help thinking she looked rather like a goldfish.

'It is a generous proposal, Felicity,' he went on, 'and I do thank you most sincerely, but I'm afraid it won't be necessary. Victoria has insisted upon taking over Edward's entire education – both boys, in fact – so I'm here to inform you neither he nor Harold will be returning to school.'

'I see,' Felicity replied. Still in a state of shock, she was finding it a little difficult to breathe. 'And the boys are happy with such a decision?'

'Yes, quite happy.'

They hadn't been to start with, Charles recalled, although Edward had accepted the necessity of the arrangement, understanding the problem Miss Coburn presented. Both boys had professed to the fact, however, that they would miss the social aspect of school; they enjoyed mingling with their friends.

'You can see your friends during the weekends,' Victoria had told them. Most of their fellow students lived on properties an hour or two's ride away.

'But we see them all together at school,' Harold had insisted, 'it wouldn't be the same.' Harold had no idea why the rules were being changed. 'I like school.'

'You'll do as you're told.' Victoria would brook no argument. 'I'm a much better teacher than Miss Coburn anyway.' And that had been that.

'Victoria herself is particularly happy with the arrangement,' Charles continued. 'She considers her brothers will provide excellent practice, for she feels she has studied long enough and has decided to offer her services part-time as a tutor next year.' He smiled like the indulgent father he was. 'To whoever wishes to employ her. I have no idea of her plans, but she so longs to be out in the real world, earning a living.'

'I see. Yes, of course. I see.'

And Felicity did. She saw only too plainly. This was all due to that little minx, that ghastly girl she so disliked. Victoria's animosity had been palpable throughout their afternoon tea last week. The daughter was jealous, it was all too evident.

Felicity knew Charles Burton found her sexually attractive, and now his hideous daughter was out to destroy any relationship that might have developed between them. She detested Victoria.

'Well, I mustn't keep you from your meeting.' Charles' smile was warm and friendly. 'I shall no doubt catch up with you again in the near future, Felicity. Perhaps at the boat regatta in Cossack? The children and I are always in attendance. As you said yourself, "quite the highlight of the year".'

He offered his hand, they shook and parted ways, Felicity thinking, *But the regatta isn't until New Year's Day!* Which only added insult to injury.

Charles sighed thankfully. The deed was done.

***

He *did* see Felicity at the regatta in Cossack on New Year's Day, but their meeting hardly aroused the same frisson of excitement, carrying neither the element of danger for him, nor the hope of success for her.

'Mr Burton,' she greeted him coolly, having left the small group of friends she was with and strolling over, parasol twirling, to where he stood on the banks of the Harding River with his children.

'Miss Coburn.' She hadn't offered her hand as she always had in the past, so he tipped the brim of his Panama hat respectfully.

'And your boys,' she said with a smile that may even have been genuine, 'how very nice to see you, Edward and Harold.' She studiously avoided Victoria, who was standing beside her brothers. But then, Victoria was taking no notice of her either, gazing out instead at the activities on the water.

'I presume your studies are progressing well?' she queried of the boys, a deliberate dig at both father and daughter.

'Yes, thank you, Miss Coburn,' Edward replied dutifully.

'I miss school,' Harold loudly announced.

'Of course you do, dear,' she agreed, her voice dripping sympathy, 'it's only natural you should.' She cast a telling glance at Charles, then turned back to Harold. 'Socialising with other children is so important for boys your age.

'Well, Mr Burton,' she said, gathering up the skirts of her pretty pastel day dress, displaying her dainty button-booted feet, 'I must not desert my friends any longer. I do hope you enjoy your day.'

'As I hope you enjoy yours, Miss Coburn,' Charles replied, once again tipping the brim of his hat. 'A very happy New Year to you.'

She nodded and sashayed away provocatively, parasol twirling, to rejoin her group, where she slid a proprietorial hand through the arm of a middle-aged man, who beamed with pleasure as she cosied up to him. She didn't glance back at Charles but her actions spoke for themselves. *Look at all you missed out on*, she was saying.

Charles was happy she appeared to have found herself a lover.

The day did indeed progress happily for all as the burgeoning crowds from Roebourne and the surrounding region gathered for their annual celebration. The Boat Regatta and Sports Day at Cossack was certainly one of the highlights of the year and had been for decades. The river and the open waters beyond were a hive of activity as far as the eye could see. With the fleet in port, there was every imaginable vessel and every imaginable boating event on display.

Luggers and schooners and ketches raced out to sea and back around the islands; smaller yacht races included cutters, sloops and dinghies, anything with a sail; and in the river itself, the most popular event of all was the four- and eight-oar races. The opposing crews came from both the ships and the townships, and again the vessels being rowed were in all varieties. There were long, narrow dinghies known as 'gigs', and there were lifeboats and skiffs and anything else that happened to be fitted with oars and rowlocks.

The action was not solely concentrated upon the vessels, however. There were swimming races featuring the strongest and fittest of all ages, while on shore there were running races held in equally fierce competition, together with long-jumping and even Japanese wrestling. No-one could deny that Cossack, a boisterous port town at the best of times, really came alive this one day of the year.

The town's pubs did a lively business too, and as the afternoon wore on and men started to become visibly drunk, Constable Jeff and the other officers who'd been posted to Cossack to police the festivities knew it would be a hard night ahead.

Charles Burton guessed as much himself and said exactly that to the young policeman. He and Victoria were seated on the verandah of Sing's Bakery and General Store, having a cooling lemonade, when Jeff passed by on his rounds.

'You'll no doubt have a hard night ahead of you, Jeff.' Charles indicated the nearby White Horse pub, where voices were already becoming raucous.

'Yes, sir,' he agreed, 'I think you may be right.'

'I'd like you to meet my daughter, Victoria,' Charles said. 'Victoria, this is Constable Jeff.'

'How do you do, Miss Burton.'

'Oh, so *you're* Jeff.' She eyed him with the keenest of interest. 'I'm frightfully pleased to meet you, I've heard so very much about you.'

Jeff was taken aback when she offered her hand. The gesture was so mature, and her manner so assured. But Charles Burton's daughter was only fifteen, wasn't she? At least, that's what he'd heard.

'Pleased to meet you, miss,' he said as he shook her hand, hoping that his, which might be grimy, wouldn't soil the pristine white of her glove.

She was studying him astutely, which he found quite unnerving. That fine-boned face beneath the boater hat, the intelligence in those dark eyes so penetrating, the very air she exuded, everything placed her in a class well above his, making him uncomfortable. But why? She was so very young.

'Is your name *really* Jeff,' she asked, 'just Jeff, and nothing else?'

'Yes, miss,' he replied.

'Honestly?' The sudden cheekiness of her smile said she didn't believe him, and the glint in her eyes held a challenge. 'That's what your birth certificate would read, is it? Just Jeff, no surname?'

'Well, no, it's a little more complicated than that ...' He wished she'd leave him alone.

Charles, seeing Jeff was uncomfortable, intervened. 'Stop that at once, Victoria. Stop pestering the poor man.'

'Sorry,' she said. But Jeff could tell that she wasn't.

'Yes, it's my guess Cossack will be a rough old town tonight,' Charles went on. 'We're about to board the next tram back to Roebourne, where our buggy is housed at the stables. Best to get the children away before the drunkards take over the place.'

Sing's Bakery and General Store in The Strand was right beside the tram tracks where the horse-drawn tram plying the route between Roebourne and Cossack would come to a stop.

'Good idea, sir,' Jeff agreed. 'No place for children.' He smiled at Victoria, who did not smile back. She clearly did not like being referred to as a child.

At that very moment, Edward and Harold bounded up from the foreshore to join them. They'd been told to keep an eye out for the tram's approach, and they'd just seen it on its way into the town centre.

'We won,' Harold announced triumphantly. They'd competed in yet another tug o' war match. 'Again! That's the third time.'

'Tram's coming,' Edward reported.

'This is the rest of my brood,' Charles said, introducing the boys to Jeff.

'*The* Constable Jeff.' Edward was most impressed and offered his hand like a grown-up, as he always did; he was a very mature lad. 'We've heard a lot about you, Constable.'

'Evidently,' Jeff replied with a glance at Victoria, who, much to his discomfort, was still studying him intensely, not in the least distracted by the arrival of her brothers.

Harold was far more than impressed by Jeff. Harold was awestruck. 'You went to sea when you were *ten*!'

'That's right. Word does get around.'

'I told them, I'm afraid,' Charles admitted. 'Sorry about that.'

'Perfectly all right, sir, it's no secret. Everyone knows. Courtesy of Sergeant Fry,' he added with a smile.

'*I'm* ten,' Harold said, openly gawking.

'Well, I wouldn't advise you to go to sea,' Jeff replied. 'It's not quite as much fun as it might sound.'

Harold nodded thoughtfully, accepting the advice from one who would obviously know.

They could all see the tram now, the sturdy bay horse pulling several empty passenger carriages along the narrow tracks on this first leg of its seven-mile trip to Roebourne.

Charles stood. 'Time to go,' he announced, gazing about at each of his brood, 'come along, children.'

Jeff again noticed Victoria's flicker of annoyance at her inclusion in the reference.

'I'll be back in a week or so, Jeff,' Charles said as they walked towards the tram, 'I'll see you then.'

'Yes, sir.'

'And try not to get into too many fights tonight,' he called over his shoulder.

'Do my best, sir.' Jeff grinned. 'Can't promise anything though, this is Cossack after all,' he called back.

Charles laughed.

Jeff watched as the horse and tram came to a stop and the family boarded. Then, as the animal set off once more, the tracks looping around the town on the journey back to Roebourne, he gave them a wave.

Victoria's gaze was still upon him as he turned and walked away. She found Constable Jeff a source of immense fascination. Her initial reaction had been very much along the same lines as her father's: this was not a young man who'd been at sea since he was ten, surely; such a man would be uncouth, ill-educated and ill-mannered. But Constable Jeff was none of these. He was good-looking, well-spoken and appeared intelligent. *How strange*, she thought. Most of all, she was intrigued by his mystery. He'd admitted his name wasn't 'Jeff'. 'It's a little more complicated than that,' he'd said. So what was it? Who was he? Where did he come from?

Her curiosity piqued, Victoria determined to find out. She would join her father on his next trip to Cossack, she decided.

And she did, Charles quite happy to humour her. She devoted so much of each day to her brothers' tuition, he considered it healthy she should have some time for herself. And besides, he enjoyed her company.

The shared trips to Cossack became a regular event over the next several months, Charles conducting his business with Benny, and occasionally carrying out some duties at the courthouse, where his presence or signature was required as a local Justice of the Peace. He was content to leave Victoria to herself for the several hours he was there, particularly as she was more often than not in the company of Constable Jeff, who, upon his personal request, had promised to keep an eye on her, which was most reassuring.

Jeff no longer found Victoria daunting. He'd come to the conclusion that she was just a young girl who happened to be extraordinarily intelligent and at times quite charming. Like the day she'd finally worn him down and he'd admitted to his name.

'Jean-François Fabron,' he'd said wearily.

'You're French,' she'd squealed, thrilled by the discovery.

'Yes,' he'd given a shrug of indifference, 'more or less.' And when he'd gone on to tell her of Sergeant Fry's horrified reaction to his name, and how the big policeman had determined he become 'J.F.' and then 'Jeff', the peal of her laughter had delighted him. That was the moment their friendship was cemented. That was when he discovered there was a side to Victoria other than the serious exterior she presented. She was a girl who liked to laugh.

'But don't you dare tell Sergeant Fry you know my real name,' he'd warned her. 'He's sworn I'm to be "just Jeff". Those were his very words. "From now on, you're just Jeff", that's what he said.' And he'd delighted in yet another peal of girlish laughter.

'I'm serious, Victoria,' he'd been forced to add – they were on a first-name basis these days, 'you're not to tell *anyone* my real name.'

Her reaction and the connection it created between the two of them pleased him. He'd played this game, allowing her to bully one harmless secret from him, but she would never know the true tragedy of his past.

'You must promise me,' he said. 'This has to be our little secret, I'm afraid.'

'Good,' she'd declared, 'that's fine by me, Jeff. I like secrets.'

From then on they'd taken to occasionally talking in French, Victoria enjoying the opportunity to improve her skills.

'Your French is really rather good,' he complimented her.

'I was coached in it by tutors from the age of six,' she said. 'I speak a little Italian and German too,' she added, not boastfully, just stating a fact. 'Father believed in as broad an education as possible for his children. Edward is also very capable. In fact, I've found Edward to be an excellent student all round.' She paused, giving the matter a moment's thought. 'Harold is still a bit of a scatterbrain, though. I have trouble getting through to him at times.'

Jeff shook his head in bewildered admiration. Victoria was such a mixture of child and adult, but both were equally refreshing.

***

The terrible accident that threatened to shatter the lives of the Burton family happened in late June, not long after Victoria's sixteenth birthday.

Charles was setting off from the homestead on his favourite horse, Lady Grey. A sturdy, high-spirited, feisty mare, he and Lady suited each other well.

'Boss, I can come with you?' a voice called, and he turned to see Alwyn Stroud sprinting after him.

He pulled the mare to a halt as the boy ran up. 'Have you chopped Nina's firewood?' he demanded.

'Um ...' Alwyn hesitated. Clearly he hadn't.

'You go back to the house right now and chop that firewood,' Charles ordered, 'and when you're done, you can saddle up and join me. I'm heading for Three Mile Gate to do a cattle count. I'll see you there.'

'Yeah, Boss.'

Watching Alwyn sprint away eagerly, Charles was glad he'd have some time to himself, which had been his intention, particularly on a day like this. He'd take things easy, enjoy the scenery, drink in the stillness and the strange beauty of the Pilbara.

It really was a glorious morning, he thought as, with a gentle pressure from his knees, Lady set off at a walk. The middle of the dry season, not a cloud to be seen, a gentle north-easterly breeze; what could be better? It would get hot as the day progressed, but right now his bush hat shielded him from the glare of the sun, and the temperature and surrounds were perfect.

He gazed across the low scrub pasturelands to the ancient hummocks beyond. These, he'd been informed by Joe, were among Earth's first dry land to have emerged from the sea, a concept he'd found unimaginable at the time. They looked for all the world like green hills, didn't they? But they weren't.

'One of the oldest landscapes on the planet,' Joe had said.

They were not at all the green, grassy hills Charles had first presumed them to be. They were sheer rock. Over the millennia, seeds had sprouted through fissures to make them appear like the sort of hillsides that would form perfect paddocks. Then, over further millennia, many of the edifices had broken into huge, crystalline blocks of rust-red rock that, although frozen by time, appeared to cascade down the slopes to the plains below.

Who would believe it, Charles thought, *who would believe such a landscape possible?* He had come to love the Pilbara.

Way in the distance, he could see Three Mile Gate, the half square mile of fenced-in land that served as a storage paddock for new stock. This was where he would do a head count of the cattle, which the stockmen had herded in just the previous week. Regular head counts had become necessary as, more and more these days, marauding bands of Aborigines would kill and steal a beast.

'And why shouldn't they?' Joe had said in defence of the natives. 'Their land has been taken over by white settlers. These plains have always been their natural hunting grounds.' With a shake of his head, he'd gone on to explain. 'Oh, I tell you, Charles, it didn't used to be like this in the early days. When I first started working for your Uncle Geoffrey, things were peaceful here between the whites and the blacks. Admittedly, those employed by the whites weren't paid much. Most were only offered food and tobacco, although Geoffrey always paid our lot a few shillings a week, but the truth is, money didn't really seem to interest them. Relations were harmonious between us all way back then. Even the natives who chose not to communicate or mingle with the whites, those who spoke their own lingo and lived in the wild, rarely caused trouble. We'd often see them crossing our property out on the hunt, but they kept their distance, and we kept ours.

'Not anymore,' he'd said with another dismal shake of his head. 'Not since the whole region was taken over by farmers, many of whom kill any blacks who threaten their stock, or else have them thrown in gaol, where the poor creatures will either be hanged or worked like dogs as government slave labour. It's a sad state of affairs for the blacks of the Pilbara.'

Charles was in complete agreement. He'd witnessed enough for himself by now; Roebourne Gaol was proof of the horrors meted out to the Aboriginal population.

Oh no, he thought as he neared Three Mile Gate. *Oh, God, no, it's going to be one of those days.* He rather regretted Joe and a couple of the workers weren't with him, as it would make the situation much easier to handle.

Several hundred yards up ahead, he could see a group of Aboriginal men, around a half-dozen in all. They were in the storage paddock, having speared a steer about fifty yards from the gate. The animal lay dead at their feet, and they were about to butcher the carcass in order to carry it off.

Charles increased Lady's speed to a canter, intent upon scaring them away. The arrival of a farmer and the use of a stern voice usually did the trick, and the natives would scatter.

'Right, you lot,' he yelled, 'get away from my cattle!'

The group turned to stare at him.

'Go on now! Get out of here! Get off my property!'

The reaction to his order was not at all what he'd expected. In only seconds, a boomerang was flying its way towards him with deadly accuracy.

It was Lady who saved the day. Even more alarmed than Charles, the mare instinctively dodged to avoid the missile, but as she did, she stumbled. Charles was thrown to the ground. Lady recovered herself and reared in terror as several spears were launched in the air, heading in their direction. The mare whirled on the spot, about to take off.

A spear lodged in the earth barely inches from Charles' face as, winded by the fall, he struggled to his feet. He needed the shotgun that was in his saddle holster, but he presumed the mare had bolted.

She hadn't. She lay on the ground, twenty yards away. Two spears were imbedded in her, one near her heart and one in her throat. Lady's body was still shuddering, but she was dead.

Charles prepared to make the dash for his shotgun, but even as he did, he saw Alwyn Stroud approaching at a gallop.

The boy pulled his horse up in spectacular fashion beside the dead mare, dismounted in a cloud of red dust and withdrew the shotgun from its holster. He fired a shot in the direction of the natives, who, rather than scattering, immediately launched two spears in return.

Charles ran towards the gate, which might provide some cover in the way of visibility, signalling Alwyn to join him. But as Charles was about to throw himself down in the bushes that grew beside the gate, he saw a death adder curled up on the ground. He twisted his body, trying to change the direction of his fall and, in doing so, struck his head on the gate post, landing heavily on his back. It was then that he felt the snake's bite.

The next shot Alwyn fired killed the snake but invited several more spears in retaliation. The boy dived down beside Charles among the bushes by the gate, virtually out of sight. The spears could not, therefore, have been directly targeted, but as luck would have it, one found its mark, driving itself deeply into Charles' upper thigh.

Alwyn let out a scream of rage and, standing boldly in full view, he pumped out the last three shells in rapid fire at the intruders, defying them to kill him.

They chose not to. The boy and the shotgun were too much for them. They scattered, disappearing into the scrubland.

But Charles didn't see any of this. His eyesight was failing. His head was spinning. The whole world was spinning. Faster and faster and yet still faster. Until everything stopped. No vision at all. Then … nothing.

***

Charles awoke to find himself in a strange bed in a room he didn't know, wearing a nightshirt and covered in a counterpane he didn't recognise. Where was he? What had happened? His head was reeling. His brain wasn't functioning. He could remember nothing.

Then out of the fog came a sound he recognised. Someone was sharpening a razor. Through the haze of his vision, he could see a man. A man was standing at the washstand not three feet from the end of the bed. He was beating out a rhythm with his razor on a leather strop. Charles dimly recognised the man's reflection, which he could see in the mirror that hung on the wall above the washstand. Or he thought he recognised the man, he couldn't be sure.

'Joe?' he queried, his voice faint, unsteady. 'Joe, is that you?'

Joe Lawson turned. 'Ah, you've come to, old chap. You're alive. Jolly good.'

'What happened?'

'Snake bite.' Joe crossed to the bedside and stood smiling down at him. 'But you got lucky. The bite was dry.'

'How do you mean?'

'A dry bite. No venom. Or at least, very little. Snakes bite with venom to kill prey, but they're also known to dry bite sometimes, as a warning to whatever frightens them.'

'You're right then.' Charles attempted a smile. 'Seems I *did* get lucky.'

'Not really,' Joe replied. 'The wound in your thigh is concerning.'

'What wound?' He was puzzled. He could feel nothing.

'A spear. Can you not remember a spear?'

'A spear,' Charles repeated, confused. 'A spear ...'

Then fractured images came into his mind. A snake on the ground ... Aborigines ... spears in the air ...

'You've been unconscious and delirious for the best part of three days, old chap,' Joe explained. 'Now, if I'm right and the bite was dry, then I'd say it was that nasty head wound, along with the spear wound to your thigh that brought you down. Serious fever. And you're not out of the woods yet. The fever may have subsided, but you'll be laid up for a while. Can't risk those wounds becoming infected, and we've got to get your strength back.'

Charles raised a hand to his head, to discover it bandaged. He tried to sit up, but the world began to swim.

'Lie back, lie back, take it easy, old man.' Joe put a reassuring hand on his shoulder, easing him down. 'As I said, you've a way to go yet.'

'How did I get here?' Charles was bewildered. 'How did …' Then a further image flashed through his mind. 'Oh, dear God.' He stared up at Joe. 'Alwyn … Alwyn was there, wasn't he?'

'Yes, and you're very lucky he was.'

'How so?'

'He scared the natives off with your shotgun.'

'That's right.' The memories now came flooding back. 'That's right. I came upon Aborigines about to butcher a steer they'd killed. I challenged them and they threw spears. Three, four spears, I don't know how many. Lady was terrified. She stumbled, I fell …'

He squinted up at the ceiling as the mare's image returned. *Poor Lady*, he thought.

'Go on,' Joe urged.

'Two hit her. I could tell she was dead. The shotgun was in the saddle holster. But before I could get to it, Alwyn was there. He seemed to come from nowhere. He grabbed the shotgun and ran to me …'

'And …' Joe prompted as Charles once again paused.

'The snake … A death adder, I think … More spears … One hit me in the leg … I don't remember anything else. I must have passed out.'

'You did.'

'So, what happened?' Charles felt a sudden stab of alarm. 'Is Alwyn all right?'

'He certainly is. Fighting fit. He brought you to my hut. Saw my horse tethered out the front, so knew I was here.'

'How on earth did he manage to do that?'

'Oh, our lad Alwyn is a remarkable fellow,' Joe said admiringly. 'He ordered his horse to lie down.'

'He what?'

'He ordered his horse to lie down, then dragged your body over the saddle, told the horse to get up and they walked you three miles back here.'

'Good grief, that's remarkable.'

'Yes, I suppose it is rather, isn't it?' Joe shrugged. 'But then Alwyn's always had a way with horses. Like many of Aboriginal blood. That's what makes them such damn fine stockmen.'

He briskly changed the subject. 'I tell you what we'll do, old chap,' he said. 'I'll pop over to the house and instruct Nina to prepare some soup. We need to get food into you as soon as we can. You haven't eaten for three days.'

He crossed to the door. 'She'll be delighted to hear you've regained your senses. Everyone will be, of course. They've all been worried stupid. Even when I told them your fever was lifting, that you were out of danger and you weren't going to die, Victoria wouldn't leave your bedside. Not until I ordered her to anyway, just this morning. I had to remind her that this was my hut, and that I wanted it back.'

He opened the door. 'While I'm away, do see if you can drink some water, old chap,' he said, indicating the glass that sat on the bedside table. 'We managed to get a bit down you now and then, but you're bound to be dehydrated.'

He made to leave and halted yet again. 'Oh, and when I return,' he added with a smile, 'I do hope you'll forgive me if I treat myself to a shave. Haven't had one for three days, and I so hate being bristly.'

Yes, Charles thought, noticing for the first time the uncharacteristic stubble on Joe's chin. *It doesn't suit you either.* Joe Lawson's fine, olive-toned skin was always impeccably smooth, which somehow suited his manner.

Then the door closed, and Charles was left on his own.

He rolled onto his side and reached for the glass, managing slowly to raise his head high enough off the pillow to take a sip, although most of the water spilled onto the bed.

Then he replaced the glass and lay back, pondering the situation.

He'd been bitten by a snake. He'd been speared in the thigh. Both wounds had been treated. How? And by whom? Furthermore, he was in a nightshirt.

It was only then the awful possibility crossed Charles' mind. He slithered his hands down under the counterpane, lifting the nightshirt, feeling the heavy bandage around his thigh, and ...

Oh my God, he realised. Beneath the nightshirt, he was naked. Completely naked.

He panicked, his mind reeling at the implications.

I'm in Joe's hut. Was it Joe who stripped me? Joe who treated me? Has he discovered the truth?

He must have, surely. But then Joe had said Victoria had

been by his bedside every day. Was it Victoria who had stripped him and treated his wounds? If so, had his secret remained undiscovered?

Charles lay there agonising over these questions and many more for a full fifteen minutes, until the door opened and there stood Joe, Nina by his side, bearing a large bowl of soup.

'Well, here we are, old chap,' Joe said heartily. 'As you can see, Nina didn't need to prepare a thing. She's had the soup ready and waiting until she knew you were up for it.'

Nina bustled over to place the bowl on the bedside table. 'Oh, Boss,' she said, beaming happily, 'so good to have you back. By golly, we was worried, the missy and the boys and me. We was so worried.'

Does she know? Charles wondered.

Joe fetched another pillow and he and Nina between them managed to prop Charles into a position where Nina was able to feed him.

Sitting on the side of the bed, Nina stirred the soup vigorously with a spoon, steam rising as shredded chicken and vegetables swirled about in the bowl.

'Got to make sure it's not too hot,' she explained. 'Had 'er simmering on the stove all day, ever since Mr Joe reckon your fever was liftin'. But we'll get this into you soon as we can. Every bit of it. Get you back good and strong, this will.'

'Thank you, Nina,' Charles replied. *Is this an act? Does she know? Does everyone know?*

'You don't mind, do you, old man?' Joe asked, waving aloft the razor he held in his hand.

'No, not in the least,' Charles replied, and as Nina slowly started to feed him the soup and he swallowed each mouthful like an obedient child, it was Charlotte who watched Joe's reflection in the mirror over the washstand. She studied his every movement, searching for any tiny nuance. But there was nothing, no sign.

If you know, you're sure as hell not giving away a thing, are you, Joe? But then you never do, do you? Always so damned enigmatic.

Charlotte continued to torture herself for the ten minutes it took Joe to shave. Never a hirsute man, and with only three days' growth, the process was relatively quick, although Joe conducted himself, as always, in leisurely fashion.

'I'll take over now, Nina,' he suggested, and having washed and dried his face, he took the bowl from her.

Nina happily agreed. 'I go tell the family, eh? Let 'em know you back with us, Boss. That all right, Mr Joe?'

'Of course it is. Give us another twenty minutes though,' Joe suggested, 'time to finish the soup. We don't want the Boss leaving any, do we?'

'Nah, that right, got to drink it all.' Nina gave a firm nod and left them to it.

As Joe sat on the bed, Charles waved the soup aside.

'No more, thanks.'

Joe voiced no insistence, seeming even to have expected as much. He placed the bowl on the bedside table and waited.

'Who undressed me, Joe? Who treated my wounds?' The questions appeared to come from Charles, but it was really Charlotte who was asking, for she had a feeling she knew.

'I did,' he replied.

She stared back at him, meeting the directness of his gaze just as steadily as he met hers.

'So you know,' she said.

He nodded, which, given the past half-hour or so of mental torture now came as no surprise to her. But what followed was totally unexpected, something that had never once crossed her mind. How could it? Why should it?

'I've always known, Charlotte. I've known since you left England. Geoffrey told me everything.' Joe smiled. 'So, you see, stripping you of your clothing to minister to your injuries held no mystery for me.'

10.

She gazed at him in utter disbelief. This couldn't be possible, surely. Could it? But his eyes told her otherwise. Yes, it could.

'You've always known,' she said, and it wasn't a question.

'That's right.'

'But …' She halted as his past comments sprang jigsaw-like to mind. 'You told me I should find myself a woman … that I should have a physical relationship with a member of the fairer sex … you said I was a young man with a young man's appetites …'

'Of course I did,' Joe replied, 'I was playing my role. Besides,' he added mischievously, 'you can't blame a chap for wanting to have a bit of fun. I enjoyed watching your reaction, which, I must congratulate you, was minimal.'

Is this why I've always found you so irritating? Charlotte wondered. *And why I'm finding you so irritating right now?*

Things were starting to fall into place, including her Uncle Geoffrey's assurances upon his deathbed. What was it Geoffrey Burton had instructed his lawyer to tell his nephew? 'Mr Lawson will ably support your endeavours in the Pilbara and is bound to prove your staunchest ally.' That's what

Andrew Goodiston Q.C. had told her in his Perth office on that day that now seemed a lifetime ago.

Yes, she thought, *of course you've known all along.*

'So you've been playing a game with me, Joe,' she said. 'I'm glad you found it so much fun.'

'We've all been playing a game, Charlotte,' he replied, displaying no reaction to the iciness of her tone, 'and a dangerous game at that.'

'You must think me such a fool.'

'To the contrary, I think you extraordinarily brave. I admit that, to start with, I was circumspect about anyone attempting what you've done, but you've succeeded, and I have nothing but admiration for you.'

'Thank you,' she said stiffly.

What else could she say? She was now suddenly and painfully aware that he had stripped her of her clothing. That he'd seen her naked body. Every inch of it. He would have had to remove all her lower undergarments as the wound from the spear was in her upper thigh, and the snake bite, embarrassingly enough, in her right buttock. And the strong crepe band she wore around her chest to disguise the swell of her breasts, it too was gone. Perhaps in order that, during her fever, she might breathe more freely without its restriction, or perhaps simply in order to bathe her, who could tell? Had he hauled it up over her head, or had he cut it off? The latter, she presumed. She was even tempted to ask. But of course she didn't.

'I'm most grateful to you for tending my wounds,' she said awkwardly instead. 'You no doubt saved my life, and I thank you.'

'No. Alwyn saved your life. It's him you must thank.'

Joe could see she was self-conscious. He could all but hear her very thoughts. But they didn't have time for any of this. They must discuss the serious issues that lay ahead.

'Nina will be back with the children soon,' he said. 'I must let you know the lie of the land before they get here.'

'Yes,' she replied, chastising herself. He was quite right. This was no time for feminine modesty.

'I noticed how closely you were studying Nina,' he said, 'I could tell you were wondering if she knew. Indeed, if anyone knew, and if so, who?'

'You noticed all that, did you?' she queried. 'All that from ten minutes in your shaving mirror.'

'I was watching you as closely as you were watching me, Charlotte.'

She nodded acquiescence and they shared a smile.

'Nina doesn't know,' he went on. 'The status quo remains as it always was. No-one but the children and I know the truth. And that's the way it shall stay.'

'I see. That's good.' Charlotte found herself thinking as Charles, which she considered an excellent sign. 'And what of you, Joe? What do the children know of your involvement in the deception?'

'Only Victoria is aware of my knowledge from the very beginning,' he replied. 'I shared everything with her. I thought it wise. We treated your wounds together, and it was only right she should feel able to trust me.'

'What was her reaction?' Charlotte asked.

'Very much the same as yours. Utter shock.'

'Yes, I can well imagine. And the boys?'

'The boys don't know the full story. They've realised over the three days you've been in my care that I'm now aware of the deception, Victoria has told me as much. But they trust me. The secret will remain between us. We're all in this together, Charlotte, all sworn to secrecy.'

'As we must be,' she agreed. 'But the boys will find it difficult to continue playing their roles in the knowledge that I've been unmasked. They had come to so accept me as their father.'

There was a tap at the door.

Joe rose to his feet. 'We're about to find out,' he said.

He crossed to the door and opened it.

Nina stood there, with Victoria and the boys.

'Here we are, Boss,' she said, bustling them inside, obviously prepared to be part of the reunion. 'Everyone real happy you're back with us.'

'Of course they are, Nina.' Joe fielded the moment impeccably, crossing to the bedside table to retrieve the soup bowl, which he thrust into her hands. 'The Boss has finished his soup. Let's return this to the kitchen, shall we?'

Nina looked down at the bowl, then back at him. 'But he ain't eat it all.' Her baleful glare told Joe this was his fault.

'The Boss has had enough, thank you,' he replied.

He ushered her out, intending to join her and leave the family to themselves, but upon his glance back, he caught Victoria's signal, a very clear shake of her head that said, *Stay*.

So he closed the door behind Nina and waited to see what would happen.

Victoria took the lead, determined to prove herself more than capable of maintaining her role.

She went to the bed, her brothers following.

'We're so glad you've returned to us, Papa,' she said, her smile glowing with such warmth as she bent down to kiss her father's cheek that Charlotte clearly read the message was for her.

Then Victoria looked to her brothers. 'We've all been worried, haven't we?'

Edward grasped his father's hand in both of his, he too determined to prove his worth. They had discussed this moment, the three of them.

'We have, Father,' he said, squeezing Charlotte's hand with such fervour that the intent of his own message was quite clear. 'We've been praying for you every single day. Twice a day, actually. Every morning and every night.'

But Harold wasn't quite up to maintaining the deception. Not now. Not yet. Harold was crying. Not out loud. But the tears were openly running down his cheeks as he climbed into bed and snuggled up beside the mother he'd been so terrified of losing.

Charlotte held him close. 'It's all right, darling,' she said, 'there, there, it's all right.' She gazed down at him, then back to her daughter and her older son. 'Everything's going to be all right,' she said, at that moment a mix of both mother and father. 'I'm so proud of you. So very proud of you all.'

It would be awkward for a while, she realised, not only for the children, but also for herself. She'd been thinking so long as a man and a father, this brief return to being a woman and a mother was confusing.

From his stance by the door, Joe found the scene touching. God, how he admired this woman.

'Up you get, now,' Charlotte said briskly, 'there's a good boy.' She was once again Charles.

Harold obediently climbed out of the bed to stand beside his sister, who took his hand. 'Yes, Father,' he said dutifully.

Victoria turned to Joe. 'How soon do you think it will be before we can return Father to the house?' she asked. 'His bed is all ready and waiting, and we miss him.'

'As soon as he feels up to it.' Joe smiled at Charles. 'What do you say, old chap?'

'I say the sooner, the better. Bring me some fresh clothes, Victoria, and we'll see how I go. Oh, and don't forget the undergarments,' he added, 'I seem to have lost mine.'

'Yes,' she said, 'Joe had to cut them off in order to treat your wounds.' Victoria knew full well the reference was specifically to the chest band. Her mother had always had two of them. *We'll have to make up another for you, Mama,* she thought, wondering where on earth they'd find the same strong crepe fabric in Roebourne. *No matter,* she told herself, *one can order anything via a catalogue these days.*

'Come along,' she said to her brothers and, still holding Harold's hand, she marched to the door, Edward following.

Joe closed the door behind them and turned to Charles. 'Admirable,' he said.

'Yes, they are, aren't they?' Charles replied.

Joe nodded. But he'd been referring to her.

'I'd better make up a pair of crutches for you, old man,' he said, 'it'll be some time before you can bear any weight on that leg.'

***

Charlotte proved correct in her assumption that things would be awkward for a while. Surprisingly enough, not so much for the children, who quickly reverted to their roles, but more for herself.

With Joe now her ally, a man who knew her secret, a man who shared in the deception, she couldn't help but view him through different eyes. She couldn't help but react to him differently. This man had undressed her, tended to her naked body. He'd seen her and touched her, and somehow she couldn't rid herself of the knowledge.

As the weeks slid into months, and she graduated from the crutches he'd made her to a walking stick, which he'd also fashioned himself, she realised that he no longer irritated her. His unruffled manner, the very composure that she'd at times found infuriating, she now saw as a sign of strength. That strange mix of Chinese and English, the casual 'old chap' and 'old man' seemed even flirtatious, and she realised, with a growing sense of horror, not only did she find him attractive, she was sexually drawn to him.

This won't do at all, she told herself. *For God's sake, pull yourself together.* The only way to continue living the lie was to think and act at all times as a man. There was no place in her life for natural female yearnings. She must distance herself from Joe Lawson.

As for Joe, he had come to recognise an aloofness in the Boss of late, which was a pity, for he very much liked Charles. He respected the reason for such behaviour though. Charlotte had become self-conscious in his presence. Understandable, he supposed. But sad.

***

Six months later, in April of 1893, Charles found himself with an even greater distraction than Joe Lawson. The shearing season was approaching. May was always the busiest time of the year, and he'd been prepared to focus himself upon it, distraction and distance being of vital importance these days. But both Joe and the shearing season took second place when, out of the blue, Victoria became a case for the gravest concern.

'You've what?' He'd been appalled by her announcement.

'I've accepted a teaching position in Cossack, Father,' she'd calmly replied. 'Two hours only, each Monday afternoon at three o'clock.'

We'll see about that, my girl, Charles had thought, but he'd kept his temper in check. Victoria was a wilful creature and confrontational tactics with her rarely ended happily.

'And how exactly has this come about?' he asked.

'I responded to an *ad hoc* request from a group of local Cossack businessmen, which appeared in the *Roebourne News*,' she said. 'They're after a person to run a two-hour class in English expression for their workers and I'm to be paid per head according to the number of students who enrol. Which might not be many to start with, but they hope to build attendance.'

She took her father's silence to signal interest, or at least she pretended to, as she went on to patiently explain.

'You see, Papa, there are quite a few European workers in Cossack who wish to settle there permanently, but their employers are aware they need a better command of English in order to communicate efficiently with the masters of cargo ships, the majority of whom are English speakers.'

Charles was fully aware of this situation. He was, after all, one of the several JPs who occasionally sat on the bench of the Cossack Court. The language barrier was indeed a drawback for the export trade, which included pearling, wool, meat and horses, principally to Singapore, Malaya and Arabia. The problem needed to be corrected for efficiency's sake if nothing else. He even knew, or had heard, that the businessmen wishing to further educate their workers had tried to secure the services of the local schoolteacher, but had been unsuccessful. He had heard also that they had arranged with the Government Education representative in Roebourne to have use of the Cossack schoolhouse in which to conduct their endeavour should they manage to secure the services of their own teacher.

He did *not*, however, know of the advertisement they'd placed in the *Roebourne News*, nor that his daughter had applied for the position. And, above all, he did not know, until this very moment, that she had been selected.

Why, he wondered, *why was she selected? Were there no other applicants?* Quite possibly yes, although Victoria would have offered an impressive application, he was quite sure of that, perhaps the best they'd received. Of one thing he was certain, however. She would not have revealed her age.

'You are sixteen, Victoria,' he said, unable to stay silent a moment longer. 'For goodness' sake, girl, you're only sixteen years old!'

'I shall be seventeen in just over two months,' she replied haughtily, sensing an impending confrontation.

'And you won't be teaching children, you'll be teaching men,' he continued, 'grown men, some of whom will no doubt be of questionable character, to say the least. Cossack can be a cesspit of depravity, my dear, a town of roughnecks and corruption. No place for a young lady! I cannot and will not allow this!'

'You can and you shall, Father,' she countered with ominous calm. Then she smiled sweetly. 'Oh, Papa, there is no need to fear for my safety, I promise you. I intend to stay at Mrs Pead's boarding house, just as you do when you sit on the bench in Cossack and are forced to stay overnight.'

He was about to speak, but she would allow no interruption.

'I'll be away from Burton Station for one night a week only. And the Police Quarters and courthouse is almost directly opposite Mrs Pead's, as you well know. Besides, Constable Jeff will keep an eye on me. You have asked him to do so in the past, and we have become well acquainted. Indeed, I consider Jeff a personal friend.' From the tone of her voice, she obviously deemed this her argument's clincher. 'So as you can see, there is no cause for concern.'

'Of course there's cause for concern,' he snapped. 'You're a *girl*. These pupils you would be teaching are not children, these are *men* we're talking about.'

Victoria remained unfazed, and there was mischief in her eyes as she suggested, still sweetly, 'Then perhaps I should dress in male attire, Papa. Perhaps I should pose as a man. Would that allay your fears? I could dress as a man and carry a gun.'

Their eyes were locked. They were staring each other down. *She's daring me*, Charles thought. *She's saying, 'Two can play at your game.'* Another thought suddenly occurred. *This couldn't be a veiled threat, could it? A threat to expose me?* Then, just as quickly, he put the notion aside. Of course not, Victoria was having fun, playing a game. She knew only too well the danger they would all face should his identity be exposed. Charles Burton was a man held in great respect throughout the Pilbara, a man of the law, a successful property owner and highly regarded boss. Should it be discovered he was a woman, the people who had looked up to him would feel humiliated. They would turn on him. He and his family would be ridiculed, hate would surround them. No, no, Victoria would never betray him, he knew that. *But, oh my*, he thought, *how she does love to play these games.*

Charles had been cornered at that moment. And he'd known it.

'There will be no need for you to dress as a man, Victoria,' he'd said. 'But yes, I would strongly suggest you carry a gun.'

And you certainly know how to use one. 'That would allay my fears somewhat.'

'Thank you, Papa.' She'd kissed him fondly on the cheek. 'I knew you'd come to see things my way.'

What other option had he? If he'd been in her shoes, he may well have played the same game, presented the same threatening argument. The two of them were so alike, they could almost read each other's minds.

And so it was, Victoria took up her position as English teacher to a motley collection of working men in Cossack's schoolhouse on a Monday afternoon at three o'clock when the children's school attendance had concluded. And despite the conversation she'd had with her father, she *did* arrive in the township dressed in male attire. Although hardly posing as a man.

Like most outback women and girls, particularly those of the Pilbara, Victoria did not ride side-saddle, as was the English custom. Burton Station did not even possess a side-saddle, and it had always been her personal preference to ride astride anyway. This necessitated the use of trousers. And when she rode, she considered a sturdy bush hat more secure, and certainly far more effective against the sun's glare, than a bonnet or a boater.

Victoria established what was to become her weekly routine on that very first Monday, which happened to be barely two months before her seventeenth birthday.

After breakfasting early, she mounted her horse, a sprightly five-year-old bay gelding called Jimmy, and left Burton Station at six am. Two saddlebags were packed with her belongings;

one including her school mistress's garb of skirt, blouse and jacket, together with toiletries for her overnight stay; the other with her school satchel, containing not only her necessary teaching materials, but the Enfield .476 handgun.

Arriving in Roebourne at around eight am, she boarded the horse-drawn tram to Cossack, which departed half an hour or so later, hitching her horse to the back of the rear carriage.

Upon reaching Cossack in the mid-morning, she untethered her horse and set off at a walk for the carriage barn and stables where the animal was to be housed for the night. She would decide the following morning whether she would return to Roebourne by tram or ride back to Burton Station.

Leading Jimmy along The Strand, she passed Sing's Bakery and General Store, then the Cingalese tailor's shop, Dalton's Bulk Beer Shop and the front door of the White Horse Hotel. She was very much enjoying this walk on this very first day of this brand-new stage of her life as a fully-fledged adult. Her head held high, her stride confident, she knew she was receiving interested glances from passers-by and those in shops and businesses, who found the sight of her intriguing.

She turned left into Pearl Street, passing the Cossack Post Office on her right, and crossed Perseverance Street with the Courthouse and Port Police Quarters on the corner to arrive at the stables, where she was greeted by its proprietor, a smiling Swedish giant aptly named 'Tiny' Sven Pedersen.

Her father had introduced her to Tiny Pedersen when, upon insisting he accompany her on a trip to Cossack to pave the way, he'd also introduced her to Mrs Pead at the boarding house. He'd had a private word with Jeff while he was there too, as Victoria had known he would.

'You will keep an eye on her, won't you, Jeff?'

'Of course, sir, goes without saying. Happy to oblige. Young Victoria and I have become good friends.'

'Glad to hear it,' Charles replied heartily. 'More than glad – relieved, in fact.' And he was.

'*God morgon*, Miss Boorton.' The big Swedish stable master took Jimmy's reins from her and held the horse as she unpacked her saddlebags. 'You today start *Engelska* speak school, *ja*?'

'I do, Mr Pedersen,' Victoria answered, lifting out the school satchel from one saddlebag and the cloth shoulder bag containing her clothes from the other. 'Three o'clock until five o'clock in the school building. Are you going to attend?'

'*Inga*.' He shook his head. 'I going at *tre* not tend.'

She took a second or so to work this out. Then, 'No.' It was her turn to shake her head. 'I said "attend", not "at ten",' and she spelt it out very slowly for him. '"Attend" is a separate word altogether. "Ten" is a number.'

'*Ja*, ten. Is gud.' Puzzlement clouded the big, bland face. 'What this is, "tend"?'

'Never mind.' She sighed. Tiny Pedersen was going to take some work. 'I'll explain in the schoolhouse. I must be off now. Goodbye.'

'*Adjo*.'

'No, not *adjo*. That is Swedish. In English we say, "goodbye".'

'Ahaa!' The jovial giant grinned broadly. 'I say goodbye.'

'Yes, that is correct. Very good, Mr Pedersen,' Victoria called back as she stepped out into Pearl Street.

She retraced her steps, turned left into Perseverance Street, walked around the Courthouse and headed for Mrs Pead's boarding house.

She slowed her pace, taking in her surrounds as she went. Cossack was hardly the most gracious of towns, she conceded. Often it was crawling with drunken pearlers, or with brash young men heading for the goldfields at Mallina, but right now, to her, this place meant freedom. Freedom to explore herself, to be whoever she wanted, to express herself however she wished. For one day a week, anyway. The prospect was exciting.

Arriving at the boarding house, she was warmly welcomed by Mrs Pead, who very much respected Charles Burton and was only too happy to be housing his daughter.

After being shown upstairs to her small, single room, Victoria washed and changed from her rough travelling attire to her neat navy skirt, cream blouse and matching navy jacket. It really was too hot for any form of jacket, she thought, even a lightweight one like this, but she was determined to make a good impression. She brushed her dark hair until it gleamed, curling it back into a neat chignon, and then joined Mrs Pead downstairs, where they lunched together in the landlady's private quarters. As a rule, she would take her meals in the boarding house dining room with the other lodgers, of whom there could be as many as fourteen, she'd been told, but this being her first day, Mrs Pead was most insistent.

'I promised your father I would look after you, my dear.'

'It's very kind of you, Mrs Pead,' Victoria replied, thinking, *I don't need anyone to look after me. I'm perfectly capable of looking after myself.* But she was grateful nonetheless. Mrs Pead was a kind woman.

Following lunch, she returned to her room, where she sat on her narrow bed, poring over her copious notes, although she knew it was highly unlikely she would call upon any of her preparation. At least, not today. The most important aspect of today's exercise would be the impression she made upon the men, the confidence she instilled in them. She would need to prove herself. How many men would there be, she wondered, and how would they react to her?

With no idea what to expect, Victoria was far from daunted. This was all part of the excitement. Her spirit of adventure was aroused and she welcomed the challenge.

At half past two, she donned her sunbonnet and gloves, picked up her school satchel and descended the stairs.

Stepping out into Perseverance Street, she marched the several hundred yards or so down to the schoolhouse boldly, where she stood in the shadows of a coolabah tree, watching as the chattering children burst out onto the verandah and dispersed in groups, going their various ways.

The children were closely followed by their teacher, who pulled the bolted door shut behind her but did not close the attached padlock, as were her instructions. The schoolhouse was to be left accessible for the tutor who would follow, the instructions having been made quite clear to each. The teacher was to retain the key to the padlock, which the tutor would close upon departing. Under no circumstances was the schoolhouse to be left unlocked. Who knew what drunks or vagrants might take over the premises during the night. Cossack could be a wild place after dark, even on a Monday.

The teacher obviously had little interest in who this tutor might be, for she did not wait to find out, nor even deign to look around. Had she done so, she might have noticed the girl observing her from beneath the foliage of the pretty, white-trunked tree nearby.

Victoria was thankful for her lack of interest. This middle-aged, purse-lipped woman who had refused to take on the tutorship of the men would no doubt be highly critical of her appointment.

When everyone had gone, Victoria emerged from the shadows of the coolabah tree and stepped up onto the little front verandah. She opened the door, entered the schoolroom and surveyed her surrounds.

A small room. A rostrum snugged up against the wall at the far end, upon it a teacher's desk and chair. A sizeable blackboard, chalk and cleaning rag on its ledge. Chairs and desks for the pupils. Fortunately not child-sized desks, she was glad to note. All in all, a very ordinary little schoolroom, just as she'd expected.

Leaving the front door open, she crossed the room, mounted the rostrum and, placing her satchel on the desk, opened it and took out her notepad, pencil and folder of papers. Beneath the folder sat the Enfield .476. A strange, but reassuring sight, she thought, as she clicked the satchel closed and placed it on the floor beside her chair.

She removed her sunbonnet. There was a hook on the wall next to the blackboard, obviously intended for the teacher. On either side of the front door were a series of hooks for the pupils' use.

She hung her bonnet on the hook and was in the act of taking off her gloves when the first of her students arrived. There were three of them, roughneck-looking workers, the type of men she'd expected. They'd come as a group and were gathered undecidedly at the door, a small cluster of confusion, confronted by the sight of her and gabbling in their own language. They had known their tutor was to be a female, but certainly not one so young!

Victoria could hear their mutters of surprise and in the babble of their words, one or two were audible, *jeune fille*, among them.

French. How very fortunate!

'*Bonjour, messieurs,*' she called. '*Entrez s'il vous plait.*' With a wave of her hand, she welcomed them in, a gesture both friendly and authoritative.

They obeyed. Automatically.

'*Asseyez-vous, s'il vous plait.*'

They sat. Again, automatically.

'*Merci. Je m'appelle Mademoiselle Burton. Bienvenue.*'

They responded with mutters of '*Bonjour, mam'selle*', then sat watching and waiting for what was to happen next.

Good, Victoria thought. But was it really going to be this easy?

It wasn't, but those first few minutes paved the way. Her manner grew in authority with each passing minute as others arrived in dribs and drabs, expressing in languages various their surprise at the sight of her. They were all taken aback. But one by one, she bade them welcome in English, instructing them to sit, and one by one, they obeyed.

By a quarter past three, she presumed this was her class. Eleven in all.

She was about to request the door be closed when Tiny Pedersen arrived.

'Miss Boorton,' he gasped apologetically, leaning heavily against the doorframe. Having run as fast as he could, and unaccustomed to running, poor Tiny was breathless. 'I sorry. Is horse. Is horse.'

'My horse?' Victoria felt a stab of alarm. 'Is Jimmy all right?'

'*Ja, ja.*' The big Swede nodded. 'Jimmy, he gud horse. Bad horse ...' Tiny shook his head forebodingly. 'Bad horse, he run. I chase ...' Words failing him, Tiny Pedersen gave a hopeless shrug of apology.

'Ah. A horse bolted from your stables ...' The translation was easy enough.

'*Ja, ja.*'

'Did you catch him?'

'*Ja.* But I be late. Sorry. I be sorry.'

'No matter, Mr Pedersen.' She waved him inside. 'Do come in and take a seat. And close the door behind you, if you wouldn't mind.'

Tiny did as he was told, sinking his giant frame gratefully into one of the chairs.

'I think we now have our full complement,' Victoria announced, gazing around at the men. A motley bunch indeed. Aged from their twenties to their fifties, all were working men, but of such disparate appearance she wasn't sure where to start. Two were Asian, which could present something of a problem, for she would have no idea how to communicate if they spoke no English. The others were Caucasian, but from where? She'd heard a little muttering in German, although she couldn't be sure; it might have been Dutch.

'Welcome, gentlemen,' she said briskly. 'We'll need to establish a roll call for ongoing classes, so let's start with some names, shall we?'

She sat, opening her notepad and taking up her pencil, then looked out at her class – to be met by a sea of blankness.

Oh dear, this won't do, she reprimanded herself. *You need to go slow, Victoria. You need to take things slowly and keep things simple.*

'Hello, everyone.' She smiled, allowing her gaze to fall on each man as very, very slowly, she introduced herself. 'I am your teacher. I am Miss Burton,' she said, putting a hand to her chest. 'And you are? Your names?'

She started with the Frenchmen, pointing first at one then another, each of them in turn reciting his name, which she wrote down in the notepad. The rest of the class quickly grasped the procedure and followed suit, after which she was able to address each man by name, asking where he came from and gently ascertaining how much English he spoke. She was gratified to discover that most of the men had a smattering of English, and that surprisingly enough the two Asians – who happened to come from Malaya – were among the more accomplished of the group, as they'd been working in Cossack longer than the others.

Throughout the entire exercise, Victoria was aware of the men's reaction to her. She was winning them over, certainly, they were accepting her authority and were prepared to trust her as their teacher. But several among them, the younger ones in particular, were eyeing her up and down lustfully. She was glad she had the Enfield with her should one of them attempt a little 'after-school activity'. Just as a warning device, no more. The sight of it would be enough to keep them in check, she was quite sure of that.

She wrote some simple phrases up on the blackboard, 'good morning', 'good afternoon' and the like.

'We shall converse in English throughout,' she told the class as the lesson drew to an end, a glance to the Frenchmen signalling there would be no further use of their mother tongue. 'You all have enough basic knowledge to learn not only from me, but from one another. I shall write up new phrases on the blackboard, we shall practise as we go, and I shall answer any queries you may have. But always in English.'

She continued to speak slowly, aware that some were understanding her well while others were getting the gist of what she was saying, and that they would talk among themselves afterwards.

'There will be strength in your camaraderie, gentlemen, for you share a common purpose.' Her smile was one of supreme confidence. 'You are, after all, Cossack workers, and that is why you are here.'

She gave a nod of dismissal, signalling class was over.

'I shall now bid you *good afternoon*, gentlemen,' she said meaningfully.

At least half the class understood her request.

'Good afternoon, Miss Burton,' came the ragged chorus of reply.

'Well done,' she congratulated them. 'I thank you for your attention, and I shall see you next week.'

As they started to file out, she turned away and began assiduously cleaning the blackboard, a clear message she was not inviting any individual attention.

She turned back to discover, thankfully, that the schoolroom was empty, and after packing her notes away in the satchel, donning her gloves and sunbonnet, she crossed to the front door and stepped out onto the verandah.

But outside the schoolroom, it appeared the rules did not apply. Several of the younger men were standing on the ground beside the steps, jostling each other, clearly prepared to compete for her attention.

She ignored them as she shut the door and clicked the padlock closed, wondering as she did whether she should display the handgun. Just a glimpse. Just a warning, no more. *A bit aggressive though, surely*, she thought, *it's five o'clock in the afternoon and still broad daylight.*

As things turned out, there was no need.

'Good day to you, Miss Burton,' a familiar voice said, and pushing past the young men, Jeff stepped up onto the verandah.

'Why, Constable Jeff,' she replied with a smile, 'how lovely to see you.'

The would-be Lotharios melted away at the sight of the young policeman known for the lightning speed of his fists.

'I've been waiting for you,' he said. 'I promised your father I'd see you home to the boarding house after your class.'

'Did you now?' She tried to sound a little arch, implying she needed no looking after, but in truth, she was grateful. She really hadn't wanted to produce the handgun. And, strangely enough, unlike her reaction to Mrs Pead's nurturing offer, she didn't at all mind the idea of Jeff looking after her. She so enjoyed his company.

'Let me carry that for you,' he said, taking the school satchel. 'Good heavens,' he remarked, upon feeling its weight, 'what on earth have you got in here?'

'A handgun,' she replied as they stepped down from the verandah, 'an Enfield .476. They're rather heavy.'

He gave her a whimsical look, this news obviously coming as something of a surprise.

'Father's idea,' she said, 'he thought a handgun might prove a deterrent should any of my students try to step out of line.'

'I've no doubt your father's right, and I've no doubt it would.'

'I'm actually rather proficient with firearms,' she said defiantly as if daring him to differ.

'I'll bet you are, Victoria.' He smiled, knowing this would be no lie. 'I'll just bet you are.'

She abruptly changed the subject. 'After seeing me safely home, where are you going, what are you doing?' she asked as they set off along Perseverance Street.

'Benny McCartney's workshop,' he replied. 'I do a check at the end of each workday to make sure he's locked the premises.'

'Ah, yes, Benny McCartney, my father's so-called business partner.' She gave a light laugh. 'A frightfully colourful character, so I'm told.'

'Yes, you could certainly call him that.'

'May I come along?'

He hesitated momentarily.

'Oh, please, Jeff,' she begged. 'It's far too early for me to be locked away at Mrs Pead's.'

He gave a shrug. 'I don't see why not,' he agreed. 'Although I must warn you, Benny's bound to be three sheets to the wind by now. He's a hopeless drunk.'

'So I've heard.'

They turned into Frazer Street and started walking down towards The Strand.

'He's a nice old bloke, though,' Jeff continued, 'we get on well, Benny and me. He can be very funny too. When he's not altogether too liquored up that is.'

Victoria smiled happily, content just to be in his company as they strolled down the street side by side, here and there, people giving the young policeman a wave or a 'g'day' as they passed. Jeff was popular with the citizens of Cossack. The good ones, that is; those who didn't break the law.

They turned right into The Strand and walked over to Benny's pearling shed where it sat on the shoaly shores of the river. The door of the workshop was wide open and Benny was seated on the front verandah of his hut next door, ubiquitous glass of whisky in hand, bottle on the floor by his feet, an all too familiar sight.

'*Mūto'i Jeff,*' Benny yelled as he saw Jeff approach.

'What did he say?' Victoria's ear was quick to pick up a foreign tongue, particularly one she didn't recognise, and she was immediately interested.

'"Policeman Jeff",' he replied, 'that's what he calls me. Or else *Pāruru Jeff*, which means "Bodyguard Jeff", depending on what mood he's in.'

'Hello there, Benny,' he called in return and a minute or so later, as they stepped up onto the hut's verandah, he made the introductions.

'Victoria, this is Benny McCartney, Benny, this is Miss Burton, who happens to be—'

'Ah, yes.' Benny's face split into its customary, ragged-toothed grin. 'The Boss's daughter, no less. How do, young miss.'

'Pleased to meet you, Mr McCartney,' Victoria said.

'*Māuruuru i te fārerera'a.*' Benny waved an expansive welcome and was about to offer them both a drink, but Jeff was having none of it.

'*Ia vai 'ōpani noa te 'ūputa,*' he said, pointing an admonishing finger at the open door of the workshop.

'Yes, yes, I know,' Benny whined, 'I know, I know. I must always lock the door.'

'What language are you speaking?' Victoria asked.

'Tahitian,' Jeff replied, still eyeing Benny disapprovingly.

'I've never heard Tahitian before.' She was fascinated. 'Where did you learn it?'

'He learned it in Tahiti, where he lived and was a rude and officious boy, just as he is being with me now!' Benny waggled an accusatory index finger at Jeff. 'Aggressive and self-important, he is.' Then to Victoria, 'But he speaks Tahitian very well. I speak it not so well these days.' He tapped his forehead. 'The words do not come anymore as they once did.'

'Say something else,' she insisted, turning to Jeff. 'Go on!'

'*E vahine nehenehe roa 'oe.*'

'Aha!' Benny exclaimed, and he grinned drunkenly, suggestively, lecherously even. 'He said you are a beautiful woman.'

'No, I didn't!' Jeff flashed a warning glance at the old pearler. 'Not like that, anyway.'

'No.' Benny shook his head apologetically to Victoria. 'No, no, I got it wrong,' he corrected himself. 'Like I told you, my Tahitian is not so good anymore. He said, you must go now.'

Victoria smiled cheekily at the old man. 'After you lock the door,' she said.

'Yes.' Benny returned a smile of resignation. 'After I lock the door.' He held a key up and rose to his feet.

'How do I say goodbye in Tahitian?' Victoria asked.

'*Nānā,*' the men replied in unison.

'Well, then, *nānā*, Mr McCartney.'

'Yes.' Benny nodded. '*Nānā, pōti'i nehenehe roa.*'

When they were back on The Strand heading for the boarding house, Victoria asked, 'What did he say to me as we left?'

'He said "*Nānā, pōti'i nehenehe roa*", which means "goodbye, beautiful girl". But he wasn't quite correct,' Jeff added thoughtfully. 'He used the word *pōti'i*, which means "girl". He should have used *vahine*, which means "woman".'

Victoria looked away to her right, over the river, and as she did, she smiled to herself. She felt beautiful right now. And she certainly felt like a woman. She always did when she was with Jeff. He was the principal reason she had applied for the position here in Cossack.

PART THREE

1893, The Pilbara, Western Australia

11.

With the shearing season upon them, Burton Station was a
hive of activity and Charles had little time to fret any further
about Victoria's weekly sojourns in Cossack. It appeared there
was little cause for concern anyway. By all accounts, her classes
were hugely successful, the numbers of her students having
doubled within only weeks. The businessmen were all too
delighted their plan had proved such a success, and the monies
the employers paid for their workers' tuition were regularly
deposited into Victoria's account at the Union Bank in Cossack.

'You're becoming a wealthy woman, my dear,' Charles
remarked. He was immensely proud of his daughter.

'Hardly, Papa,' she laughed, but in truth, she was proud of
herself.

'All that fretting I did for nothing,' he said. 'I should have
known better. You're more than capable of looking after
yourself.'

So, Charles focussed instead on the chaos that
surrounded him. The shearers had arrived and were housed
in their huts, and the shearing shed itself was a scene of
utter madness. Here, men competed with all the insanity
that only top-gun shearers could. Charles and Joe had

hired the best, as they always did, and the competition was furious, as it always was.

After the weekly clip had been assessed, baled and stamped, the bales were taken by dray to be stored in the warehouse at Roebourne. At the end of the shearing season, the year's entire wool clip would be transported by bullock train to Cossack, from where it would be shipped to buyers all over the world.

The wool from Burton Station was not of the same class as the high-quality merino fibre produced in the colonies of Tasmania and New South Wales and Victoria, where the pastures were rich and the stock carefully bred by experts. The Burton wool was Pilbara wool, of durable strength from durable stock. Sturdy, strong and practical, like the land itself, this wool was respected for its sheer resilience.

Charles was kept happily distracted throughout the shearing season, following which there was the further distraction of Victoria's seventeenth birthday. Or he had presumed the occasion would be a distraction. He and the boys had made a trip into town to buy presents, and to collect those ordered from a catalogue at the post office, Nina had baked a cake especially, and Alwyn had hand-painted a boomerang as his personal gift. They were to have a party. And then ...

'What do you mean you haven't invited Joe?' Victoria demanded. 'Of course, Joe must come. Good heavens above, Joe's *family.*'

'Yes, yes, I know dear,' Charles had replied. 'I'm sorry,' he'd added with a vague wave of a hand, 'I haven't seen much of him lately, I simply forgot to ask him, that's all.' He ignored the oddly quizzical glance from his daughter.

The birthday party proved an enormous success and, Charles had to admit, principally due to Joe.

'I didn't know you played the violin,' he said in amazement when Joe turned up on the night with a bottle of champagne under one arm and, most bizarrely, a violin tucked under the other.

'I don't, old chap,' Joe replied, 'well, yes, I do just a little, but I'm not very good, and I don't even refer to the thing as a violin.'

He plonked the champagne down on the breakfast room table, which was well and truly set up for the party, and held the instrument aloft like a trophy.

'This is my fiddle,' he announced to Charles and the children, 'which I offer as part of the evening's festivities. I must warn you, however, my repertoire is limited. I can play only Scottish songs and reels and jigs.'

'Why on earth is that?' Victoria demanded.

'The British family my mother worked for as an amah in Hong Kong were Scots,' he explained. 'Or rather, the father was, the mother was frightfully English. Anyway, I was taught the violin along with their son, Douglas. Being the same age, we were schooled together.' He raised a humorous eyebrow. 'The violin was for Scottish melodies at "Daddy's" insistence, I don't think the fellow was particularly musical. In any event, those are the only ones I remember. Douglas has no doubt gone on to Chopin and Mozart.'

'Good heavens, I didn't know any of this,' Charles remarked with interest. It explained quite a lot about Joe Lawson, he thought.

'Oh, there's a great deal you don't know about me, old chap.' Joe grinned. 'I'm quite the man of mystery.'

'Play something, Joe.' Harold was already jumping up and down, very much in a party mood. 'Play something, play something.'

So, Joe did: 'The Bonnie Banks o' Loch Lomond'. And there was no looking back after that. The tone of the evening was set.

Charles relaxed more and more as the night wore on. They ate copious amounts of roast mutton and drank endless toasts to Victoria, to family, to Nina's food and to her cake, which was a triumph. Needless to say, throughout the toasts, Nina kept herself and Alwyn well away from the champagne, both sticking instead to her homemade lemonade.

And throughout the party, there was Joe and his fiddle. Following the meal, they moved into the living room, where he was in hot demand, with 'Comin' Thro' the Rye', 'My Bonnie Lies Over the Ocean', and even 'Wee Willie Winkie'.

'The very first song I was taught,' he said, 'I must have been all of ten.' And to his surprise, the whole Burton family sang along with him.

'I taught them "Wee Willie" when they were little,' Charles laughed.

Alwyn loved the reels and the jigs best. With a natural sense of rhythm, he made up his own steps, whirling about like a dervish in perfect time to the music, Nina clapping along. Harold joined in the dance, albeit a little clumsily.

Victoria is quite right, Charles thought, watching on, *Joe is most certainly family. We share a bond. And now more than ever, I mustn't let anything form a rift between us.*

Following the meal and the toasts and the dancing came the gift-giving segment of the evening, which proved a definite highlight.

Victoria adored the hand-painted boomerang from Alwyn, and she was most appreciative, or so she said, of the football from Harold, but it was Edward's gift of an atlas that took first prize.

'Oh, Edward,' she breathed, running her hands over its pages with reverence, 'this is wonderful, truly wonderful. Did you purchase it via a catalogue?'

'Of course,' he said, 'just as you taught me.'

But Edward's atlas was to be outdone by his father's choice.

'Oh, Papa ...' Victoria was rendered all but speechless as she drew out the green silk gown from the layers of tissue paper in its box.

'Oh, Papa ...' She held the garment up against herself and twirled on the spot. 'How beautiful ... Where did you ...'

'Catalogue,' Charles said. 'Same as Edward. We've all learned from you, my dear, as you can see. We ordered the gifts some time ago and collected them from the post office just last week.'

She couldn't stop twirling, the silken fabric rustling and swirling about her, a sea of emerald green in the lights of the candles and kerosene lamps.

'Why don't you try it on?' Charles suggested. 'Nina, you might go with her and lend a hand perhaps?'

'Sure, Boss.'

Nina gathered up a lighted candelabra and as the two disappeared to Victoria's bedroom, Edward, Alwyn and

Harold took the football out onto the front verandah where they kicked it around, leaving the men to chat together.

'Looks like you've made a real hit with the dress, old chap,' Joe said.

'Yes, she's become quite fashion-conscious of late,' Charles replied. 'I had to study up on what the latest look is for young women. I have no idea what they're wearing these days. It's all in the catalogues of course, with pictures and descriptions, but I'm glad I got it right.'

'You certainly did that, I'd say.' Joe took a sip of his drink. The champagne now gone, the two were sharing a bottle of beer.

'Yes, it appears I did, didn't I?' Charles said, relieved. 'It's all to do with her Monday nights in Cossack,' he went on. 'She likes to dress for her evening meals at the boarding house. Don't ask me why. Mrs Pead does serve up an excellent evening repast, and her guests are invariably interesting company I've found, but the dress code is hardly formal.'

'Perhaps she's just enjoying being the attractive young woman she is,' Joe said.

'Yes, I've no doubt that's it,' Charles agreed. 'And I must say, she has every right to enjoy herself. She works so hard. To and from Cossack, teaching those workers on Mondays, then back here teaching the boys for the rest of the week, including Saturdays. I'm very proud of her.'

'As you should be, old man.'

They raised their glasses in a mutual toast.

'Your fiddle has certainly been a triumph,' Charles said. 'All this time and I've been totally unaware of the musical fellow my partner was. You're a mystery indeed, Joe. Do you ever play it when you're with the men?'

'Oh, yes, quite often, when we're sleeping rough around the campfire.' Joe's smile was easy and relaxed, the smile of a true friend. 'The Boss usually isn't around then, so he doesn't get to see.'

'Ah, yes.' Charles nodded, equally relaxed, feeling neither threatened nor confronted. It was true, he rarely camped out with the men. 'Mystery solved.'

'What do you think?'

There was a swirl of colour as Victoria twirled into the room, closely followed by Nina, candelabra held high.

'Isn't it glorious,' Victoria said delightedly, parading in front of them. 'The perfect fit, the perfect colour, the perfect style.' Another swirl. 'What do you think?'

'Perfect in every way,' Charles agreed. 'Green really is your colour.'

'Not just *any* green, Papa,' she corrected him, 'this is *emerald* green.'

'Of course.' Charles smiled. 'Silly me.'

The gown really did suit her, he thought. Simply cut, with high, puffy sleeves at the shoulder, it tapered elegantly to a slender waist, then into a full-length skirt with a rhinestone-edged hemline. *The latest fashion for young women*, he'd read in the catalogue. *And that's what she is*, he thought admiringly. *She's a young woman now. My little girl is all grown up.*

'Thank you, Papa.' Victoria bent down to kiss his cheek.

'You look quite lovely, my dear,' he said, and as their eyes met, his daughter read the message in his with absolute clarity.

'I feel quite lovely,' she agreed, and her smile said, *Yes, Mama, you're right. I'm all grown up now.*

Unable to resist a glance in Joe's direction, Charles knew instantly their exchange had been recognised for exactly what it was. But, again, he didn't feel threatened. *Joe is an ally*, he told himself, *not a threat*. They even shared a smile, signalling their joint relief that any tension between them was now a thing of the past.

***

Victoria couldn't wait to show off her new gown at the first available opportunity, which would be when she next invited Jeff to join her for dinner at Mrs Pead's boarding house. She had done so already on two occasions, having the extra expense added to her account privately, in the knowledge that Jeff's wage as a policeman was minimal. It was her way of thanking him for escorting her to her lodgings after class.

She decided the following Monday would be the perfect occasion. After all, he could hardly refuse to celebrate her birthday.

When the day arrived, she was so excited the mere thought sent her pulse racing to such an extent she could barely concentrate upon her class. The emerald-green gown was hanging up in the wardrobe of her little room at Mrs Pead's, waiting to be worn, ready to be admired. Being silk, it was barely rumpled at all from its ride to Cossack in Jimmy's saddlebag.

'I turned seventeen last week,' she announced as he joined her on the verandah of the schoolroom. He was always there waiting when she locked up after class, even though, as they both well knew, his protection was no longer necessary. She was perfectly safe these days. They simply enjoyed each other's company.

'Did you now? A grown-up girl of seventeen,' he said indulgently. 'Then I wish you a happy birthday, Victoria, and offer you my heartiest congratulations.'

'Thank you.'

He took the school satchel from her. It wasn't as heavy as it had been in the past, for she no longer took the handgun to class. 'No need for it,' she'd said when he'd queried her, 'there's never a threat from my students.' Which was true, she was so popular with her class that any troublemaker would be dealt with by the pupils themselves.

'I thought, given my recent birthday, that you might like to join me for dinner at Mrs Pead's,' she suggested as they set off down Perseverance Street.

'Can't this evening, I'm afraid,' he said. 'I have to write up a report for Sergeant Fry.'

'Oh.' She was instantly deflated, and more than a little taken aback by the casual manner of his response. 'Really?' She felt slighted, and it showed in her tone, which clearly said, *You're refusing to celebrate my birthday?*

'I'm sorry, Victoria.' He sensed she was peevish, but there was little he could do about it. 'We had a nasty incident here in Cossack last night. Very nasty, in fact. A knife fight at the White Horse Hotel turned into a riot. Several were wounded and one man was killed. Sergeant Fry's arrived in Cossack and wants a detailed report on his desk first thing in the morning.'

'I see.' She supposed she had to. But she was bewildered as they crossed Frazer Street and continued to walk on. 'Aren't we going to check up on Benny?' she asked.

'I already have. Need to start on this report as soon as possible.'

'Oh.' She was further irritated. As a rule, she accompanied him to Benny's workshop, which she very much enjoyed. Today wasn't progressing at all as she'd planned.

Jeff bade her farewell outside the boarding house, knowing she was disappointed. Cross even. She could be demanding at times, particularly when she didn't get what she wanted. Victoria, so eminently readable, was never one to disguise her feelings.

'I tell you what,' he suggested as she took the school satchel from him, 'why don't we go for a ride tomorrow morning after I've handed my report in to Sergeant Fry? I'm sure he'll let me have an hour off, particularly when I tell him it's to celebrate your birthday. He's a great admirer of your father's.'

Her glowing smile signalled all was instantly forgiven. 'Yes,' she said, 'what time?'

'Eight o'clock? At the stables?'

'Eight o'clock it is. Jimmy and I will be waiting.'

Closing the door behind her, she bounded happily up the stairs. There was something to look forward to after all. Hardly as exciting as the prospect of toasting her birthday and showing off her glorious new gown, but that could wait until next week. In the meantime, the gown would join the small wardrobe of clothes Mrs Pead kindly kept in store for her these days.

Having worked herself into a state of excited anticipation, Victoria was not prepared, however, to spend the entire night sitting upstairs in her poky little room. Good heavens, it was only five-thirty. Nor did she wish to join the other lodgers, pleasant though they were, for dinner. She would venture forth instead and walk down to the river, where she would sit by the shore and enjoy the breeze off the water. Cossack would hardly be dangerous on a Monday night, and she would avoid the busy pub areas.

She informed Mrs Pead she would not be dining as she wished to study in her room and gratefully accepted the sandwich Cook made up for her instead.

After eating, she changed from her schoolteacher navy blue into her riding trousers and rough shirt. Best not to advertise her gender, she decided. At a passing glance, people would presume she was a man. And just to be safe, she took her cloth shoulder bag with the Enfield revolver, its weight resting reassuringly by her side.

Then, while the lodgers were dining, she crept downstairs and out into the street, warning herself that she must make sure to return before ten o'clock. The front door of the boarding house was locked each night on the dot of ten.

A quick look up and down Perseverance Street assured her the town was relatively quiet, as she had presumed it would be, and intending to avoid the central area with its lights and its pubs, she turned right and set off on her way out of Cossack.

She passed the Malay camp on her left and then beyond that, the Chinatown tents to her right, knowing that just one hundred yards further would see her free altogether from the township and alone on the sandy soil of the foreshore.

Once there, she made her way down to the Explosives Wharf, where it stood on the river's edge, a marine light marking its presence. The wharf was exclusively for the loading, unloading and storing of explosives – for government use, the clearing of land, the building of roads – and people rarely came near the place. She'd walked here once before with Jeff when he'd been giving her a guided tour of Cossack and its surrounds.

Seating herself on a mooring bollard at the wharf's edge, Victoria marvelled at the stillness of the night and the brightness of the moon reflected in the water. The sky was cloudless, the stars were brilliant, and the moon itself was a glorious golden ball. A full moon, she realised. Perhaps that's why she was so restless.

The gentlest breeze came off the water, relieving the stifling heat of the evening. Good God, even now in the middle of the dry season, which would be winter to those down south, it was hot up here in the Pilbara.

But so very beautiful, she thought, looking out over the tangled growth of mangroves silhouetted in the moonlight and listening to the gentle lap of the water.

Then, suddenly and with a sense of shock, she realised she was not alone. She'd heard something. What was it? A cough. A man's cough. And then something else. Another man. Another man laughed. The sounds were coming from behind the explosives storage shed not twenty yards away.

Victoria stood, instinctively reaching into her cloth bag, her hand wrapping itself around the handle of the Enfield revolver. She would quietly steal away, she decided. To stay might well be to court trouble.

She turned to go but then heard a voice. A child's voice, raised in protest. A cry, perhaps of pain.

'Who's there?' she called.

Scuffling noises and mutters reached her through the darkness, then the outline of a man appeared from behind the explosives shed.

'Well, well, what do you think you're doing here, lad?' he called.

'No business of yours, sir,' she answered, feeling her pulse quicken. What were these men up to?

Her voice was the giveaway.

'Ah, not a lad at all, I see.'

The man came nearer, squinting for a closer view of her. And where she stood in both the marine light and the moonlight, he could see her clear as day.

'My, my, what do we have here,' he slurred lasciviously. 'What a looker you are, missy.' He was well drunk, she could tell.

As he spoke, a young Aboriginal girl, no more than nine or ten years old, darted out from behind the shed. She ran straight past the man and then straight past Victoria and threw herself off the wharf into the river

Victoria gazed after her, alarmed. The child had disappeared altogether. She could see nothing but the moon's reflection rippling on the now-ruffled water's surface. What had happened to the girl? What was she to do?

'Don't worry about her, darlin',' the man said dismissively. 'She's a black. They can swim like fish. She's headed for her mob's camp on the other side of the river. It's low tide, what's more. She'll swim it easy.'

'But she was only a child,' Victoria muttered in outraged disbelief. 'How could you …?'

'She's a black!' the man snapped. 'A heathen! She was getting no more than she deserved! Or she was about to. That is …'

Victoria noticed his gaze shift to over her shoulder.

'… That is, until you interfered.'

'I take it your friend has now circled behind me and is approaching my back,' she said.

'Whatever gave you that idea, darlin'?' His grin was malevolent. 'But it happens to be right. Oh, my lovely, you are now in a lot of trouble.' He was all but licking his lips in anticipation.

'I'm afraid I must contradict you.'

Victoria drew the Enfield from her shoulder bag. Not for one second had her hand relinquished its grip. She raised the revolver and aimed the barrel directly at the man's head. 'It is you who is in trouble. You and your friend.' She tilted her head, as if listening intently. 'Your friend who I sense has lost his nerve, and is thinking of running away,' she added.

She smiled as she heard the man run off. 'Oh, dear, now you're alone. How sad.'

'You slut!' Sweat instantly beading, the man tried to bluff his way through the abject fear that now fell upon him. 'You filthy slut, who do you think—'

'Turn your back and get down on your knees.' Victoria's voice was as cold as ice.

The man did so, terrified, realising just how much trouble he was in. This girl was going to kill him. He'd seen the murderous look in her eyes. He wanted to run. He wanted desperately to run away like his brother, Arnie. But his body was frozen to the earth as he knelt motionless, waiting for the inevitable bullet.

Victoria marched up behind him and swung her arm with all the strength she could muster, sending the magazine of the heavy revolver crashing into the side of his skull. Then she stood back and watched his unconscious form drop to the ground, where it began bleeding into the dirt.

She turned and looked about, hoping no-one had seen her. No-one, thank God – the place remained deserted.

Then, sensing movement to her right, she turned and saw the young Aboriginal girl, who had climbed back out of the river and was standing on the wharf. Their eyes met, locking together momentarily. Then the girl grinned, teeth flashing white in a cheeky face, before once again she leapt from the wharf, disappearing into the moonlit black waters.

Victoria returned the Enfield to her shoulder bag, knelt and felt the man's pulse. He was alive. And there didn't appear to be copious amounts of blood, although it was difficult to tell in the dark. She would leave him here to be discovered in the morning. Either dead or alive, he might bleed out through the night, but she didn't particularly care. Men like him didn't deserve to live anyway.

What sort of vile people are you? she thought as she took her leave. *This place attracts the very dregs of humanity.*

Back at the boarding house, having returned unobserved, she carefully cleaned the handgun upstairs in her little room, although in the light of the kerosene lamp she could see no particular evidence of blood. She felt no fear, no guilt.

Although, remembering those ruffians who had attempted to rob them at Burton Station several years previously, she did wonder whether or not this meant she had killed another man. To have killed two men by the age of seventeen was something few young women could boast, she supposed. But if this were to prove so, she refused to suffer any pangs of conscience. Both had deserved to die.

***

The following morning, Jeff was three-quarters of an hour late arriving at the stables. Jimmy was all saddled and eager, dancing on the spot, as impatient as Victoria was to get going.

'Is not for Constable Jeff to be late,' Tiny Pedersen remarked after they'd been waiting together for a full fifteen minutes.

'It's not *like* Constable Jeff to be late,' she automatically corrected him, simply a matter of habit.

'Yes, I like very much Constable Jeff. Is good man.' Tiny was puzzled. 'What? You *not* like? How this can be?'

Victoria heaved a sigh. Tiny Pedersen remained an uphill battle. 'No, that's not what I meant at all.'

'What then is you mean?' Tiny asked eagerly. He loved to learn.

The query regrettably led on to much discussion. 'Like' had always been such a simple word for Tiny Pedersen. An easy word too. 'I *like*, I *not* like,' he insisted. To discover something could be 'like this' or someone not 'like that' was extremely interesting, but also very complicated. As for it being 'not like Constable Jeff to be late', that was incomprehensible.

Victoria was relieved when Jeff finally arrived at a quarter to nine.

'Did you sleep in?' she demanded, as Tiny went off to saddle one of the police horses that were housed at the stables.

'To the contrary, I've been up since six o'clock.'

'Oh? How come?'

'A man known to us, a fellow called Bart Cameron, was found by some Chinese market gardeners down near the Explosives Wharf,' he explained. 'He'd been bashed in the head.'

'Oh, dear. He was dead, then?'

'No. Ugly wound, but he'll live. When we interviewed him, he said he'd been attacked by a madwoman who'd come out of the dark and coshed him for no apparent reason.'

'How odd.'

'Yes, that's what we thought. Although Bart's a nasty piece of work and he was no doubt up to something unpleasant. Anyway, it required another report. I'm sorry I'm late.'

'You're forgiven.'

He didn't die then. Victoria supposed she was relieved. At least it meant she'd only killed one man. *So far.*

They rode to Settlers Beach, on the coast a mile out of Cossack, where they galloped their horses along the broad, white sands, the animals loving the ride as much as they did themselves. Then they dismounted and walked beside the foreshore, taking off their boots and relishing the feel of the coarse, coastal sand beneath their bare feet.

They didn't talk a great deal, they didn't feel the need as they gazed out at the beauty of the ocean, at the rugged coastline, and Jarman Island a mile or so out to sea. Here was where the majority of ships anchored, sending lighters up the inlet to the port of Cossack, delivering or collecting cargo and passengers.

Jeff watched her as she drank in the view. This was the Victoria he liked best. There seemed so many Victorias: the authoritative schoolteacher who commanded a class of working men; the precocious student who'd been studying law from the age of thirteen; the spoilt young 'missy' who was so demanding of attention. He'd come to know them all, and all were interesting, but this one was his favourite. The unpretentious, commonsense, down-to-earth Victoria in her trousers and her man's shirt and her bush hat. A mix of child-like girl and highly competent young woman, she was such a complex creature.

Back at the stables in Cossack, as he returned his police horse and Victoria collected Jimmy's saddlebags, already packed for her journey, she wrung a promise out of him. Or at least, as much of a promise as he could commit to.

'My invitation to dine in order to celebrate my birthday still stands,' she said in that imperious manner she sometimes adopted. 'You must promise me faithfully that you'll come to Mrs Pead's next Monday.' It sounded very much like an order.

'I promise,' he agreed. 'Unless there's a knife fight at the White Horse or someone gets coshed,' he added. 'There's no accounting for what can happen in Cossack.'

'True,' she said. But she made him shake hands on the deal.

He accompanied her to the tram stop in The Strand. Given the morning's workout, she would not overtax her horse by riding him all the way to Burton Station. Jimmy would walk along behind the tram, and she would ride home from Roebourne.

But during the tram trip, which she always enjoyed, Victoria did not relax and take in the passing landscape as she usually did. She made her plans instead. The exhilaration of that morning and the intense pleasure of Jeff's company had inspired her to take action. She was seventeen now, and the gown was waiting in the wardrobe allotted her at Mrs Pead's. The moment had arrived, she decided.

***

'I'm going to return to my law studies, Father,' she announced to Charles the following Friday.

'Good heavens above, Victoria,' he exclaimed, 'you teach every day of the week. Where on earth will you find the time?'

'There's always Sunday,' she said airily. 'I don't teach the boys on Sundays, and I very much miss my studies.'

He supposed he wasn't surprised, remembering the intensity of that young girl sitting all alone on the back verandah, hunched over her books.

'I can't seem to find the first volume of *The Oxford History of the Laws of England* though,' she said. 'I do believe you had it with you when you were researching a case.' She knew perfectly well that he had.

'Yes, I did, my dear. It's with several other law books and journals of mine in the Magistrate's Chamber at the Cossack Courthouse.'

'Ah.' She knew that perfectly well too. 'Would you mind awfully if I collected it when I'm in Cossack next week?'

'Not at all. You'll have to do so on the Monday, though. Court's in session on the Tuesday.'

'Yes, of course.' She already knew that, she'd checked. 'I'll call in and collect it straight after class.'

'Excellent. I shall lend you my set of keys.'

It had been that easy.

Now all she had to do was pray that everything would go according to plan; most importantly, that Jeff would not let her down.

Bearing in mind the disappointment of the previous week, her opening query when he met her on the schoolhouse verandah after class that Monday was brazenly direct.

'You *are* going to keep your promise, aren't you?' she demanded. 'You *are* going to dine with me at Mrs Pead's tonight?'

'I am,' he replied. 'There has been neither knifing nor coshing in Cossack over this past day or so.'

'I'm very glad to hear it. And we're now going to check up on Benny?'

'We are,' he said, taking the school satchel from her.

'Oh, good.' She smiled, and started chatting away nineteen to the dozen as they walked together.

En route to Benny's workshop, they passed right by the courthouse, but she made no mention of the fact that she needed to call in and collect a book from the Magistrate's Chamber. She was too distracted, talking far too much and far too fast; the book could wait until later.

After spending a pleasant fifteen minutes or so with old Benny and ascertaining that the workshop was secured, Jeff escorted her back to the boarding house.

'I shall see you at seven,' he said.

'Yes. Seven o'clock on the dot,' she agreed. 'In exactly one and a half hours. I can't wait.'

He was charmed, she was so child-like in her excitement. 'And we shall toast your birthday, Victoria, I promise.'

'Yes. We shall.'

He was punctual, arriving on the dot of seven as promised, and sat in the front parlour of the boarding house awaiting her, a small bunch of flowers in hand. He hadn't bought the flowers, it was true, but he had gone to some trouble to acquire them, walking out of town to where they grew in abundance on the side of the road. It was the beginning of the wildflower season, and they made a pretty bouquet, the vivid red of the Sturt's desert pea, the fluffy lavender of the mulla mulla blossom and the rich gold of the acacia wattle.

Victoria was nearly ten minutes late. Deliberately. She wanted to make an entrance as she came down the stairs, which led directly to the front parlour, where she knew he would be waiting. And she'd gone to such trouble. She'd even packed a set of curling rags and tongs in Jimmy's saddlebag, and her long, dark hair, usually drawn back in a chignon, was now framing her face in soft ringlets. She'd added a pinch of colour to her lips and cheeks too. And above all, there was the gown; cut in a way that accentuated the slenderness of her waist and the curve of her back, and in a colour that so suited her complexion. How could she fail to impress?

He was in such deep conversation with one of the lodgers, however, several of whom were seated in the parlour awaiting the announcement of dinner, that he didn't notice her entrance. He didn't even give her a glance.

Victoria found this intensely irritating. Although she was gratified to see he'd brought flowers.

'Good evening, Constable Jeff,' she said.

Looking up, he froze at the sight of her. The very reaction she'd wanted. Her irritation vanished in an instant.

He stood, as did each of the gentlemen in the parlour, four in all.

'Good evening, Mr O'Connor.' After nodding to the two other lodgers, regulars she knew, Victoria greeted the middle-aged man to whom Jeff had been chatting. Patrick 'Paddy' O'Connor was a local landowner; Victoria and her family were well acquainted with the O'Connors and their tribe of five. 'What sees you at Mrs Pead's, may I ask?'

'I sail on the morning tide, Miss Burton,' the Irishman said. Paddy had been calling this girl 'Victoria' for the full five years he'd known her, but looking as she now did, such a liberty seemed cheeky, if not downright rude. It must have been a good six months or so since he'd last laid eyes on her, and she had clearly blossomed into an elegant young lady. 'A trip home, via Singapore, to visit my ailing father before he departs this mortal coil.'

'Oh, dear, I'm sorry to hear your father is unwell.'

'It's to be expected. He's a goodly age. Approaching ninety.'

The door to the dining room opened and the maid appeared.

'Dinner is served,' she announced, and stood aside waiting as, one by one, the lodgers filed past. Jeff and Victoria chose to dally before following them.

'Happy birthday,' he said, handing her the flowers.

'How pretty. Thank you.' She put her nose to the bouquet and breathed in the aroma. The flowers had no particular fragrance as such, but she loved their freshness and the smell of the land.

'You look beautiful, Victoria,' he said. 'That's a lovely dress.'

'Yes, *isn't* it,' she enthused, giving a twirl on the spot, drinking in his admiration. 'A birthday present from Father, he has such wonderful taste. Isn't it just glorious.'

'It certainly is.' *Oh, no, my dear girl*, he thought, *it is you who is glorious*. How had he failed to notice, among all the Victorias he'd come to know, that she'd turned into such a beauty? She was radiant. Radiant and womanly. *Where has the child gone?* he wondered as he offered her his arm.

'I'll put those in water for you, miss, and place them in your room,' the maid said, taking the flowers from Victoria as they passed her at the door.

'Thank you, Alice, that's very kind,' she replied. And she sailed into the dining room, aware of the eyes that signalled the admiration of every man present.

Several more joined the gathering over the following ten minutes. There were eight lodgers currently staying at Mrs Pead's boarding house. A mixed bag of late-season wool buyers, two Perth lawyers on an extended business trip relating to yet another miners' dispute at the goldfields of Mallina and, with the overnight arrival of Paddy O'Connor, the ranks had now swelled to nine. The only female present at the table was young Victoria Burton, which was quite often the case on Mondays, unless a visiting businessman happened to be accompanied by his wife.

The conversation at the table was convivial as always, and when the carafe of red wine was passed around to accompany the roast beef, Jeff raised his glass.

'I wish to propose a toast,' he said, adding with a smile to Victoria, 'as I promised I would.' Then to the table, 'Raise your glasses, one and all, and let us drink to Miss Burton's birthday.'

There were cries of surprise and 'congratulations' as everyone raised their glasses.

'To Miss Burton's birthday,' they chanted, following Jeff's lead.

Victoria's look to him was accusatory, while also signifying her gratitude that he had not announced which particular birthday they were toasting. She had no wish for it to be known she had just turned seventeen.

'Today is not really my birthday,' she admitted a little shamefacedly. 'I am a fraud, I fear, for my birthday was well over a week ago.' But her admission was made with such charm she was instantly forgiven, and another bout of congratulations followed.

Victoria remained scintillating company throughout the evening, keeping everyone entertained, even flirting a little here and there. Which was no hardship. Feeling as lovely as she did tonight, flirting came easily to her. But it was all in order to impress Jeff.

'You were quite the belle of the ball, Victoria,' he remarked after dinner, when they returned to the parlour.

'Which was all your fault,' she said. 'It was you who insisted upon turning everything into a party.'

'I was only following through on my promise to toast your birthday.' He gazed around for the maid. 'Shall we order some tea?' In the past, they'd had a cup of tea in the parlour before he took his departure.

'Oh, dear.' She looked suddenly caught out. 'Oh, dear, I just remembered.'

'What? What is it, Victoria?' He was concerned. She seemed worried.

'I have to go to the courthouse.'

'At this time of night, whatever for?'

'I need to fetch a book from the Magistrate's Chamber.'

'What on earth are you talking about?' He was dumbfounded now.

'I need a law book from Father's collection there,' she explained. 'It's imperative for my studies during the week, and I can't pick it up tomorrow, as the Court will be in session.'

'Yes, it will.' He knew that only too well; he was to be in attendance as Court Constable the following morning.

'Oh, dear, I'm so sorry, Jeff,' she said, 'it completely slipped my mind. I'll just pop up to my room and get the keys Father lent me.'

He stared after her as she disappeared up the stairs to return only minutes later, wearing a cape over her dress and clutching her father's set of keys.

'I won't be long,' she said, 'only fifteen minutes or so. You wait here and we'll have tea when I get back.'

She was already making for the front door, but he beat her to it.

'Don't be ridiculous, Victoria, I'm not letting you out on the streets alone at this time of night.'

He offered her his arm and they left together for the courthouse. As she had planned they would.

'You should have told me about the book this afternoon,' he said as they went, 'we could have collected it on the way to Benny's.'

'Yes, I know,' she admitted. 'I forgot. How silly of me.'

The Magistrate's Chamber, which led off from the courtroom, was not in the least grand. A rather poky affair with a desk, two hardback chairs, a small bookcase and a single bed. Here, a visiting magistrate or JP could spend the night if there were no rooms to be had elsewhere, which was known to have happened on occasion, particularly at the height of the pearling season.

They stepped inside and Jeff struck a match, lighting the oil lamp that sat on the desk as she hunted for the book.

Victoria had been in the Magistrate's Chamber before. She knew this room well enough and found the book with little trouble. She'd known exactly where it would be: in the lower shelf of the bookcase, along with her father's sundry collection.

As she stood, Jeff was about to snuff out the wick of the oil lamp, but she stopped him.

'No, wait,' she said, and placing the book on the desk, she crossed to the door, which they'd left ajar, and closed it. Then she turned to him. 'I'm glad we're alone.' She dropped her cape to the floor and stood there before him in the emerald-green gown, knowing she looked captivating. 'I wanted to share my birthday with you Jeff. Just you and no-one else.'

She crossed to him where he remained motionless by the desk, the oil lamp still glowing, and placing a hand on his chest, looked deeply into his eyes, her face only inches from his. 'Do you understand what I'm saying?'

'Yes.' He did. All of a sudden and only too well. 'Yes, I believe I do.' He removed her hand from his chest. 'But we can't, Victoria,' he said gently, 'we can't and we mustn't do this.'

'We can and we must,' she replied.

She took up his hand once again and cupped it against her breast, holding it there, insistent, demanding. He could feel beneath the swell of her flesh the depth of her breathing, even the pump of her heart.

'I'm sorry, my dear,' he said, firmly this time. 'I cannot and will not oblige.'

But Victoria was not prepared to take no for an answer. Her well-planned seduction was not about to end like this. Tonight was the night she was to lose her virginity. She had determined it should be so.

'You can and you will, Jeff.' She was thrusting herself against him now, in a blatant attempt to arouse him, which was certainly having its effect. 'You know that you want to, don't you,' she breathed, aware of his erection through the silk fabric of her gown. 'You know that you want me, admit it. You do, don't you, Jeff,' she chanted, each thrust driving him mad. 'You want me. *You want me.*'

And to his shame, she was right. He could resist no longer. The urge was overwhelming. Dear God, how long had it been since he'd had a woman?

Their coupling was swift, hardly the way Victoria might have wished. Not that she'd expected anything romantic, knowing that her brutality in taking the lead would only invite brutality in return. But they hadn't even undressed, which rather surprised her. She'd removed her lower undergarments and he'd downed his trousers, no more than that.

She'd steeled herself for the pain, which had not been overly intense, and when it was done, there was a little blood on her petticoat, but fortunately none on the bed. And even more fortunately, she discovered, none on her lovely new gown, although being emerald green, it was difficult to tell in the dull glow of the oil lamp.

Despite the lack of emotional involvement, Victoria refused to be disappointed. She'd lost her virginity and that had surely been the object of the exercise, she told herself as she smoothed down the bedcover and donned her cape.

'Oh,' she said with a smile, and she picked up her father's copy of *The Oxford History of the Laws of England*, 'I mustn't forget my book.'

Jeff didn't return the smile. He didn't even look at her. He appeared in a state of shock. Which she supposed was hardly surprising.

'Don't feel guilty, Jeff,' she said apologetically, 'it was all my fault.'

'Come on,' he replied and he snuffed out the lamp, 'I'll take you back to the boarding house.'

He didn't say a word during their walk back to Mrs Pead's and Victoria had the good taste to stay silent, sensing she was the one who should probably feel guilty.

'I don't suppose you'd like a cup of tea?' she asked at the front door. 'There's plenty of time.' It was well before ten.

He shook his head.

'Why don't we go for a ride tomorrow morning?' she suggested brightly.

'I can't,' he said, his tone terse. 'Court's in session and I'm to be in attendance.'

'Oh. Yes, of course. Well, I'll see you next Monday then.'

He said nothing, but turned and walked off into the night.

12.

Victoria had had a full week to consider her actions of the previous Monday and having given the matter a great deal of thought, she now wondered whether Jeff would be waiting for her at the end of today's class. His shocked reaction to their sexual encounter and his abrupt departure after escorting her back to the boarding house that night had left her very much in doubt. He might wish never to see her again, and she supposed she could hardly blame him.

But to her vast relief, he was there. Had he not been, she would have sought him out, for she desperately needed to talk to him.

It was Jeff himself, however, who got in first.

'We need to talk, Victoria,' he said as he joined her on the verandah.

'Yes,' she agreed, 'we do.'

'Let's go somewhere quiet.'

He didn't look at her as they began walking down Perseverance Street on their way out of town, and she didn't chatter away as she usually did, but remained obediently silent, wondering where his choice of 'somewhere quiet' might be.

Of course, she thought, when they arrived at the Explosives Wharf. 'No-one ever comes here,' he'd said when he'd given her his guided tour of Cossack and its surrounds. 'Nice place to sit and have a quiet think by the river.' Which was precisely why she'd come here that night.

And someone else had come here that night too, hadn't they, she thought, *someone bent on raping a child.*

She seated herself on one of the mooring bollards at the wharf's edge, the very one she'd sat on that night while she'd had her 'quiet think by the river'.

Jeff sat beside her on the wharf, gazing out over the water, still reluctant to meet her eyes, it seemed. But she didn't give him a chance to begin whatever it was he wanted to say. Instead, she leaned in towards him urgently, eager to make amends.

'I'm sorry, Jeff,' she said, 'I'm so terribly, terribly sorry.'

He turned to her. 'What for?' he asked bluntly.

'I used you. I used you wantonly, shamelessly,' she insisted. 'And I had no right.'

He continued to stare at her with eyes that were dull. Disinterested. He didn't look at all like the Jeff she knew. The man who had shared with her, and her alone, his real name. Jean-François Fabron, the man with whom she spoke French on occasion, the man with whom she laughed, the man who teased her and treated her sometimes as a child and sometimes as a woman. She had ruined their friendship.

Victoria detested herself at that moment. *How could I have been so shallow?* she thought.

'I had no right to do what I did,' she went on, desperate to get through to him. 'I wanted to know what it was like … Sex, I mean … I wanted to lose my virginity … I wanted—'

'It doesn't excuse what I did, Victoria. It doesn't in the least excuse my behaviour.' She'd not regained his interest. Not even a flicker. He returned his gaze to the river. 'I just wanted to let you know that I intend to resign from the police force. I shall hand in my notice to Sergeant Fry this week and leave Cossack.'

She stared back at him, appalled. 'But why? Why on earth would you do something as drastic as that?'

'Oh for God's sake, girl, listen to yourself,' he snapped, turning back to her. 'You're seventeen years old! I defiled you. I robbed you of your virginity! How am I supposed to live with myself after taking advantage of you in such a way?'

'But I *wanted* you to.' She all but screamed the words out in her frustration. 'Didn't you *hear* what I said? I *wanted* you to! I *wanted* to lose my virginity. I was literally *begging* you to take it. To *ravish* me, to—'

'All right, all right, calm down,' he said, looking about anxiously, although there was no-one within earshot. 'You don't need to have that relayed all around Cossack.'

But she'd finally got through to him. He was at last prepared to talk.

'It's not only what I've done to you, Victoria,' he admitted. 'It's what I've done to your father. I've betrayed his trust. He placed you in my care. I was to protect you from the very act I perpetrated upon you, which would always have been the fear uppermost in his mind. Surely the fear uppermost in the mind of any girl's father.'

She looked him boldly in the eye. 'You mean rape.'

'Yes, of course I mean rape.'

'But you didn't rape me,' she declared. '*You* didn't rape *me*! *I* raped *you*!'

Jeff gave a bark of laughter. He couldn't help himself. 'Oh, Victoria,' he said, shaking his head helplessly, 'you are such a child.'

'I am *not* a child.' The remark infuriated her. 'I am seventeen, yes, but I cannot remember when I was last a child.' Should she tell him she had killed a man when she was thirteen? she wondered. Would that perhaps impress?

Her high dudgeon continued to be a source of amusement, but Jeff had further serious news to impart.

'There is the added fact that your father is virtually my employer,' he went on. 'I receive remuneration from Charles Burton for checking on his pearling interests here in Cossack.'

'You're talking about Benny McCartney?'

'That's right. I am paid one pound a week to keep an eye on Benny and ensure the work premises are secure at all times. So, you see,' he added with a shrug of resignation, 'your father has even further reason for detesting me. I've been trusted on all counts and found sadly wanting. If I was Charles Burton, I'd have me run out of town. Or thrown in gaol. Or I might even have a bullet put in my head. I certainly deserve all he could throw at me.'

'So you're running away for fear of the retribution my father might seek?'

She was deliberately goading him, and he knew it, but he refused to rise to the bait.

'If that's the way you choose to see things, Victoria, then yes.'

'The act of a coward, in my opinion.'

'An opinion to which you're entitled.'

Well, that tack isn't going to work, she decided. But there was another possible angle, wasn't there?

'What if I'm pregnant?' she demanded.

'What?'

'What if, after you've run away, I discover I'm pregnant?'

She felt a surge of triumph in the pause that followed. *Aha, you didn't think of that, did you?*

He hadn't and was stymied for an answer. Such an outcome was most unlikely, but he was prepared to encompass it. 'Very well, I shall remain in Cossack long enough for us to know either way,' he conceded with dignity. 'In the remote chance this should prove so, we will speak further. If not, I will take my leave.' He stood. As far as he was concerned, the conversation was over.

Victoria jumped to her feet.

'Jeff, listen to me,' she begged, 'please, please listen.'

'Have you stopped playing these games of yours?'

'Yes. Yes, I have, I promise. Please hear me out.'

He nodded.

'I will not have you ruin your life because I threw myself at you. Can we not put this behind us? We had such a fine friendship, why must we destroy it?'

'We can't just pretend this didn't happen, Victoria,' he said gently, aware now that she was genuinely pleading.

'Why not? Why must you leave Cossack? You've built

yourself a life here. You have friends and a career. Why, you told me yourself just recently that Sergeant Fry intends to promote you to Senior Constable. That's something to be proud of. Everyone here respects you, Jeff.'

He was looking at her so kindly, Victoria presumed her argument had fallen upon fertile ground.

'My father finds you the most admirable of men.'

'Exactly.' His smile was, if anything, just a little patronising. 'In which case, how can I look him in the eye? How can I look any of them in the eye, these people who so respect and admire me?'

Victoria realised that perhaps she may have overplayed her hand. 'If I were to tell my father what happened,' she said rebelliously, 'and if I were to tell him the *way* that it happened,' she added, 'he would understand.'

Jeff laughed out loud. 'No, he wouldn't, Victoria. He'd kill me. And he'd have every right.'

Ah, but you don't know my father the way I do, she thought. *You don't know my father at all.*

'Come along now,' he said, 'I have to get back to work.'

'You won't leave, though, will you?' she begged as he started briskly walking back towards town. 'Promise me, Jeff, please.' She was forced to skip a little in order to keep up with him. 'Promise?'

'I won't leave until we know you're safe,' he agreed. *Again, that exasperating mix of child and woman*, he thought. *She's utterly impossible.* 'I promise.'

***

Charles Burton's reaction to the news his daughter had lost her virginity was not as explosive as Jeff had predicted it would be.

'You've what?' he demanded, barely able to believe his ears.

'I've lost my virginity, Father,' she repeated. 'Intentionally. Just one week ago. I set out to do so with great deliberation, and I accomplished my aim.' Then she stood back and awaited the fireworks that would follow.

Victoria had fronted her father the very next day, shortly before lunchtime on the Tuesday when she'd returned from Cossack. She'd sought him out where he was in the home paddock with Joe Lawson, branding the newly arrived cattle.

'You're home early,' Charles called when he saw her approaching. As a rule, she didn't arrive home until mid-afternoon.

'I didn't catch the tram to Roebourne,' she said, giving a wave to Joe, who was in the act of releasing a steer. 'I left straight after breakfast and rode here directly. Can we have a talk?'

'Of course. Fire away.'

'In private.'

'Oh.' Charles exchanged a glance with Joe, and Joe gave a nod and took the branding iron from him. 'Of course, Victoria,' he said. 'It's nearly time for lunch anyway. Let's head on home.'

They walked back to the homestead together, but once there, Victoria was not content to chat in the front sitting room.

'My bedroom,' she said. 'The boys will be home for lunch any minute.'

'Oh. *That* private,' Charles said meaningfully.

'Yes.'

'Very well.'

They adjourned to her bedroom, and that's when she'd come out with her brazen statement.

'I've lost my virginity, Father,' she said, right to his face.

He'd been so flabbergasted, she'd even had to repeat herself. And then she'd stood back to await the fireworks, which, surprisingly enough, were a little slower in coming than she might have expected.

'I see,' Charles replied coldly. '*Intentionally*, you say. With *great deliberation*?'

'That's right.'

'And who, may I ask, was the lucky recipient of your attentions?'

'Constable Jeff.'

Again, the reaction was not the immediate outrage Victoria had expected, and again her father's tone was icy.

'And where exactly did this "surrendering of your virginity" take place?'

'In the Magistrate's Chamber at the courthouse.'

Her statement elicited no response, apart from a look of sheer disbelief.

'Remember how I borrowed your keys, Father,' she said, 'in order to collect the law book I wanted?' She picked up the volume of *The Oxford History of the Laws of England*, which sat on her bedside table, and plonked it down on the bed before him. 'As I told you, I set out with great deliberation. This was no accident, believe me. I planned on losing my virginity.'

Charles looked blankly at the book, then back at his daughter. 'You and Jeff had sexual intercourse in the Magistrate's Chamber?'

He seemed more dumbfounded than outraged, which Victoria found vaguely amusing. She even wondered whether she might laugh.

'How could you *do* such a thing, Victoria!' Charles' tone was condemnatory now. 'How could *Jeff* do such a thing! Good God, girl, he's a member of the Cossack Police Force! How could he—'

'He didn't!' Victoria was no longer tempted to laugh. 'I told you, Father, he didn't! I threw myself at him! I gave him no choice—'

'Of course he had a choice! Every man has a choice!'

'Not Jeff. Not then. Don't you understand? I did everything humanly possible to seduce him. I even ripped off my own underwear!'

'Why?' Charles demanded. 'Why in God's name would you do such a thing?'

'Because I wanted to know what it was like,' Victoria all but yelled. 'I wanted to experience sex!'

The words hung there between them. Loud. Abrasive. Shocking.

The very words I said myself, Charlotte thought, recalling the admission she'd made to her father and Eleanor all those years ago. Her father had been shocked. But Eleanor had understood.

'I'm not you, Mother!' In her desperation, Victoria was now the accuser, the confrontation now between mother and daughter. 'I could never deny my sexuality. I could never live the lie you do. I'm a woman and I intend to live my life as a woman. Can't you understand? I wanted to know what sex was like. I *needed* to know what sex was like. And I chose to find out with Jeff.'

Just as I needed to know what sex was like, and just as I chose to find out with Tom Philby, Charlotte thought, remembering how she, too, had ripped off her own clothes in her desperate urge to discover.

'Yes,' she said, 'I do understand.' She sat on the bed, patting the counterpane, bidding her daughter join her.

At which point, Victoria caved in. 'Oh, Mama ...' There were tears in her eyes as she crossed to sit beside her mother. 'I so admire your bravery, I honestly do. But are you really prepared to live the rest of your life as a man?'

Charlotte shook her head. 'There will be no need, my dear. We will return to England one day.' *Sooner than you think*, she told herself. The five years were nearly up, the debt owed to her uncle all but paid off, and the family's honour restored. But she wouldn't let Victoria know any of this. Not yet. They could not afford to let their guard down. In fact, she decided, this must be the only time they speak together as mother and daughter until they were home in England.

'Tell me, Victoria, what are Jeff's views on this?'

'He says he's going to hand in his resignation to Sergeant Fry and leave Cossack.'

Charlotte nodded. Such a decision did not surprise her. Jeff was an honourable young man.

'I've blackmailed him into staying long enough to ensure I'm not pregnant, but he'll leave immediately we know this to be the case. Which means that I've ruined his life.'

'Yes, it would appear you have.'

'He's riddled with guilt. Even believes that he raped me. And he's convinced you'll kill him if you find out.'

If I were a man, perhaps I would, Charlotte thought. *But then my father didn't kill Tom Philby, did he? Perhaps all men are not alike.*

'Was it worth it, Victoria?' she asked.

'The sex? No, not in the least. But I hadn't expected it to be,' Victoria said, 'not the first time anyway. I only chose Jeff because I wanted him to be the one. I love him, you see.'

'You love him?' The statement came as a complete surprise.

'Yes,' Victoria replied with conviction. 'Yes, I do.'

'You're only seventeen,' Charlotte gently reminded her.

'So everyone keeps telling me.' There was a steeliness in Victoria's eyes now, and an edge to her voice. 'But we both know I'm not a child and haven't been for some time, don't we, Mother?'

Yes, we do, Charlotte thought.

'Besides,' she added glibly, 'many young women get married at seventeen these days.'

'Good grief, is that what you want?'

'Not necessarily. But I don't want Jeff to leave Cossack. I want to get to know him better. Oh, not in *that* way,' she said in response to her mother's suggestively raised eyebrow.

'He's so shocked by what happened he wouldn't come near me physically. But I *do* love him, Mama, and I'd like to find out if one day he might come to love me.'

Oh, my dear, you are lucky, Charlotte thought. *How I envy you the experience.* Charlotte had never once been in love herself. 'So, what can we do to make Jeff change his mind, I wonder?' she said thoughtfully.

'I've no idea,' Victoria admitted, 'but I doubt you'd be able to get through to him. He's so ashamed he said he'd never be able to look you in the eye.'

'Then I shall just have to look him in his,' Charlotte replied. 'I shall say nothing of what happened between you, but perhaps I can lend him some confidence. We'll see what we can do.'

They both heard the slap of the door to the breakfast room and the sound of boys' voices. Edward and Harold had arrived home for lunch.

Charles rose to his feet. 'Come along now, time to eat.'

'Yes, Father.'

And they left to join the boys in the breakfast room, where Nina and Alwyn were about to serve up.

***

Charles paid a visit to Cossack that Friday, arriving at Benny's workshop towards the end of the workday in the knowledge that Jeff was bound to turn up at around that time.

The pearl workers had just left, and Benny was in his customary position on the verandah, lounging on his old sofa, bottle on the floor, glass in hand. He was already well and truly drunk, but he jumped to his feet at the sight of Charles Burton.

'Ah, Boss,' he called in greeting, 'what a pleasant surprise. I was just about to lock up.' And he immediately and ostentatiously set about doing so, making a great show of the procedure and chatting away as he did. 'Haven't seen you for a while. I trust all is well.'

'Yes, very well, thanks Benny, we've been busy with the shearing season.'

'Yes, yes, of course. Would you care to join me for a drink?'

'Why not? Just a quick one, eh?'

Benny's face cracked into its ragged-toothed grin, and he disappeared into the shack to fetch another glass.

Charles pulled a chair up beside the sofa and they toasted each other as they sat.

'Good to see you, old friend,' he said, and Benny beamed with pleasure.

Then barely five minutes later …

'Mūto‘i Jeff,' Benny called his customary greeting as Constable Jeff walked up to the shack.

Jeff had seen Charles Burton seated with Benny on the verandah. He couldn't bear the thought of facing Victoria's father, but he had no option. He couldn't exactly wait until the man had gone – the two were sharing a drink and, who could tell, he might be there for some time.

'Hello, Benny,' he called back. Then as he stepped up onto the verandah. 'Hello there, Mr Burton.'

'Hello, Jeff, good to see you,' Charles said.

'Join us for a drink?' Benny offered, picking up the bottle and waving it about with dangerous largesse.

'Can't, mate,' Jeff replied, 'still on duty.'

'I'm all locked up, *Pāruru Jeff*.' The old man gleefully waggled the key to the workshop's padlock, which he wore on a piece of string around his neck. 'You can't catch me out today.'

'I'm glad to see that, Benny. I'll leave you to it, then.' He nodded to Charles Burton. 'Good afternoon, sir,' he said.

Charles downed the remnants of the cheap whisky, burning his throat in the process. It really was filthy stuff. 'Hang on a tick, Jeff,' he said. 'I'll walk back to the station with you. Time I was leaving, and my horse is tethered there. Thanks for the drink, Benny.'

'Any time, Boss.' Benny waved the two men farewell and poured himself another glass.

'I believe congratulations are in order,' Charles said as they set off for the station several hundred yards away.

'Oh?' Jeff glanced a query.

'I saw Sergeant Fry in Roebourne the other day, and he told me you're to be promoted to Senior Constable.' Charles hadn't seen Sergeant Fry, and the Sergeant hadn't told him the news, he'd heard it from Victoria.

'Yes, sir.' Jeff gave a nod, but didn't meet the older man's eyes, focussing instead on the track that led up the slope away from the shore.

'That's quite an honour, my boy,' Charles said, 'particularly for one who's been in the force such a relatively short period of time. It takes most young chaps years to get promoted.' He gave a hearty laugh. 'Why, many of the senior constables I know are bordering on middle-aged. Yet you're how old?'

'Twenty-three, sir.'

'An achievement indeed.' Charles nodded his approval. 'Sergeant Fry clearly thinks very highly of you.'

'It would appear so, sir, and I'm honoured that he should.' Jeff's gaze remained firmly focussed on the police station he could now see up ahead. Only a minute or so to go. He couldn't wait for this interminable exchange to be over.

'You have a very promising career ahead of you, son,' Charles said. 'You should be proud of yourself.'

'Yes, sir.' *Proud!* Jeff thought with a sense of self-loathing. *If you only knew!*

They walked on in silence, until they arrived at the police station, where Charles' horse was tethered by the water trough. Charles came to a halt beside the trough. He was by now determined the young man should look him in the eyes.

'I want to thank you, Jeff,' he said.

'Thank me? For what, sir?' And Jeff was finally forced to meet Charles Burton's gaze.

'For looking after my daughter as you do. I am most grateful, believe me.'

Grateful! Jeff felt like screaming out, 'Grateful for what? I *raped* your daughter!' But after being unable to meet the man's gaze, for some unknown reason he was now unable to look away. Charles Burton's piercingly dark eyes, so perceptive and so like his daughter's, were drilling into his.

'I suspect Victoria may be just a little in love with you, Jeff,' Charles said.

Jeff recognised the man's tone was meaningful. *But meaningful of what? What was he saying?*

'Better take care there, lad.'

He was issuing a warning. But a warning to whom? A warning of what?

Then, unexpectedly, Charles smiled. A warm smile. Friendly, trusting. 'Well, I must be off.' He turned away, tightened the girth of his saddle and mounted his horse. 'Goodbye, Jeff.'

And Jeff was left wondering what on earth had just happened.

Charles had collected the mail from the Roebourne Post and Telegraph Office on his way to Cossack. It had included a letter from his father, the sight of which had pleased him, for there'd been a dearth of news from Yorkshire lately and he'd wondered if there might be cause for worry.

It was after dark when he arrived home. The family had eaten and were gathered in the sitting room. He said nothing to Victoria of his trip to Cossack or of having seen Jeff. What would be the point? He would not converse with her again on a woman-to-woman basis, and he had no idea of the effect his meeting had had upon Jeff.

He ate the meal that Nina had put aside for him and took his father's letter to the privacy of his bedroom, where he read it by the light of the kerosene lamp. He would share its contents with his children tomorrow, but in the meantime he wanted to assure himself all was well.

Dearest Charles, William wrote,

I do apologise for this belated reply to your latest missive. Indeed, this belated reply to your last several missives enquiring whether all is well. I am so sorry to have worried you as I obviously have.

I can happily inform you that all is now well, but it has not been so for the past several months. In fact, I believe at one stage it was very much a case of touch and go. I had a heart attack, you see. Can't really recall what happened, but they found me up on the hill overlooking the valley. Your favourite spot, remember? Where you and Byron would ride when you were a boy. Evidently, I was just lying there, and it was at first presumed I'd fallen from my horse, as he'd returned riderless to the stables. Upon Reginald Langton's examination, however, it proved to be a heart attack. At least, that was the good doctor's opinion, for which I am eternally grateful as I have been spared the embarrassing assumption of poor horsemanship on my part. I certainly have no memory of falling from my horse, but I do recall feeling a vice-like pain in my chest up there on the crest of that hill as I looked out over the view that we both so love. I suppose I must have lost consciousness and toppled from the saddle.

Anyway, son, doctor's orders are now that I am to take things gently, and I am doing just that. In truth, I'm being shamelessly mollycoddled. Eleanor is

*pampering me like a spoilt child, spending far more
time up here at Pendleton than she ever did in the past,
which I have to say I am very much enjoying. She is
thoroughly devoted to my wellbeing, for which I am
most grateful, knowing as I do how much she must be
missing London.*

*I have no wish to concern you with my enquiry,
Charles, but I am interested to hear of your current
progress. You have been in the Pilbara for close to five
years now. Are there any plans afoot to return home?
I miss you, dearest son, and I miss my grandchildren.
Do give Victoria, Edward and Harold my love and ask
them to write to their doting grandfather.*

*I'm sorry this letter is so short on news, but there
really is not much more to report from Pendleton.
I just spend my days lolling around, and as you of
all people know, I am not normally one to choose a
lazy existence. Something I shall have to get used to, I
suppose. For a while anyway, until I regain my strength.*

*My thoughts are with you always, dearest Charles,
Your loving father.*

Charlotte's mind raced as she stared down at the letter. There
was so much she could read between the lines. Her father
knew only too well of her five-year plan, they had discussed
it together at length before her departure. Was he now calling
upon her to come home? Did he fear he might die before the
return of his grandson, who was destined to become the next
Squire of Pendleton?

And what of Eleanor? What were the intentions of that detestable woman in so devoting herself to William Burton? Did she expect to marry him on his deathbed? And if so, to what advantage? Knowing Eleanor, there would surely be an ulterior motive.

Charlotte read and re-read the letter, before taking up her pen and replying. And in doing so, she was forced to mention the name of the woman she so loathed. Not once in responding to her father's letters had she referred to Eleanor, although William had written of her often, always in the hope he might bring about a reconciliation between his mistress and his daughter.

Dearest Father, she wrote,

Do you want me to come home? Do you need me? Do you wish to have your grandchildren nearby? If such is the case, I am prepared to make the arrangements for our departure immediately. I had planned on returning towards the end of this year or in early '94 in any event. Please let me know if you need me there earlier.

Charlotte gritted her teeth as she then wrote:

It is a relief to know that Eleanor is taking such good care of you. What are your plans with regard to her show of devotion, may I ask? Do you intend to make her your wife?

Throwing caution to the wind, she didn't care how scathing she might sound as she continued. To voice her feelings otherwise would be sheer hypocrisy. Besides, she wanted to warn her father, although she doubted he would heed her, just as he had not heeded her in the past when it came to Eleanor.

I am aware Eleanor refused your offer of matrimony all those years ago, Father, but perhaps she now perceives things a little differently. It may be advisable to practise caution.

She would leave it at that. Her father would know exactly what she was saying, and although he would dislike the implied criticism of his mistress's intentions, it might at least give him pause for thought.

Dearest Father, please forgive the practicality of this letter, I wish only to do what is best for you. Believe me, the news of your heart attack and your ensuing frail health has disturbed me deeply. I long to be with you, to take care of you, to be your capable right hand as I was throughout the whole of my youth. Or at least as I wished to be and perhaps perceived myself to be. You are everything to me, Father. You always have been. We are father and son like no other, are we not?

There could surely be no clearer message than that.

It is late at night here, and the children are abed. They will write letters to you in the morning, and I shall post this from Roebourne tomorrow.

In the meantime, I am thinking of you, Father, and willing with all my heart that you make a full and speedy recovery.

Your loving son, Charles.

Charlotte then undressed, donned her man's nightshirt and extinguished the lamp, after which she lay in the dark, wondering what her father's reply might bring. Were her days in the Pilbara numbered? Was she soon to return to England and, in doing so, once more live her life as a woman? Things had become suddenly and jarringly confusing.

***

To young Constable Jeff, everything about his life seemed confusing. What path lay ahead? Where was he to go? What did the future have in store for him?

'Do you have any news for me?' he asked when he met Victoria at the schoolhouse after class on Monday. If by any chance she had discovered she was pregnant, that would at least provide an answer to the rest of his life. Perhaps not the life he'd wanted, but ...

She shook her head. 'I won't know for another two weeks, Jeff,' she said.

He nodded, resigned to the fact he must live in this limbo for a further fortnight.

'Are we going to check on Benny?' she asked hopefully.

'I already have.'

'Oh.' She was disappointed, she would have so liked some time with him.

'Do you mind if we talk?' he asked. 'Something strange happened the other day and I feel the need to tell you.'

'I don't mind at all,' she said, trying not to sound too eager. 'We'll go somewhere quiet, shall we?'

He nodded, and automatically they headed for the Explosives Wharf. He was silent as they went, obviously preoccupied, and she wondered what had happened.

When they were seated together on the wharf, he came out with it immediately.

'I saw your father on Friday,' he said.

'Oh, yes?' Victoria was only mildly surprised by the news. Although her father had said nothing of his visit to Cossack, she would hardly have expected him to keep her informed of his actions. Now, however, she found herself holding her breath, wondering what had come to pass between the two of them.

'Yes, he was having a drink with Benny when I called in on my rounds. He was extremely pleasant,' Jeff said. 'Said Sergeant Fry had told him of my impending promotion. He congratulated me, said it was a big step up to Senior Constable for a chap my age, wished me well with my career, and ...'

'And?' Victoria prompted as he paused, shaking his head, obviously nonplussed.

'He was so damn nice, I didn't know where to look,' Jeff said. 'All I could think of was, *If you only knew what I'd done, you'd kill me.* And then ...' A further pause. 'And then it got even worse. He thanked me for looking after you, Victoria. I mean he actually *thanked* me.'

'What did you say?'

'Nothing. What *could* I say? I just stared back at him. And somehow I couldn't look away, it was as if he was trying to tell me something. Then he said he thought you might be a little in love with me and that I'd better take care. But he didn't say it in anger, it was more as if he was warning me as a friend.'

Jeff, clearly in a state of bewilderment, now appealed to her. 'What on earth did he mean, Victoria? He can't possibly know what happened. But why issue the warning? What was he saying?'

He was saying it's over to me, Victoria thought. *He has successfully distracted you, and he's saying the rest is now up to me.* She felt an overwhelming surge of gratitude. *Thank you, Mama.*

'Father is a very direct man, Jeff,' she said, 'and a very honest man. He was simply telling the truth. I *am* a little in love with you, I told him so myself. And he was issuing you a warning. A warning to beware of me. It's as simple as that.'

Victoria laughed at the concern she could see in his eyes. 'Oh, there's no great cause for anxiety, I assure you,' she said. 'My declaration of love can be put down to mere girlish infatuation. Which is the way I'm sure Father sees it, just as I'm sure it's the way all men would see it. Such romantic pronouncements are hardly uncommon among female adolescents who tend to dramatise their emotions.'

Her dismissive comment in no way referred directly to herself, but to the sort of girls Victoria personally considered vacuous romantics. Her light-heartedness was putting him at his ease, however, so she continued in the same vein.

'Of course, you have yourself to blame in part for my infatuation,' she said playfully. 'You should never have shared your secret with me as you did.'

'What secret?'

She was pleased to note her ploy had successfully distracted him further. 'Your name, of course. The fact that you're not Jeff at all, but Jean-François Fabron. You should never have shared that secret with me.'

'I only did so because you nagged it out of me,' he protested. 'You badgered me for weeks.'

'Nevertheless, you told me. And you swore me to silence, what's more.' She gave an imperious flick of her head. 'The trust you placed in me was profound, Jeff. I, and I alone, am the only person who knows your real name.'

'You don't, actually.'

'What?'

'Jean-François Fabron is not my real name. I was christened John Francis Boyle and I'm not even French.'

Her slack-jawed amazement was so comical he burst out laughing. 'I'm sorry,' he said, 'but when you adopt that superior attitude, I simply can't resist the opportunity for one-upmanship.'

'I am betrayed,' she replied with more than a touch of theatricality, 'utterly betrayed. To think that you lied to me!' Victoria couldn't have been happier. Their banter had dispelled the awkwardness that had sat so uncomfortably between them. For now, anyway. At this moment it felt as if their old friendship had been, if not restored, at least rekindled.

'I didn't really lie,' he admitted. 'I've been Jean-François Fabron since I was fourteen, and I'm more French than English. Or at least I consider myself so.'

Then he told her his story. Briefly. How he'd adopted the surname of the French skipper who had been like a father to him. How the skipper and crew had lost their lives in a typhoon off the coast of Tahiti. And how he'd been rescued by a Polynesian fisherman called Tavi Amaru.

'That was when John Francis Boyle ceased to exist,' he said.

'In which case, you're forgiven,' she declared magnanimously. 'Now that I know all your secrets, I forgive you.'

'Yes,' he said. 'You know all my secrets now. Nothing more to tell.'

She didn't know all his secrets. She didn't know he had married Tavi Amaru's daughter. She didn't know that, at the age of seventeen, he'd fathered a baby girl, that he and Raina and little Miri had been so content living with Tavi and his extended family. Those days had surely been the happiest of his life. She didn't know that typhus had wiped out the whole of his beloved Tahitian family, leaving him devastated. There was a lot she didn't know about him.

'It's good for friends to share secrets,' Victoria announced. Now in deadly earnest, she was really referring to lovers, but that would come later. A return to friendship was enough right now. 'Secrets form bonds between friends,' she said.

She was thoughtful for a moment. Then … 'I have a secret I could share with you, Jeff. If you would like me to, that is.'

He was unsure whether he should encourage any further intimacy, but she appeared eager to confide, and it seemed heartless to say no.

'If you wish,' he said, 'yes, of course.'

Victoria wondered what his reaction would be if she told him about her 'father', the fact that the man he so admired was a woman. That would certainly be the sharing of a 'secret'. She smiled to herself at the mere thought of the response she would get should she so betray her mother.

'You remember, several weeks ago, a man was discovered right here at the Explosives Wharf in the early hours of the morning. He'd been attacked, and you had to make out a report.'

'Yes, of course I remember.'

'He said a madwoman came out of nowhere and coshed him.'

'Yes. That's exactly what he said.'

'I was that madwoman.'

'You what?'

As he stared back at her in disbelief, Victoria felt triumphant. 'There! That's my secret. You are now sworn to silence.'

She realised that as he was, after all, a policeman, she really should show some justification for an action tantamount to attempted murder.

'But before you judge me,' she added hastily, 'that man was a very bad man and he was—'

'Of course he was a bad man,' Jeff interrupted brusquely. 'You're talking about Bart Cameron, one of the vilest men in the whole of the Pilbara, who should be gaoled and the key thrown away. What the devil were you doing roaming around at night, Victoria? How incredibly foolish of you. And what brought you here, of all places?'

'You had told me it was a nice place by the river to sit and have a quiet think.'

'In the dead of night?'

'It wasn't in the dead of night, it would have been barely nine o'clock.'

'That is the dead of night in Cossack,' Jeff replied, 'that's when things happen, Victoria. Why the hell were you here?'

'I wanted to sit by the river and have a quiet think,' she repeated, 'and this was the place you told me to come. Besides,' she added sulkily, 'you'd refused to join me for dinner at Mrs Pead's. I didn't want to sit in that little room all by myself.'

So it's my fault, he thought, *how typical of Victoria to be so cantankerous. Particularly when she feels cornered.*

'All right,' he relented, hands submissively in the air. 'I'm spoiling your story. Tell me what happened that night.'

'Well,' she said, off and running, 'you're quite right, Jeff, he was the vilest of creatures this what's-his-name ...'

'Bart Cameron.'

'Yes, him. Bart Cameron and another man were bent on committing the most heinous of crimes that night. A truly unspeakable act! They were about to rape an Aboriginal girl. A child! She would have been no more than ten. Can you believe that?'

Jeff nodded. Yes, he could. He knew the Cameron brothers.

'I had the Enfield in my shoulder bag,' she went on. 'You see, I was not so "incredibly foolish" enough to "roam around at night" without my revolver.'

'Good girl.' He acknowledged her retaliatory comment with a smile.

'I was fortunate enough to come upon them before they'd harmed the child,' she continued, 'and the hand gun did the rest. I coshed Bart and his friend ran away.'

'That would have been his brother, Arnie,' Jeff said. 'Arnie's known to be a coward. Luckily enough for you. Between the two of them, they may well have overpowered you.'

No, they wouldn't, Victoria thought, *I would have shot them both before they had the chance. And what's more, they knew that.*

'The girl escaped,' she concluded. 'Brave little thing. Jumped off the wharf and swam across the river.'

'Yes, the local mob's camp is on the other side. Lucky escape indeed,' he agreed. 'Lucky escape for you too, Victoria. The Cameron brothers are a dangerous pair. I've had many a run-in with them in the past. They'd have raped you as well if they'd had half a chance.'

Oh, yes, she knew that to be right. She'd seen the look on Bart's face before she'd drawn the gun.

'I'd recognise Bart Cameron if I saw him,' she said. 'I've kept an eye out for him ever since that night, but I haven't seen him around town.'

'I'm not surprised. I'd say after his run-in with you, he would have headed to the goldfields at Mallina. The brothers share their time between here and the goldfields, where they're also known to cause trouble. Bad eggs, the two of them. Scum of the earth.'

Jeff looked her up and down with renewed respect. 'So a mystery has been solved, Victoria,' he said. 'You're the madwoman who came out of nowhere and coshed Bart Cameron.'

'I am,' Victoria admitted with pride. 'And we have now shared secrets, you and I. As true friends do.'

She offered her hand and they shook. As true friends do.

13.

Victoria proved not to be pregnant. Which didn't in the least surprise her. Their coupling had been so brief, so frantic, it was difficult to believe it could have led to conception. Although she rather wished it had. Not that she wanted a child, but it would have kept Jeff in Cossack.

'I have news,' she said abruptly when he met her on the schoolhouse verandah two weeks later. 'You're free to leave.'

'Good. I'm glad. You're far too young to be a mother.'

'I agree.'

'Do you want to come with me while I check up on Benny?'

'Of course.'

Then, as they made their way down to the foreshore, he told her he'd decided to stay in Cossack, that he'd accepted the promotion offered by Sergeant Fry. 'Which I suppose now makes me a career cop,' he said.

'Good. I'm glad.' She echoed his words by way of reply, but as she did, she blessed her father. *This is all your doing,* she thought. 'You'll make a wonderful career cop, Jeff.'

They were back on the firm footing of friendship. She would take care not to abuse the delicacy of the relationship she had come so close to destroying. But she vowed also that one day he would love her. *You'd best heed Father's warning, Jeff*, she thought happily. *You'd best take care.*

***

William Burton's reply to his son's query arrived in the early spring, and the contents of the letter, which started out in a lighted-hearted vein, came as somewhat of a surprise to Charles.

Dearest Charles,

I must apologise for the fact that my enquiry about your current progress aroused in you such concern. This was really not my intention. I certainly do not need you galloping home to Yorkshire with your children in order to be at my deathbed. I am not quite the doddery disaster you assumed from my previous missive – how very indulgent I must have sounded. Truly, my boy, although perhaps not as hale and hearty as I once was, there is life in me yet, I can promise you. I have reached the ripe old age of seventy-five, this is true, but given Eleanor's tender ministrations, I have every intention of living to eighty or perhaps even for a whole further ten years. This is how young she makes me feel.

And while speaking of Eleanor, I understood instantly that your well-meaning 'advice' regarding matrimony was offered as the direst of warning, which I have to admit, upon reading I found highly amusing.

Charles was taken aback by the comment. Amusing? He'd been quite sure his father would take offence at his implication of Eleanor's ulterior motives regarding matrimony.

I appreciate the care you have for my welfare, Charles, and above all the care you have for our beloved Pendleton, but I must tell you, dear boy, that I had already proposed to Eleanor. I did so a good three months ago. And she refused me! Again! Most men would find this the ultimate humiliation, do you not agree? To be refused by the same woman twice! Yet she tends to me with all the loving care of a wife, which I find extraordinary. She has even moved to Pendleton now, where she devotes her time solely to me. I can only construe this devotion as evidence of her love. How else am I to interpret such selflessness, I ask you?

How else indeed, Charles wondered. What the devil could the woman be up to? There was not a shred of selflessness in Eleanor. He read on.

Now I must add here, dear boy, and this on a serious note so please do heed me. Eleanor and I both know how you feel about her. She is aware that up until now, you have not even been able to bring yourself to mention her name in your letters. We have talked of this fact, which saddens us both.

Charles all but snorted his derision out loud as he read that. Eleanor? Saddened? Hah! Then, reading further, he came to an abrupt halt.

Eleanor is so saddened indeed that she intends to write to you, Charles.

That woman was going to write to him? Charles was outraged. How dare she! What did she expect to gain? His thanks for her devotion to his father, the man she had all but destroyed through her avarice? Charles vowed there and then he would not read a word she wrote. He would tear up her letter.

But William, knowing exactly what his son's reaction would be, gave explicit instructions.

I wish you to read her letter, son, whatever it is she intends to write. I have no idea what this may be, for she says she will not share it with me, but she very much wishes to communicate with you. Do not destroy her letter, Charles, I beg of you. Read it for my sake, son. Contact between the two of you would so please me.

Naturally, Eleanor understands the rules. In fact, when I read your last letter out to her, she agreed with your comment. We are indeed 'father and son like no other'. She very much admires the strength of our bond.

Charles was further outraged to learn his father read out his letters to Eleanor. It had never occurred to him that

William Burton might share their letters with his mistress. William wrote,

She intends to send you her letter a week from now, in order that you should have had time to read this before its arrival.

Clearly Eleanor, too, expected her letter would be destroyed unread, had Charles not received in advance his father's instructions.

In the meantime, dearest son, follow through with whatever plans you have made. Do not alter the course of your life to suit me. I shall survive. And I shall be here to welcome you home to Pendleton when the time is right.
Your loving father.

Charles did not respond immediately to William's letter, deciding instead to wait until he had read whatever it was Eleanor had to say. He would make no comment to his father upon the contents of her communication, apart from the fact he had obeyed instruction and read the damn thing. But the prospect of having to do so was odious to him.

He waited a fortnight before visiting the Roebourne Post and Telegraph Office, just to ensure Eleanor's letter had arrived by then. And it had. There it was, addressed to Charles Burton, Esq. of Burton Station.

Charles was not surprised by the hand, which he had hitherto not seen. It was elegant, yet bold and assertive, just as he would have imagined Eleanor's hand to be. And her name was clearly marked with a flourish on the back of the envelope, like the statement that was no doubt intended. Yes, he thought as he stood examining the letter in the foyer of the telegraph office, he would certainly have torn the thing in half and thrown it in the nearest rubbish bin had he not received his father's instructions.

Upon returning to the homestead in the late afternoon, he took the letter directly to his study, where he intended to give it a cursory read before then writing to his father. But within the very first paragraph, Eleanor had gained his attention.

My dear Charles,

I know William has insisted upon your reading this letter and I am aware the task will be abhorrent to you ...

She had certainly read his mind there, Charles thought, his eyes skimming the page further.

... So I shall not delay in getting straight to the point. Your father will have intimated that all is well with regard to his health, but this is not so. He has determined to trivialise the situation in order to prevent your worrying. He feels ridden with guilt that his last letter aroused in you such concern. As I said to him, 'Of course it would, my dear, your son does

not know you have had a heart attack.' He must surely realise such news would arouse concern in any child.

The truth of the matter is, Charles, that your father's condition remains extremely delicate. He must not exert himself, for if he does, he risks a further heart attack, which, the second time around, would more than likely prove fatal. However, as you know, William is not a man who enjoys an idle life. It takes a great deal of nagging to prevent him from expending his energy. This is why I have now moved to Pendleton in order to be with him at all times. Which brings me to the purpose of this letter.

I know you believe I have an ulterior motive in my devotion to your father. William and I shared a laugh at the virtual accusation you voiced in your letter. But this is not so. It may have been once, many years ago. But time changes one's perspective, does it not? I have no devious plan to rob you of your inheritance, Charles, nor to encourage the selling off of any further Pendleton lands. I am no threat to you, my dear. I wish only to look after your father, and this I intend to do. Put my actions down to those of a lonely old woman, if you will.

She's talking to me now, Charlotte thought. *Eleanor is talking directly to me as a woman.*

I shall share a secret with you, Charles, one that William does not know. I have sold the townhouse.

379

I have purchased a small apartment in central London and invested the balance. When the time comes, I shall require a modest income by way of support. Men, particularly you men of the landed gentry, my dear, have never understood the needs a single woman such as I face. Especially later in life.

She means I have never understood the need a single woman such as she faces, Charlotte thought. *And perhaps she's right. Perhaps I never have.*

In closing, dearest Charles, I want you to know that your father is well looked after. I intend to care for him until his death, as I know he wishes me to. After which, I shall leave you in peace at Pendleton. When William is gone, my dear, you will never see me again, I can assure you.
With fondest regards from your one-time friend,
Eleanor

Charles leaned back in his chair and stared down at the two pages of script on the desk before him, written in that boldly elegant hand. Eleanor had surprised him.

Then, pushing the pages aside, he opened his writing pad and his inkwell, took up his pen, and began his reply.

Dear Eleanor,
I shall be brief. I had not intended to respond to your letter. In fact, as I'm sure you suspected,

I would not even have read it had Father not demanded I do so.

However, I respect your honesty, which I must admit came as a surprise, and shall answer with an honesty equal to yours.

I believe you when you say you have no ulterior motive, and am most relieved to hear this, although I am mystified as to why you would refuse Father's offer of marriage. I seek no answer and have no right to enquire, but given your current devotion to his care, it seems odd you should have no desire to become his wife.

There is one enquiry I would like to make of you, however. You say you wish only to look after my father, and suggest I put your actions down to those of 'a lonely old woman'. These are powerful words, Eleanor, or at least I find them so, particularly given my previous knowledge of you. If it is true you are lonely and in need of company, then to which should I attribute your current devotion to my father? Are you driven by love? Or by necessity? I should be most interested to know.

In the meantime, I am grateful for your care of Father. I agree he does need to be well tended. Like you, I am fully aware if he were not regularly nagged, he would certainly risk doing himself damage.

I shall be returning to Pendleton in the early part of next year, I should think around March or April – autumn here, spring in England. Always strange to contemplate. Not that one would ever recognise autumn in the Pilbara, where there is not a single deciduous tree to be found. This is probably why there are only two seasons recognised in this part of the world. The Wet and the Dry. Terms eminently understandable to those who live here.

I wish you well, Eleanor, and shall no doubt see you in the spring.

Regards,

Charles Burton

He wrote a brief missive to his father announcing his plans and entrusted both letters to Alwyn Stroud the very next morning, with instructions for the lad to ride into Roebourne and post them. Then, his communications inspiring the need to make arrangements, he informed Joe of his intentions.

They were doing a head count of stock at Three Mile Gate, the very spot where Charles had come under attack. Ever since then, orders had been issued that no man must patrol on his own, be it the Boss or a worker. The band of marauding Aborigines had been altogether too dangerous that day.

'I'll be leaving in around six months, Joe,' Charles announced as they sat on their mounts overlooking the storage paddock, steadily counting the cattle that were grazing.

'Oh.' Joe was taken aback. 'Where for?' he asked.

'England. I'll be going home to Pendleton.'

'Really?' The normally unflappable Joe Lawson made no attempt to disguise his astonishment. 'I thought you were here for the long haul, old chap. I mean, I had presumed you were settled in the Pilbara forever.'

'No, no, that was never the plan,' Charles replied. 'I always had in mind five years. It'll be a little more than that, in fact, closer to six. Time enough to pay off Father's debt to Uncle Geoffrey, which was always my aim.' His smile was triumphant. 'And we've done it, you and I, haven't we? Burton Station is not only mortgage-free, it's thriving.'

'It certainly is, Charles. My word, yes, you've done a grand job.' Joe was flummoxed. The news was not only unexpected, it was highly distracting. *You'll be returning home as Charlotte, won't you?* He had accepted her as Charles for so long, it came as a shock to see her as Charlotte. But now, looking at her, he could see her as nothing else, and he felt uncharacteristically ill at ease. He averted his eyes.

'I could never have done any of this on my own, Joe,' Charles said, 'as you very well know. I'd have been lost right from the start had it not been for you.'

Joe shrugged. 'Just following Geoffrey's instructions, old man, and you're a very quick learner, I'll give you that.'

He's self-conscious, Charlotte thought. She recognised why. *But there's no need to be, Joe. You've known all along. You're the only one who ever knew, the only one who still does.*

'It will be strange,' she said, 'returning to my previous life.'

'Yes,' he replied, turning to her. 'Yes, I should imagine it would be.'

She had instantly put him at his ease, and just for this moment, they knew they could speak openly.

'I shall not tell the children of our return to England yet,' she said. 'Best to leave it until the last minute. Easier to maintain the deception that way.'

'Essential, I should think.'

'I shall miss you, Joe.'

'And I shall miss you, Charlotte. Very much.'

They shared a smile, then looked back at the cattle.

'I've completely lost count,' Charles said.

'Me too, old chap. Better start all over again.'

***

These days, Jeff was sporting two chevrons on the upper sleeves of his uniform.

'Very impressive,' Victoria had said the first time she'd seen them. 'Was there a special ceremony to recognise your promotion?'

'Of course not.' He'd given her a quizzical look, wondering whether perhaps she was joking, but it hadn't appeared so. 'I was just handed the chevrons and told to sew them on.'

'Really?' She was genuinely surprised. 'That doesn't seem fair.' She inspected the sleeves of his uniform. 'Very nice stitching,' she said, 'you did an excellent job.'

Their friendship these days was more solid than ever, and as 1893 drew to a close, Victoria was convinced the depth of her affection was reciprocated. Despite the fact there was no further need of his protection during daylight hours, Jeff joined her every chance he had, simply because he enjoyed her company. Surely this was a sign.

He loves me, she thought, *he just doesn't know it yet*. But she must tread carefully, she warned herself.

Then about a fortnight before Christmas, something happened that lent her further confidence. Something totally unexpected.

Jeff was accompanying her to the tram stop in The Strand early on Tuesday morning. She hadn't brought her horse to Cossack this week, instead leaving Jimmy stabled in Roebourne. She always did so when she knew Jeff would be unable to join her for a ride the following morning, as was the case today, when he was required in court.

The Strand, being the major thoroughfare of Cossack, was relatively busy even at this hour, shops and businesses setting up for the day. As they passed the White Horse Hotel, the bulk beer shop and the Cingalese tailor's, people openly greeted them, some recognising the English teacher in her neat navy-blue skirt, cream blouse and pretty sunbonnet, but most acknowledging the young policeman.

They returned the greetings, but as they approached Sing's Bakery and General Store, Victoria came to a sudden halt.

Beside her, Jeff halted too, wondering what had so caught her attention.

In front of them, by the main doors to the store, stood a young Aboriginal girl of around ten, and her eyes were fixed upon Victoria, just as Victoria's eyes were fixed upon her.

Jeff wondered what could be passing between them. Then, even as he watched, the girl dived into the store and re-emerged only seconds later, dragging a woman, who appeared to be her mother, by the hand.

Boldly declaring something in her native tongue, the girl pointed at Victoria and the woman unhesitatingly crossed to her.

She stood before Victoria for several seconds, which seemed quite a long time, neither of them moving. Then she placed her hand on her heart.

'Thank you, missus,' she said. 'Thank you for my girl.'

Victoria nodded in recognition and they maintained eye contact for several more seconds, which again seemed a long time, before the woman abruptly turned and walked away.

The girl stood for a moment or so longer. Then came the smile. As cheeky as Victoria remembered it. After which, she scurried off down the street after her mother.

'What was that all about?' Jeff asked as they continued on their way.

'She's the girl the Cameron brothers were about to rape that night,' Victoria said. 'I'm surprised she recognised me. I was wearing my bush hat and trousers at the time.'

Jeff was thoughtful as they arrived at the tram stop. 'Would the brothers recognise you?' he asked.

'I don't know,' she said. 'Arnie wouldn't, he crept up behind me. And Bart thought I was a lad at first. He was delighted to discover I wasn't when he heard my voice and came in for a closer look, but I can't be sure he'd recognise me in the light of day.'

'I think you should carry your revolver at all times, Victoria,' Jeff advised.

'I always do at night,' she replied. Then, catching the glance he flashed her, she quickly added, 'On the very odd occasion when I venture out alone, that is.'

'You should carry it whenever I'm not with you,' he instructed. 'I'd be happier that way. The brothers are bound to return to Cossack, and Bart Cameron would most certainly kill you for what you did to him. He'd make sure there were no witnesses, of course, but he would hunt you down and kill you, Victoria.'

'I'll do as you say, Jeff, I promise I will,' she dutifully responded. But all she could hear was, 'carry it whenever I'm not with you, I'd be happier that way'. All of which surely meant that he loved her.

'I must get back to the station and prepare for court,' he said.

'Will you be able to join me for an early morning ride next Tuesday?' she asked.

'Should be. Yes, I would think so.'

'Good.' She smiled. 'I'll bring Jimmy with me.' She couldn't wait.

***

Eleanor's response to Charles' query had arrived well before Christmas. She had obviously replied immediately to his letter. *Dear Charles*, she'd written,

> *You enquire whether my current devotion to your father is driven by love or necessity. The answer is simple. I find it impossible to tell the difference.*

Your mystification about why I would refuse your
father's offer of marriage is far more complicated, as I
am really not altogether sure myself. Perhaps I simply
do not wish to be perceived as one of 'the landed
gentry', a class which I secretly despise ...

Eleanor was being playful, Charles decided, evading the
question, which in fact he had not asked.

It may have been Eleanor's intention to sound playful, but
there was an element of truth in her answer. She had detested
the Marquess and his friends and all they stood for.

Or perhaps, my dear Charles, I simply did not wish to
remain being seen in your eyes as an opportunist. Who
can tell?
Needless to say, I did not share all of your letter
with William. I read out to him only the interesting
bits and pieces about autumn in the Pilbara, or rather
the lack thereof, and the seasons of the Wet and
the Dry, facts about which I knew nothing. He was
fully aware of all this and far more from his brother,
Geoffrey. I must say, I felt extraordinarily ignorant.
Your father is most excited about the prospect of
your return in the spring and is currently writing to
tell you so, in which case I shall keep my letter brief.
I look forward to seeing you, Charles, and wish you
and your family a safe, and perhaps even pleasurable,
voyage home, if this is at all possible. I personally
can think of nothing more ghastly than any form of

extended sea travel myself. The channel crossing is
horrific enough.
With warmest regards,
Eleanor

William Burton's reply to his son's letter, which had also been awaiting Charles at the Roebourne Post and Telegraph Office, was equally brief.

Dearest Charles,
I cannot begin to tell you how overjoyed I am at the
prospect of your return to the motherland. I long to
see my son and my grandchildren back home here at
Pendleton.
I also cannot begin to tell you how delighted I am
that you have written to Eleanor. I have wished with
all my heart that the bond between the pair of you
could be restored. This makes me unbelievably happy.

Well, yes, Charles supposed there had perhaps been a bond of some sorts restored. Who could tell? He would never really know where he stood with Eleanor. But then did anyone?

She would not let me read your letter to her, sharing
only snippets with me. Just as she will not allow me
to enclose herein the one she has now written to you,
obviously for fear I may read it. My goodness, how
secretive she is being, and what a waste of postage
stamps, sending the two letters off to Australia

*individually. But who am I to disobey a woman's
wishes? Particularly a woman like Eleanor, who as
you well know, Charles, is a force to be reckoned with.*

*This will most likely be the last correspondence we
shall exchange before your arrival home, son, so I will
keep this letter brief as Eleanor says she has done hers.*

*Suffice to say, I wish you and the children a safe
journey home. From those long-ago accounts you sent
me of the thrilling sights you all experienced on the
voyage out to Australia, I have no doubt there will
once again be much adventure on the high seas.*

*As I have told you on previous occasions, Charles,
I am extraordinarily proud of you. Indeed, I sometimes
find myself lost in wonder. How did a son of mine
come to be so very brave, and so very wise?*

Your loving Father

Charles didn't reply to Eleanor, but he did to his father.
There would be ample time for a final letter to reach home
before their embarkation for England, and he couldn't resist
a response to William's eminently readable comment to
Charlotte.

*Your son became brave and wise because you raised
him bravely and wisely, Father. You made him aware
that anything is possible. I am pleased to inform you
this happy circumstance continues to be so.*

*As has been reported in previous letters, my
mission here in the Pilbara has been accomplished.*

*Uncle Geoffrey's debt has been repaid, Burton Station
is thriving and it is time to come home.*

*I have not read your last several letters out loud to
the children the way I normally would for the simple
fact they do not know of our imminent return to
England. They have been told of your heart attack as
you're aware – you will have received their cards and
well wishes – but I am yet to inform them of the voyage.*

Charles knew William Burton would understand the reasons
why his grandchildren were being kept in ignorance of their
return home; that he would recognise the game must be
played out until the very last minute.

*And you are quite right, Father. Victoria, Edward and
Harold will be excited beyond measure at the prospect
of another adventure on the high seas. Oh, you cannot
imagine what sights we beheld! I yearn to behold yet
more.*

But above all, I long to see you.

Your loving son, Charles.

***

Settlers Beach had become the favoured choice of location for
Victoria's occasional early morning ride with Jeff. She only
wished these outings could be a regular occurrence every
single Tuesday, but he reminded her that he did, after all, have
a job. To which she would give a reluctant sigh of resignation.

This particular Tuesday, barely a week before Christmas, their outing held a special significance for Victoria. She had a plan.

'There's no class next week because Monday happens to be Christmas Day,' she said as they strolled beside the shore, barefooted, boots and reins in hand, horses docilely following. They'd had their gallop along the broad coastal beach, racing one another as they so often did, and now they walked peacefully back to where they'd started. To where the track wound its way up the hill to the rough dirt road that led the mile or so from Cossack to the point of Reader Head.

'Could you by any chance be given the day off?' she casually enquired.

'I could, yes,' he answered, 'but I offered to be rostered on instead.'

'Oh? Why?'

'We were asked our preference and I thought I'd leave it available for those with families.' He shrugged. 'Christmas Day doesn't mean much to me.'

'It does to me.'

'Of course it does, Victoria,' he said with a smile, 'you have a family.'

She halted abruptly. 'I consider you family, Jeff,' she declared, 'and I'd like you to spend Christmas Day with us.'

He paused, turning to look at her. Her tone had been peremptory. It had sounded very like an order.

She grinned excitedly. 'Our Christmases are wonderful, truly they are. We have a lucky dip. Nothing lavish, just lots of little presents and we all take pot luck. Nina always cooks up a marvellous feast, and we pull Christmas crackers and wear paper hats. I order these up especially from the catalogues. It's such fun. And this time we'll get Joe to play Scottish songs on his fiddle like he did at my birthday. And, oh, Jeff, the boys will be so thrilled if you're with us. They admire you hugely. Do please, please say you'll come.'

He heaved an inward sigh, albeit with a wealth of affection. From the peremptory to the child-like, she was once again the chameleon.

'I can't, Victoria. I'm working.'

'But you said you'd been given the option,' she persisted, 'you could easily change your roster.'

'Perhaps, yes, but there are other things to consider ...'

'Like what?' She stared up at him demandingly. 'You tell me what.'

'Your father, for instance. Why on earth would your father wish to—'

'It was Father's idea, actually.'

'What?'

'It was Father's idea to invite you.'

'Why would he do that?'

'Because he knew I wanted you to come. He knew I wanted you to be there.'

Jeff gazed at her uncomprehendingly.

'He's like that, my father,' she went on blithely, 'he quite often seems able to read my mind. In fact, I really do think he can.'

Victoria had been wondering how to broach the declaration she intended to make today. This was not the way she'd intended, but it might possibly be the most effective, she decided. Her father could well be the key to her plan.

'Father was adamant, Jeff,' she said. 'He really would like you to come to Burton Station for Christmas Day.'

Jeff studied her shrewdly. 'What is it you're up to, Victoria? What are you playing at?'

'I have something I wish to tell you,' she said. She dropped the boots she was carrying onto the sand, and he could see she was now in deadly earnest. 'Can we sit for a minute or so? Do we have the time before you need to get back to work?'

'Yes. Although the weather's going to turn soon.'

He dropped the boots he was carrying also, and they sat together on the sand, arms looped around knees, reins still loosely in hand, the horses standing peacefully by.

She gazed out to sea for a moment or so, where the clouds were gathering in ominous formation. 'Do you remember that time when Father spoke with you in Cossack? That time when he spoke to you about me?'

Jeff nodded warily.

'You told me exactly what he said to you that day. He said that he thought I might be a little in love with you, and he warned you that you'd better take care.'

Jeff nodded again. Not warily this time, but, with eyes fixed upon her, he seemed to be wondering where this was leading.

She smiled. 'I don't want to frighten you,' she said, 'but I'm afraid Father was right.' Dropping the horse's reins, she reached her hand up, gently touching his cheek, and he didn't flinch. Then, repositioning herself in the sand, she was on her knees, her head a little higher than his, and she was looking into his eyes.

'I love you, Jeff,' she said.

She kissed him with a wealth of tenderness, and again he didn't flinch. He didn't return the kiss, but he didn't pull away. Perhaps in a state of shock, he allowed it to happen.

'There,' she said, sitting back on the sand, 'that wasn't too difficult, was it?' She grinned happily and retrieved the horse's reins, although Jimmy hadn't moved a muscle. 'You do know that you love me, don't you?'

He did. But he wasn't going to tell her so. Not yet.

'You're still only seventeen, Victoria,' he said.

'I'll be eighteen next year,' she replied meaningfully.

He stood, extending his hand to her. 'We must go,' he said, hauling her to her feet. 'The weather's about to turn nasty.'

They headed for the track up the hill.

'You will come to Burton Station for Christmas, won't you?'

'Yes, I'll come to Burton Station for Christmas,' he replied. *I'd better. It appears Charles Burton and I may have something to talk about.*

The torrent of rain rolled in from the sea and they were drenched by the time they got back to Cossack. But neither of them cared.

***

Victoria's announcement to the family over dinner that she had invited Constable Jeff to Burton Station for Christmas

Day was met with whoops of excitement from her brothers, as she had known it would be. Her father was amenable, as she had expected him to be, but there was an element of censure.

'You might perhaps have consulted me first, Victoria,' he said.

'I would have, Father, if he was simply a guest,' she boldly responded, 'but as it turns out, I'm inviting him as family.' Then she dropped the bombshell none of them could possibly have expected. 'You see, this is the man I'm going to marry.'

Edward and Harold were gobsmacked.

'Has he asked you?' Edward demanded.

'No. But he will.'

'How do you know?' Fifteen-year-old Edward, always a forthright boy, was highly suspicious. 'How can you be sure?'

'I just *know*, Edward,' she said with that superior tone her brother so detested. 'Women can sense these things the way men cannot.'

'I can't wait for Jeff to be part of the family,' twelve-year-old Harold piped up. 'He'll be the best brother-in-law ever! He can tell us stories about being at sea and all the places he's seen and ...'

As the chat went on, Charles said nothing. But when dinner was over, he requested Victoria join him in his study.

They didn't sit. Charles propped himself on the edge of his small office desk, arms folded across his chest, and Victoria remained standing.

'Am I supposed to take this outrageous declaration of yours seriously?' he demanded.

'Yes, Father, you are.' She could tell he was annoyed. More than annoyed; he may even have been simmering with anger. But the customary control he exercised remained in place. She always admired him for that.

'And assuming Jeff *does* wish to marry you,' Charles said icily, 'when precisely do you presume this marriage will take place?'

'Next year,' she replied. 'I *presume*,' she said, mocking his tone, 'when I have turned eighteen.'

Charles stood to confront her.

'You will not be here next year for your eighteenth birthday, Victoria,' he sternly announced. 'You will be at home in Pendleton, where you belong. We leave for England in three months.'

Victoria stared back at him in a state of disbelief.

Charles felt his anger instantly subside. Given his daughter's resolute strength of character, together with her acute intelligence, it was sometimes all too easy to forget she was still little more than a girl. A girl, furthermore, who considered herself very much in love. He had been too harsh.

'I'm sorry, my dear, but I couldn't share my plans with you earlier,' he said. 'And I shan't tell the boys until the last minute, for obvious reasons, which I know you will understand. But I have booked our passage. We sail at the end of March.'

'*I* don't.' Having recovered from her shock, Victoria met her father's gaze with steely eyes.

'I beg your pardon? You don't what?'

'I don't sail at the end of March. I shall not be going with you.'

They stared each other down like duellists.

'This was always your plan, was it, *Father*? You always had an end in sight.' Returning to Pendleton had never once occurred to her, and she felt strangely angry, foolish even, as if she should have known. 'You had an end in sight right from the start,' she said, which sounded very much like an accusation.

'I did,' Charles replied firmly. 'It was essential.'

'Yes. Yes, of course it would be. You wouldn't have been able to do what you did otherwise, would you, Father?'

The question being rhetorical, Charles said nothing.

Victoria changed tack, but once again her words sounded accusative. 'I thought you believed me when I told you I loved Jeff.'

'I did,' Charles replied. 'I believed you then and I believe you now. But young love doesn't necessarily last, my dear, and you have a life to return to in England. We all do.'

'You, perhaps. And the boys. Edward most certainly. But not me, Father. My life is here. Here with Jeff.'

Charles felt himself begin to soften. He longed to take her in his arms. Oh, how dearly he loved this daughter of his. But he would not drop his guard. Not this time.

'You're sure of Jeff, are you?'

'Yes, quite sure.' Victoria's smile was confident. 'He's not ready to admit it yet, but he loves me.'

'Then I shall look forward to his company at Christmas,' Charles said with a brisk nod, and they left things at that.

***

The Christmas party was in full swing, just as Victoria had promised Jeff it would be.

He'd arrived at around lunchtime. His horse had been brushed down, watered and housed in the stables and he'd been settled into one of the worker's huts not far from the homestead, where he was to stay the night.

Despite the fact it was over a hundred degrees in the shade, they'd dined on two well-stuffed roast chickens, a leg of mutton and copious baked vegetables smothered in gravy. Charles' Uncle Geoffrey had been a great believer in traditional Christmas luncheons and Nina was well trained. Had there been a turkey to hand, she would have cooked that, and she even knew how to make an excellent plum pudding, complete with brandy sauce.

There had been eight crowded around the old, scarred breakfast table: Charles and his three children; Nina and Alwyn Stroud, who, although serving the food, were virtually family; Joe Lawson; and then of course there was Constable Jeff.

Jeff had been a little self-conscious in Charles' presence at first. 'Thank you very much for inviting me, Mr Burton,' he'd said upon arrival.

'No need to stand on ceremony, lad,' Charles had replied jovially, shaking his hand in warm welcome. 'I think, given it's Christmas, you can make it Charles, what do you say?'

'Yes, sir. Thank you, sir.' Such familiarity did not come easily to Jeff.

But as the Christmas crackers had been pulled and the paper hats donned and the meal steadily devoured, he had relaxed. Very much so. He'd never experienced a family Christmas before, and the bonhomie around the table had delighted him. The glasses that were clinked in endless toasts, the joshing of the boys, the banter between the men, the laughter and the chatter and the general chaos; everything had converged to make him feel at home.

He'd regularly caught Victoria's eye. It had been difficult not to – she'd spent a great deal of the time looking at him. Her every glance had said, *See, I told you it would be wonderful*, and his every glance in return had said, *You're right, I agree*.

They hadn't left the table until four o'clock in the afternoon. Everyone had helped with the clearing up, after which they'd proceeded to the sitting room, where they'd immediately set about making yet more mess as they addressed the lucky dip.

Jeff hadn't known what to bring, so he'd played it safe and purchased two jars of boiled sweets from Sing's Bakery and General Store. Everyone liked sweets, didn't they? But as packages were untied and wrapping paper flung all around the place, an eclectic selection, both practical and bizarre, was revealed, from a curry comb and a mouth organ to a ball of string.

Swaps had taken place afterwards, Alwyn opting for the ball of string, in which no-one had appeared interested, and which had been his offering in the first place. Alwyn considered string exceedingly useful. And judging by the amount that had been thrown around with the wrapping paper, he was quite right.

Now, the lucky dip over, glasses were replenished, Joe produced his fiddle and they were into the singalong. Joe surprised them all. He'd been practising, he said, preparing for this very day, and he could now play Christmas carols. 'Not very many,' he warned, 'and not very well, but I'll give it a go.'

Raucous renditions of 'Jingle Bells', 'O Come All Ye Faithful', 'Hark! The Herald Angels Sing' and 'Silent Night' followed.

'You're an excellent singer,' Victoria said admiringly as Jeff lent full voice to the hymns.

'Tahitians love hymns,' he explained. 'I used to sing with all my friends in church, especially at Christmas. The whole of French Polynesia loves Christmas.'

They completed two renditions of each hymn, after which Joe apologised. 'Sorry,' he said, 'I only know those four. It'll have to be Scottish songs now.'

But no-one minded. Dusk was creeping in, lamps were lit, and the festivities continued. They sang to the Scottish ballads they knew, and they danced to the jigs and reels Joe played, Harold attempting to join in on the mouth organ he'd claimed from the lucky dip, but failing miserably. Which again, no-one minded. At one stage, Nina disappeared to the kitchen for a half an hour or so and re-emerged with trays of chicken and lamb sandwiches and Christmas cake, which, much to everyone's surprise, they hungrily devoured. Then at long last, the day was over.

Joe said his farewells and left, Nina and Alwyn departed for their cottage nearby, and a lighted kerosene lamp was placed on the sitting room table in order for Jeff to see his way to the worker's hut.

'I'll accompany you, shall I?' Victoria suggested hopefully. 'We wouldn't want you to get lost.'

'No, I'll be fine thanks,' he replied with a smile. Then he turned to her father. 'I've had a splendid day, thank you, sir,' he said. Relaxed though he was, Jeff somehow couldn't quite bring himself to embrace the use of 'Charles'. 'I must say, it was undoubtedly the best Christmas I've ever had,' he added.

'Excellent.' Charles shook his hand warmly. 'We've enjoyed your company, lad, I'm glad you could come.'

The boys chorused their 'goodnights' and disappeared to their room.

'We'll see you for a late breakfast, Jeff,' Charles instructed. 'Say, around eight?'

'Thank you, sir, yes, I shall be here.'

Charles, too, disappeared to his room, leaving the couple alone. He had no intention of spying, but he wondered nevertheless what they might get up to.

'*I'm* glad you could come too,' Victoria said, closing in on Jeff, offering her face up to him.

'Goodnight, Victoria,' he said.

'Aren't you going to kiss me?'

'Of course I am.'

He bent and gently kissed her on the cheek, which didn't satisfy her in the least.

Her arms were suddenly around his neck and her body snuggled against his as she whispered in his ear, 'I could come to your hut when everyone's asleep.'

She didn't expect for one minute he would agree to such a suggestion, but his response nonetheless surprised her. He threw back his head and laughed out loud.

'You're determined to shame me, aren't you?' he said.

'Yes,' she cheekily replied, 'I'm determined to shame you into marrying me.'

'Go to bed, Victoria.'

'Not until you kiss me.'

He bent and once again kissed her, still chastely, but this time on the lips.

'There,' he said, 'you've been kissed. Now go to bed.'

He picked up the kerosene lamp and left, quietly closing the door behind him.

14.

The following morning, Charles couldn't resist a passing comment to his daughter as, together, they set the table for breakfast.

'I half expected you to pay a visit to the worker's cottage last night,' he said with the droll raise of an eyebrow.

'I would have if I'd thought it would work,' she replied. 'I even suggested it to Jeff, but of course he refused. He actually had the temerity to laugh.' She smiled. 'He did kiss me though. A nice, chaste, brotherly kiss, Father,' she added with mock primness. 'He is an honourable man, you know.'

'Yes, I do believe he is.'

Charles, already worried, had made his remark in play, but her reply now further concerned him. So many questions needed answers. Was Victoria's assumption Jeff loved her mere girlish fantasy? What were his intentions? She'd said herself that he'd not yet made any declaration of love. And a brotherly kiss, although indeed honourable, did not sound promising.

He reluctantly decided there was only one option open to him. *I shall have to have a chat with this young man.*

Breakfast was another hearty meal. Lamb chops, boiled potatoes and eggs mopped up with damper and lard, the sort of breakfast devoured by hungry men about to set off early for a hard day's work. But today being Boxing Day, there would be no early start, only the most essential of tasks would be addressed and these in more or less desultory fashion.

Edward and Harold begged Jeff to stay and kick the football around with them, but he refused the offer.

'Sorry, boys,' he said, 'I'd like to, but I'm on duty this afternoon. Have to get back to Cossack.'

After once again thanking Charles Burton for his hospitality, Jeff picked up his kit bag, ready to fetch his horse from the stables. Victoria was all too willing to accompany him, but Charles intervened.

'Why don't I come with you, Jeff?' he said. 'We can have a little man-to-man chat on our way to the stables.'

'Yes, sir, I'd like that very much.'

Both men had expected Victoria to make some sort of objection or at least insist upon joining them, but she didn't. Instead, she hung back, eyeing them astutely, knowing she would be their topic of conversation.

'I'll see you at the regatta next week, Jeff,' she said amiably. There was to be no class the following Monday, which was New Year's Day. The whole of the area would be celebrating Cossack's annual Boat Regatta and Sports Day.

'Yes, I'll see you then, Victoria.' Jeff grinned. 'Thank you for a Christmas that was every bit as wonderful as you promised it would be.'

'My pleasure.' She gave him a wave and watched the two men as they walked off together. *You're going to confront poor Jeff, aren't you, Father?* she thought. *You don't trust me when I tell you he loves me, and you're going to demand he inform you of his intentions.*

She refused to allow the thought to annoy her, however.

And you, Jeff, what will you tell Father? Will you tell him the truth? Because you do love me, you know you do. But are you ready to admit it?

Victoria felt supremely confident. In herself more than anything. Even if Jeff was not yet prepared to profess his love, she was quite prepared to wait. And for as long as it took. *It's only a matter of time*, she thought.

'I'll get straight to the point, Jeff,' Charles said as they stepped down from the front verandah and set off briskly for the stables. 'There's something you should know. Something Victoria will not have told you.'

'Oh, yes, sir?' Jeff was intrigued. Charles Burton was not only deadly serious, he appeared worried. What could be wrong?

Charles didn't alter his pace. If anything, he sped up a little, eyes focussed directly ahead. 'I have booked the family's return passage to England,' he said. 'We leave towards the end of March.'

'Oh.' They continued walking, but it was obvious Jeff was shocked by the news. 'You're right, sir. She did not tell me that.'

'Victoria refuses to obey me,' Charles went on, spelling everything out plainly. 'She says she will not come with us, but maintains her place is here with you. She claims that she loves you and is convinced you love her in return.'

'I see.' It was Jeff who then came to a halt, and the two turned to face each other. *Little wonder the poor man's worried*, Jeff thought.

'So, as I'm sure you'll understand, I need to know your stance on this situation,' Charles said. He was starting to feel a little awkward. The young man did not appear particularly confronted. If anything, he seemed self-assured, confident even. In which case, was he about to dismiss all this talk of love as mere girlish fancy on Victoria's part? Charles hoped he was, for then, between the two of them, they could bring her to her senses. But it did leave him feeling rather foolish.

'Do you love my daughter, Jeff?' he demanded.

'Yes, Mr Burton, I do.'

'Ah.' The answer was so instant, so unequivocal, that Charles was momentarily stumped for an answer. *Where do we go to from here?* he wondered. But Jeff had the answers and was quick to put his mind at rest.

'As a matter of fact, sir,' he said, 'I had wondered whether I should say something to you on this trip out here to Burton Station. I've thought upon the matter a great deal, I must say, but decided to wait until after Victoria's eighteenth birthday. Now, however, given the circumstances, I believe this is the right time.'

'Yes?' Charles waited breathlessly.

'I should like to ask for your daughter's hand in marriage, sir.'

From the homestead's front sitting room, Victoria was peering through the flywire door. They weren't even halfway to the stables yet! But they were in avid discussion and they appeared quite amicable. There were even nods shared between the two of them. *This looks promising*, she told herself. Then, after several more minutes, they started walking on.

A multitude of thoughts were teeming through Charles' brain. He had agreed to Victoria's engagement, even though he considered her far too young. He had further agreed that she and Jeff would marry when she'd turned eighteen. Which, in his opinion, was still far too young, although as he reminded himself, *I was only eighteen myself when I wed, wasn't I? And then not for love. How lucky Victoria is.* And he couldn't think of any son-in-law he'd rather have than Jeff. It would mean that he would be leaving behind his only daughter when he returned to England, and that's where the true heartache lay.

Oh Victoria, my darling, Charlotte thought, *how I shall miss you!*

They'd reached the stables. Charles stood to one side as Jeff saddled his horse.

'Would you like to come back to the homestead and break the joyful news to your fiancée?' he asked.

'No, thank you, sir, I'll be late enough as it is. I shall leave that to you.'

Jeff mounted his horse and grinned down at the man who was to be his father-in-law. 'Goodbye, Charles,' he said. 'I'll see you at the regatta.'

He looked so absurdly happy and young and handsome, and so completely in love, Charles thought. *Oh, Victoria, you lucky girl.*

'Goodbye, Jeff,' he said, 'see you next week.'

***

As always, New Year's Day in Cossack was a kaleidoscope of colour and activity. Myriad boats of every description dotted the waters while, on the shore, people of all sorts and from all walks of life were either in fierce competition or on parade in their finest, simply milling about socially. There was something for everyone at Cossack's annual Boat Regatta and Sports Day.

Charles Burton and his children arrived on the horse-drawn tram in the middle of the day, having housed their buggy and pair at the stables in Roebourne. Victoria was so eager to see Jeff she had considered riding directly to Cossack, but she didn't wish to appear at the regatta in her men's trousers and bush hat, particularly as this was the day when she would celebrate her engagement.

Jeff was there to greet the tram's arrival. He'd been keeping an eye out for her all morning.

She jumped from the carriage before it had even come to a halt, looking lovely in her sky-blue summer dress and pretty straw bonnet, and ran to him.

He took her in his arms, having little option – she had so launched herself at him – and they kissed. On the lips. Right out there in the open for all to see.

Jeff quickly broke away, aware this was highly unethical; he was in uniform after all. But his delight was nonetheless undisguisable.

'It's all right,' she laughed. 'You're allowed to kiss me. We're engaged!'

'Yes.' He smiled. 'We are.'

Charles and the boys had stepped from the tram and now joined them.

'Congratulations, you two,' Charles said.

Edward offered his hand. 'Welcome to the family, Jeff,' he said formally, while beside him Harold jumped about excitedly echoing his congratulations.

Jeff thanked them, a little overwhelmed and painfully aware of the attention they were attracting from the many passers-by.

Victoria wasn't in the least self-conscious. 'We'll have to buy me an engagement ring now, won't we?' she demanded.

'Yes,' he agreed, 'although I don't know where we'll find anything to your taste around here.'

'I'll order exactly the one I want from a catalogue,' she said with a serene smile.

'Come along, boys.' Charles rounded up his sons. 'We'll leave you two to celebrate,' he said as they moved off. 'Don't forget though, Victoria, the poor lad *is* on patrol. Let him do his job.'

'I can tag around with you while you're on patrol though, can't I?' she murmured, tucking a proprietorial arm through Jeff's and snuggling up close.

'I don't see why not,' he agreed. 'Although I think we'll observe a little distance,' he added, disengaging their arms. 'Your father's right, I *am* on duty.'

Not wishing to cause him embarrassment, Victoria behaved herself, but she was determined to bask in this day. And bask she did. As they bumped into several of the locals she knew, she shared the news. Personally, she'd have preferred to crow it out loud to one and all from the rooftops, but she was select in her choice and discreet in her broadcasting.

Mrs Pead was the first. The kindly boarding house owner was mingling among the crowds on the riverbanks watching the yacht races and greeted them warmly.

'Good day, Miss Burton, Constable Jeff, and a very happy New Year to you.'

'It is indeed a very happy New Year for us, Mrs Pead,' Victoria said. 'I simply must share the news with you.' She leaned in confidentially. 'We don't have the ring yet, but Constable Jeff and I have just become engaged. Apart from the family, you are the first to know.'

'Oh, my dear.' Mrs Pead beamed from one to the other. 'I am so happy for you both.' There followed a kiss to Victoria's cheek and a handshake to Jeff. 'So very, very happy.'

Then came Sven Pedersen.

'Constable Jeff and I are engaged, Mr Pedersen,' Victoria said, and the giant Swede pumped Jeff's hand effusively. The news didn't really surprise Tiny at all. On the times when the two had met at his stables for their early morning ride, he could have sworn they were in love.

She even told Benny, when they passed by his hut, where he sat on his verandah. 'We're engaged, Benny,' she said.

The old pearl worker congratulated Jeff in Tahitian and offered them both a drink.

'Can't, Benny,' Jeff said, 'I'm on duty.'

Victoria was surprised to discover none of the locals knew of their engagement.

'Why didn't you tell anyone?' she asked. 'You've had a whole week to spread the news.'

'Didn't think you'd want them to know until you had the ring,' he said.

'I want the whole *world* to know,' she declared.

As it turned out, someone else *did* know.

Victoria was delighted when none other than Sergeant James Arthur Fry swooped upon them. He'd just arrived in Cossack for the regatta.

'I do believe congratulations are in order,' the big Police Sergeant's voice boomed in her ear. 'Heard the news from your father in Roebourne last week, Miss Burton,' he said as he doffed his hat to her. He shook Jeff's hand with a bone-crushing grip. 'And as for you, young man, well done! I'd say you've scored the pick of them all.'

'So would I, sir,' Jeff agreed.

Victoria couldn't have been more pleased. Sergeant Fry travelled the area a great deal. He'd no doubt been spreading the news all around the district. She certainly hoped he had.

As the day progressed, Jeff's policing services were rarely called upon in an active sense, his mere presence and those of his fellow constables appearing sufficient deterrent to any would-be troublemakers.

At one point he was required to break up a wrestling match that was out of control, the umpire unable to part the competitors, who seemed intent upon killing each other. And now and then, on entering the rowdy hotel bars, his stern voice of authority was required, perhaps even with the threat of arrest. But little else. After which he would rejoin Victoria, who was waiting outside.

It was in the late afternoon when the chilling moment occurred.

Jeff was checking out the bar of the Weld Hotel, Victoria waiting some distance off. He had warned her to keep well clear of the entrance, for by now the crowds inside were getting rowdier and drunker.

Two men barged past her on their way to the Weld, one of them bumping into her roughly. No word of apology, he was too bent on getting to the bar. Annoyed, she whirled about and just for an instant looked directly into the face of Bart Cameron.

He took no notice of her at all but walked straight on.

She stood watching as he and the man with him, presumably his brother, Arnie, disappeared into the bar.

Only moments later, Jeff appeared. 'The Cameron brothers,' he said, 'they're here.'

'I know. Bart just bumped into me,' she replied. 'I looked him right in the face.'

Jeff was alarmed. 'What was his reaction? Did he show any sign of recognition?'

'No. Not a flicker. Mind you, he was in a hurry.'

'We must get you out of here, Victoria,' he said, ushering her away. 'It's not worth the risk.'

'I'm to meet Father at Sing's Bakery and General Store shortly anyway,' she said, 'we're taking the late afternoon tram back to Roebourne.'

'Very wise,' he agreed. 'Cossack will soon be a town full of drunks. Even more than usual,' he said wryly. 'Always is on New Year's Day.'

Jeff was thoughtful as they walked on towards the tram stop. 'I should have known the brothers would turn up for the regatta,' he said. 'Let's hope they don't intend to stay long. Either way, there's bound to be trouble tonight. Particularly with those two in town. And particularly at the Weld, which is always their choice of bar.'

Charles was already waiting at Sing's Bakery and General Store, sitting in the shade of the verandah with a cup of tea.

'The boys will be along soon,' he said. 'They're keeping their eye out for the tram, milking everything they can until the last minute as usual. Want a cup of tea?' He directed the query to Jeff.

'No, thanks, sir, better not be seen slacking. I'll get back to my rounds.'

The men nodded their goodbyes, and Victoria edged to one side with Jeff to make her own farewell.

'A whole week until next Monday,' she muttered petulantly. 'I don't think I'll be able to bear it.'

'Yes, you will, Victoria,' he said with a smile. 'Think of all the fun you'll have looking through your catalogue.'

'Yes, there is that, isn't there?' She returned his smile. 'I'll have a ring all picked out by then and I'll bring the catalogue to show you.'

'I shall look forward to seeing it.'

He kissed her lightly and was about to go, but she put a hand on his arm and stopped him.

'Jeff,' she said, 'when we marry, will I be known as Mrs John Frances Boyle or Mrs Jean-François Fabron?'

There was such a sparkle in her eye he couldn't tell whether her question was inspired by genuine interest or mere playfulness.

'Whichever is legal, I suppose. Jean-François Fabron would be my choice, but ...' He shrugged. 'It will make no difference. This is the Pilbara. Around here, you'll be known as Mrs Jeff.'

Victoria's laugh was one of pure joy. It was exactly the right answer. She couldn't have asked for a better one.

Charles had been discreetly watching the farewell between the young lovers, and the peal of joyous laughter from his daughter now filled him with a mix of emotions. Victoria was so in love and he was happy for her. He trusted Jeff, who would make an excellent husband. But when he left in only three months, would he ever see his daughter again? Would she ever return to England? He doubted it. And he could never return to the Pilbara himself. He wondered, too, if, when she was married, Victoria would ever tell Jeff the truth about her 'father'.

She will have every right, Charlotte thought, *particularly when the children arrive. She will wish her children to know of their one remaining grandparent and of their heritage. I wonder what Jeff's reaction will be.*

'The tram's nearly here, Father,' Edward yelled. The boys were racing up from the shore.

Charles drained the last of his tea and stood.

***

Jeff's prediction proved correct. There was trouble that night. Particularly at the Weld Hotel and particularly from the Cameron brothers. Or so it seemed to him.

The whole of Cossack was a cauldron of drunkenness, which was always to be expected on New Year's Day and the end of the regatta's festivities. Jeff had anticipated as much. But when he entered the bar at the Weld Hotel, he was doubly annoyed that the trouble appeared to be coming from the area he'd predicted. The Cameron brothers, and specifically Bart. Given his worries for Victoria's safety, how he wished these two could disappear from the face of the earth.

There was goading and shoving and aggressive behaviour among a bunch of men at the end of the bar, a fight clearly about to break out, and guess who was in the middle of it? None other than Bart, backed up by his wimp of a brother, Arnie.

Jeff muscled his way through the pack, which quickly parted when they realised this was the young cop with the lethal fists. He grabbed Bart by the collar of his rough work shirt and jammed him back against the bar.

'We don't want your kind here, Cameron,' he snarled. 'If you and your brother know what's good for you, you'll get out of town.'

Bart held his hands up submissively. 'What did I do, Constable?' he protested in all innocence. 'What did I do? You tell me.' He looked around at the others, particularly his brother. 'C'mon, you tell me, what did I do?'

Arnie immediately came to his assistance. 'Yeah,' he said belligerently, always buoyed up in Bart's presence, 'what are you picking on him for? That's not fair. He hasn't done nothin'.'

'Not yet perhaps.' Jeff knew he'd overreacted. 'But you were about to, weren't you, Bart?' He released the man's collar, aware he had no right to lay in with his fists the way he would have liked. 'Can't help yourself, can you? Trouble follows wherever you go. Well, I'm giving fair warning. I've got my eye on you.' He cast a withering glance at Arnie. 'You and your brother. You're not welcome in Cossack.'

Powerless to do more than issue a threat, he turned and strode out of the bar, aware of the sneering and jeering from the Camerons behind his back. God, how he prayed they'd heed his warning and get out of town, hopefully before next Monday, when Victoria returned.

But the Camerons didn't get out of town. Admittedly, there were two ferocious cyclones over the next several days. Twelve luggers were lost and the steamer *Anne* damaged, as was the sea wall of Cossack. But all fatalities had taken place at sea. The cyclones shouldn't have prevented the Camerons from leaving.

Jeff came upon them any number of times throughout the week. And whenever he did, Bart mocked him, pretending to cower with fear in his presence, Arnie giggling at the joke. The mere sight of them infuriated Jeff.

Then, on Sunday night, things came to a head.

***

Jeff entered the bar of the Weld Hotel to a familiar sight: a Cameron was bullying a defenceless man. But this time it wasn't Bart, it was his younger brother, Arnie. Bart was nowhere in sight.

Bart's absence was unusual, for Arnie Cameron was a spineless man who lived entirely in the shadow of his elder sibling. An inveterate coward with a big mouth, he offered his opinions all too readily, knowing he was under his brother's protection. Arnie liked talking tough, and he had a particular fondness for assaulting those unable, or at least unlikely, to defend themselves.

This time it was little 'Irish Pat' Kelly. A kind man, known as a bit of a soft touch, and therefore at times taken advantage of, Irish Pat was certainly not one inclined to retaliate to any form of violence. An easy target.

'You're as weak as piss, Pat,' Arnie was sneering in a perfect imitation of his brother. 'You're a person that life has given up on, that's what you are.' He pushed the small Irishman in the chest. 'Answer me, man. Am I right or am I wrong?' he jeered into Irish Pat's frightened face. 'You're a weakling that life has deserted, admit it now, aren't you?'

'Well, what do we have here?'

Arnie swung around to see none other than Constable Jeff standing in the doorway.

'If it isn't Arnold Cameron, the toughest man in the Pilbara,' Jeff said, 'giving life advice to the downtrodden.' He stepped smartly up to Arnie and grabbed him by the lapel. 'And without his big brother to back him up, what's more.'

Arnie spun his head about, eyes searching the bar, and

realised with a sickening sense of shock that his brother was nowhere to be seen. *Shit*, he thought, *Bart must have gone outside for a piss.*

'And just what did you intend to do to the little Irishman?' Jeff demanded threateningly.

'Nothing,' was all Arnie could reply. He was terrified. 'Nothing at all. Just having a bit of fun.'

'I think you might have been intending something like this.' Jeff held Arnie at arm's length and punched him squarely in the nose, cracking it like a duck egg.

Arnie Cameron fell to his hands and knees, blood pouring from his flattened nose into the sawdust covering the floor.

'I clearly recall,' Jeff broadcast loudly for all to hear, 'that I told you and your brother you're not welcome in Cossack. I told you so only last week and you're both still here! Why is that?'

He paused, but Arnie didn't reply.

'I'm talking to you!'

He leaned over Arnie, declaring, once again at the top of his voice, 'This is a first and final warning to you and your brother. You've got one day to get out of Cossack.' He was angry now, his pent-up frustration with the Camerons rising to the fore. 'If you don't comply, I'll come looking for you both. And I'm telling you here and now, I'll be carrying a gun, which means you *won't* be arrested!'

There was silence in the bar, everyone seemingly frozen.

Jeff looked over to the barman. 'Right!' he announced. 'That's it for tonight! You can all get home to your beds! The pub's shut. As of now!'

Deathly silence reigned as he marched out of the doors and into the night.

***

Jeff spent the next hour and a half walking off his anger. He passed Benny's place, thinking if the old man was still up he might join him for a drink, but the hut and adjacent workshop were both in darkness. He checked the locks once again, simply through habit, then began a final roam of the streets. Hardly a soul about and on a Sunday evening, which in the old days used to be busy.

He shook his head. It seemed to him these days that Cossack was dying, a thought that saddened him. It was over three years now from when he'd first arrived in the spring of 1890, and since then, the place had diminished considerably. The sea trade still survived, wool and beef seemed secure, but the pearling business had mostly moved to Broome, several hundred miles up the coast. And those mining boom years of rough adventurers pouring into town had cooled to a trickle of young, hopeful men less inclined to drink and fight. Nowadays, young men appeared to be looking to their futures. A new century was beckoning, after all. There was more and more talk lately of Australia coming into its own as a nation. The Commonwealth of Australia no less, a country in its own right under the sovereignty of the British Crown.

Contemplative now, Jeff was no longer angry as he walked along the deserted Strand. At the corner of Pearl Street, he halted and looked up to where, on the right, the brand-new stone courthouse was starting to take shape. Destined to be the finest building in Cossack, it was scheduled for completion in 1895.

Strange, he thought, *that they should design an edifice as grand as that just as the town is threatening to die away.*

He crossed Pearl Street.

Ah, well, the new courthouse might well stand as a monument one day when Cossack ceases to exist. Such is the power of architecture.

Turning to gaze out over the moonlit river, his mind wandered aimlessly from the filthy hovels of his childhood in London's Limehouse and Whitechapel to those boulevards of Paris, where the architectural beauty had so overwhelmed him. Then to the tropical islands of French Polynesia, to the magnificence of the Marquesas, their jagged volcanic mountains rising into the clouds like the spires of great cathedrals. He smiled to himself. *Nature is surely the greatest architect of all.*

Thoughts of the islands brought with them thoughts of his family. Of the family who had adopted him in Tahiti, of his wife and his child. *We were so young when we wed*, he thought, *barely seventeen, although quite normal in Tahitian culture.*

Sad that the marriage had been so short-lived. It had been less than a year before pretty Raina and baby Miri had been taken from him, together with the whole of his extended family. Wiped out in a single typhus blow, along with so many others. The curse visited upon the innocent islanders by the white colonialists.

Jeff remembered how he'd liked being married, and how he'd liked being a father. He could now look forward to being both all over again.

Now there's Victoria, he thought, *my beautiful, maddening, complex Victoria, whom I could swear I fell in love with on that first day we met.*

He would tell Victoria all of this when he saw her tomorrow, he decided, and he wondered at the reaction he was bound to get. He could just hear her.

'What? You've been *married*? And you never *told* me! How *dare* you keep a secret like that!'

Yes, that's exactly what she'll say.

Time to head home. He'd cut through behind the post office for a final check on the stockyards before calling it a night. A fresh head of stock had been delivered earlier in the day and you never knew who might be prowling around in the hours after dark. Someone perhaps with an eye to stealing a steer?

He was ten yards into the gloomy passage between the post office and the new Customs Bond Store when he realised he was not alone. He was being followed.

He stopped and turned. A man's silhouette was all he could see.

'Step forward and show yourself,' he demanded.

The man took several steps towards him and Jeff recognised who it was. 'Well, well, if it isn't Bart Camer—'

The sound of the gunshot was deafening in the confines of the alleyway. The bullet hit Jeff in the stomach like a blow from a sledgehammer. He staggered several feet backwards though he maintained his footing. But he knew he was a dead man. The heavy-calibre bullet had ripped his gut and smashed his spine.

'That's for my brother ...'

Bart Cameron's voice rang in Jeff's ears. He was aware of the man coming closer. Then he fell on his back and stared up.

But he stared up at what?

He couldn't see Bart. All he could see was a vision of Victoria. His glorious Victoria. She was smiling down at him. Mockingly, lovingly, teasingly, everything that Victoria was ...

'And this one's from me.'

Jeff didn't hear the gun discharge. He sensed only a thump as the bullet entered his heart, killing him instantly.

15.

Victoria hadn't brought Jimmy with her this Monday, stabling him instead in Roebourne, where she'd changed into her attractive summer dress before catching the horse-drawn tram. Her feelings were along similar lines to those of last week, when she'd come to the regatta: she had no wish to arrive in Cossack in her rough riding clothes. Everyone there would now know she was engaged and she wanted to look pretty as she walked down The Strand, accepting the congratulations that were bound to be on offer. And she very much wanted to look pretty for Jeff as they leafed through the catalogue she carried in her cloth shoulder bag. She had selected three choices of rings and couldn't wait to show him. Instead of going for an early morning ride on the Tuesday, they would meet for a cup of tea in the front sitting room at Mrs Pead's boarding house, where they would study the catalogue. And perhaps, if there was no-one else around, they may even kiss and cuddle the way fiancés were wont to do. Mrs Pead herself certainly wouldn't mind.

The moment she stepped from the tram, Victoria sensed something was amiss. *We're in a brand-new year*, she thought, *where are the happy people?*

Walking along The Strand, she received no offers of congratulations as she'd expected, and not a word came in answer to her several 'Happy New Years'. In fact, many of the locals she knew seemed to be averting their eyes as she passed.

How odd. What have I done?

Then when she turned into Pearl Street she saw, on the opposite side of the road, Sergeant Fry and four constables, obviously having arrived from Roebourne. They were standing in the laneway next to the post office building.

I suppose that explains it, she thought, *something bad's happened and the police presence has thrown a shadow over the town. What on earth could it be?*

She continued on into Perseverance Street, unsettled now by the silence.

She looked across the road to the schoolhouse and saw the large figure of Tiny Pedersen sitting hunched on the school steps. He appeared to be waiting, and he rose as she approached him.

'Hello, Mr Pedersen,' she said with a smile. But her smile quickly faded, met by the torture she could see in the big Swede's eyes. 'Something's happened, hasn't it?' she asked, unnerved.

No answer came.

'What are the Roebourne Police doing in Pearl Street?'

As Sven Pedersen stood gazing silently at her, she noticed his lip was trembling.

'Is everything all right, Tiny?'

'Not all right.' He shook his head and a tear coursed its way down his cheek.

It was the tear that did it. Victoria's body ran cold, and a sick feeling swept through her. 'What is it, Tiny? Tell me,' she demanded. 'What is it?'

'Is not good.' The big Swede shook his head. 'Is why no-one come here today.' He pointed at the school door. 'No class for you today.'

She began to shake. 'It's Constable Jeff, isn't it? It is, isn't it?' she demanded. 'Constable Jeff has been hurt.'

'Constable Jeff not hurt. Constable Jeff dead.'

'What?' She clutched the big man's hand, fearing her legs would give way. Her mind was spinning so dizzily she felt she might faint. 'When? How?' she managed to gasp.

'Someone. Last night. They shoot him.'

Victoria tore her hand free and ran back across Perseverance Street, gasping for air, staggering as she went. Then, all of a sudden, she came to a halt. Drawing herself erect, she took two deep breaths. *Stop it*, she commanded herself. Another deep breath. *Get control.* She breathed out steadily and slowed her pace as she walked down to the corner of Pearl Street, where she stood looking across at the gathering of policemen.

Fry noticed her immediately. He had seen her pass by some minutes before and had been expecting her to reappear. He knew Tiny Pedersen was waiting for her at the schoolhouse. She met his eyes now, and with what appeared to him a demanding glare. Then, before he could cross to her, she was striding purposefully towards him.

Fry watched her approach. *She knows*, he thought. *My God, but you have to admire her. She knows that the man she loves, her fiancé no less, is dead. Yet look at her. She's one tough young woman, Victoria Burton.*

He nodded to the constables, who drifted to one side, and as he stepped forward to meet her, she offered her hand.

'Good day, Sergeant Fry,' she said.

'And to you, Miss Burton.'

Beneath the fine lace of her glove, he could feel her hand was cold and he could see in her eyes the deepest distress, but he could see also that she was determined to hide it.

'There's been a bit of bad business,' he said. Which he realised was surely the understatement of all time as far as this young woman was concerned, but being the customary manner in which he expressed himself, he could think of no other way to voice the situation. 'I presume you have gleaned what has taken place.'

'Yes, Sergeant,' she replied, 'I have *gleaned* that Senior Constable Jeff ...' Victoria nearly stumbled over the name but quickly recovered herself, '... is dead. Murdered, I assume?'

'Yes, shot in the heart. He would have died instantly, which is at least something of a blessing, wouldn't you agree?'

'I would. Do we know who did it?'

There was fury in her eyes, and he couldn't help but notice her clenched fists and fixed jaw.

'No. We have no witnesses. No report from anybody.'

'And your thoughts, personally?'

'This is police business, Victoria.' Fry softened his response. This helpless anger of hers could be doing her no good. 'I'm not allowed the privilege of making assumptions about events that occurred prior to the killing—'

'Events,' she interrupted. 'Events that occurred prior to the killing? Events, such as what?'

'Well, it appears Jeff flattened Arnie at the Weld, but—'

'Arnie?' she queried. 'Arnie Cameron?'

'Yes.' He nodded. 'In the pub last night. Arnie was picking on little Irish Pat and Jeff apparently—'

'Was Bart Cameron involved?'

'Evidently not. He was there prior to the altercation and returned to the pub several minutes later.'

'Will you arrest them?' It sounded very much like a demand.

'On what grounds? As far as can be ascertained, they've done nothing to warrant being arrested.'

'Oh, come on,' she snapped. 'It's obvious! The entire population of Cossack must know the Camerons killed Jeff. Or Bart, anyway, Arnie wouldn't have the guts. Have you even spoken to the brothers?'

'Of course I have,' Fry snapped back in reply, her interrogation annoying him.

'And?'

'They denied any knowledge of the crime. Bart Cameron told me he found his brother on the floor of the pub and, after straightening his broken nose, they rode out of town, heading for Mallina. But Arnie complained about the pain so much they decided to camp on the track and early this morning they returned to Cossack to hopefully see a doctor.'

Victoria glared at him. 'And you *believed* them?'

'No!' It was Fry's turn to be angry. Angry, above all, at his own powerlessness. 'I didn't believe a word of it!' He glared back at her. They were at loggerheads now. 'But I have no evidence, not one shred! How can I arrest them, charge them with murder and present them to the court when I don't have a witness? Not one! Nobody has yet to claim they even heard the gunshots!'

'I'll be a witness for you,' she said desperately. 'I'll say anything you want me to say. I'll—'

'Stop it! Stop it, Victoria!' He could see she was starting to crumble. 'That would mean perjuring yourself in a court of law and that would make you no better than them.' Oh, God, how he felt for her! 'You have a life to live, my dear. Don't let this destroy you. Jeff wouldn't want—'

'John,' she interrupted. 'His name was John. John Francis Boyle.'

'Really?' Fry was confused. 'But I thought he had some sort of French name ...'

'He did. Jean-François Fabron. He was that too. He was ...' Victoria shook her head helplessly. She wanted to explain. She wanted to tell him Jeff's story. But she was incapable, the tears now rolling down her cheeks.

Oh, God, what have I done? the big policeman thought. He reached out and drew her to him, where she willingly rested her forehead against the barrel of his chest, fighting to stifle the sobs that threatened.

He patted her back in a clumsy but successful attempt to comfort her and, within only seconds, she had her breathing under control.

'Where is he?' she asked, her voice muffled against him.

'In the cells at the rear of the station.'

'The cells?' She looked up, her tear-streaked face aghast. 'You've put him in the cells?'

'There's no-one else in custody. He's alone.'

She nodded, sniffing back the tears, wiping her cheeks, and, having recovered herself, drew away from him.

Fry went on to explain the official procedure he'd planned, aware she was keen to stifle any further show of emotion.

'We've arranged to bury Jeff later this afternoon, Victoria,' he said. 'Word has been posted around Cossack, and I sent a man out to Burton Station before I left Roebourne this morning. Your father will already be on his way here and may well arrive within the next hour or so.' *Which will hopefully be of some comfort to you*, he thought.

She nodded once again. 'May I see Jeff's body?'

He was taken aback. Such a thing was highly unorthodox. But how could he refuse?

'Yes,' he said. 'Give me half an hour and meet me at the cells.'

'Thank you, Sergeant,' she said. 'I'm sorry for the outburst.' She even attempted a smile. 'I'm all right now. I shall meet you in half an hour.'

Victoria spun on her heel and walked off, head held high, knowing she must get to the privacy of her room at Mrs Pead's as soon as possible, where she could fall apart altogether.

***

Precisely half an hour later, Victoria joined Sergeant Fry at the entrance to the cells.

The big policeman unlocked the door and indicated she enter.

'He's down the end, in the last cell. I can give you only five minutes, Victoria. It's not correct for you to be here at all.'

Fry closed the main door behind him and Victoria was left alone in the narrow passageway where three small stone cells led off to the right. The cells' doors were open, allowing the light to flood in through their single-barred windows, forming a pattern on the walls of the passage as she walked to the cell at the end.

The door to this one was closed, but not locked. She pulled it open to reveal what was obviously a body, lying on the ground, covered in a tarpaulin.

She knelt beside it, hauled back the tarpaulin, and there he was. The bullet wounds were horrendous, but Sergeant Fry had been right, she realised. They were fatal to the point he would have felt no pain in the seconds before death claimed him. She was glad for that.

It was his face though, the expression on his beautiful face, that so moved her. Jeff appeared completely at peace. He might have been asleep, she thought, dreaming of something glorious. There was even the faintest smile on his lips.

She lay down beside him on the rough dirt floor, head resting on his shoulder, and she gazed at his face, tears once again flowing. Her Jeff. Her beautiful Jean-François Fabron.

'Oh, my love,' she whispered. 'Oh, my dearest love.'

Five minutes later, she met Fry at the main door to the cells, dry-eyed, rigid-backed and resolved. Those several minutes had been enough. She had said her goodbyes. But young Victoria Burton knew she would never be the same again.

'Thank you, Sergeant Fry,' she said.

***

The impromptu funeral of Constable Jeff late that afternoon was impressive. One might even have presumed it to be the burial of a most important citizen that had been planned for some time. But it wasn't. It was just Jeff.

Upon Sergeant Fry's request, a priest from the Holy Trinity Anglican Church in Roebourne had arrived to conduct the graveside service, and it seemed the whole of Cossack had turned up to pay their respects.

The whole of Cossack except for the Cameron brothers, Victoria thought as she stood among the crowd, scanning the cemetery grounds that looked out over the river. She was thankful the Camerons had not made the pretence of attending, for had she seen them, she doubted she'd have been able to control herself. She'd thought they might turn up in a further effort to cover their guilt, but they'd obviously felt no need.

She was thankful, too, to have her family beside her. Her father and her brothers had arrived in Cossack, all three on horseback, having ridden directly from home, and with them was Joe Lawson.

All in all, a fitting tribute to you, my darling, Victoria thought, gazing about at the crowd. Again, she was rigid-backed and tearless. She'd done her crying. Besides, there were plans to be made.

***

Charles worried for his daughter. When he and his sons and Joe Lawson had arrived in Cossack on that terrible day, they'd been of comfort to Victoria, he could tell. Despite the fact she was keeping herself tightly in control, he knew their presence was of the utmost importance to her. Which was probably why the boys had managed to maintain their own level of control, he decided, for when news of Jeff's death had reached them at Burton Station, they'd all been deeply affected. Harold had openly wept, and Edward, although known for his ability to maintain a stiff upper lip, had been so shocked, he'd nearly followed suit. Even the inscrutable Joe Lawson had been visibly horrified to learn of Jeff's cold-blooded murder.

On arrival, they'd gathered around Victoria, showing support for which she had been grateful. She had wholeheartedly accepted her father's embrace, but had still not allowed herself any open display of grief.

Charles had even been prepared to break the rule he'd sworn he would abide by until their departure for England.

'Shall we find a quiet corner where we can speak openly, my darling?' Charlotte had whispered in her daughter's ear as they'd embraced.

'No, Father, that won't be necessary. Although I thank you for the offer,' Victoria had whispered back in all sincerity.

Charles had very much admired her stoicism at the time. But now, these weeks later, he worried that she should remain so remote. He'd expected her anguish to find an outlet at some stage. She was still grieving, he had no doubt, for grief manifested itself in so many ways, but her preoccupation with work seemed to him unnatural. He would even have preferred she weep and wail, at least then he might have comforted her. He might have served some purpose. As it was, he felt helpless.

'Victoria, my dear,' he said, 'are you not perhaps taking on too much? Do you really think these extra classes in Cossack are necessary?'

'I do, Father, yes,' she said firmly. 'I have more students than ever now, and they need me.'

'But you could be resting, my dear,' he suggested, 'you could—'

'And *I* need *them*, Father,' she said, aware of his concern and his desire to be of comfort. 'Don't you see, Papa?' she added gently. 'The classes are a distraction for me. They serve a purpose.'

'Yes, yes, of course.' *Surely you should be spending less time in Cossack, rather than more*, Charles thought, *where everything there must be a reminder of Jeff.*

He knew better than to pressure her any further, though. She would heal when they returned to England, he told himself. They were due to depart in less than two months now, and when they did, who could tell? Perhaps when they were back home at Pendleton all this might be relegated to an awful dream, the stuff of nightmares. He could only hope so.

Victoria's extra classes did indeed serve a purpose. In the days following Jeff's murder, she had been able to think of nothing but killing Bart Cameron. She had decided to take justice into her own hands. If the law could not prevail and Cameron were not to stand trial for murder, then she considered it only right she should be his executioner. However, she was too clever to make the mistake of taking immediate action. She had bided her time, the death of Bart Cameron assured in her mind. All she'd had to do was plot his demise with logic and simple common sense.

She was aware that in order to achieve Bart Cameron's death, she must be in Cossack on a more regular basis. Increasing her English tutorage to two afternoon sessions a week, one on Monday and one on Wednesday, she now stayed at Mrs Pead's until her return to Burton Station on the Thursday. This allowed her to keep track of the Cameron brothers' whereabouts, for they spent as much time at the Mallina goldfields as they did in Cossack. Many a nefarious activity was conducted around Mallina, after which they would return to Cossack in order to drink and carouse and God only knew what else.

These days she left her horse at the stables in Roebourne and caught the tram, aware that, should she be seen in her rough riding clothes, Bart Cameron might well recognise her. And as the weeks passed, she waited for the opportunity to present itself.

Then one day, it did.

Strangely enough, it was little 'Irish Pat' Kelly who provided the inspiration for a plan of the greatest simplicity.

Irish Pat attended her classes religiously despite the fact that English was his only tongue. He did so merely because of his two closest friends, a pair of young Dutchmen he'd taken under his wing. Bram and Daan Vandergrift had decided to refine their extremely poor knowledge of English, and Irish Pat's idea of a good friend was one who helped his mates. How he could possibly have helped them refine their linguistic ability in any practical sense was beyond comprehension, but he was determined to show support.

On this particular Monday, Victoria arrived at the schoolhouse to discover a number of men waiting on the verandah, as they so often were, chatting away, as they so often did. Today's group included Irish Pat and his two Dutch mates, which was not surprising as they were usually among the early arrivals.

After greeting the men, she unlocked the door and they followed her inside like so many obedient sheep, Pat, in his high-speed Irish brogue, continuing to chat about the occasional letters he received from his brother in Perth. Apparently, the postman left them for him with whichever barkeeper was on duty at the Weld Hotel, the Weld being his favoured drinking hole. Pat boasted that he simply collected a letter whenever it was waved in the air.

'They do that for lots of folk,' he said cheerfully, 'right regular postmen they are at the Weld.'

You gorgeous little leprechaun, Victoria thought, as she

set her things out on her teacher's desk. *Could it really be that simple? And even if not, it's certainly worth a try.*

She sat, and while waiting for the rest of her students to arrive, printed a note on a sheet of paper, which she sealed in an envelope, addressing the envelope also in print.

When her class had concluded and sixteen big, rough men rose and rushed for the door, no doubt headed for the pubs, Victoria called to Irish Pat and beckoned him to her desk.

Irish Pat was mystified, but only too happy to be singled out by the pretty young teacher.

'You go on,' he said to Bram and Daan, 'I'll see you there in a jiffy.' And he reported to the desk at the front of the classroom.

'Patrick,' Victoria said in her best teacher's voice, 'I just wanted to tell you I am most pleased with the way you accompany the Vandergrift boys to class. You're a good friend to them both, you certainly are.'

Pat, lost for words, could only stare at the beautiful girl who had called him Patrick. Like most of the men in Cossack, he was just a little bit in love with Miss Burton.

'Um,' he began. 'Er ...'

'Would you be on your way to the Weld Hotel bar, by any chance, Patrick?'

There, she'd said it again.

'Well, um, er ...' He remained a little tongue-tied. The last person to call him Patrick had been his mother. And then, back in the old country, many years past.

'Could you possibly give this to the barkeeper for me?' Her smile was radiant as she handed him the envelope.

Pat looked down at the name on the envelope. Bart Cameron. He froze. This note was for Bart Cameron!

'Could you do that for me, Patrick?'

He heard his name again but continued to stare at the envelope. Then he looked up at her, his expression one of the deepest concern.

Her radiant smile faded. 'And if not for me, perhaps you might do it for Constable Jeff,' she suggested meaningfully.

Jesus, Mary and Joseph, his brain screamed. *Is she crazy?*

'Miss,' he managed to stutter, 'are you sure you got the right name on this?'

She looked him directly in the eyes. 'I'm not only sure, Patrick, I'm absolutely positive.'

What Pat saw there was utter fearlessness. 'You do know who you're communicating with, don't you?' He shook his head and looked around the room, but the others, of course, had all departed. 'He's a terrible man, that he is, miss.'

'I know.' Her eyes continued to hold him with their sheer daring. 'I know, Patrick.' She held her hand out. 'In which case, if you'd rather return the envelope, we'll say no more on the matter.'

'No!' he exclaimed, clasping the envelope firmly to his chest. She was planning something. He didn't know what it was, but he was prepared to be a part of it. 'I shall see this to the barkeeper for you. Constable Jeff was a great human being, and I hold you, Miss Burton, in equal esteem. You've the heart of a lioness. I shall see this to the barkeeper. I shall let you know when it has been delivered, what's more. And I shall take our conversation to the grave, I swear, or my name's not ...'

He paused, having been about to say 'Irish Pat', but instead drew himself to his full height of five feet and three inches and declared, 'Or my name's not Patrick Augustus Kelly.'

The radiant smile reappeared. 'And you, sir,' she said, 'have my friendship for life, or my name's not Victoria Elizabeth Burton.'

***

It was during class on the Wednesday afternoon two days later that Irish Pat, with a glance and a conspiratorial nod, confirmed to Victoria that her letter had been handed by the barkeeper at the Weld Hotel to the recipient for whom it was intended.

She nodded her thanks in return. *What do you know about that? Good things come to those who wait.* It was time for her to make her move.

Victoria had planned exactly what she was going to do. She could only hope now that Bart Cameron would take the bait.

The following day, as she was leaving the boarding house, she invited Mrs Pead to join her for morning tea on The Strand.

'Such a lovely day, out,' she said, 'and I don't leave until lunchtime, when I intend to catch the midday tram.'

'I'd be delighted, my dear.'

Mrs Pead was only too willing to spend time with this unbelievably brave young woman. The way Victoria Burton had soldiered on so stoically these past few weeks since the shocking death of her fiancé ... No words could describe Mrs Pead's admiration. But then, they were outback women, weren't they? Outback women born to shoulder their bereavement and get on with the job at hand. Mrs Pead herself was made of the same stern stuff.

Over a pot of tea at Sing's Bakery and General Store, the two chatted happily, Victoria offering greetings to all who passed their table, ensuring her presence in Cossack was noted by many. She also told others, as she had Mrs Pead, that she intended to take the noon tram to Roebourne and continue on horseback to Burton Station.

Then, with a great deal of show, Victoria waved goodbye to Mrs Pead and did indeed leave on the noon tram.

In Roebourne, she had a Devonshire tea at Renshaw's General Store. She sat in the store's teashop throughout the remainder of the afternoon, completing her school paperwork and chatting to Alma, the Renshaws' youngest, who worked there.

Then, at five o'clock, she bade Alma farewell, saying she was going to the stables to retrieve her horse and head home to Burton Station.

At the stables, she changed into the riding apparel that was kept in Jimmy's saddlebags and tipped the young lad who saddled her horse. She informed him, quite unnecessarily as far as he was concerned, that she was on her way home to Burton Station, and he wished her a safe journey.

Once well clear of Roebourne, however, she swung her horse around and set off at a trot back to Cossack. She didn't follow the tram tracks, but stayed well concealed behind the tree line.

Finally, about half a mile from the lights of Cossack, she dismounted and strapped about her hips the belted holster containing her Enfield .476. This too had been stored in Jimmy's saddlebags, awaiting the moment when it would come into play.

Leaving Jimmy tethered, she walked on, circling the town unseen until she found herself a hundred yards distant from the Explosives Wharf. And there she settled down to wait.

***

They were right on time. Ten o'clock, as her note had suggested. It had read:

BART, BIG JOB COMING UP AT MALLINA. BIG MONEY.
PLENTY FOR ALL OF US. EXPLOSIVES WHARF 10 O'CLOCK
THURSDAY NIGHT. TELL NO-ONE. COME ALONE.

Bart Cameron had taken the bait. But he hadn't come alone, as her note had stated he should, had he? He'd brought his damned idiot brother, Arnie, with him.

Oh well, Victoria thought, *two for the price of one. All the better. You both deserve to die.*

The two men were armed, she noted, obviously wary in case this might be a trap. Which was not good. But she noted also that both men were slightly the worse for wear from the grog they'd consumed, which could prove to her advantage.

Rising stealthily from her hiding place among the coastal scrub, Victoria drew the revolver from its holster and, keeping low, crept closer to the wharf.

Closer and then closer she came until, finally reaching the last of the scrub, she stepped out into the glow from the marine light on the Explosives Wharf. She wanted them to see her, to know who she was, so she kept the revolver concealed by her side. Better they should have a good look before she killed them.

Thirty feet away, seeing what they thought was a man, the brothers raised their weapons in a warning, just in case this might be a trap of some sort.

'State your business,' Bart called out. 'Was it you left the note at the Weld? And if so, what's this about?'

But Arnie's eyesight was better than his brother's. 'Hey, Bart,' he said, 'it's not a bloke. It's a—'

Then Bart recognised exactly who it was. 'It's that bitch,' he said. 'It's that mad bitch who coshed me.'

Victoria raised the Enfield.

'And she's got a—'

They were Arnie's last words.

Victoria's first shot hit him on the bridge of his already-damaged nose and he dropped to the ground, dead.

Her second shot hit Bart Cameron in the stomach and, with a grunt, he fell flat on his back. But as his arm made contact with the ground, his revolver exploded and Victoria felt the bullet hit her boot. The shock upon impact was horrific, but she ignored it and, marching the thirty feet to where he lay, she kicked the weapon from his hand and stood over him.

He lay staring helplessly up at her, anger and hatred plainly written across his face.

'You,' he snarled in agony, his body already reporting his imminent death. 'Why the hell ...'

'You shouldn't have killed Jeff,' Victoria said coldly. She raised the Enfield, about to finish the job.

Then his hand flashed out with the speed of a snake, something she'd not expected. Grabbing her leg, he pulled her to the ground. But as Victoria fell, she fired.

The bullet hit him directly between the eyes.

And that was it. The game was over.

Victoria rose to her feet and looked down at him. Only briefly. Then she turned and walked away.

Once again circling the town and keeping well out of sight, she made her way back to where Jimmy was tethered.

Her foot was hurting now, throbbing with each step, and she wondered how bad the wound might be. Hopefully she would be able to conceal it.

During the ride home, with no weight on the foot, however, the pain was far less. A good sign perhaps?

Back at Burton Station, she lit the lamp in the stables and watered Jimmy and brushed him down before retiring herself.

The first hint of dawn was streaking the sky as she crept into the homestead. She went straight to her room and in the light of a kerosene lamp placed a towel on the floor, hauled off her bloodied riding boot and examined the damage.

A flesh wound only, she was thankful to note, a nasty one certainly, but no bone broken. The bullet had glanced across the side of her boot, leaving a heavy gash in both leather and flesh, just below the ankle.

She fetched the basin and water jug from the wash stand and cleaned the wound as best she could, then wrapped several neck scarves about her ankle and foot, forming a makeshift bandage. She would look after it properly in the morning.

Returning the bloodied water basin and towel to the wash stand, she covered the whole lot with a woollen shawl from her cupboard. She would look after the evidence in the morning too.

Stripping off her clothes, she donned her nightdress, slipped into bed and was asleep within minutes. It had been a very long night.

She was rudely awakened at nine o'clock. By none other than her father.

'Wake up, sleepyhead!' Charles exclaimed. 'You've missed breakfast,' he said as she groggily came to.

'Oh, yes.' She hauled herself into a sitting position. 'I'm sorry, I must have slept in.' A rather obvious statement, she realised.

He was standing there gazing down at her. And a little strangely, she thought.

'You were very late getting home last night,' he remarked, 'or should I say this morning.'

'Ah ...' She wasn't sure how to respond to that.

'I was worried when you hadn't returned by dinnertime, Victoria,' he said. Clearly an accusation.

'Yes, Father, I'm sorry I couldn't let you know—'

But his eyes were flickering around the room, seeking evidence, and it was all too obviously there.

'Bit hot for a shawl, wouldn't you say?' He crossed to the washstand and pulled the shawl aside to reveal the basin with its bloodied water and towel.

'What happened, Victoria?' Still an accusation, but now mingled with concern.

'That's why I was so late coming home, Father ...' Victoria's mind was frantically searching for a story that might sound valid. 'On the way back from Roebourne, Jimmy and I had an accident. He was startled by something, I didn't see what it was, but he shied and I fell. I must have hit my head and lost consciousness. For how long I really couldn't tell, but it was dark when I regained my senses ...'

She trailed off, aware her father wasn't listening. His eyes had scanned the room and he'd seen her boots, which she really should have hidden under the bed.

He picked up the damaged one, examining it closely. 'This happened in the fall, I take it?'

'Yes, that's right.' She pulled back the coverlet, sat up and swung her legs over the side of the bed, displaying the bandaged foot. 'I don't quite know how, but the boot and my foot both suffered in the fall.'

Rubbish, Charles thought, *nothing but a bullet could cause this sort of damage.*

He put down the boot. 'Let's take a look, shall we?'

Kneeling on one knee, he placed her wounded foot on the other and proceeded to undo the neck scarves that served as a bandage.

'You're lucky,' he said when the wound was revealed. 'Very lucky that it was only a glancing blow, and from the side. Your ankle could well have been shattered otherwise. You'd have been a cripple for the rest of your life.'

'Yes,' she admitted. They both understood exactly what he was saying.

Rising to his feet, Charles sat beside her on the bed. 'What have you been up to, Victoria?'

She knew there was no point in trying to evade the issue any longer.

'Righting a wrong, Father,' she replied, meeting his eyes boldly. 'You'll find out soon enough.'

***

The bodies of the Cameron brothers had already been discovered. They'd been found by passing market gardeners in the first light of dawn, around the same time Victoria had arrived back at Burton Station.

Upon being informed of the murders, Sergeant Fry had his instant suspicions. Could this be the work of young Victoria Burton? he wondered. In her frustration at the lack of legal action, had she taken on the role of executioner?

Fry considered the only daughter of Charles Burton, a man for whom he had the utmost respect, one of the smartest and toughest young women he'd ever known. Victoria was certainly capable. Fry was quite convinced she'd killed a man at thirteen years of age. Following the confrontation four years previously when Burton Station had been attacked, her father had maintained he'd killed all three men himself. But the wounds to the bodies had told an altogether different story. Charles Burton had used a shotgun, hadn't he? And one of the deceased had received a bullet through the eye. Much as Burton had insisted he was responsible for all killings, Fry had always been doubtful. He remained convinced to this day that Victoria had been involved. One tough young woman indeed.

Loath as he now was to find evidence against Victoria Burton, Fry was duty-bound to make enquiries. A dual murder could not go uninvestigated.

However, a trip to Cossack and intensive questioning both there and in Roebourne revealed not a suspicion in the world. By late morning of that very same day, Fry was satisfied that Victoria Burton's alibis were all well-established. *Not only tough*, he thought, *but smart.*

He considered making a trip out to Burton Station, mainly to put Charles Burton's mind to rest. Victoria's father would surely have suspicions of his own and would no doubt be worrying.

But as it turned out, there was no need. Charles Burton himself paid a visit to Roebourne Police Quarters late that afternoon.

Sergeant Fry invited him into his office with a signal to the young constable behind the front desk to bring them a pot of tea.

'To what do I owe the honour, Mr Burton?' Fry said expansively as he settled back in his chair.

Charles made the pretence of settling comfortably into his own chair, but he was wary, watching for any giveaway sign from the Sergeant.

'I heard about the murders in Cossack,' he said. 'Wondered if you'd come up with anything?'

'Ah, yes, the Cameron brothers. Word does travel fast, doesn't it?'

'Always,' Charles agreed, 'when it's something as interesting as murder. So how is your investigation going?'

'Dead end, I'm afraid.' Fry smiled reassuringly, eager to put Charles Burton's mind at rest. 'No leads to be found anywhere. Neither here in Roebourne nor in Cossack. I'd say this was a vengeance killing, some sort of payback tied up, more than likely, with their disreputable dealings in Mallina. The Camerons were involved in all sorts of sticky business around the goldfields. I'll send a man up there to make some enquiries. Doubt we'll come up with anything, though.'

'I see.' Charles certainly did see. Victoria had obviously covered her tracks, for which both he and Fry were grateful. 'Well, good luck with it all, Sergeant.'

'Thank you.' Fry leaned in conspiratorially. 'Mind you, Mr Burton, I doubt the Cameron brothers will be deeply mourned. A most unsavoury pair. I, for one, am convinced it was they who killed Constable Jeff, the finest of men.'

'Yes, I would hazard you're right there,' Charles agreed. 'A very great loss, our Jeff.'

'Ah, the tea,' Fry exclaimed as the Constable appeared with a tray, 'and gingerbread biscuits, excellent. I shall pour, thank you, Constable.'

He waved the young policeman away and picked up the pot.

'I believe you will shortly be returning to England, Mr Burton,' he said as he started to pour.

'Yes,' Charles said, 'that is correct. Only a month or so now.'

And they settled down to chat, the unspoken, but crystal-clear, understanding shared between them. This business would be swept under the carpet.

Once again, justice has been served in Pilbara fashion, Charles thought. He still didn't altogether approve, but there were times when he had to admit it really did work out for the best. *And who can argue with that?*

16.

Victoria had admitted the truth to her father that morning, but she'd refused to discuss the matter in any detail. 'The Cameron brothers are dead,' she'd said bluntly, no more than that.

Charles had, quite naturally, been shocked. 'But how?' he'd stammered. 'What did you …?'

'You need have no cause for concern on my behalf, Father,' she'd assured him, 'I left no evidence.' Then she'd added, as if it would surely be of some comfort, 'And you must admit, men like that deserve to be killed.'

The same words she'd said on that day nearly four years ago, Charles remembered, and delivered in the same ruthlessly detached way.

Then she'd sprung out of bed, wincing as her wounded foot took her weight.

'I simply must have breakfast,' she'd demanded. 'I've had nothing but a Devonshire tea since yesterday afternoon and I'm starving.'

'We'll see to that foot first,' Charles had insisted.

After which he'd spent the rest of the morning wondering what on earth he should do, until his decision to visit Sergeant Fry had finally put his mind at rest.

Now, as the days passed and he saw the re-emergence of his daughter, Charles understood the reasons for her strangely remote manner over the past several weeks. She had been planning the murder of the Cameron brothers, or perhaps, as she saw it, their executions.

He felt oddly relieved in this knowledge, for she now appeared to be back to her old self. Whatever that was. With Victoria it was sometimes difficult to tell, her nature could be so variable. But she seemed content. From time to time, Jeff even featured in her conversation, not in any maudlin sense, nor in anger, but just in passing reference, as if he was still with her.

Which he no doubt still is, Charles thought, *and quite possibly always will be.* How he envied his daughter a love like that!

Charles was thankful to see Victoria happy again. He would not, after all, have to wait until they were home in England for her to heal. She had already healed. It may have taken the murder of two men to do it, he thought with a strong sense of irony, but she had healed herself right here in the Pilbara. How fortuitous and how timely. The family could now return to Pendleton free of worry.

***

Two weeks before their departure, he gathered his children together in the breakfast room.

'We will be leaving in a fortnight,' he announced to his sons and daughter, who were seated on the bench opposite him.

The boys looked back at him blankly.

'Leaving for where?' Edward asked.

'England,' Charles replied.

More blank looks, this time jaws agape with surprise.

'Singapore first,' he went on to explain. 'We set sail for the island of Singapore on the twenty-eighth of March, then after staying several days there, it's on through the Suez Canal and finally to the port of Liverpool. We are going home, boys,' he declared, 'home to Pendleton.'

Edward was the first to recover himself. Being fully aware of the responsibilities that lay in store for him as the future Squire of Pendleton, he had always known they must go home at some stage. He simply hadn't expected it to be so soon. Rather, some time when he'd reached adulthood, he'd supposed. But he nodded, accepting the news.

Harold didn't know what he'd expected. He'd never even thought of the future. Life was a day-by-day proposition to Harold, who lived always for the moment. Now, the prospect of further adventures sounded immensely thrilling. More sea voyages, the island of Singapore, the Suez Canal. He couldn't wait. He grinned excitedly at his father.

But Charles needed to issue a warning. 'You must understand that our return to England means the return to our previous way of life. Our previous *relationship*,' he said tellingly. 'You do understand me, don't you?'

Both boys nodded.

'Until we disembark at Liverpool, however,' he went on, 'we shall continue as we are.' He met the eyes of each of his children in turn, signalling the importance of his instruction.

'On board ship I shall remain Father to my sons and my daughter. Understood?'

'Yes, Father,' the boys chorused.

'But I shan't be with you, Father,' Victoria said. It was neither a rebellion nor a confrontation of any sort, just a simple statement.

Charles was bewildered. 'What do you mean, Victoria? Of course you will be with us.'

'I told you months ago that I was staying here,' she replied patiently. 'I told you I was staying here with Jeff. We were to be married. You accepted that.'

'Yes, my dear, of course I did,' he replied gently and with equal patience. 'But Jeff is no longer here. When he died, I rebooked your passage.'

'You shouldn't have done that.'

He looked at her sharply, but she had not intended to be rude.

'I am sorry, Father, that you misread my intentions,' Victoria said, 'and I apologise for any inconvenience I may have caused you. But I am staying here.'

'Boys,' Charles ordered, 'you may leave the table and report to Joe. He's bound to have work for you.' A brisk nod. 'Off you go now.' And the boys up and left.

Charles glared across the breakfast table at his daughter. Now was confrontation time, he decided. Now he would lay down the law.

'I cannot allow you to stay here on your own, Victoria,' he said. 'You must see that!'

'I shall not be on my own, Father, I shall be with Joe and Alwyn and Nina and the whole team of Burton Station—'

'Don't be foolish, girl,' he snapped. 'I mean alone with no family, far away from your home ...'

'But this is my home, Papa, don't you understand?' Victoria didn't snap back, as was her wont whenever a voice was raised to her. Instead, she quietly spelled out the truth to him. 'This is where I belong. This is where Jeff is, and where I will stay for the rest of my life. He and I both belong here. I shan't leave.'

Her declaration was so indisputable, Charles was shocked into submission, the bubble of his complacency exploding right before his eyes. He'd been blindly lulled into a sense of security and was now about to lose his daughter all over again, he realised. And he was about to lose her not to a man this time, but to a phantom.

His face must have mirrored the pain he felt, because Victoria rose and, circling the table to sit on the bench beside him, placed a comforting hand upon his shoulder.

'Please, Papa,' she said, 'please don't be sad. I shall be happy here, I promise you I shall. Oh, I have such plans, truly I do!'

He could hear the excitement in her voice and swivelled about to face her. He took both her hands in his, but he couldn't find the words. He couldn't think of what to say.

'I'm a Pilbara woman now, don't you see,' Victoria announced triumphantly. 'When you return to England, I shall take your place. I shall work alongside Joe and Alwyn, and I shall manage Burton Station just as you did. I have been following your procedures and your progress every step of the way. This is to be my future.'

The two sat locked together, staring into each other's eyes, and as they did, all pretence fell away, leaving only honesty and admiration in its wake.

'I do not have your bravery, Mother, nor your courage,' Victoria said. 'I could never do what you have done. I *will* run this station though, and I will run it well. Not as a man. But as a woman.'

'Oh, my dear.' Charlotte smiled. 'Do you not think that will take bravery and courage?'

'Not when the way has been paved for me as you have done, Mama. No.' Victoria shook her head vehemently. 'You are the bravest person I have ever known.'

Mother and daughter embraced, holding each other close, feeling one another's heartbeat. Then when they parted, the mask was back.

'I wish you every happiness, Victoria,' Charles said, but the eyes that met his daughter's were those of Charlotte.

'And every *success* too, Father,' Victoria replied. 'Every *success*! I told you I had plans, and I do.' Her face lit up eagerly as she went on to explain, 'I have been making enquiries over this past fortnight and there are many ways in which I feel we can expand our interests here in the Pilbara. As you well know, Roebourne has undergone a period of rapid population growth over the past several years due to the recent depression that has so affected the eastern colonies. The collapse of the Melbourne land boom has brought people flocking to the Pilbara and business opportunities abound in the region ...'

Charles studied his daughter, fascinated. 'Making enquiries over this past fortnight ...' *Yes*, he thought, *that would have been during the two weeks since you killed the Cameron brothers. Oh, my dear, you have been busy.*

'There is movement afoot too,' Victoria went on, 'that a request be put forward to the Forrest Government to identify a site at Point Samson for a deep-water wharf, thereby alleviating the need for lighterage in transporting cargo and passengers, as is now the case at Cossack. This will be a great boon to our business, Father,' she said. 'I shall certainly lead the district's residents in pushing for this enterprise to go ahead.

'And there is further news from the Pilbara goldfields that a geologist's tests have revealed the possibility of vast iron deposits in the region.' There was no stopping Victoria now. 'Who can tell, Father? The future of the Pilbara may well lie in the discovery of minerals. Or iron ore at least. There are so many opportunities to explore ...'

Charles heard himself laugh. 'And you, my dear, will be the one to do it,' he said. *Oh, my darling, I shall miss you most dreadfully, but I shall certainly not worry about you.* 'You'd better inform Joe of all this,' he said.

'Yes, with your permission, I intend to,' Victoria replied. 'I shall tell him right now, if I may, Father.'

'You may.'

***

'Only a week to go,' Joe said. 'You all packed and ready?'

'More or less,' Charles replied. 'There's bound to be something I've missed, but I doubt it'll be anything I'll need at Pendleton.'

They were mucking out the stables. It was a job that could have been consigned to a couple of station hands, but by unspoken consensual agreement, they'd decided to tackle it together. A way of being alone, perhaps? Yes. They both knew that.

The place was silent. Not even the snort of a horse or the chomp of hay to be heard. The horses were all out with the men on muster or peacefully grazing in the home paddock. Just the smell of dung and animal sweat and straw. They loved the smell of the stables, they'd both agreed.

'You'll miss all this, won't you?' Joe said.

'Oh, yes,' Charles agreed, 'I certainly will. Strangely enough, not *this* in particular,' he added, looking around the stables and breathing in the odour. 'The stables at Pendleton look and smell very much the same, as I suppose all stables do. But I'll miss everything else about the Pilbara.'

'Are you looking forward to being home in Pendleton?' Joe asked.

His gaze was so intense, it was as if he was trying to see inside Charles' mind. At least, that was the way it appeared to Charles, who tried to answer as honestly as possible.

'That's a very difficult question,' he said. 'I'm really not sure.'

They'd given up any pretence of work now and were seated on the floor, leaning up against the wall of one of the stables that they'd mucked out.

'Let's take a bit of a breather, old chap,' Joe had suggested, although neither had been in the least tired. It seemed the ideal opportunity to talk.

'I'm looking forward to seeing Father,' Charles said. 'And the countryside too. The Yorkshire dales are beautiful, Joe, so very beautiful.'

'Yes, I can imagine. I've seen the postcards your father sent to your uncle. Geoffrey always maintained he did it to torment.'

Joe's scrutiny remained so intense that Charles felt compelled to offer a confession.

'I'm not quite sure how much I'm looking forward to returning to who I am though,' he said.

Joe nodded. It was the question he'd been asking.

'Charles Burton has so taken over my life now, and for so very long, that I fear he may be difficult to leave behind.'

'Oh, I think you'll manage, Charlotte,' Joe said with a smile.

He had forced her to reveal herself, as had been his intention, and she smiled back at him, grateful for this final connection.

'I cannot thank you enough for all you have done for me, Joe,' she said. 'For your strength and your support and above all your loyalty. I could never have done what I've done without you.'

'I think you can do anything, Charlotte, anything you put your mind to.'

He reached out and took her hand in his, turning it over, examining the callused palm, the grimy, chipped fingernails.

'A working man's hand,' he said, shaking his head in mock disapproval. 'This won't do at all. You'll have to take more care of yourself back at Pendleton.'

'Never,' she declared. 'I work in the fields at home, you know. I labour alongside the workers. I always did, even as a child.'

The touch of their hands was special to her. She wondered if it was to him. He was smiling that enigmatic Joe Lawson smile that had so irritated her in the early days, but which she now found attractive.

'One can hardly call the grazing lands of the Pilbara "fields",' he said wryly, and as he released her hand, she could have sworn he did so with an element of regret, 'but I shall miss labouring alongside you, Charlotte.'

'Then you should come to Pendleton,' she boldly replied. 'We always need good workers there.' Her eyes held a challenge.

If she'd expected a playful response in typical Joe Lawson style, she didn't get one. His reply came in all seriousness.

'How would you and I fit in such a world, my dear?' he said. 'England is not kind to Orientals, nor to those who choose to fraternise with them.'

'Of course there is an alternative solution,' Joe went on, this time with a mischievous glint in his eye. 'You could always come back here as a woman. Your own sister, perhaps? Charles' sibling. Uncle Geoffrey's niece. How's that for an option?'

They laughed. He was being facetious now. But they were both aware some sort of declaration had been made.

'You will write to me, won't you, Joe?' she asked.

'Oh yes,' he promised, 'I'll write to you, Charlotte.'

***

Over the following week, there was many a farewell from neighbouring farmers, and from citizens of Roebourne and Cossack. Charles Burton and his family were well respected by all. The workers and staff of Burton Station, too, gathered together offering their well wishes, the reaction among some quite emotional.

Nina was distraught. 'Dunno what we gonna do without you, Boss,' she said, mopping up her tears with a voluminous man's handkerchief, of which she appeared to have many. These had belonged to Geoffrey Burton, Joe informed Charles.

'Hardly surprising,' he said, 'she was your uncle's mistress, or she became so, in the latter years of his life.'

Charles was most surprised. 'I didn't know that.'

'There's lots of things you don't know, old chap,' came Joe's customary rejoinder.

Alwyn, too, was visibly affected. Now a strong, capable nineteen-year-old, Alwyn Stroud owed a great deal to Charles Burton.

'I'd still be in gaol if it wasn't for you, Boss,' he said as he fervently shook Charles' hand. But unlike Nina, Alwyn didn't feel the need to shed tears, mainly because Miss Victoria was staying and she above all was his true hero. He could read and he could write, and all because of her. He worshipped the very ground Miss Victoria walked on.

Then came the early morning, shortly after dawn, when Joe drove Charles and his family to Cossack, Victoria insistent upon coming along with them to say her final goodbyes. 'You're not getting rid of me, Father, until the very last minute,' she declared.

Given the sizeable amount of luggage they were carrying, they travelled by dray, Victoria up front with the men, the boys piled into the back with the trunks and cases.

As they journeyed the well-worn route, Charles was reminded of that first trip they'd made from Cossack to Burton Station. Which happened to have been in this very same dray, he mused. Everything had seemed so strange to him then. It had been the first time he'd met Joe Lawson and he remembered his shock upon discovering the man was Chinese. Or rather half Chinese.

'My mother was Chinese, my father English,' Joe had said in those clipped tones of his, and then he'd gone on to explain the origins of his name.

Charles couldn't even remember what Joe's real name was now, but he did recall it was a very funny story, the way he'd become simply 'Joe Lawson'.

'A perfectly ghastly bilingual disaster,' Joe had said at the time. 'Your Uncle Geoffrey found it frightfully funny.'

With the sturdy horse trotting on, the boys chatting away in the back and Victoria absorbed in the passing scenery, Charles had become lost in his thoughts of the past. But beside him, Joe seemed somehow to have divined them. Possibly because he'd been thinking along the very same lines.

'Might as well be yesterday, eh, old chap?' he said.

'Yes, perhaps,' Charles agreed, 'or else a lifetime ago. I'm not sure which.'

With the dray approaching Cossack, Victoria struck up a passionate conversation.

'You see, Father, the importance of a deep-water wharf at Point Samson? You see what a boon it will be? No more lighters running to and fro between port and anchorages. Cargo loaded and passengers boarded directly onto ships. The speed, the efficiency, the all-round capabilities this will offer,' she continued. 'The sooner we can persuade the government to get this enterprise under way, the better.'

'Yes, my dear, I can quite see that,' Charles patiently agreed.

Half an hour later, they stood on the stone wharf, watching as their luggage was loaded onto the lighter to be transported to Jarman Island, where Charles and the boys would board the waiting ship at anchor. They would then stay aboard overnight until the ship set sail on the early morning tide. Now was the time for final farewells.

Victoria hugged her brothers. 'You'll be off to a proper school soon,' she said, tousling Harold's hair. 'I bet you'll miss my nagging.'

'I bet I won't,' he replied.

And the ultimate compliment from Edward: 'I bet they don't have teachers at Eton who are half as good as you.'

Both boys hugged Joe too. Joe was family after all.

'We'll write,' Edward promised.

Then Victoria hugged her father. 'Goodbye, Mama,' she whispered, 'I'll miss you.'

'As I will you, my darling,' Charlotte whispered back, and they clung to each other for just that moment longer.

Charles' last contact, however, was with Joe.

'Goodbye, Joe,' he said as they shook. 'Look after Victoria for me.'

'It'll be more a matter of *her* looking after *me*, I'll wager,' Joe replied. 'She's a formidable young woman, your daughter.'

'Yes, she is that,' Charles agreed.

He and the boys boarded the lighter, and as the sailors cast off the lines and the vessel pulled away from the wharf, they stood on the deck, waving goodbye.

'Don't forget to write, Joe,' Charles called.

'Of course I won't, old chap. Promise.'

They both knew his promise was being made to Charlotte.

EPILOGUE

YORKSHIRE, 1903

'Yes, you're quite right, my dear,' Eleanor agreed, 'it's a very pretty view. In a *bucolic* way,' she added with a faint air of distaste, 'very *pastoral*. Personally, I prefer something a little more exciting. The outlook from St Paul's, say, or the Tower of London, where you can feel the throb of the city.'

Charlotte threw back her head and gave the hoot of laughter that Eleanor's performance deserved, and which Eleanor herself had expected. The two had become the most unlikely of friends over the years and these days enjoyed each other's company.

It was a fine morning in early autumn, and they were seated on horseback at the crest of the hill gazing out over the panorama of the Yorkshire Dales, the picturesque village of Otley in the distance, Pendleton House and the farmlands nestled in the valley below. Charlotte's favourite view.

Upon arriving at the crest of the hill, Eleanor had refused to dismount. 'I am perfectly comfortable where I am, thank you,' she'd said, so they'd both sat where they were, horses held on a loose rein, allowing the animals to graze.

Charlotte had been amazed to discover upon her return from Australia all those years ago that not only could Eleanor Witterson ride, but that she was a fine horsewoman, and that she accompanied William Burton on his morning ride every single day of the week.

'A gentle excursion only,' Eleanor had explained, 'nothing too strenuous. But the doctor maintains a daily outing is good for him, and he certainly enjoys it.'

'I didn't know you could ride,' Charlotte had said.

'Of course I can ride, although certainly never *astride* as some do,' Eleanor had replied disdainfully. 'During my younger years, a regular jaunt along Rotten Row was *de rigueur* for any young lady in London society.'

Then later that same morning, she'd demonstrated her skills in the side-saddle, perfectly attired in her green velvet riding habit, complete with chin-strapped silk top hat, as she'd set off at a trot beside William. Charlotte had found the sight bizarrely amusing.

Eleanor, in turn, had been amused by Charlotte's naiveté. Had the girl never heard of the Pretty Horsebreakers? Obviously not. But then she was born and bred a country lass, so it was hardly surprising.

Eleanor had joined the ranks of the Pretty Horsebreakers at the age of seventeen. Beautiful young women, impeccably attired, riding beautiful horses, impeccably turned-out, attracted boundless attention in Hyde Park's Rotten Row. They not only proved an excellent advertisement for the local livery stables, who provided the animals free of charge for that very reason, but in parading their skills as they did, these young ladies were quick to gain the attention of men from the upper echelons of society.

It had certainly worked for Eleanor. She had gained any number of wealthy lovers over the years, before culminating in the triumphant conquest of the Marquess of Farnsworth. Riding had proved an essential skill.

'I shall be moving back to London shortly,' Eleanor said, looking out at the view that, secretly, she did find rather impressive, although she'd never admit it. 'My real estate agent informs me the tenant has vacated my apartment, and it's time I returned to the city.'

'You don't have to go, you know,' Charlotte said, 'you're quite welcome to stay on at Pendleton.'

'No, no, my dear, I *do* have to go. There is a time for everything and it is now time for me to return to my city life.' Dismissing the view with a wave of her hand, she turned to smile at Charlotte. 'I do still detest the country, you know. Nothing but your father could have kept me here this long.'

William Burton had died six months previously. He was now interred in the family crypt beneath the floor of the old church, and Charlotte still felt his loss deeply. She was grateful though that he'd lived to the fine old age of eighty-five. *A good innings*, both women had agreed.

'He wrote to me that he might live for another ten years after his heart attack,' Charlotte had told Eleanor at the time of her father's death, 'and as it turns out, he did. I think all due to you. He said you made him feel young.'

'Really?' Eleanor had raised an elegantly quizzical eyebrow. 'Well, that's something of a miracle. Approaching sixty as I am, I would have thought I had no elixir of youth left to offer,' she said wryly.

Eleanor was in actual fact sixty-nine, but had for years professed to be in her fifties. Having decided she would never turn sixty, this was as old as she would ever become.

'So you *did* love him,' Charlotte declared, her tone a mix of accusation and triumph. 'You wrote to me once that you found it impossible to tell the difference between love and necessity. But to have lived with a man in a place you detest for all these years? Come along, Eleanor, admit it! You loved my father!'

Eleanor shrugged, clearly determined not to be cornered. 'Being loved is sometimes enough. I shall miss that.' She was momentarily thoughtful for she did, surprisingly enough, wish to be honest. As honest as she could be, when she really didn't have the answers.

I have been trained to love for the whole of my life, she thought, *or to display all the signs of love. Over time, it becomes difficult to tell the difference between pretence and reality.*

Eleanor was finding Charlotte's interrogation just a little confronting, as Charlotte obviously intended she should. But Charlotte couldn't be expected to understand, could she, that love was a business.

'I shall miss your father, Charlotte,' she admitted, 'and I shall miss his love.' Yes, she decided, she was prepared to go that far. 'I shall miss also being needed,' she said. 'There's that too.'

'Indeed there is.' Charlotte smiled, satisfied with the answer. 'I can understand you would feel that way. And what's more, I know exactly what you mean, Eleanor. I'm feeling rather redundant myself,' she said, recognising as she did a familiar refrain. She was echoing the sentiments of Joe's last letter.

I'm beginning to feel just a wee bit superfluous, Joe had written.

> *Victoria runs Burton Station with unmatchable efficiency, as you can well imagine, and as you will know from the accounts she herself has sent you of our progress. Your daughter is way ahead of me, Charlotte, and the men all love and respect her, particularly Alwyn, who is now station foreman and nigh on as efficient as the Boss herself. I do at times fear I've become redundant, and as I shall turn fifty-five this year, I wonder whether I shouldn't just give it all away …*

Charlotte adored Joe's letters, which were always written fondly and with the intent to amuse. As were her own letters to him. Their correspondence was of great importance to them both.

'With Father now gone and the boys at Oxford,' she said, 'I'm at a bit of a loss as to what to do with my life.'

'We're both at a crossroads then, are we not?' Eleanor said with a brittle smile. *You at least* have *a life, Charlotte,* she thought, wondering what would await her on her return to the city. She would be lonely. There would be no more lovers. But society beckoned, and that would just have to be enough.

Taking up the slack of her reins, she lifted her horse's head from the grass. 'Let's return for morning tea,' she suggested.

'Excellent idea,' Charlotte agreed, following suit.

They kept their horses on a tight rein, taking care they shouldn't stumble as they wended their way slowly down the stony hillside. Then, once on the grassy flats, Eleanor gave a slight tap of her left heel to the flank of her mount and was away.

Charlotte, too, set off at a swift canter towards Pendleton House, the two riding neck and neck for a minute or so. But, breaking into a gallop, Charlotte very soon drew away, and Eleanor watched admiringly as she streaked on ahead.

The girl certainly can ride, she thought, much as she disapproved of the inelegant style. Astride and in breeches, long black hair flying! *Good God, she doesn't even wear a hat!*

Whenever they pitted themselves against one another, Charlotte always won, which slightly irked Eleanor. Reminding herself that, at forty-five, the girl was a whole generation younger didn't really salve her irritation, for she was quite sure her own skill as a horsewoman had not diminished. Good grief, the only problem she'd had in her youth was taking care never to best her beaus in a race. Particularly the Marquess. To outride the Marquess would have been unforgivable.

'Well done,' she said, arriving at the stables where Charlotte had dismounted and was already in the act of unsaddling her horse. 'As usual.' Eleanor always accepted defeat graciously. Or appeared to. 'I'll see you up at the house,' she said, leaving the stable boy to look after her mount. 'Don't be too long,

I'm simply dying for tea.' It also irked her that Charlotte took forever brushing down her horse. A pure waste of time. That's what stable hands were for.

The tea was set out in the front sitting room of the west wing and Eleanor was already on her second cup when Charlotte arrived.

'The girl served the scones warm,' Eleanor said accusingly, 'they'll be cold by now.'

'I don't mind,' Charlotte replied. 'Ivy knows I prefer them cold anyway.' No matter how many times she reminded Eleanor of the maid's name, Ivy always remained 'the girl'. As did the other two housemaids. Charlotte was aware this was not due to any memory lapse on Eleanor's part, but rather a reminder to servants of their lowly status, and while she did not in the least approve, she'd given up trying to change Eleanor's attitude. Eleanor was Eleanor and always would be.

Charlotte plonked herself down on the chaise longue, leaned forward and started pouring herself a cup of tea, Eleanor openly casting a stern look of disapproval at her stockinged feet. Eleanor loathed slovenliness. Riding boots were always left at the side entrance, yes, but surely Charlotte could place a pair of slippers there in readiness rather than parading about like this indoors. And her hair. So messy! Eleanor herself was freshly coiffed, her top hat resting on the nearby sofa, her feet in dainty satin slippers. But she'd given up trying to change Charlotte's habits. Charlotte was Charlotte and always would be.

'When do you plan on returning to London?' Charlotte asked as she sipped her tea.

'Within the month, I would say,' Eleanor replied. 'Certainly by the end of October anyway.'

'So soon?'

'Yes, I want to be comfortably established in the apartment before winter sets in.'

'That means you won't be here when the boys return from Oxford?'

'Afraid not.'

'They'll be disappointed.' They would be too. Eleanor was at her witty, sparkling best with Edward and Harold, who enjoyed her company. But then Eleanor was at her witty, sparkling best in the presence of all young men, so long as they were not of the working class. 'You'll miss the big celebration in the village when Edward is officially recognised as the new Squire of Pendleton,' she said. 'The Mayor is to host a ceremony in the Town Hall and there's bound to be much partying in the square afterwards.'

'Yes, I'm aware of that,' Eleanor replied, not bothering to hide her indifference; she could well do without the villagers. 'It really does seem so silly, doesn't it,' she said, 'that Edward be required to go to all the trouble of completing a law degree, only to return home and become a gentleman farmer.'

Charlotte laughed. 'Yes, I quite agree. Family tradition, I'm afraid. Father and Uncle Geoffrey found it amusing too. "Just something all Burton men *do*," they used to say.' She placed a scone on her side plate, cut it in two and started slathering both halves with butter. Charlotte was very fond of butter.

'Harold has another three years of study, but he'll go through exactly the same procedure,' she said, 'ending up with a full law degree under his belt, but one which will never be put into practice. Seems such a waste of time, doesn't it? But that's men for you, I suppose.'

Eleanor gave a 'humph'. *That's landed gentry for you,* she thought scathingly.

'Or rather *English*men,' Charlotte corrected herself. 'A man's qualifications and talents certainly wouldn't go to waste in Australia. Not in the Pilbara anyway.'

She paused, reflecting upon the rough justice that had been served in the Roebourne Court. *It had worked though, hadn't it? Oh, yes, it had certainly worked.*

'You don't even need the qualification,' she said thoughtfully, 'just a little knowledge and talent enough to make it up as you go along.'

Eleanor was studying Charlotte closely, that strong-boned, androgenous face. She was noting, too, the change in Charlotte's manner and speech as she relived some element of the past. *How very interesting,* she thought. *Dear me, yes, you would have made a most impressive young man. Handsome too.*

'I would have enjoyed meeting you as a man, Charlotte,' she said in all seriousness. 'Who knows,' she added flirtatiously, 'I might even have set my cap at you.'

Charlotte burst out laughing and hoed into her scone. Eleanor could be such fun.

But Eleanor wasn't out to have fun. She was far too curious.

'How did you find life as a man,' she asked, 'was it easier?'

Charlotte gave the matter a moment's thought as she chewed. 'Easier than being a woman, is that what you mean?'

'Of course that's what I mean.'

'Difficult to say, really. Nothing's easy in the Pilbara, and certainly not for a woman. I doubt I could ever have accomplished what I did had I not been a man.' Her smile was rueful. 'Although it appears Victoria is managing famously. But then she's part of a new breed, isn't she? Victoria is a modern woman.'

Charlotte ignored her scone as she warmed to her theme. 'Did you know, Eleanor, that Australian women have now been granted the vote? Just last year it was. *The Commonwealth Franchise Act 1902*, Victoria informed me. She's been fighting the suffragette cause for a number of years now, attending meetings in Perth. Australia is the second nation in the world to have achieved such progress, she tells me, following New Zealand. And not only can Australian women vote, they can stand for election in the Federal Parliament.'

Charlotte shook her head in wonderment. 'Oh my goodness, times have changed. I wonder how long it will take for England to become so enlightened.'

Eleanor was not remotely interested in the enlightenment of Australian politics, nor of England's, for that matter. This had not been her enquiry at all.

'Oh, come along now, Charlotte,' she said with a touch of impatience, 'I asked if you found life easier as a man. Simple question. Surely you must have discovered this to be so. Everything is easier for men. Always has been, always will be.'

'I'm surprised you should say such a thing.' Charlotte studied the older woman shrewdly. 'You of all people. You've practised control over men with the greatest success for the whole of your adult life.'

'Yes, this is true,' Eleanor admitted, 'but only through manipulation. Hardly because I've been apportioned any power of my own.'

'You've always had power of your own,' Charlotte said, 'and you've always known how to wield it. You're a strong woman, Eleanor. I believe strong women can achieve almost anything. You and I have both proven this to be true, wouldn't you say?'

The question was rhetorical, Charlotte redirecting her attention to her scone, signalling an end to their conversation. They were travelling on dangerous ground now. She wasn't sure whether, deep down, she would ever truly forgive Eleanor's treachery.

Sensing an element of disapproval, Eleanor pursed her lips and returned to her tea. What a fruitless discussion. She and Charlotte never agreed upon anything.

Several minutes later, the butler arrived.

'Excuse me, Miss Charlotte,' he said, 'but young Barnaby's just returned from Otley with the mail. Would you like it brought in here?'

'Yes, please, Teddy,' Charlotte said eagerly, finishing off the second scone.

'And Baker,' Eleanor barked imperiously as the man turned to go, 'did the boy fetch me a newspaper?'

'Yes, ma'am, he did.'

'Good. Have that brought in too, if you would.'

'Yes, ma'am.'

'Thank you, Teddy,' Charlotte said, sharing with him a wink and a smile. She found it amusing that, in Eleanor's eyes, Teddy was now deserving of recognition. Just as all maids were 'the girl' and all footmen were 'the boy', Teddy, having long ago moved through the ranks from footman to head butler, was addressed by his surname these days.

A moment later, young Barnaby appeared with the mail on a small silver salver, which he placed beside the tea tray on the table, and a folded newspaper, which he handed directly to Eleanor.

She accepted it without a thank you and without even a glance at the boy. Then, unfolding it, she settled down to read.

'Thank you, Barnaby,' Charlotte said, and the lad, a gauche youth of around seventeen, offered a grateful nod and disappeared.

Sifting through the mail, Charlotte gave a yelp of delight. 'Another letter from Joe,' she exclaimed. 'And so soon. How lovely.'

Eleanor didn't bother looking up from her newspaper. When was there *not* a letter from Joe, she wondered, and when was it *not* lovely?

'Oh my goodness.' A minute or so on, another yelp from Charlotte. 'He's just turned fifty-five.'

How extraordinarily uninteresting, Eleanor thought, eyes still focussed upon her newspaper. 'Yes, he told you in his last letter he was turning fifty-five this year, don't you remember?' she said drily. Charlotte continuously quoted bits and pieces from Joe's letters, and the man's name constantly featured in her conversations. Eleanor found it quite tiresome.

Charlotte read on in silence, which to Eleanor was a merciful blessing. Then finally …

'Oh dear.' Lowering the letter to her lap, Charlotte looked up, confused.

Eleanor deigned to look up from her newspaper and their eyes met.

'What is it, Charlotte? Is something wrong?'

'He's suggesting I meet him in Hong Kong.'

'What on earth for?'

'Neutral ground, he says.'

'What in heaven's name does *that* mean?'

But Charlotte just shook her head, bewildered.

'Oh, for God's sake, read it to me,' Eleanor growled. 'Read it out loud.'

Charlotte obligingly took up the letter. 'I'll just read the end bit,' she said, 'the bit where he talks about Hong Kong.

And now, my dear Charlotte, I have a proposition to put to you. At fifty-five years of age, I have come to a decision. I intend to quit the Pilbara and return to my long-ago home of Hong Kong. I am not quite sure what I shall do there, but I shall not be idle. The excitement of Hong Kong does not invite laziness, and I may even go into business with my half-brother, Douglas. He's not actually my half-brother at all, but the son of the British family who all but adopted me and we grew up together. A frightfully nice chap, we've reconnected after all these years.

Anyway, I wondered whether perhaps you might
like to join me there. Being neither England nor the
Pilbara, you understand, but rather 'neutral ground'.
I would love to show you Hong Kong, Charlotte,
knowing as I do how such a place would appeal to
your spirit of adventure.

Do give the matter some thought, my dear.
With fondest wishes,
Your old friend, Joe

The letter landed back on Charlotte's lap and she once again looked up to meet Eleanor's eyes.

'What do you make of that?' she asked.

What do I make of that? Good God girl, are you blind? 'What do *you* make of it, dear?' Eleanor asked sweetly. 'Which is surely more to the point.'

'Um ...' Charlotte was uncharacteristically at a loss. 'I really don't know,' she admitted. 'I'm flattered that Joe wants to show me Hong Kong. And the adventure aspect does appeal, but ...'

She got no further than that before Eleanor exploded. 'He doesn't want to show you Hong Kong, he wants to share his life with you!' She shook her head in bewilderment. 'Good grief, the blindness of the two of you knows no bounds. You've been writing love letters to each other for years without knowing it, and now, when the man finally recognises the fact and comes up with an offer, you can't see it for what it is.'

'Oh.' Charlotte stared back at her, stunned, Eleanor's outburst making sudden, and complete, sense. She remembered that day in the stables. The touch of Joe's hand, the hint of a declaration ... *Of course. She's right!* It was a revelation.

Eleanor was aware her words had hit home. 'Oh, my dear Charlotte,' she said patronisingly, but not without an element of affection, 'for someone as brave and as intelligent as you are, you can be so remarkably stupid.'

The broadest smile spread across Charlotte's face. She was aglow with sheer happiness.

'Yes, I can, can't I,' she said.

Eleanor couldn't help but think how beautiful she looked. How beautiful, and how womanly.

'A pity you're beyond childbearing age,' she said. 'The children of inter-racial relations, particularly Eurasians, are so exceptionally good-looking.'

But Charlotte didn't hear her. She was re-reading Joe's letter.

ACKNOWLEDGEMENTS

First and foremost, my love and thanks to that brilliant man, Bruce Venables, who happens to be my husband. You're always inspirational, Brucie – this time more than ever. Big thanks.

I am deeply indebted to my good friend Chris Dawson, or should I say, 'Christopher John Dawson, 32nd Squire of Weston Hall, Yorkshire'. Thanks, Chris, for so generously sharing with me the detail of your ancestral home and history, all of which was invaluable.

Thanks also to Karratha Library and Sarah Barton's wonderful team there, particularly Taylor Coventry, who was librarian and historian during my research trip to the Pilbara in the early planning stages of this book. Taylor has since left her position at this wonderful library, but the assistance she offered was extraordinary, way and above the call of duty. Thanks, Taylor, you're a gem.

I'd like to acknowledge, too, Tracey Poultney and Denyce Crawford of the Karratha Tourism and Visitor Centre, who were most helpful during my visit.

The team too at the Karratha International Hotel were most pleasant and obliging, making for a comfortable stay in the Pilbara.

Many thanks to my agent and publicist, Karen Reid, for her friendship, support and expertise in all things literary. And of course, a big thanks to my old mates, Sue Greaves and Susan Mackie-Hookway, who always assist with their support and encouragement. Also to IT experts Colin Julin and Rob Graham, without whom I would have drowned in a sea of technological disasters many times over.

Finally, my thanks to my publisher, Roberta Ivers, editors Rachel Cramp and Kylie Mason, designer Hazel Lam, and the whole of the hardworking, helpful and jolly nice team at HarperCollins Australia.

Among my research sources, I would particularly like to recognise:

William Vavasour: The Squire of Weston, 1798–1833, Mary Creaser, B.Ed.

Cossack Gold, W.L. Lambden Owen, (1933) Facsimile with additions, Hesperian Press, Western Australia, 1984

Roebourne: 150 Years 1866–2016, City of Karratha, 2016

Claremont Yacht Club, 100 Years of History 1905–2005, edited by Rob Nunn, Claremont Yacht Club

BOOK CLUB QUESTIONS

1. The Pilbara is one of the oldest places on the planet, with rock formations dated to more than 3 billion years old. The Earth itself is 4.5 billion years old. What other places around the world can lay claim to such ancient beginnings?

2. The Pilbara has long been renowned for its reserves of precious metals, from gold to iron ore and more. How different do you think the Pilbara is now compared to the setting of the novel?

3. Evidence shows that Aboriginal people have been living continuously in the Pilbara for at least 30,000 to 40,000 years before European colonisation, which began in the mid-1800s. The novel touches on the clash between Aboriginal custodianship and European ownership of country. Discuss.

4. Charles successfully hid who he really was in the six years he spent in the Pilbara. Can you name any figures from history or literary history who were able to do the same? Do they have anything in common?

5. How are Victoria and Charlotte similar and dissimilar? Do you think their attributes are innate, or have they been shaped by the countries and the cultures they grew up in?

6. For a long time, Charlotte considers Eleanor to be a rapacious opportunist, intent only on spending William Burton's fortune. But is Eleanor simply a certain woman of her time, doing the best she can to live her life in the way she is accustomed? Do Charlotte and Eleanor have anything in common?

7. Thanks to the attractions of the Pilbara – the grazing country, the gold and the pearls – people from all over the world flocked to this part of Australia. How many languages did you notice in the novel? How many cultures from around the world were living in the Pilbara in the story?

8. Honour and justice are two themes in the book. In what ways are honour and justice different between Yorkshire and the Pilbara?

CONNECT WITH JUDY NUNN

Website

www.judynunn.com.au

JudyNunnAuthor

CONNECT WITH HARPERCOLLINS

Website

www.harpercollins.com.au

HarperCollinsAustralia

HarperCollinsAustralia

HarperCollinsAustralia